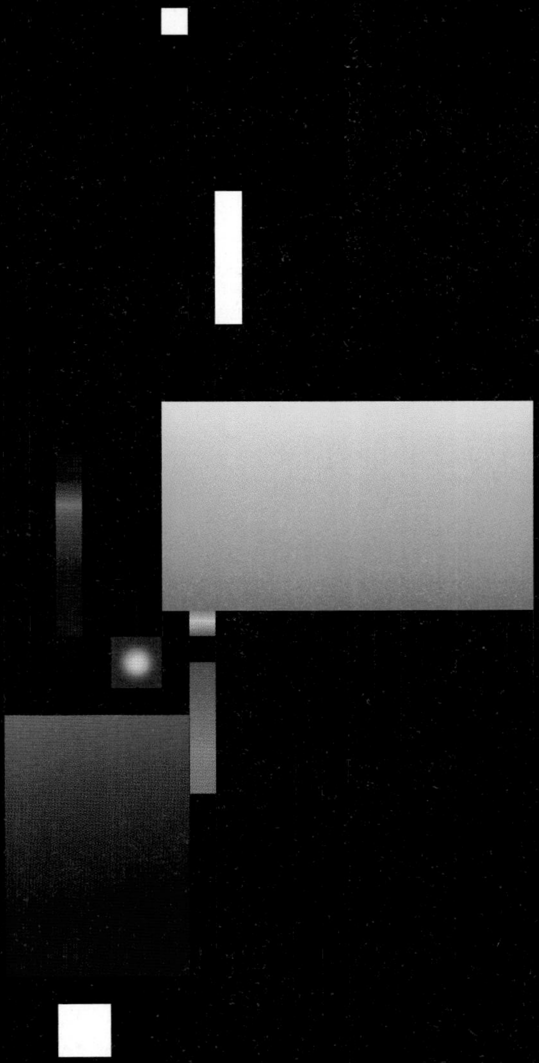

vol.1

DRIFTER™

Drifter
Volume
01

Originally published as DRIFTER #1–5

Ivan Brandon
Script

Nic Klein
Full color art and cover

Clem Robins
Lettering

Tom Muller
Logo and design

Sebastian Girner
Editor

Nic Klein
Original series cover artist

Esad Ribic, Cliff Chiang, Jason Latour, Becky Cloonan, Marko Djurdjević, Rafael Albuquerque, and Skottie Young
Original series variant cover artists

OUT OF THE NIGHT.

DRIFTER created by Ivan Brandon and Nic Klein
AN OFFSET COMICS PRODUCTION

imagecomics.com

Image Comics, Inc.
—Robert Kirkman: Chief Operating Officer /
Erik Larsen: Chief Financial Officer / Todd McFarlane: President /
Marc Silvestri: Chief Executive Officer / Jim Valentino: Vice-President /
— Eric Stephenson: Publisher / Kat Salazar: Director of PR & Marketing /
Emily Miller: Director of Operations / Corey Murphy: Director of Retail Sales /
Jeremy Sullivan: Director of Digital Sales /Randy Okamura: Marketing Production Designer /
Branwyn Bigglestone: Senior Accounts Manager / Sarah Mello: Accounts Manager /
David Brothers: Content Manager / Jonathan Chan: Production Manager /
Drew Gill: Art Director / Meredith Wallace: Print Manager /
Addison Duke: Production Artist / Vincent Kukua: Production Artist /
Sasha Head: Production Artist / Tricia Ramos: Production Artist /
Emilio Bautista: Sales Assistant /Jessica Ambriz: Administrative Assistant /

ISBN: 978-1-63215-281-7

DRIFTER VOL 1. First Printing. June 2015. Published by Image Comics, Inc. Office of publication: 2001 Center Street, Sixth Floor, Berkeley, CA 94704.

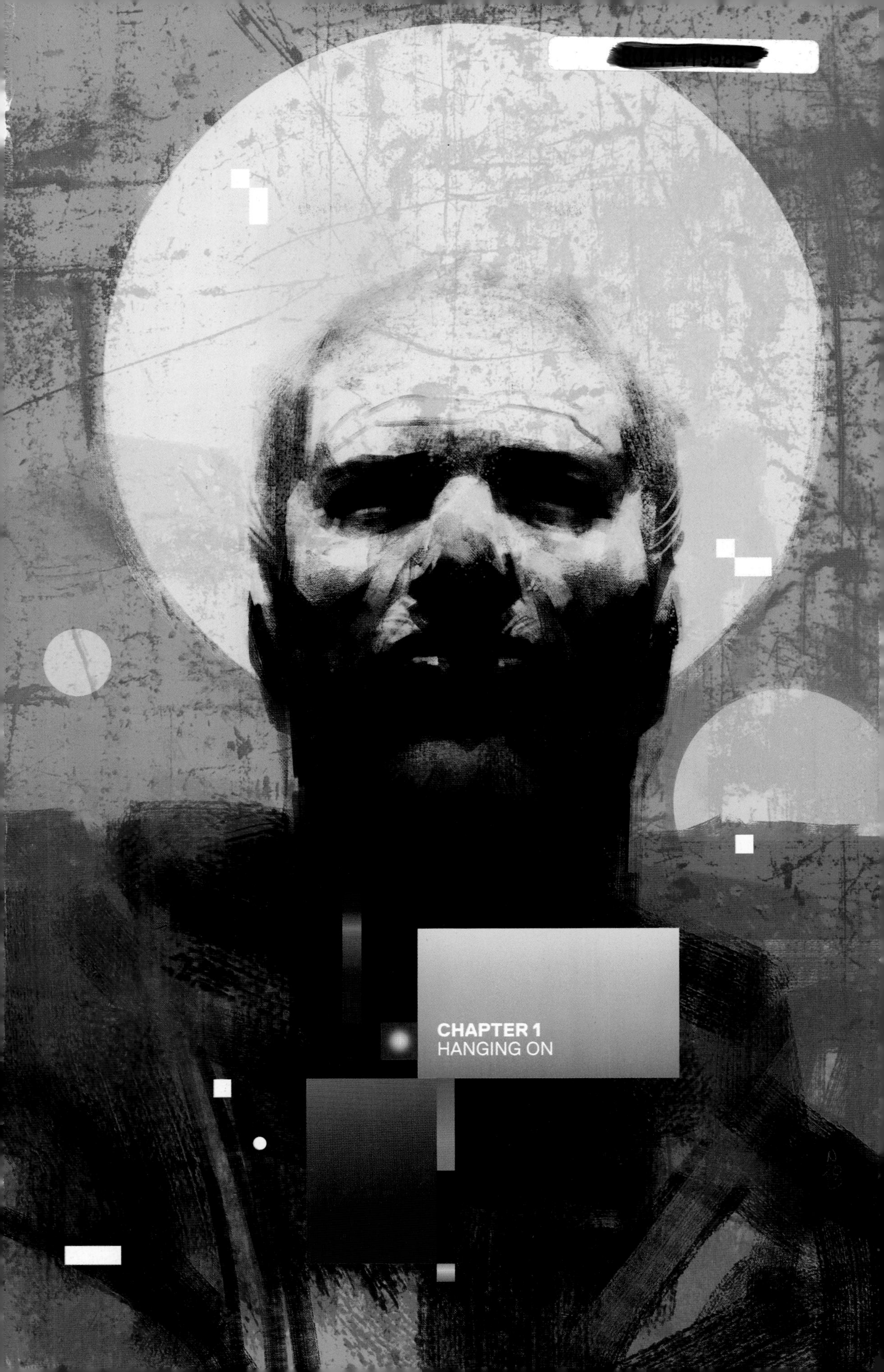
[redacted]
CHAPTER 1
HANGING ON

UNIDENTIFIED PROJECTILE BREACH IN AFT PANEL LL27

METHANE OVEREXPOSURE
IN SOUTHEAST
PROPULSION GALLERY

ENGINE **11** OFFLINE

ENGINE **13** OFFLINE

ENGINE **15** OFFLINE

PERSONAL DISASTER IS IMMINENT

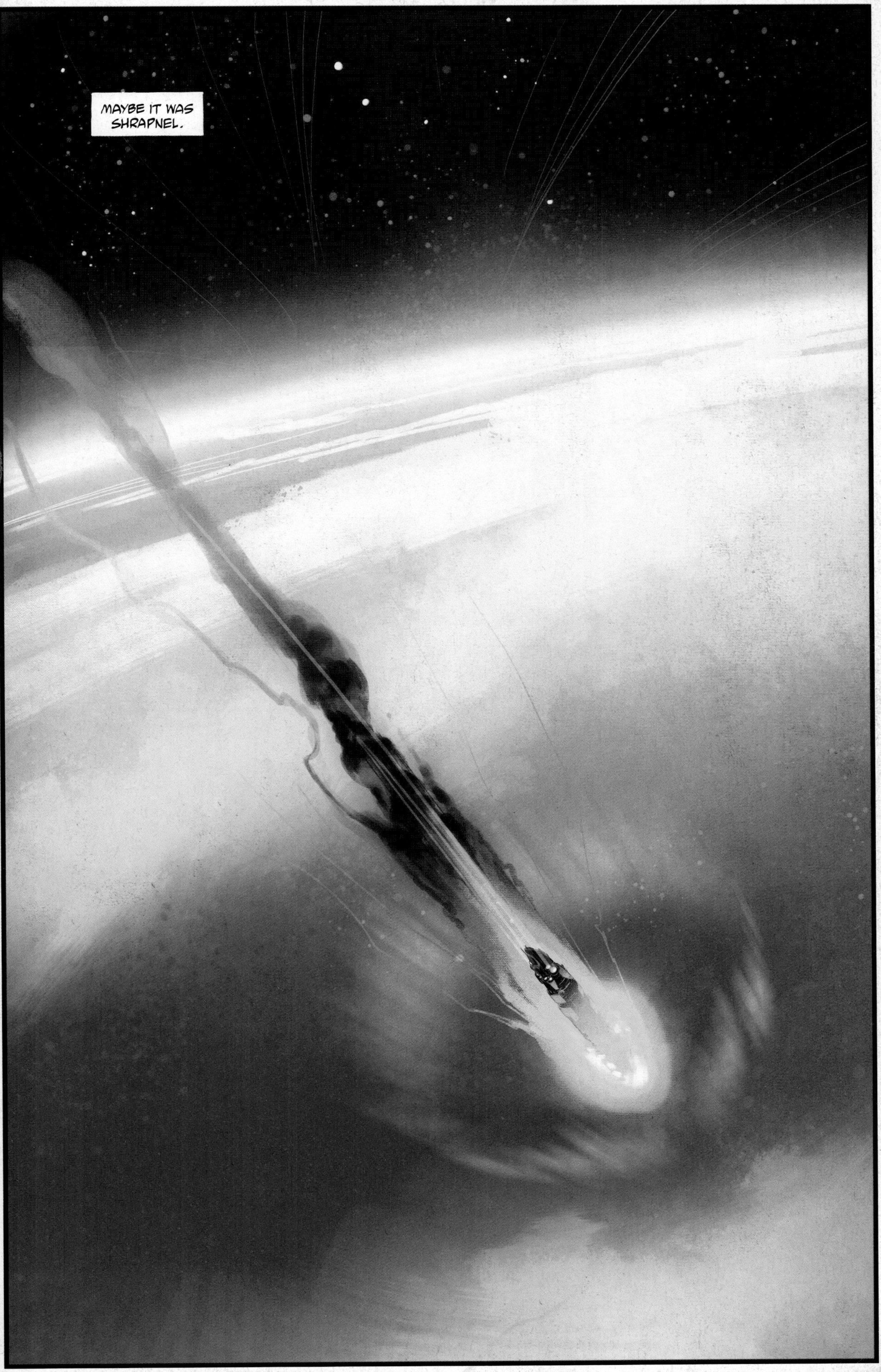
MAYBE IT WAS SHRAPNEL.

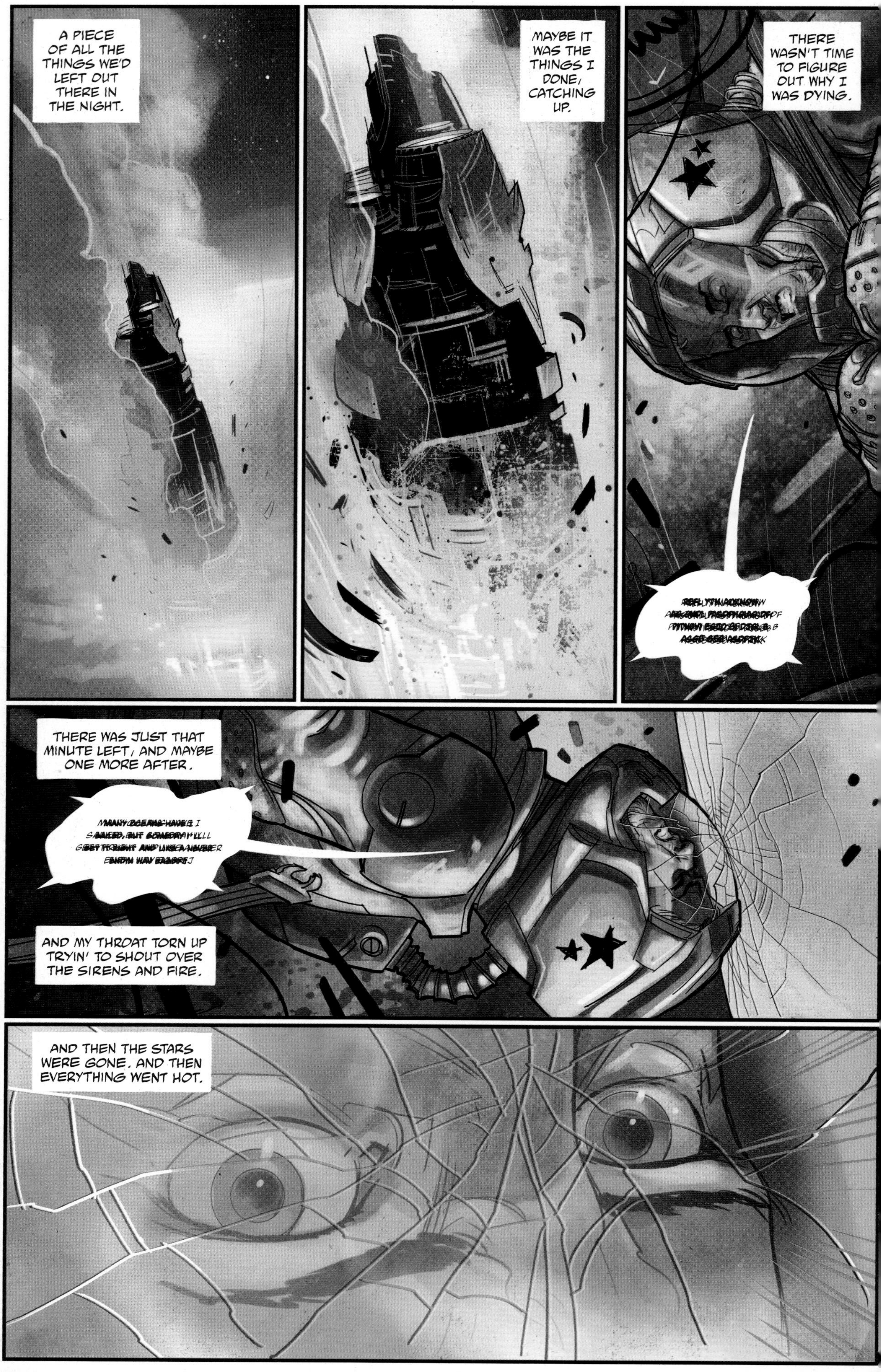
A PIECE OF ALL THE THINGS WE'D LEFT OUT THERE IN THE NIGHT.
MAYBE IT WAS THE THINGS I DONE, CATCHING UP.
THERE WASN'T TIME TO FIGURE OUT WHY I WAS DYING.
THERE WAS JUST THAT MINUTE LEFT, AND MAYBE ONE MORE AFTER.
AND MY THROAT TORN UP TRYIN' TO SHOUT OVER THE SIRENS AND FIRE.
AND THEN THE STARS WERE GONE. AND THEN EVERYTHING WENT HOT.

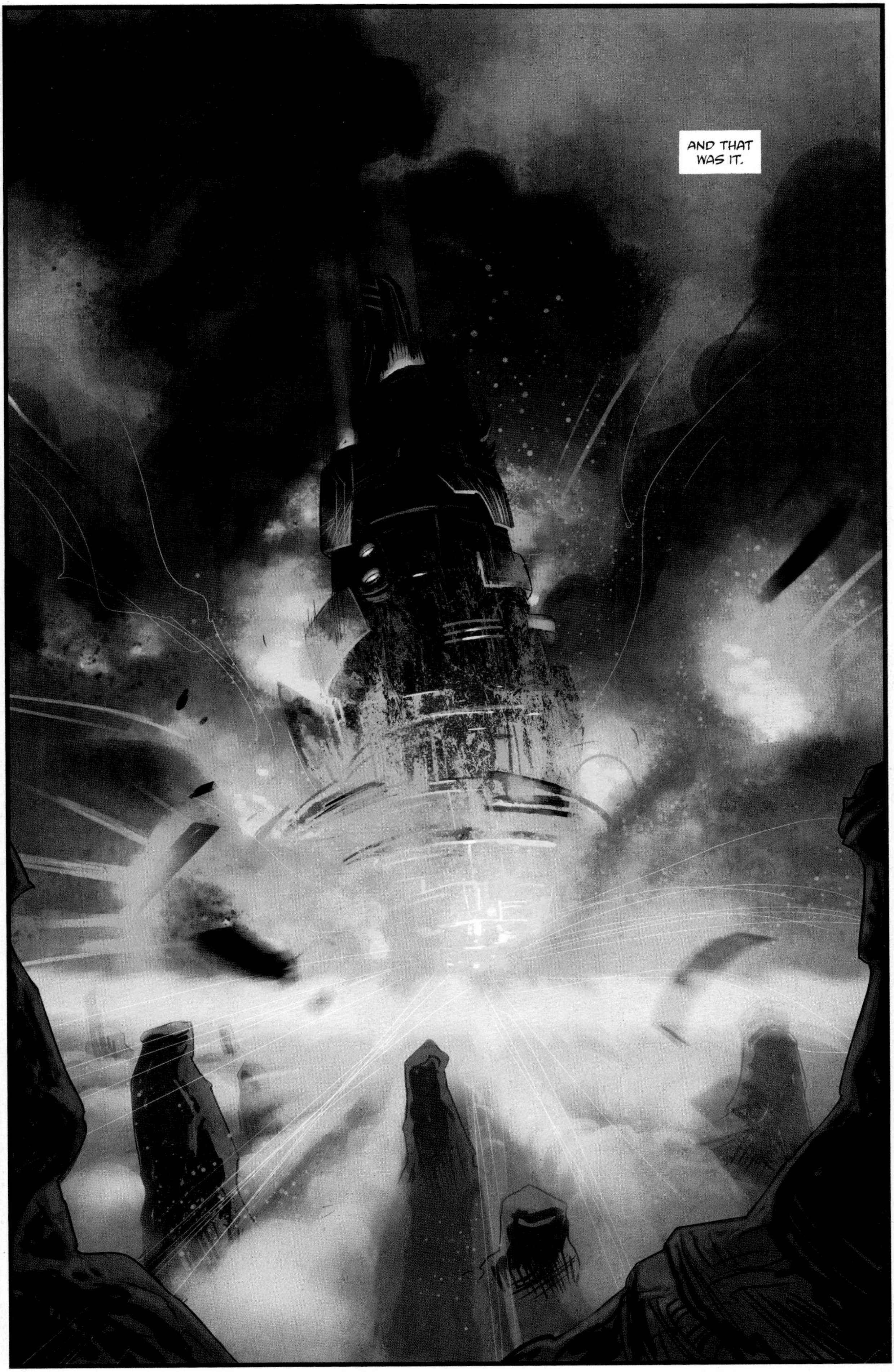
AND THAT WAS IT.

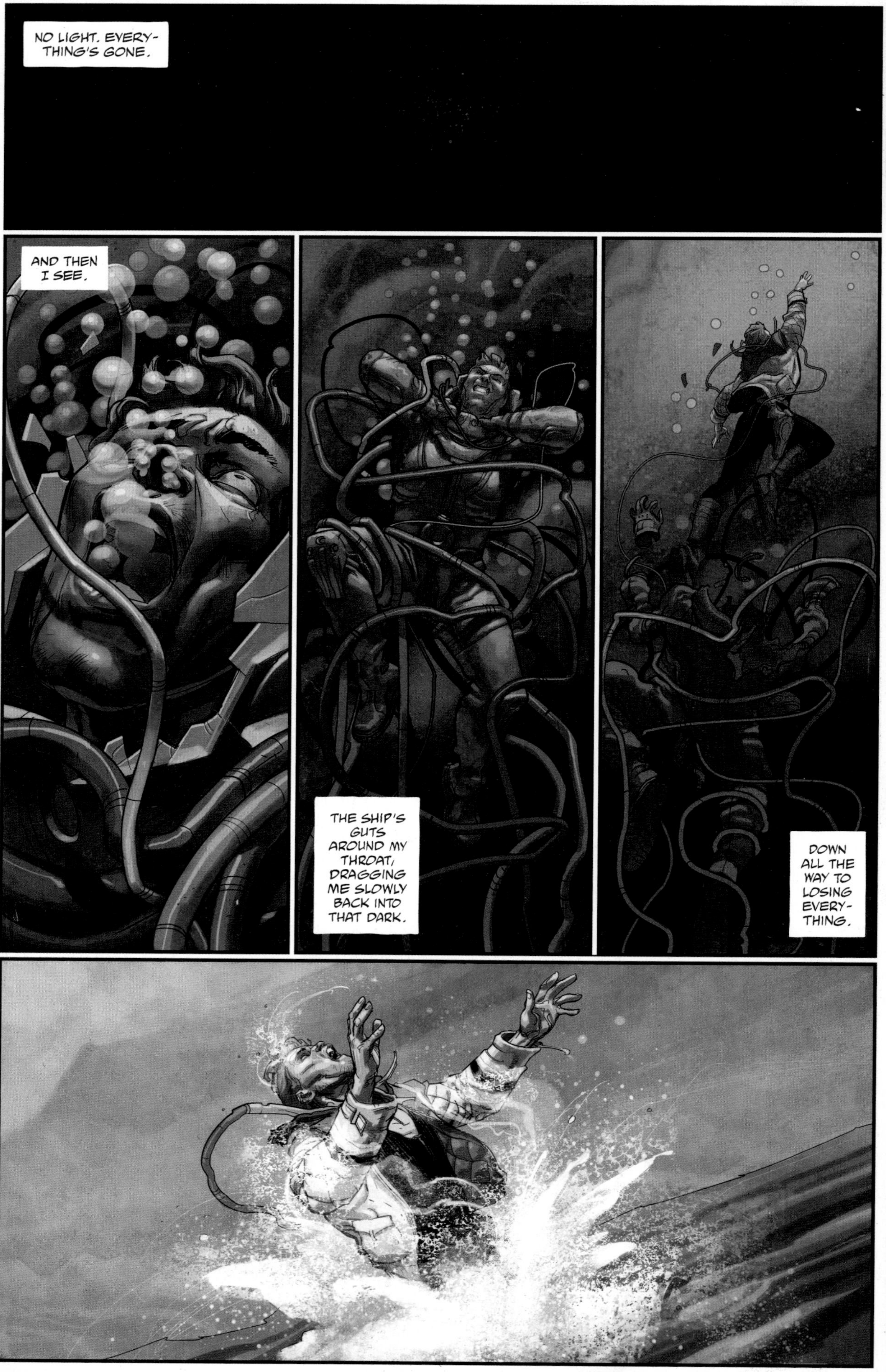
NO LIGHT. EVERY-THING'S GONE.
AND THEN I SEE.
THE SHIP'S GUTS AROUND MY THROAT, DRAGGING ME SLOWLY BACK INTO THAT DARK.
DOWN ALL THE WAY TO LOSING EVERY-THING.

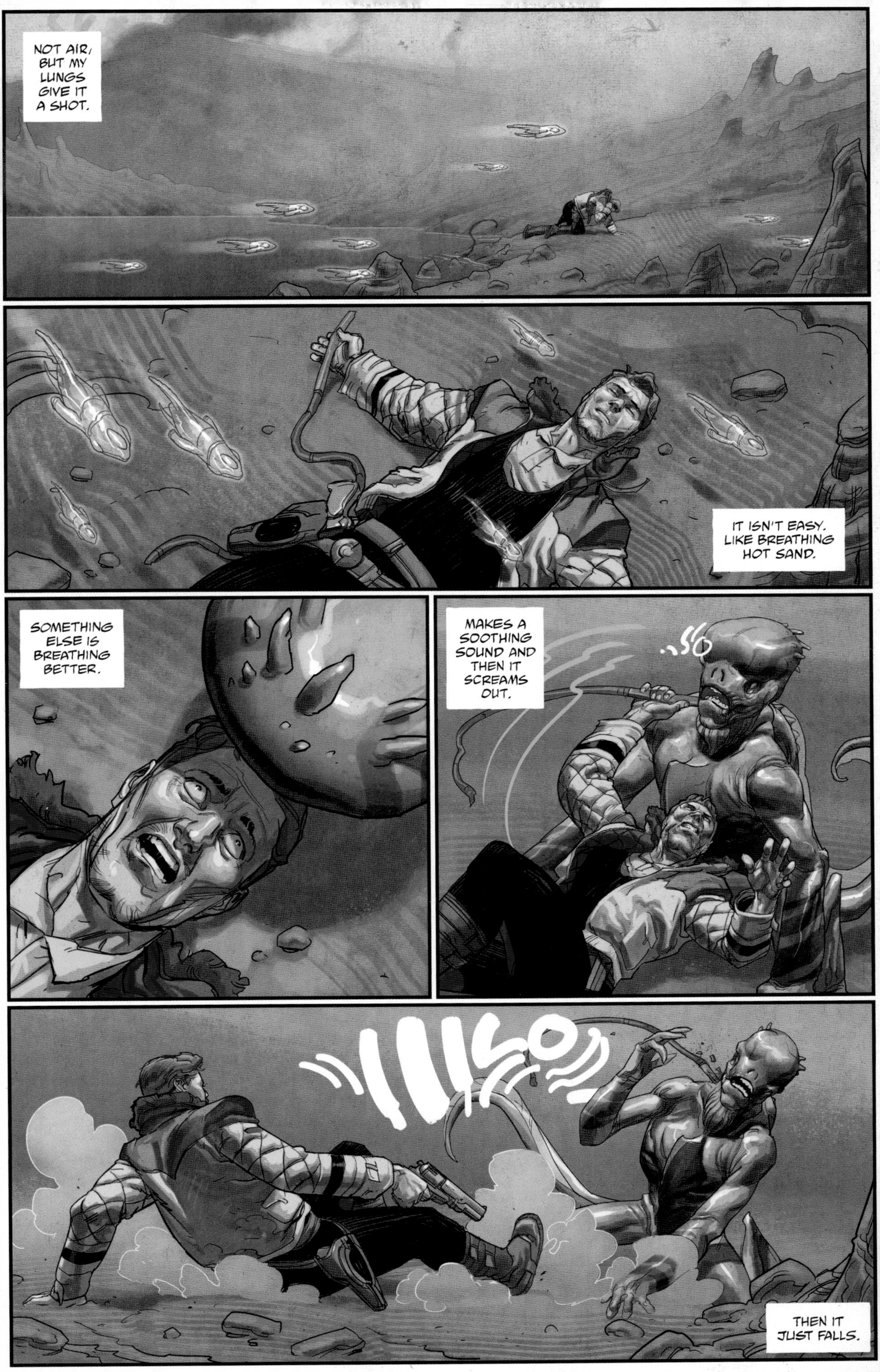
NOT AIR, BUT MY LUNGS GIVE IT A SHOT.
IT ISN'T EASY. LIKE BREATHING HOT SAND.
SOMETHING ELSE IS BREATHING BETTER.
MAKES A SOOTHING SOUND AND THEN IT SCREAMS OUT.
SO
SO
THEN IT JUST FALLS.

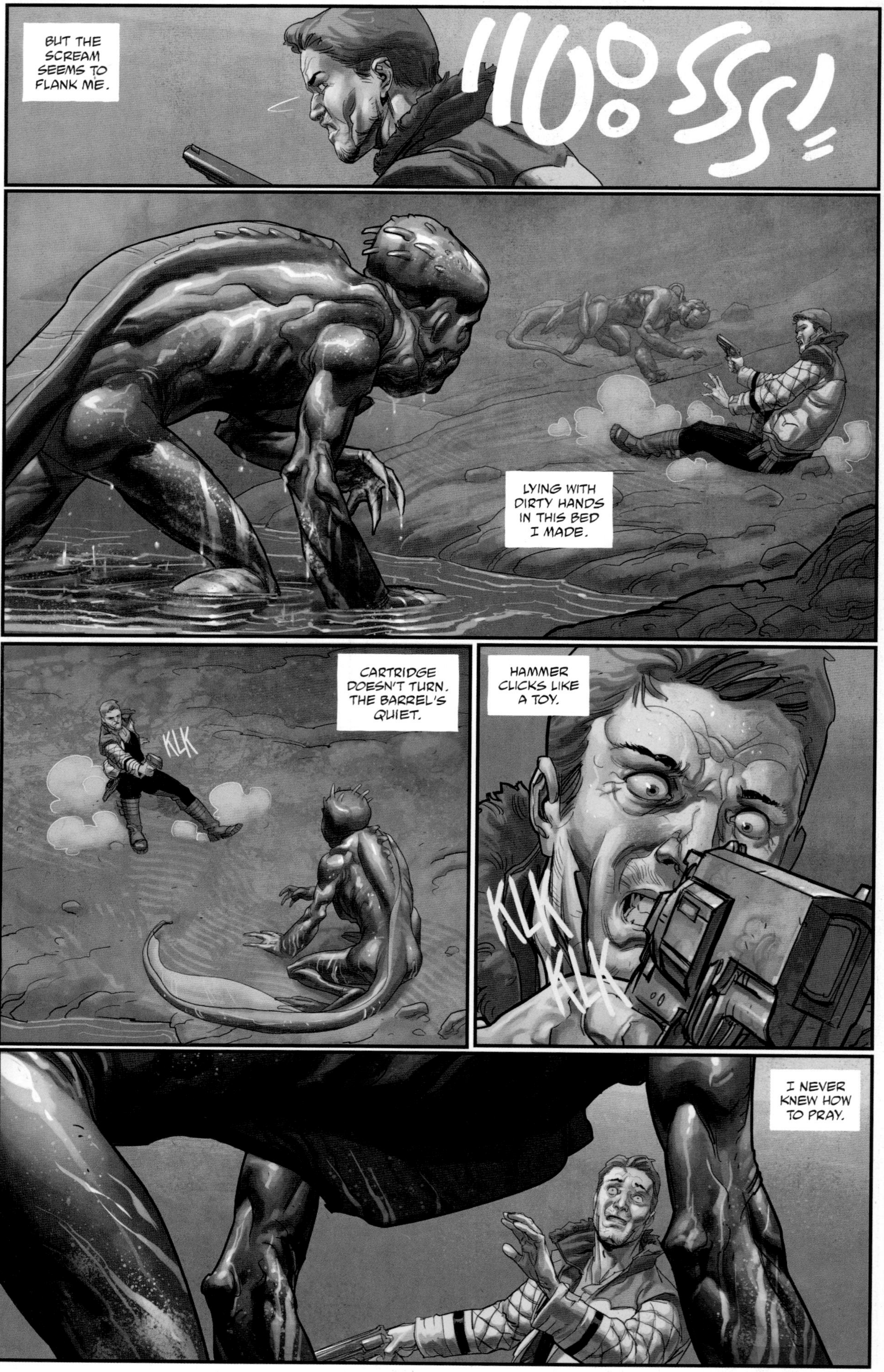
BUT THE SCREAM SEEMS TO FLANK ME.
LYING WITH DIRTY HANDS IN THIS BED I MADE.
CARTRIDGE DOESN'T TURN. THE BARREL'S QUIET.
KLK
HAMMER CLICKS LIKE A TOY.
KLK
KLK
I NEVER KNEW HOW TO PRAY.

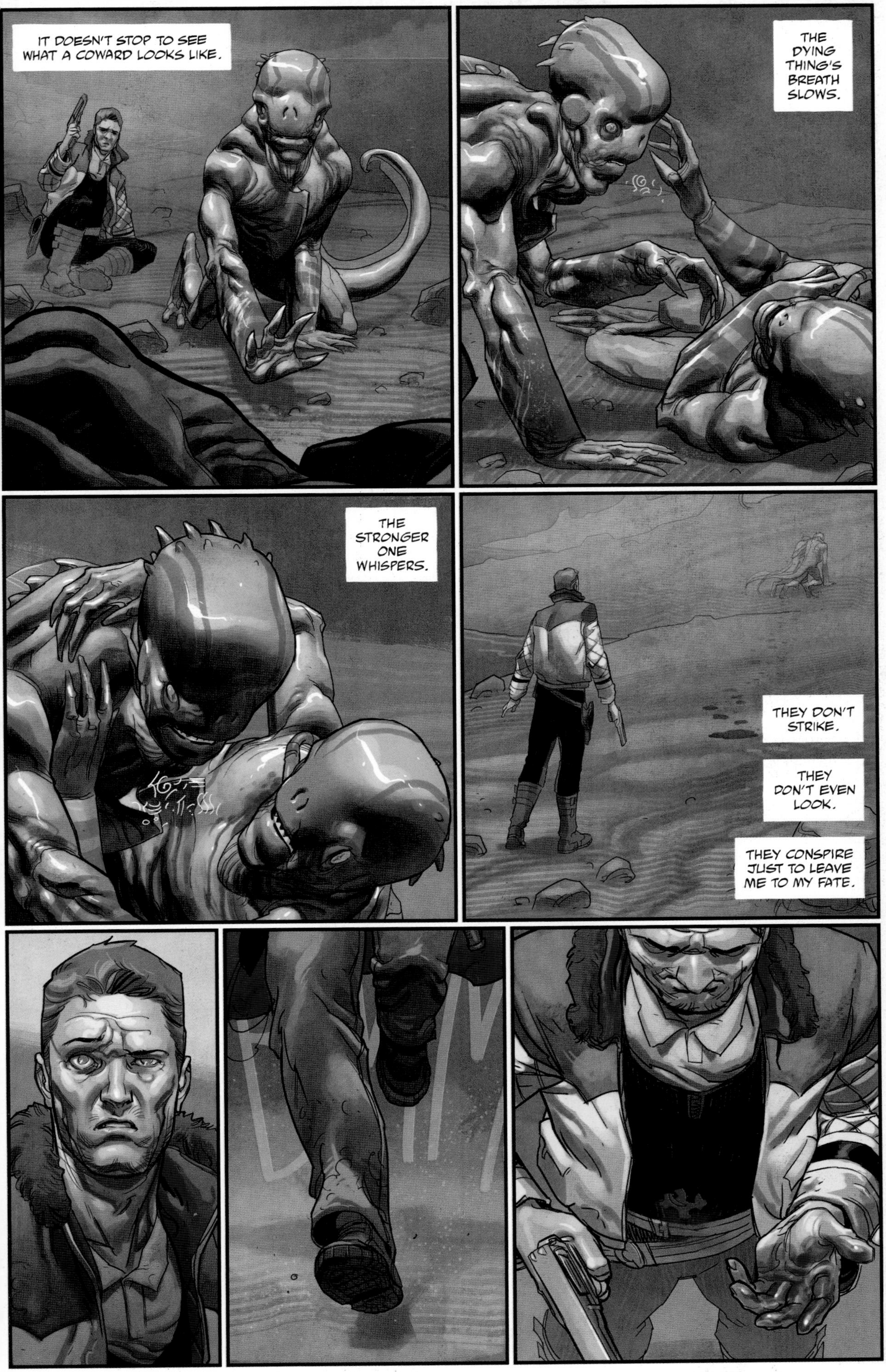
IT DOESN'T STOP TO SEE WHAT A COWARD LOOKS LIKE.
THE DYING THING'S BREATH SLOWS.
THE STRONGER ONE WHISPERS.
THEY DON'T STRIKE.
THEY DON'T EVEN LOOK.
THEY CONSPIRE JUST TO LEAVE ME TO MY FATE.

AND THAT FATE COMES RUNNING.

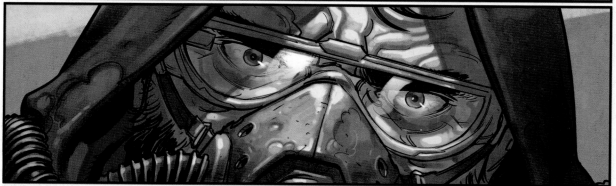

FELL OUT OF THE SKY JUST TO DIE HERE IN THE DIRT.

WHAT DO YOU WANT ME TO *DO?* *TELL* ME. COME ON.

JUST THIS. NOTHING. JUST *BE* HERE.

AND WHO *YOU* HERE WITH, LEE?

MEET A GIRL LIKES TO LOOK IN YOUR EYES, IT'LL FIX WHAT'S WRONG IN YOU.

UNTIL THE DAY THAT SHE LOOKS THROUGH YOU. LOOKING AT SOMETHING YOU CAN'T SEE.

I'M LOOKING AT YOU, JONAH. I'M HERE WITH *YOU.*

HELLO. *HELLO?*

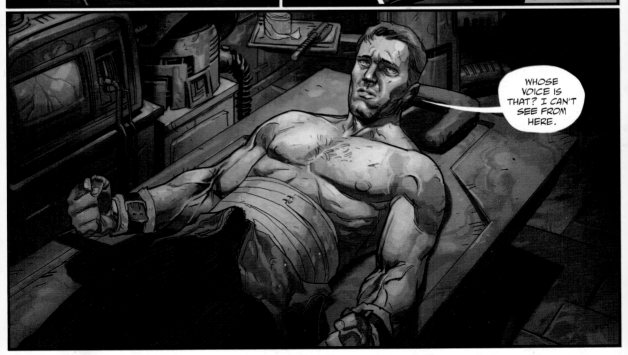

WHOSE VOICE IS THAT? I CAN'T SEE FROM HERE.

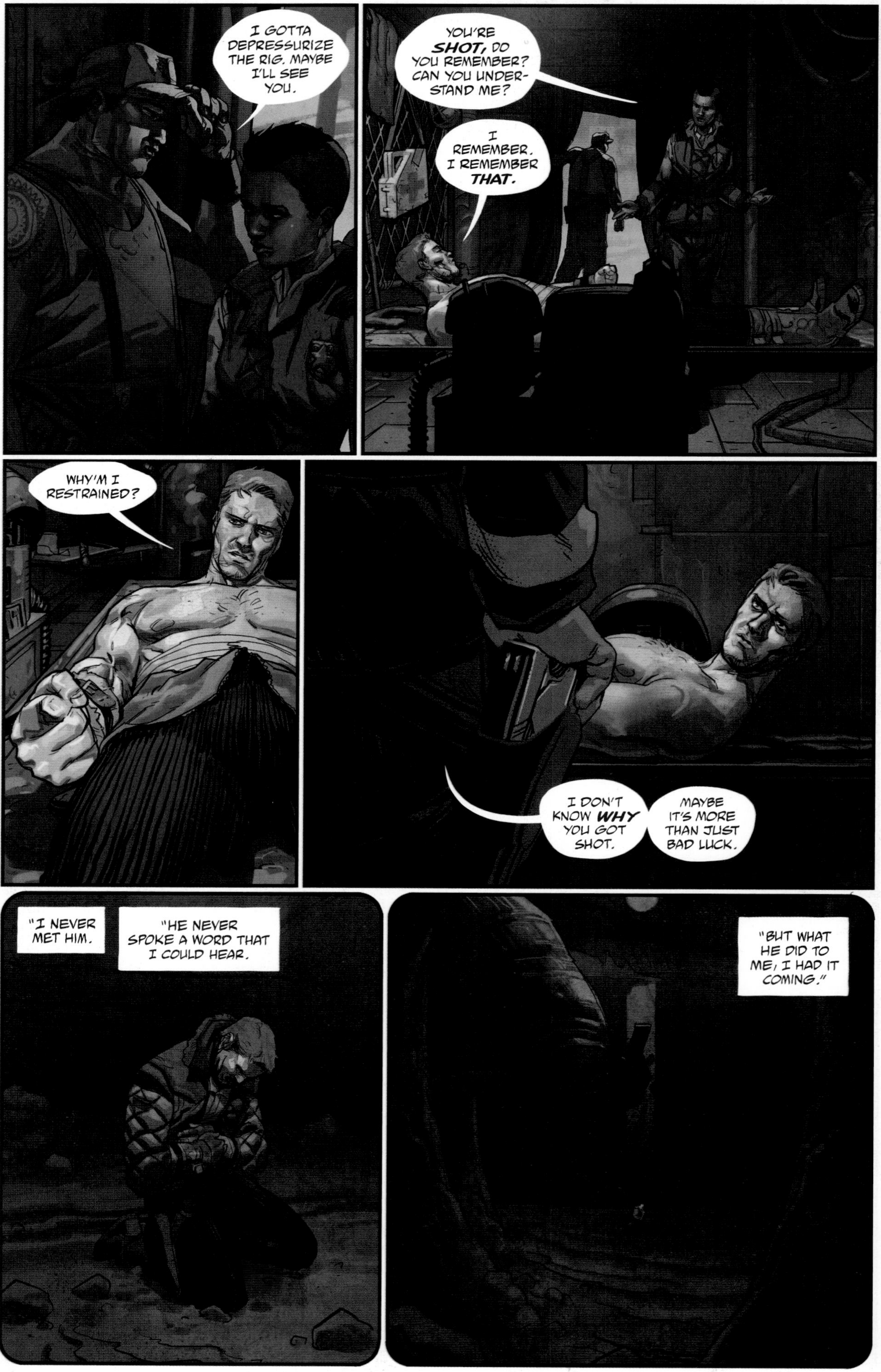
I GOTTA DEPRESSURIZE THE RIG. MAYBE I'LL SEE YOU.
YOU'RE **SHOT,** DO YOU REMEMBER? CAN YOU UNDERSTAND ME?
I REMEMBER. I REMEMBER **THAT.**
WHY'M I RESTRAINED?
I DON'T KNOW **WHY** YOU GOT SHOT.
MAYBE IT'S MORE THAN JUST BAD LUCK.
"I NEVER MET HIM.
"HE NEVER SPOKE A WORD THAT I COULD HEAR.
"BUT WHAT HE DID TO ME, I HAD IT COMING."

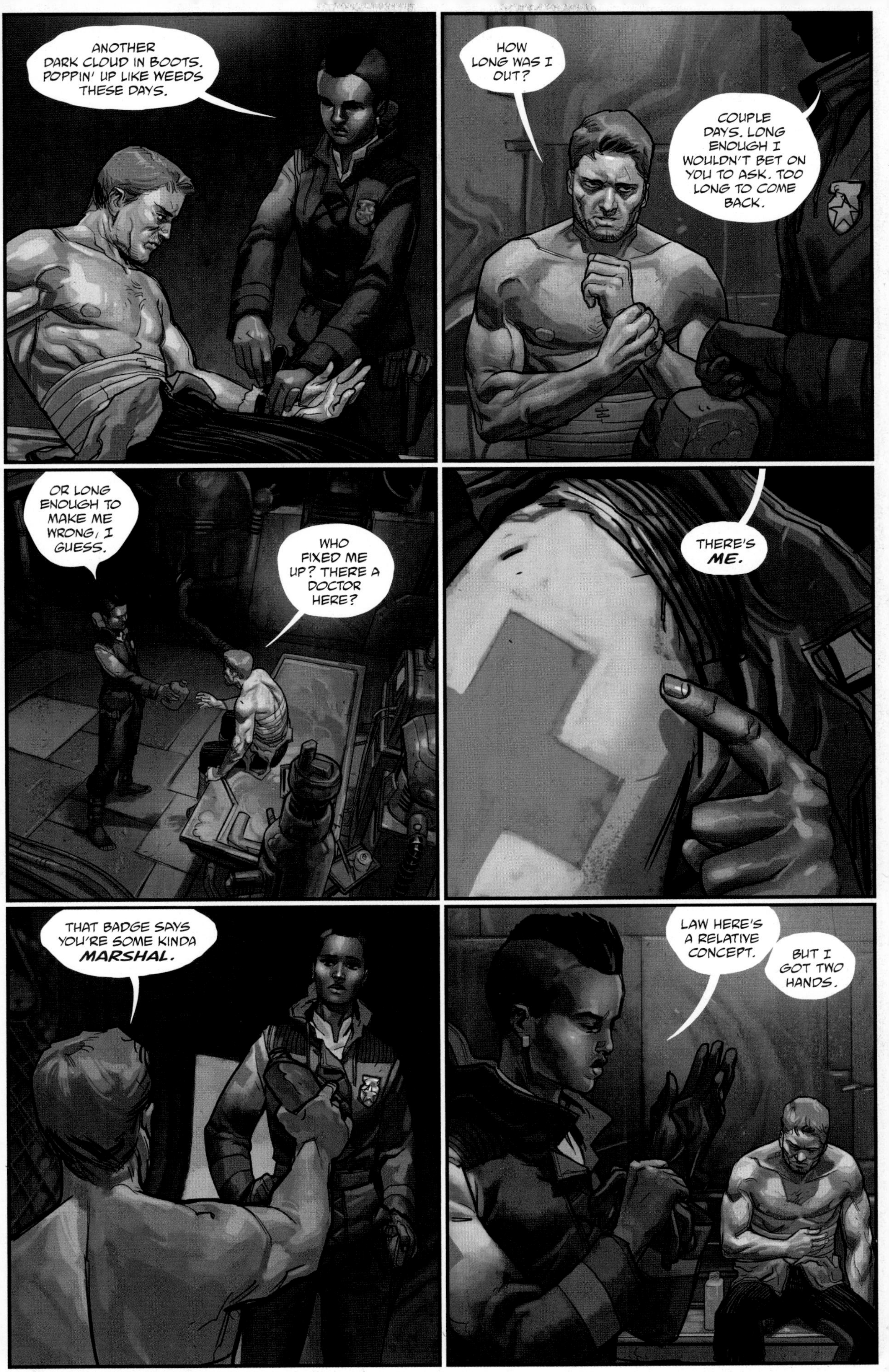
ANOTHER DARK CLOUD IN BOOTS. POPPIN' UP LIKE WEEDS THESE DAYS.
HOW LONG WAS I OUT?
COUPLE DAYS. LONG ENOUGH I WOULDN'T BET ON YOU TO ASK. TOO LONG TO COME BACK.
OR LONG ENOUGH TO MAKE ME WRONG, I GUESS.
WHO FIXED ME UP? THERE A DOCTOR HERE?
THERE'S **ME.**
THAT BADGE SAYS YOU'RE SOME KINDA **MARSHAL.**
LAW HERE'S A RELATIVE CONCEPT.
BUT I GOT TWO HANDS.

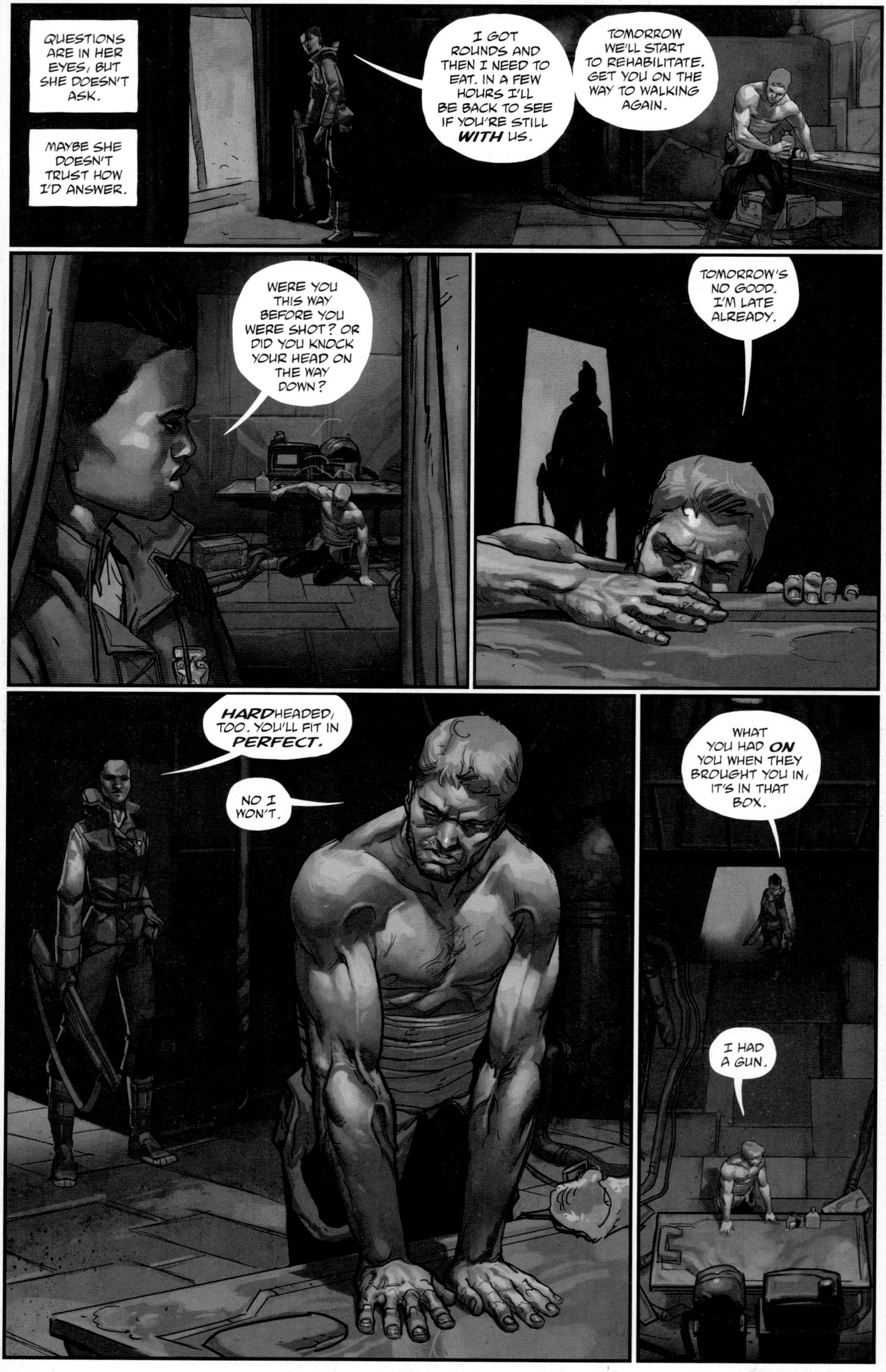
QUESTIONS ARE IN HER EYES, BUT SHE DOESN'T ASK.
MAYBE SHE DOESN'T TRUST HOW I'D ANSWER.
I GOT ROUNDS AND THEN I NEED TO EAT. IN A FEW HOURS I'LL BE BACK TO SEE IF YOU'RE STILL WITH US.
TOMORROW WE'LL START TO REHABILITATE. GET YOU ON THE WAY TO WALKING AGAIN.
WERE YOU THIS WAY BEFORE YOU WERE SHOT? OR DID YOU KNOCK YOUR HEAD ON THE WAY DOWN?
TOMORROW'S NO GOOD. I'M LATE ALREADY.
HARDHEADED, TOO. YOU'LL FIT IN PERFECT.
NO I WON'T.
WHAT YOU HAD ON YOU WHEN THEY BROUGHT YOU IN, IT'S IN THAT BOX.
I HAD A GUN.

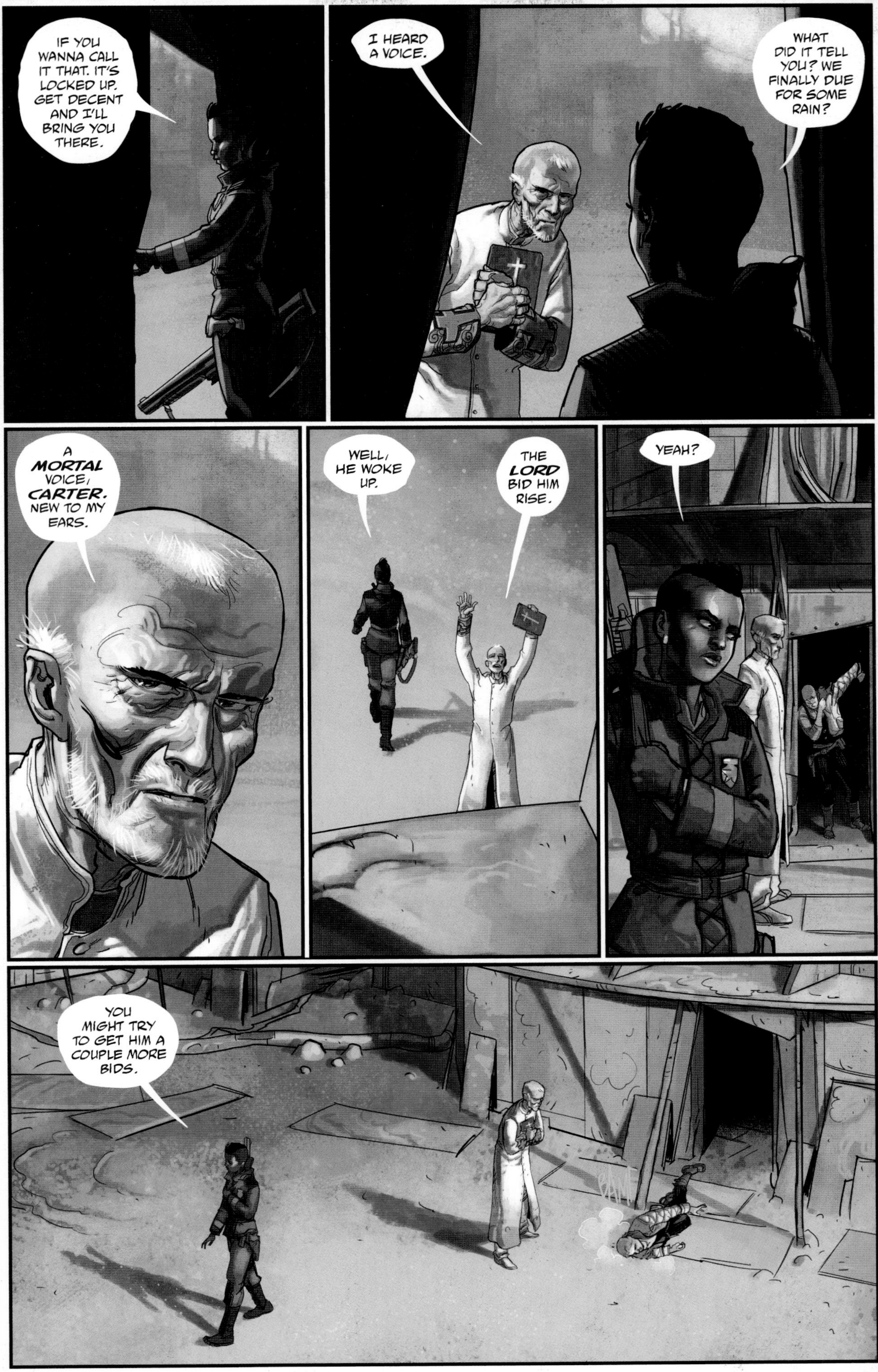
IF YOU WANNA CALL IT THAT. IT'S LOCKED UP. GET DECENT AND I'LL BRING YOU THERE.
I HEARD A VOICE.
WHAT DID IT TELL YOU? WE FINALLY DUE FOR SOME RAIN?
A MORTAL VOICE, CARTER. NEW TO MY EARS.
WELL, HE WOKE UP.
THE LORD BID HIM RISE.
YEAH?
YOU MIGHT TRY TO GET HIM A COUPLE MORE BIDS.

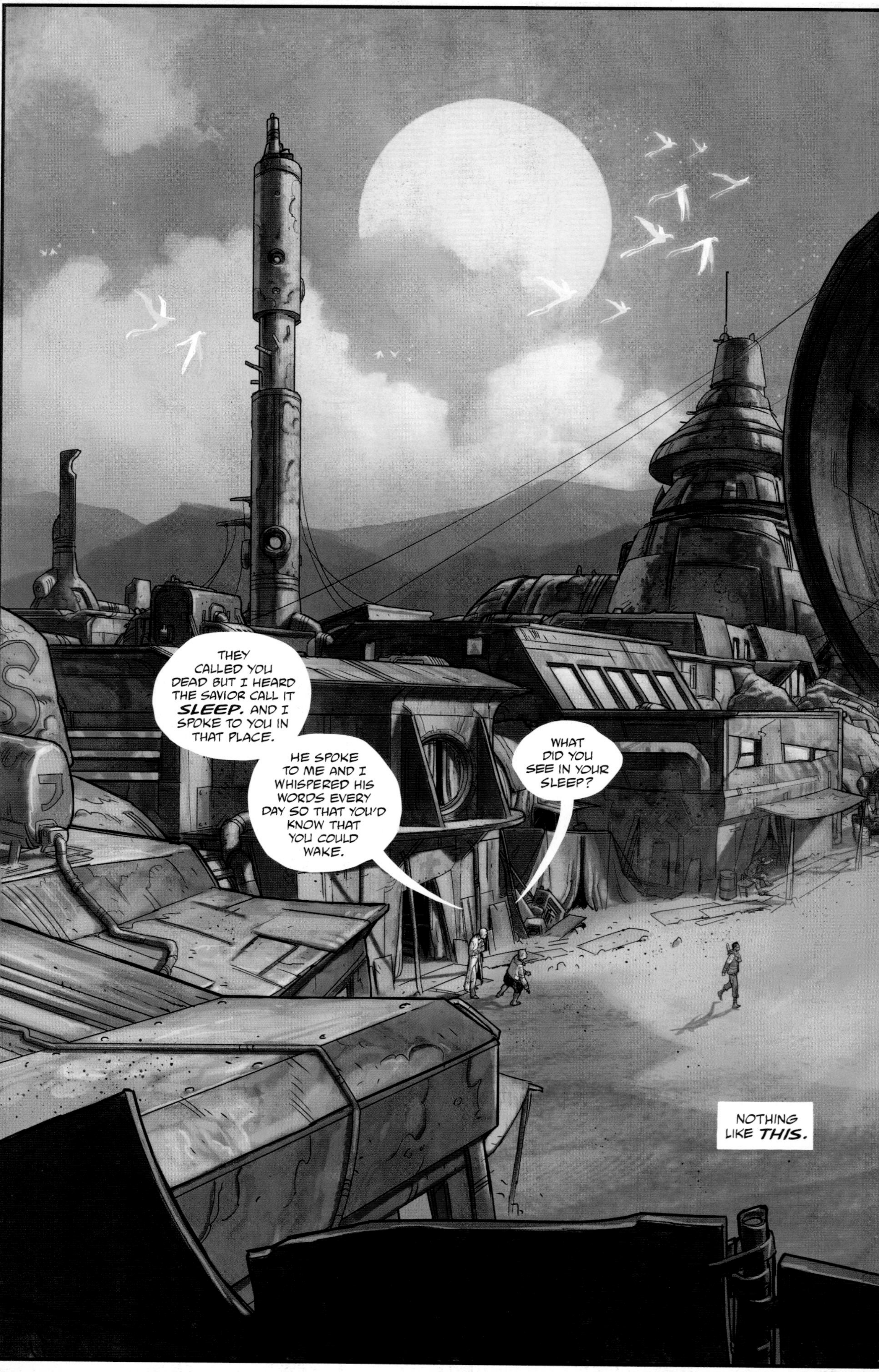
THEY CALLED YOU DEAD BUT I HEARD THE SAVIOR CALL IT SLEEP. AND I SPOKE TO YOU IN THAT PLACE.
HE SPOKE TO ME AND I WHISPERED HIS WORDS EVERY DAY SO THAT YOU'D KNOW THAT YOU COULD WAKE.
WHAT DID YOU SEE IN YOUR SLEEP?
NOTHING LIKE THIS.

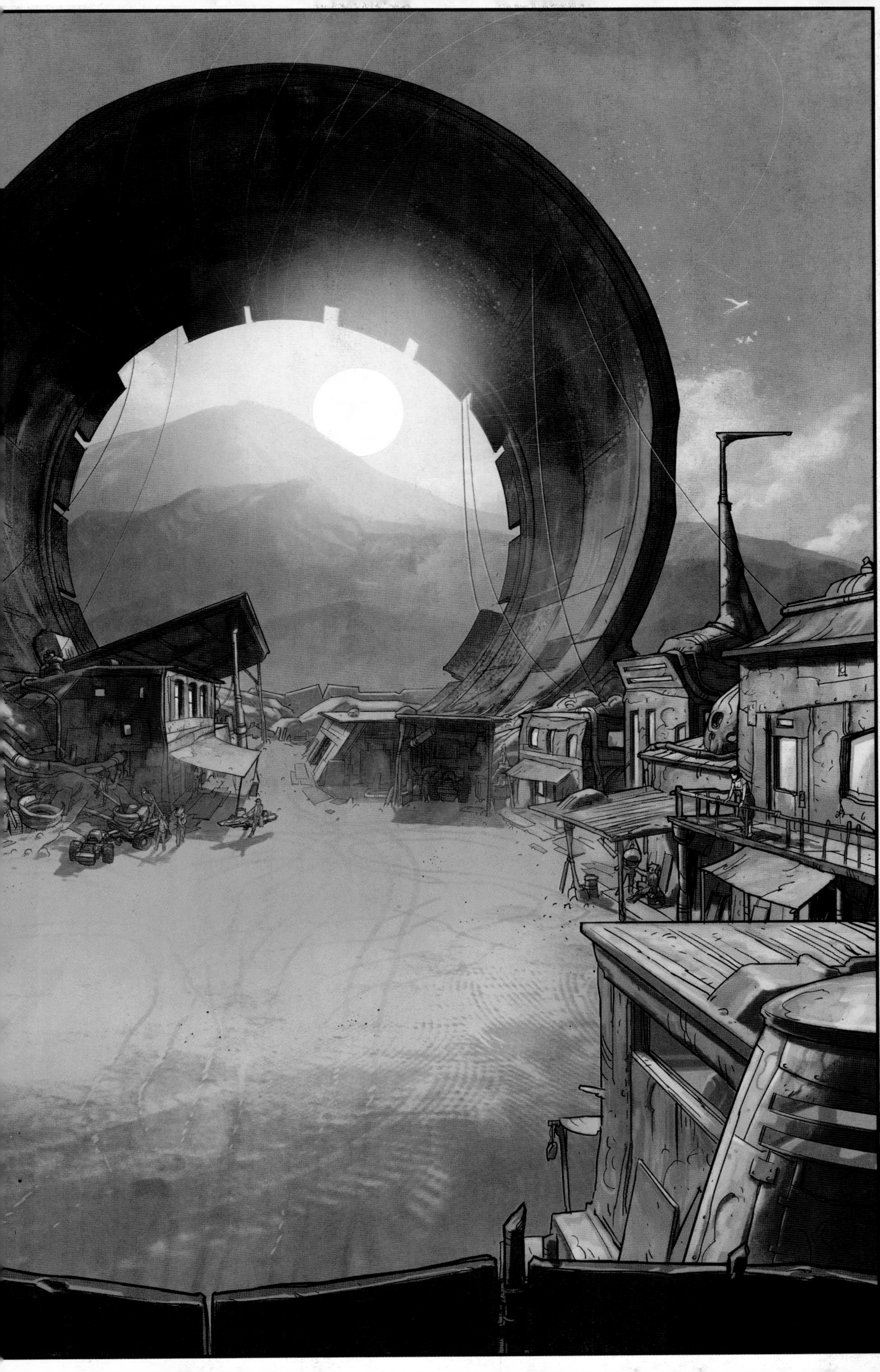

I DREAMT OF YOU LIKE *THIS* TODAY. RISEN. ARRIVED.

ARRIVED TO *WHERE?* WHAT KINDA PLACE ARE WE?

THEY CALL IT GHOST TOWN. WHAT KINDA PLACE, I GUESS WE'RE WORKING AT. WHAT KINDA PLACE IT'LL *BE.*

WHERE CAN I GET MY HEAD RIGHT?

MISTER?

IS THERE A *BAR?*

TAKE HIM TO IT. TELL BIG TO LET HIM HAVE HIS GUN OUT OF THE SAFE.

I'VE GOT A LOT TO DO TODAY.

WHAT DO THEY TAKE HERE FOR MONEY?

ALLOW ME TO ARRANGE IT.

EARS RING LIKE A SIREN. WHATEVER BLOOD I HAVE, IT MOVES UP TO MY HEAD.

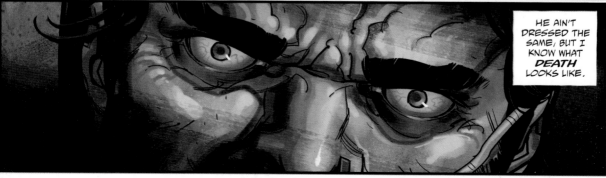

HE AIN'T DRESSED THE SAME, BUT I KNOW WHAT *DEATH* LOOKS LIKE.

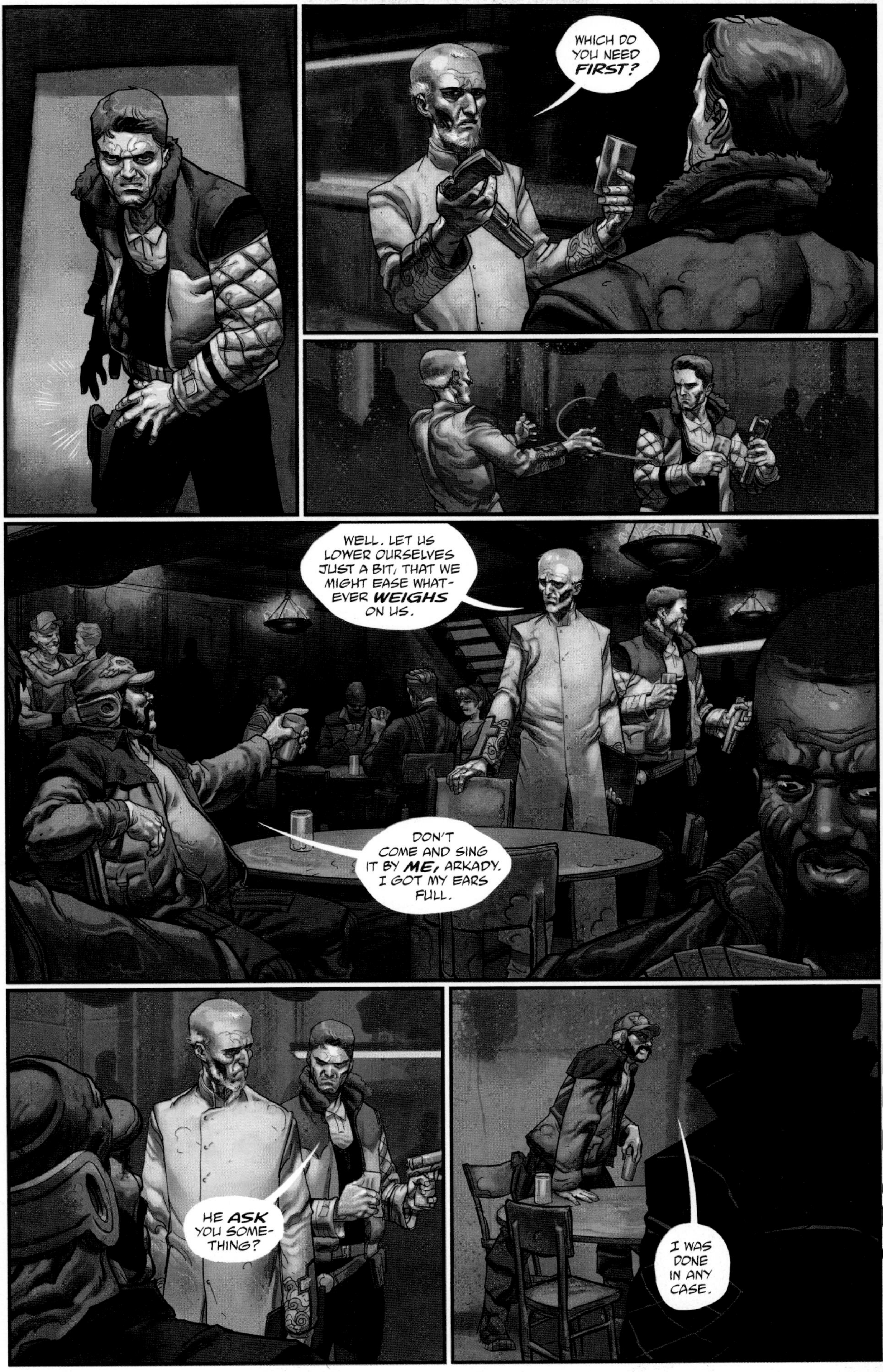
WHICH DO YOU NEED FIRST?
WELL. LET US LOWER OURSELVES JUST A BIT, THAT WE MIGHT EASE WHATEVER WEIGHS ON US.
DON'T COME AND SING IT BY ME, ARKADY. I GOT MY EARS FULL.
HE ASK YOU SOMETHING?
I WAS DONE IN ANY CASE.

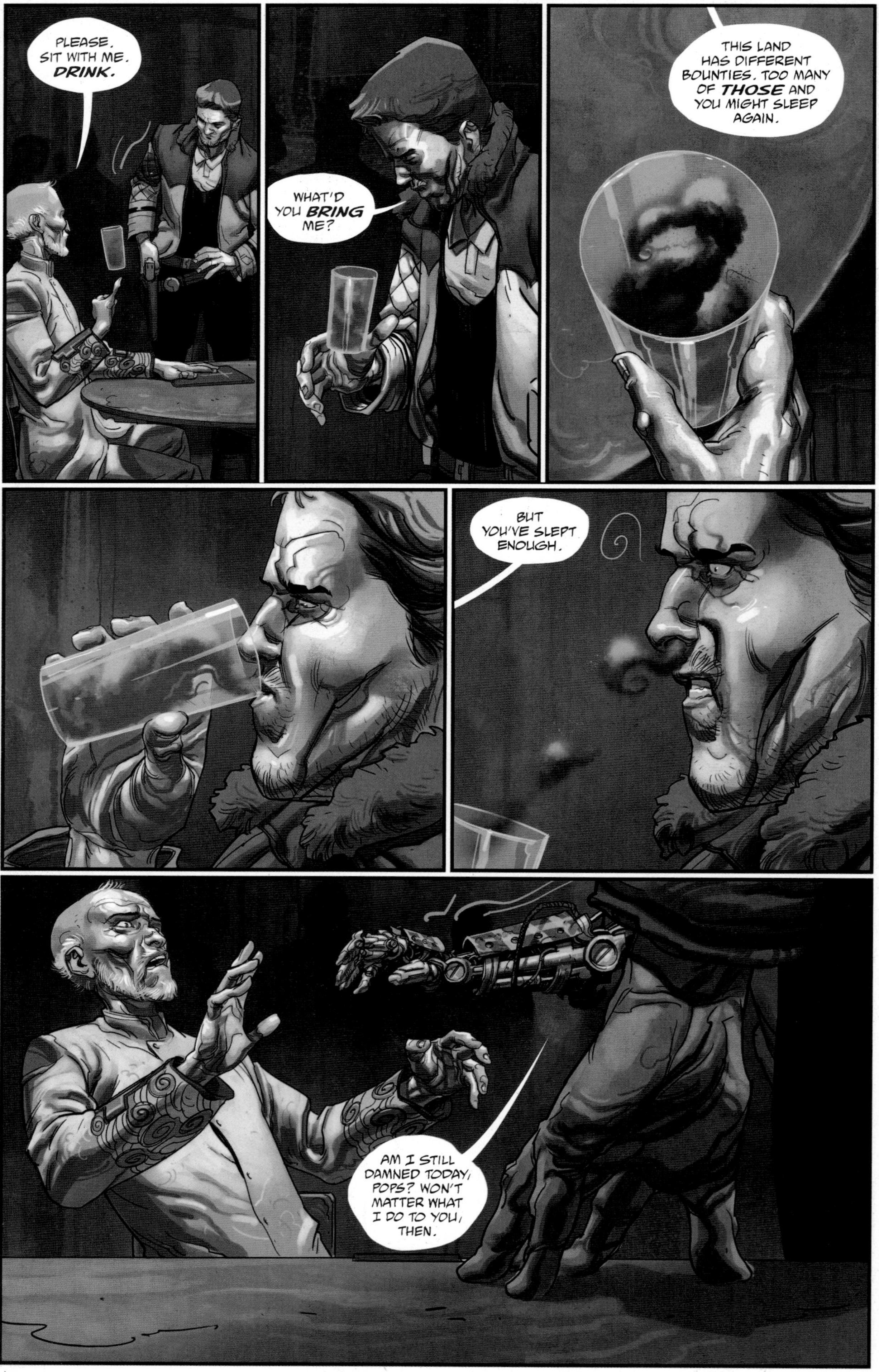
PLEASE. SIT WITH ME. DRINK.
WHAT'D YOU BRING ME?
THIS LAND HAS DIFFERENT BOUNTIES. TOO MANY OF THOSE AND YOU MIGHT SLEEP AGAIN.
BUT YOU'VE SLEPT ENOUGH.
AM I STILL DAMNED TODAY, POPS? WON'T MATTER WHAT I DO TO YOU, THEN.

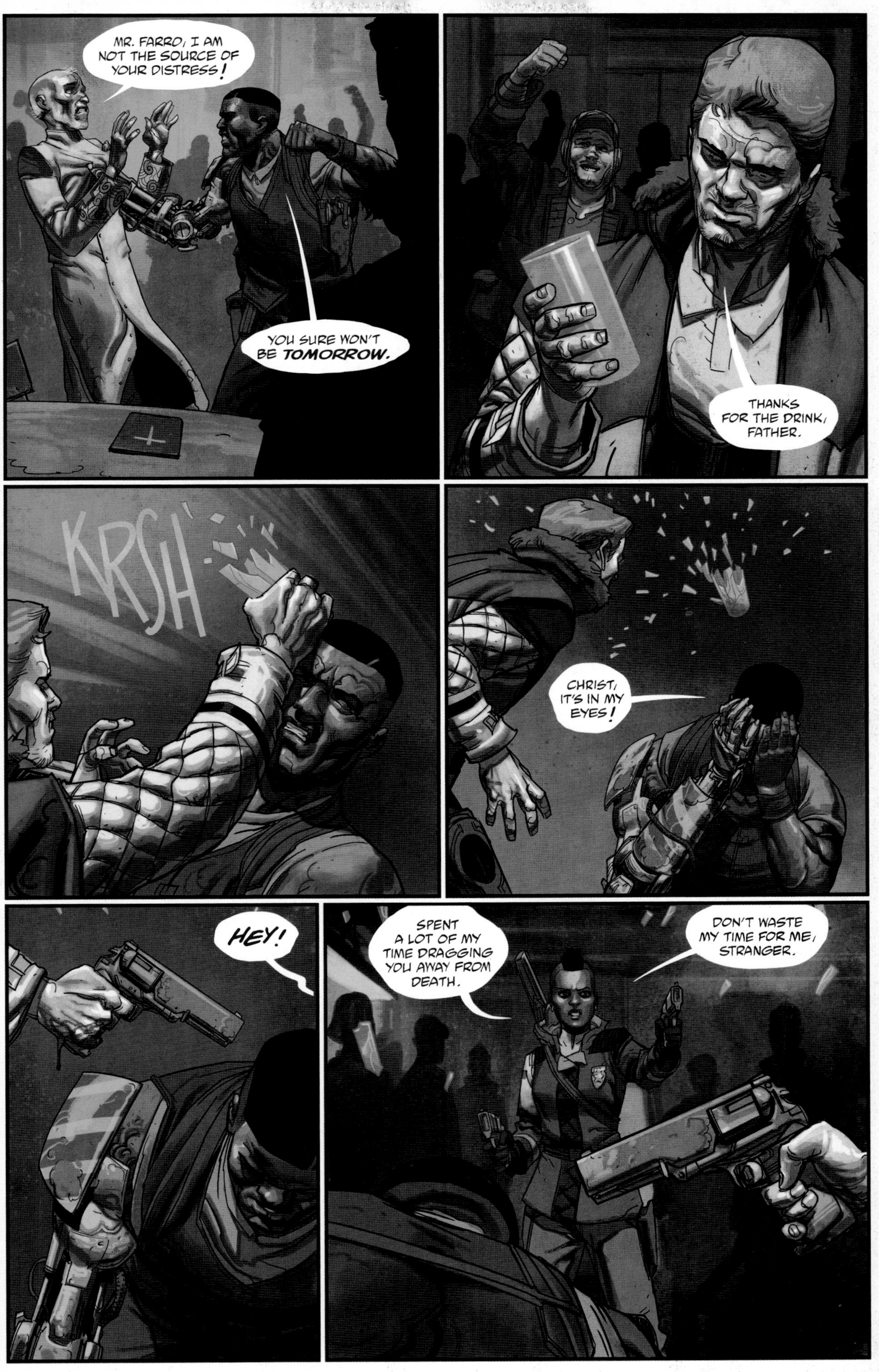

MR. FARRO, I AM NOT THE SOURCE OF YOUR DISTRESS!
YOU SURE WON'T BE TOMORROW.
THANKS FOR THE DRINK, FATHER.
KRSH
CHRIST, IT'S IN MY EYES!
HEY!
SPENT A LOT OF MY TIME DRAGGING YOU AWAY FROM DEATH.
DON'T WASTE MY TIME FOR ME, STRANGER.

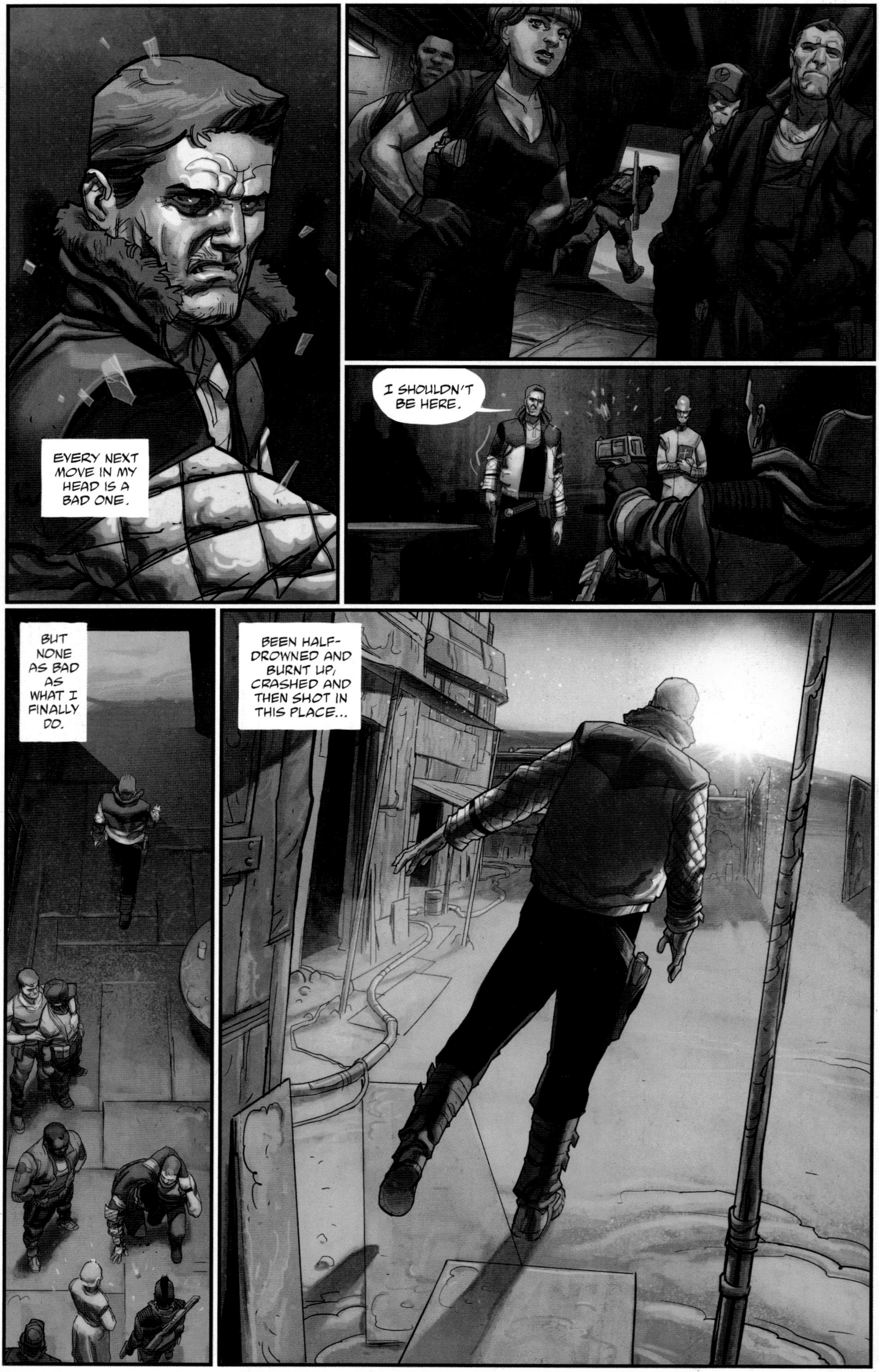
EVERY NEXT MOVE IN MY HEAD IS A BAD ONE.
I SHOULDN'T BE HERE.
BUT NONE AS BAD AS WHAT I FINALLY DO.
BEEN HALF-DROWNED AND BURNT UP, CRASHED AND THEN SHOT IN THIS PLACE...

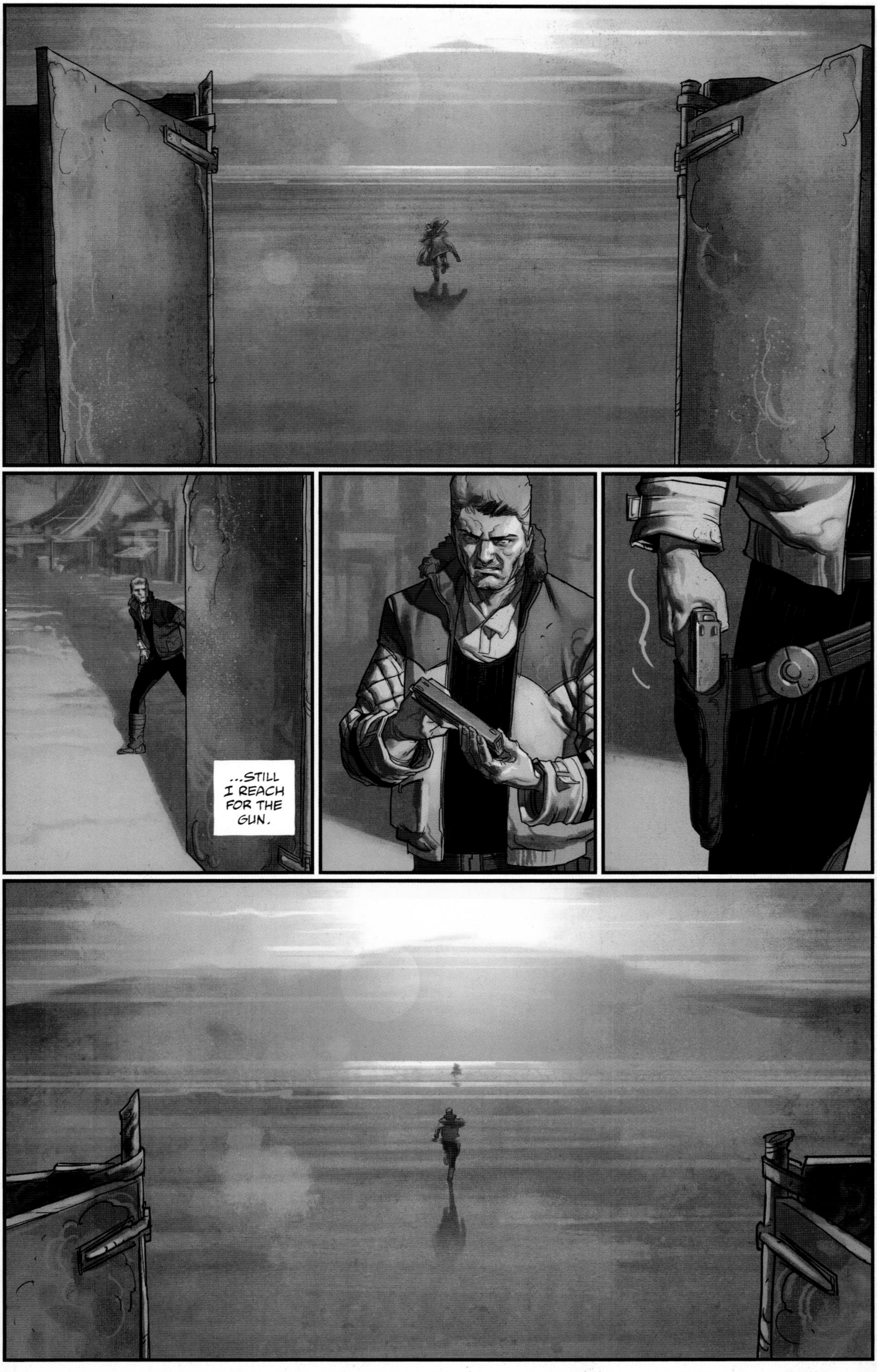
...STILL I REACH FOR THE GUN.

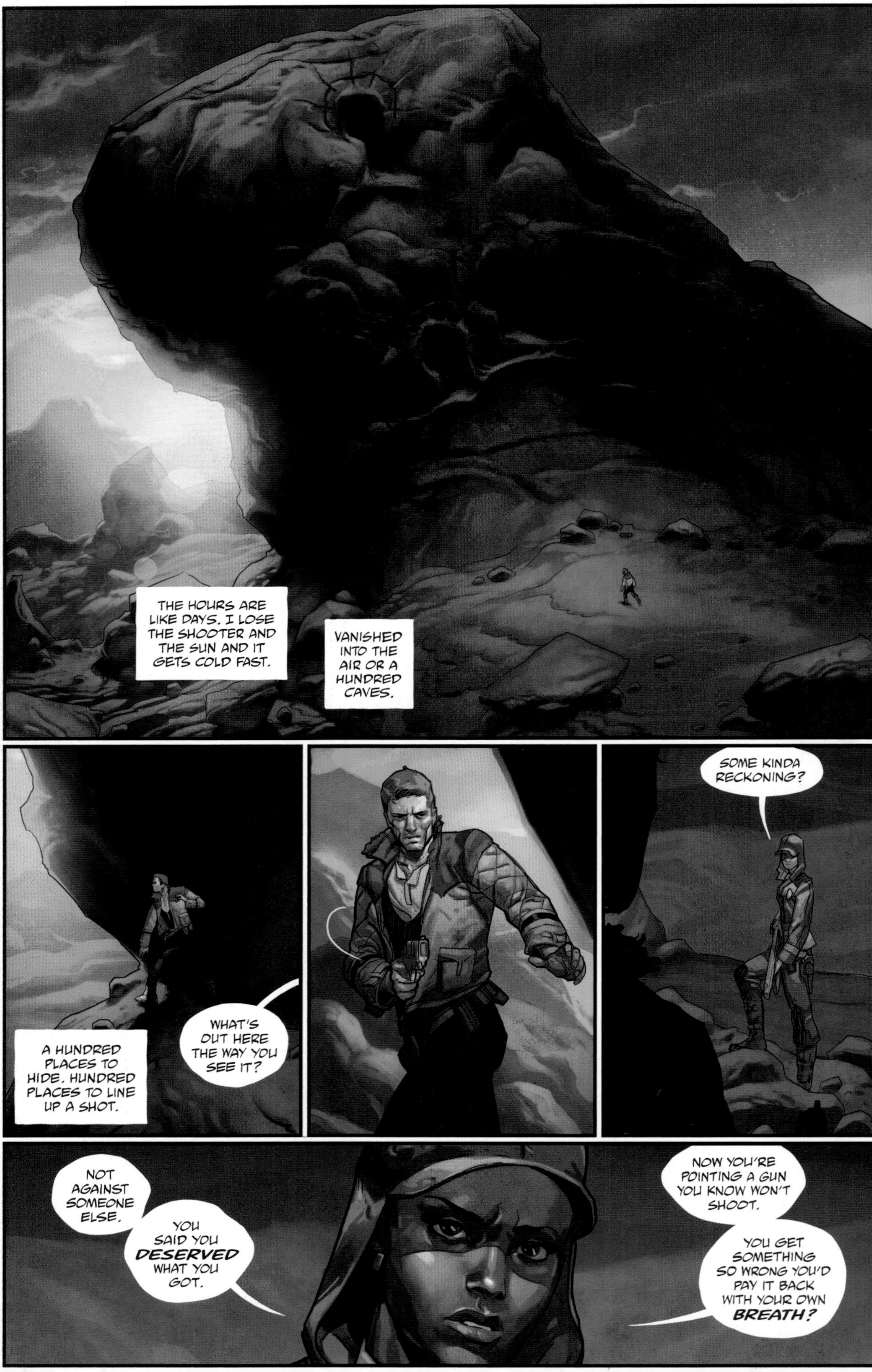
THE HOURS ARE LIKE DAYS. I LOSE THE SHOOTER AND THE SUN AND IT GETS COLD FAST.
VANISHED INTO THE AIR OR A HUNDRED CAVES.
A HUNDRED PLACES TO HIDE. HUNDRED PLACES TO LINE UP A SHOT.
WHAT'S OUT HERE THE WAY YOU SEE IT?
SOME KINDA RECKONING?
NOT AGAINST SOMEONE ELSE.
YOU SAID YOU **DESERVED** WHAT YOU GOT.
NOW YOU'RE POINTING A GUN YOU KNOW WON'T SHOOT.
YOU GET SOMETHING SO WRONG YOU'D PAY IT BACK WITH YOUR OWN **BREATH?**

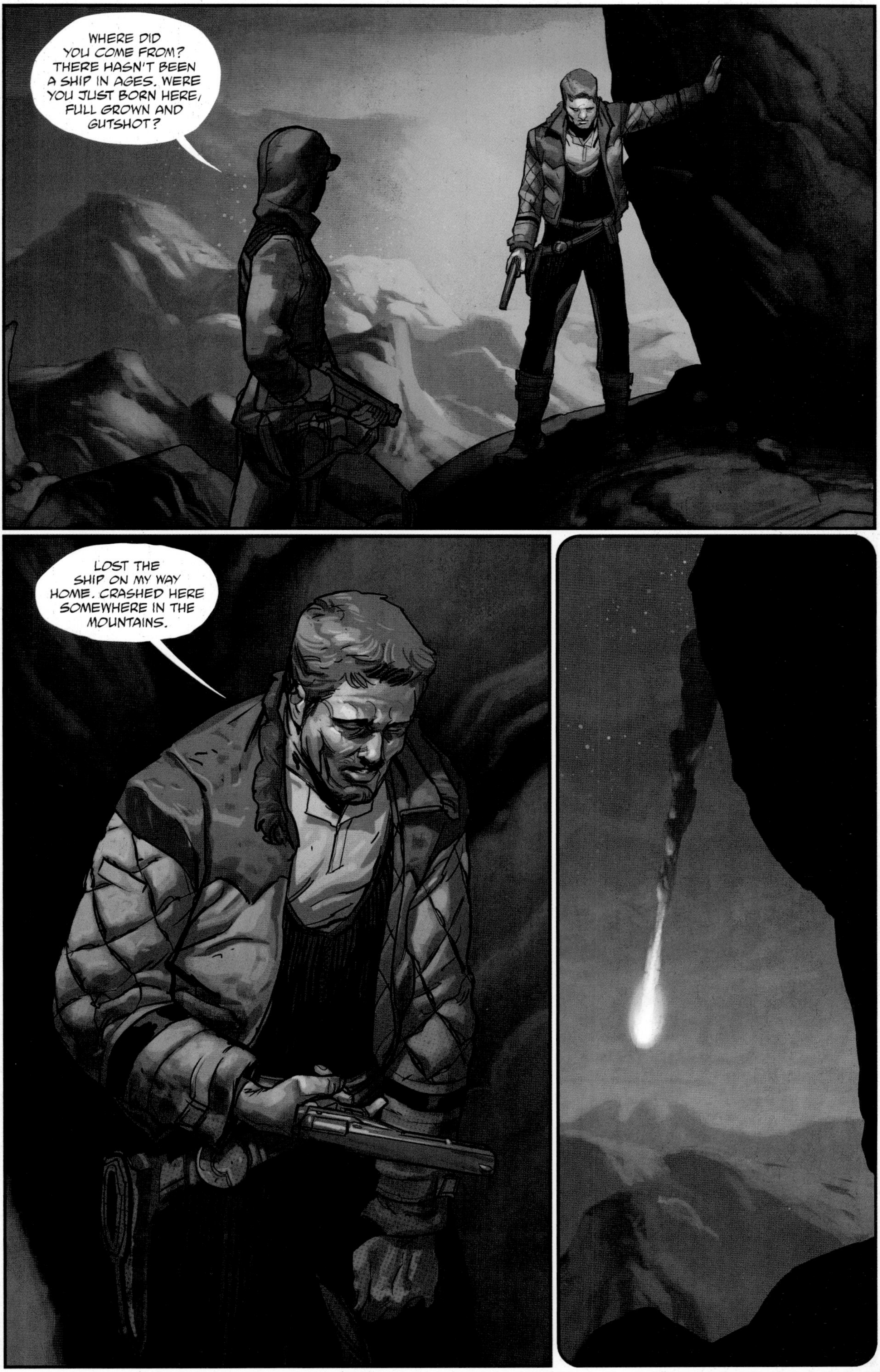
WHERE DID YOU COME FROM? THERE HASN'T BEEN A SHIP IN AGES. WERE YOU JUST BORN HERE, FULL GROWN AND GUTSHOT?
LOST THE SHIP ON MY WAY HOME. CRASHED HERE SOMEWHERE IN THE MOUNTAINS.

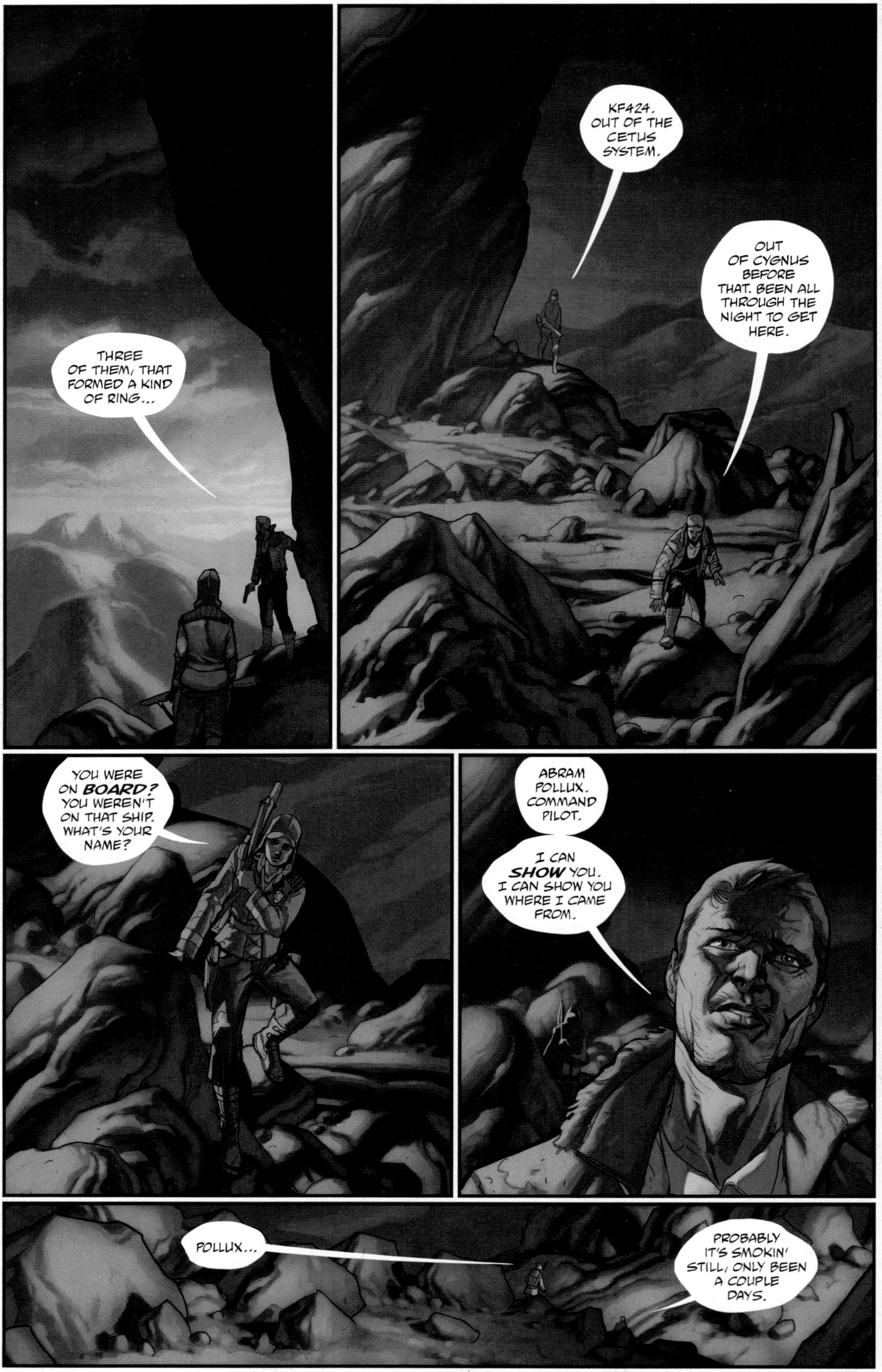
THREE OF THEM, THAT FORMED A KIND OF RING...
KF424. OUT OF THE CETUS SYSTEM.
OUT OF CYGNUS BEFORE THAT. BEEN ALL THROUGH THE NIGHT TO GET HERE.
YOU WERE ON BOARD? YOU WEREN'T ON THAT SHIP. WHAT'S YOUR NAME?
ABRAM POLLUX. COMMAND PILOT.
I CAN SHOW YOU. I CAN SHOW YOU WHERE I CAME FROM.
POLLUX...
PROBABLY IT'S SMOKIN' STILL, ONLY BEEN A COUPLE DAYS.

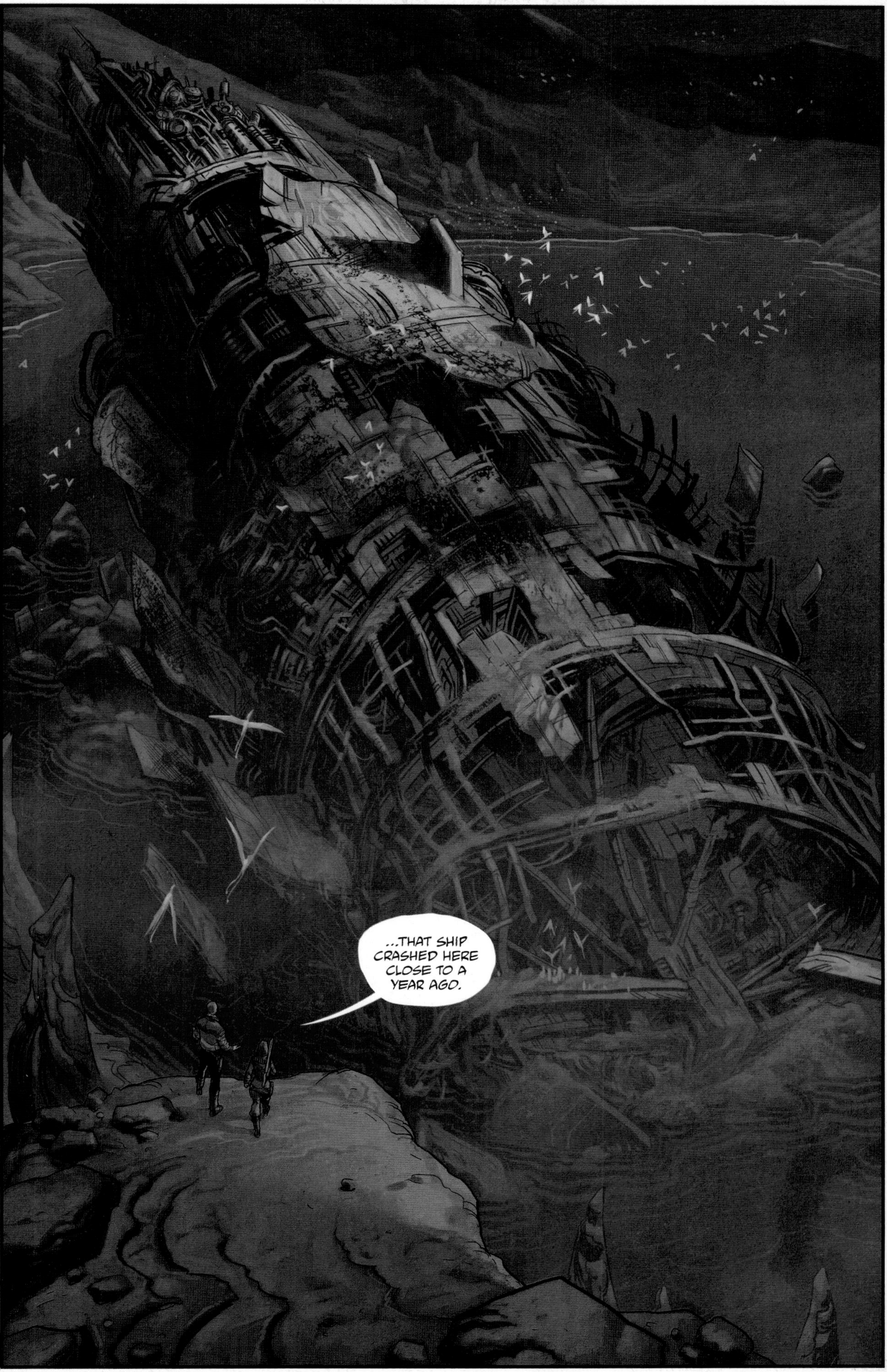
...THAT SHIP CRASHED HERE CLOSE TO A YEAR AGO.

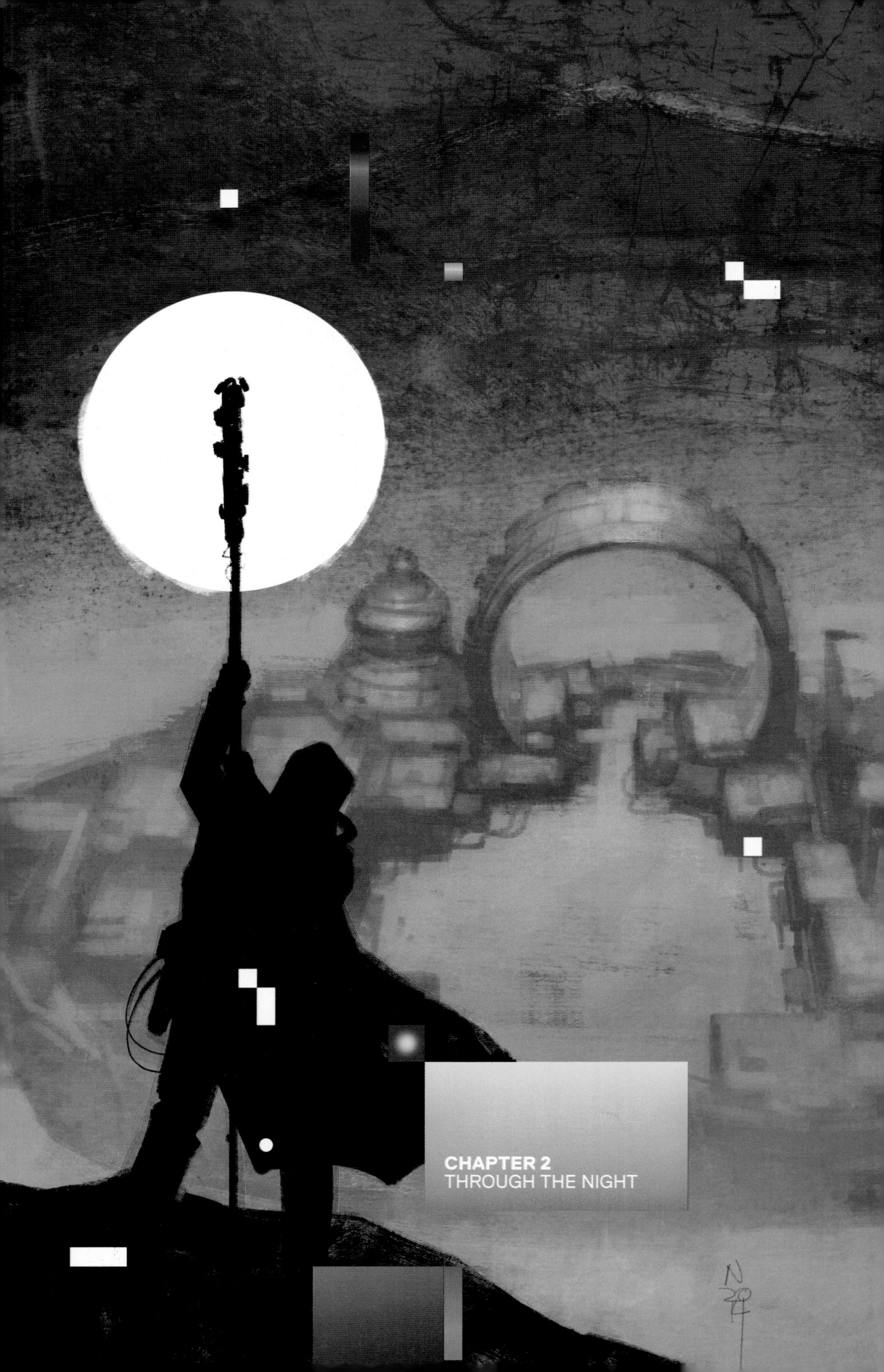
CHAPTER 2
THROUGH THE NIGHT

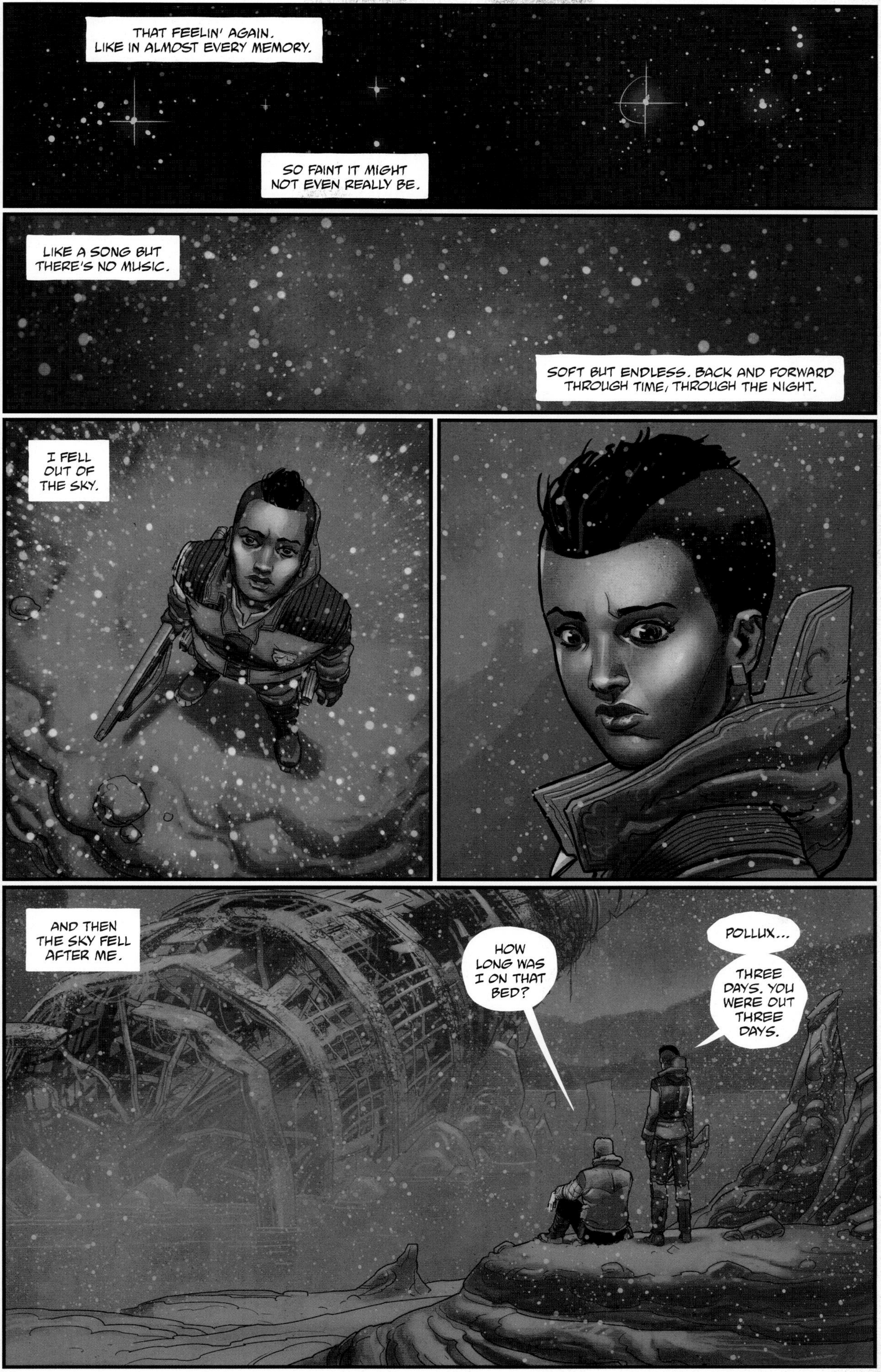
THAT FEELIN' AGAIN. LIKE IN ALMOST EVERY MEMORY.
SO FAINT IT MIGHT NOT EVEN REALLY BE.
LIKE A SONG BUT THERE'S NO MUSIC.
SOFT BUT ENDLESS. BACK AND FORWARD THROUGH TIME, THROUGH THE NIGHT.
I FELL OUT OF THE SKY.
AND THEN THE SKY FELL AFTER ME.
HOW LONG WAS I ON THAT BED?
POLLUX...
THREE DAYS. YOU WERE OUT THREE DAYS.

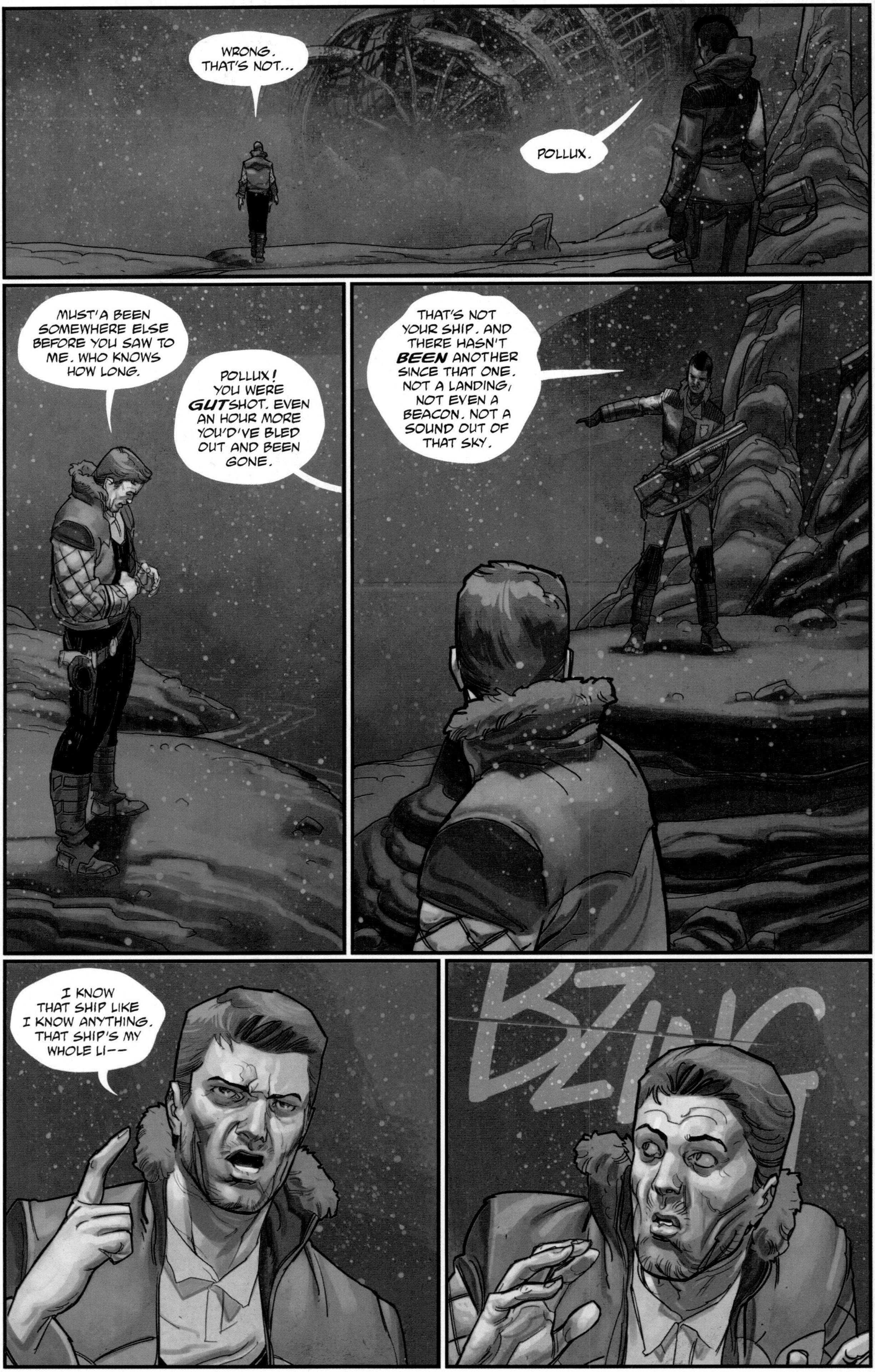
WRONG. THAT'S NOT...
POLLUX.
MUST'A BEEN SOMEWHERE ELSE BEFORE YOU SAW TO ME. WHO KNOWS HOW LONG.
POLLUX! YOU WERE GUTSHOT. EVEN AN HOUR MORE YOU'D'VE BLED OUT AND BEEN GONE.
THAT'S NOT YOUR SHIP. AND THERE HASN'T BEEN ANOTHER SINCE THAT ONE. NOT A LANDING, NOT EVEN A BEACON. NOT A SOUND OUT OF THAT SKY.
I KNOW THAT SHIP LIKE I KNOW ANYTHING. THAT SHIP'S MY WHOLE LI--

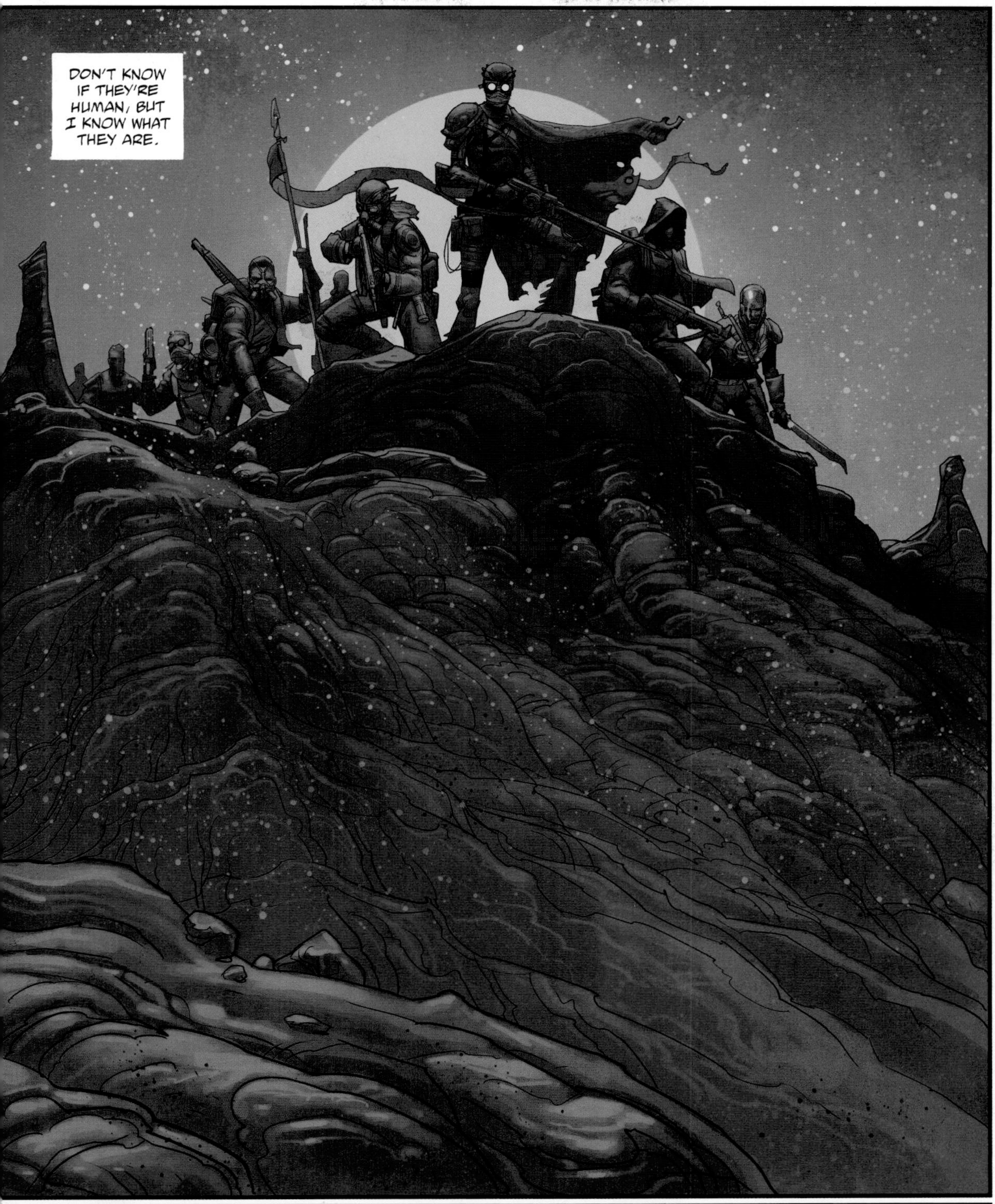
DON'T KNOW IF THEY'RE HUMAN, BUT I KNOW WHAT THEY ARE.
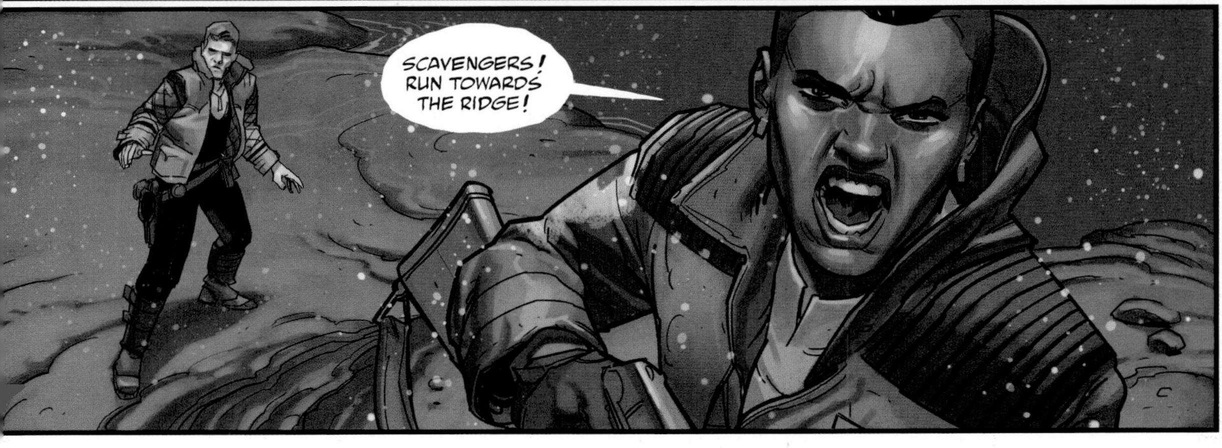
SCAVENGERS! RUN TOWARDS THE RIDGE!

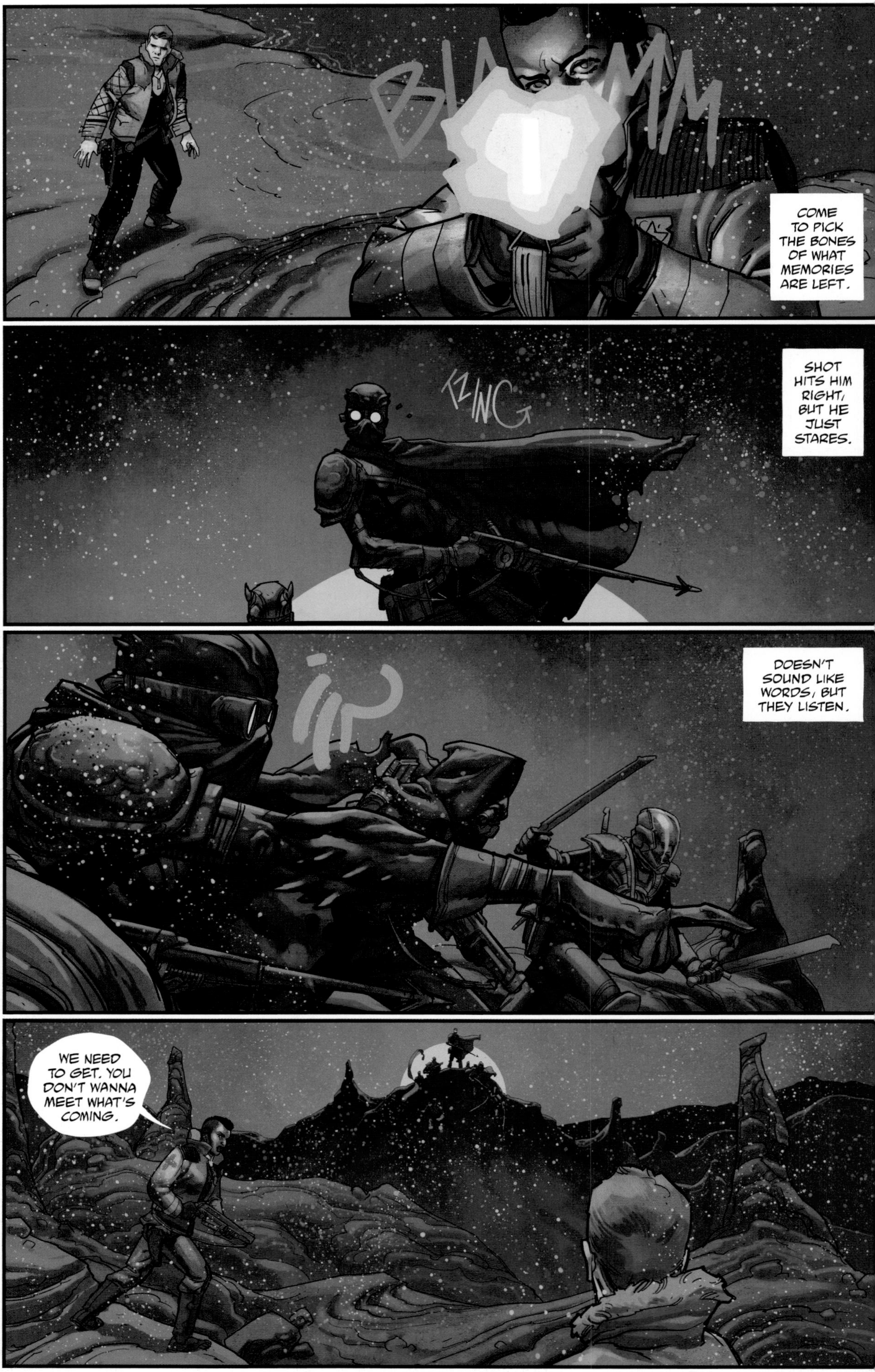
BLAMM
COME TO PICK THE BONES OF WHAT MEMORIES ARE LEFT.
TZING
SHOT HITS HIM RIGHT, BUT HE JUST STARES.
DOESN'T SOUND LIKE WORDS, BUT THEY LISTEN.
WE NEED TO GET. YOU DON'T WANNA MEET WHAT'S COMING.

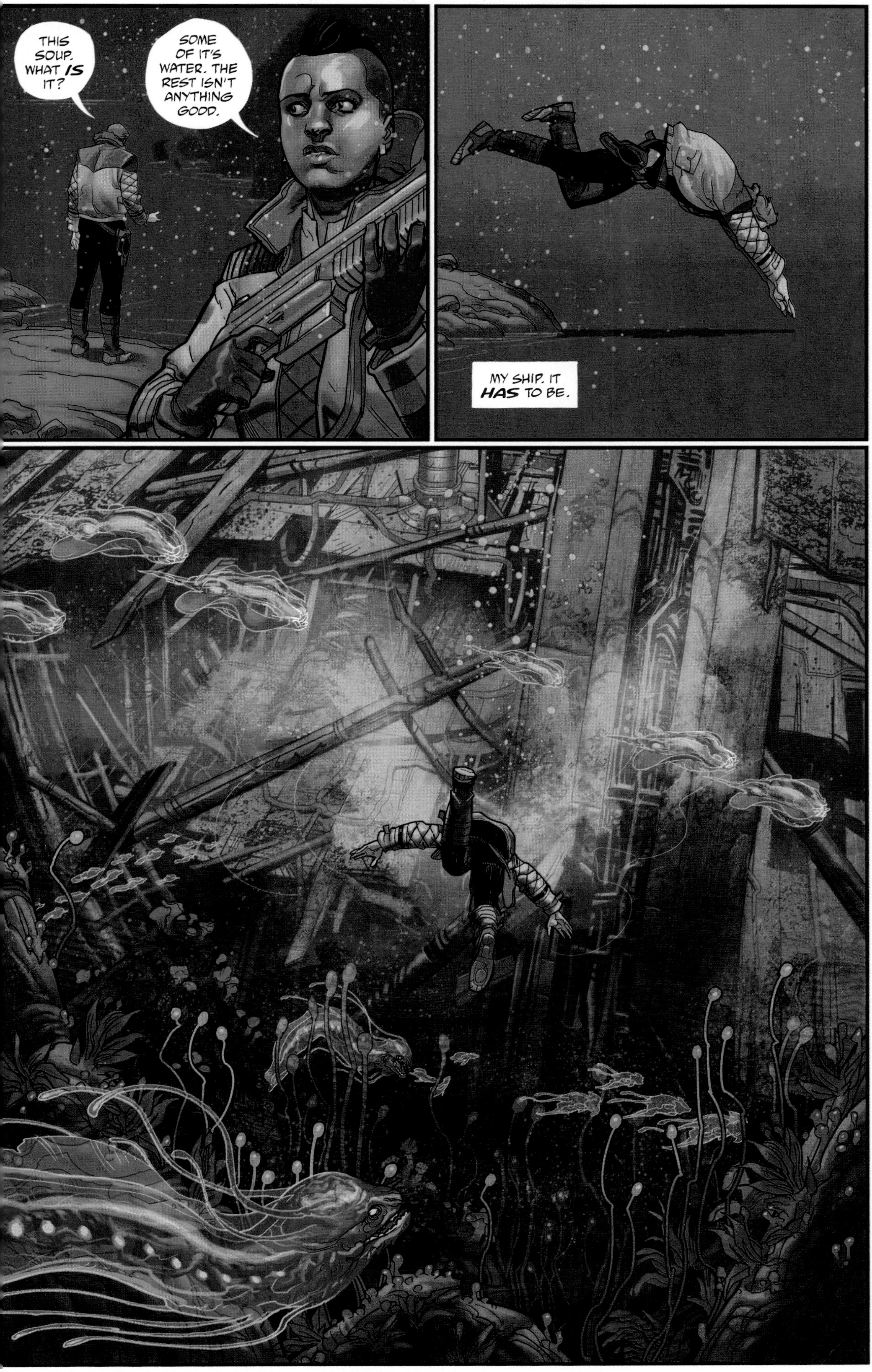
THIS SOUP. WHAT IS IT?
SOME OF IT'S WATER. THE REST ISN'T ANYTHING GOOD.
MY SHIP. IT HAS TO BE.

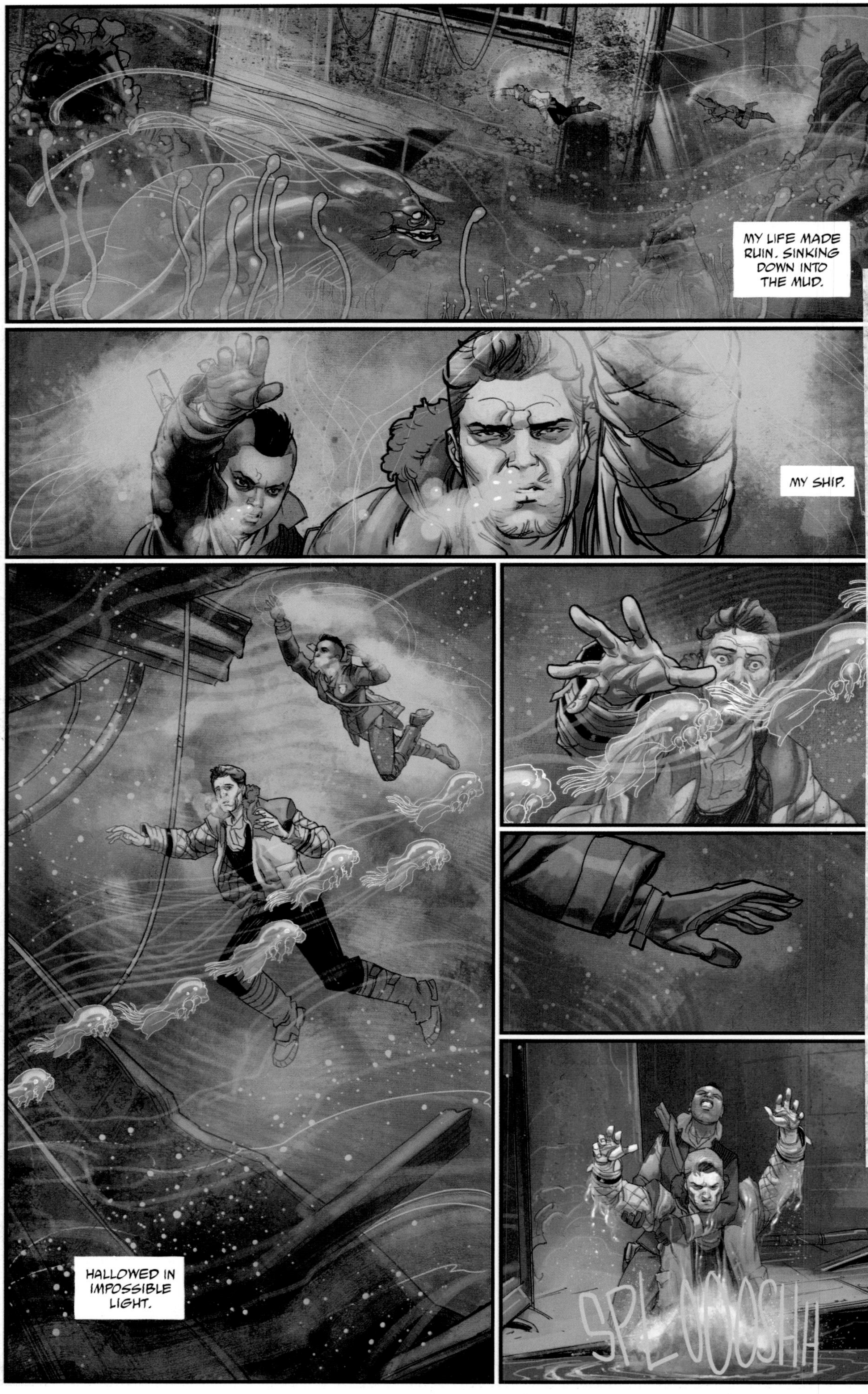
MY LIFE MADE RUIN. SINKING DOWN INTO THE MUD.
MY SHIP.
HALLOWED IN IMPOSSIBLE LIGHT.
SPLOOOSHH

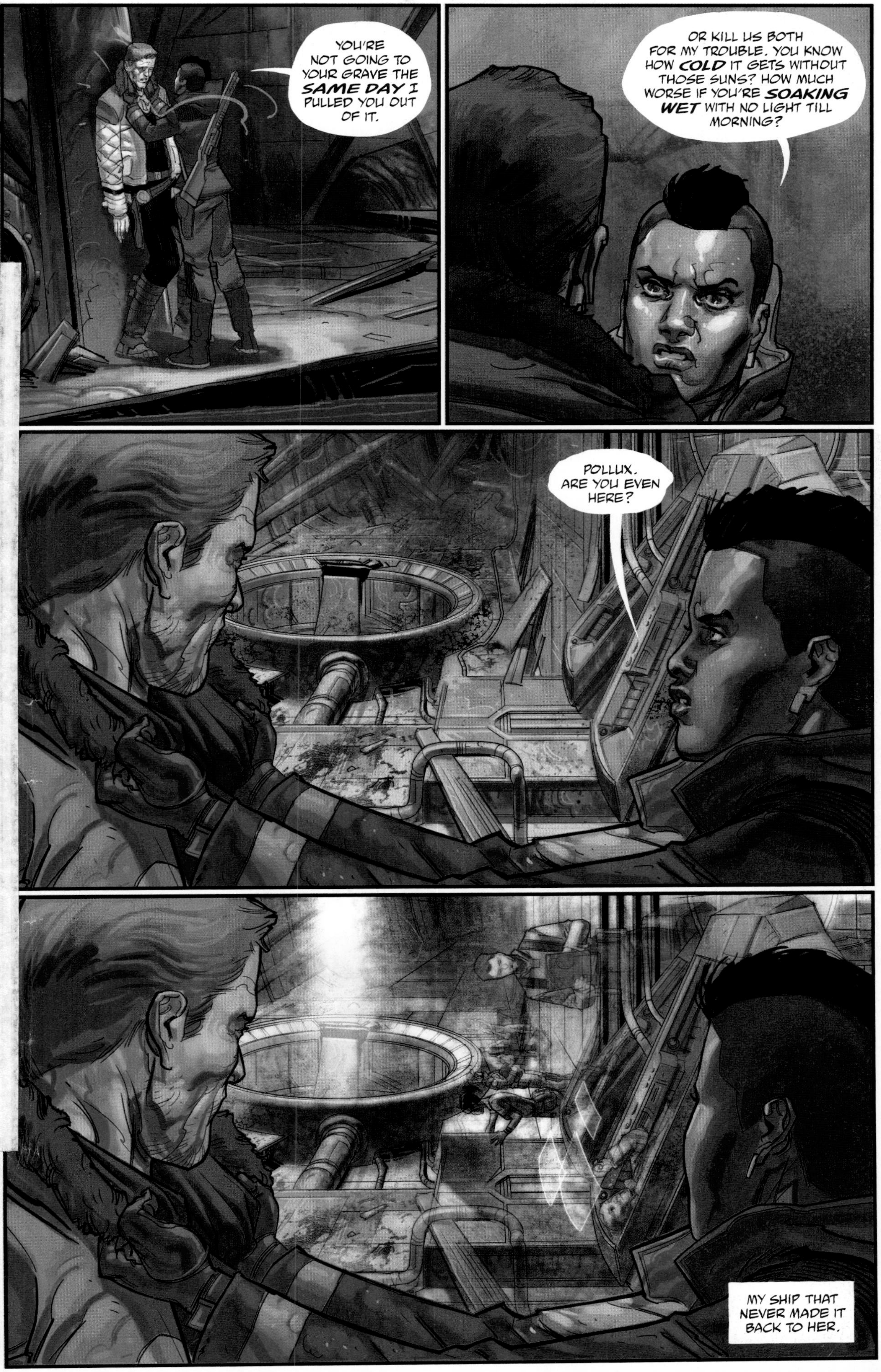
YOU'RE NOT GOING TO YOUR GRAVE THE SAME DAY I PULLED YOU OUT OF IT.
OR KILL US BOTH FOR MY TROUBLE. YOU KNOW HOW COLD IT GETS WITHOUT THOSE SUNS? HOW MUCH WORSE IF YOU'RE SOAKING WET WITH NO LIGHT TILL MORNING?
POLLUX. ARE YOU EVEN HERE?
MY SHIP THAT NEVER MADE IT BACK TO HER.

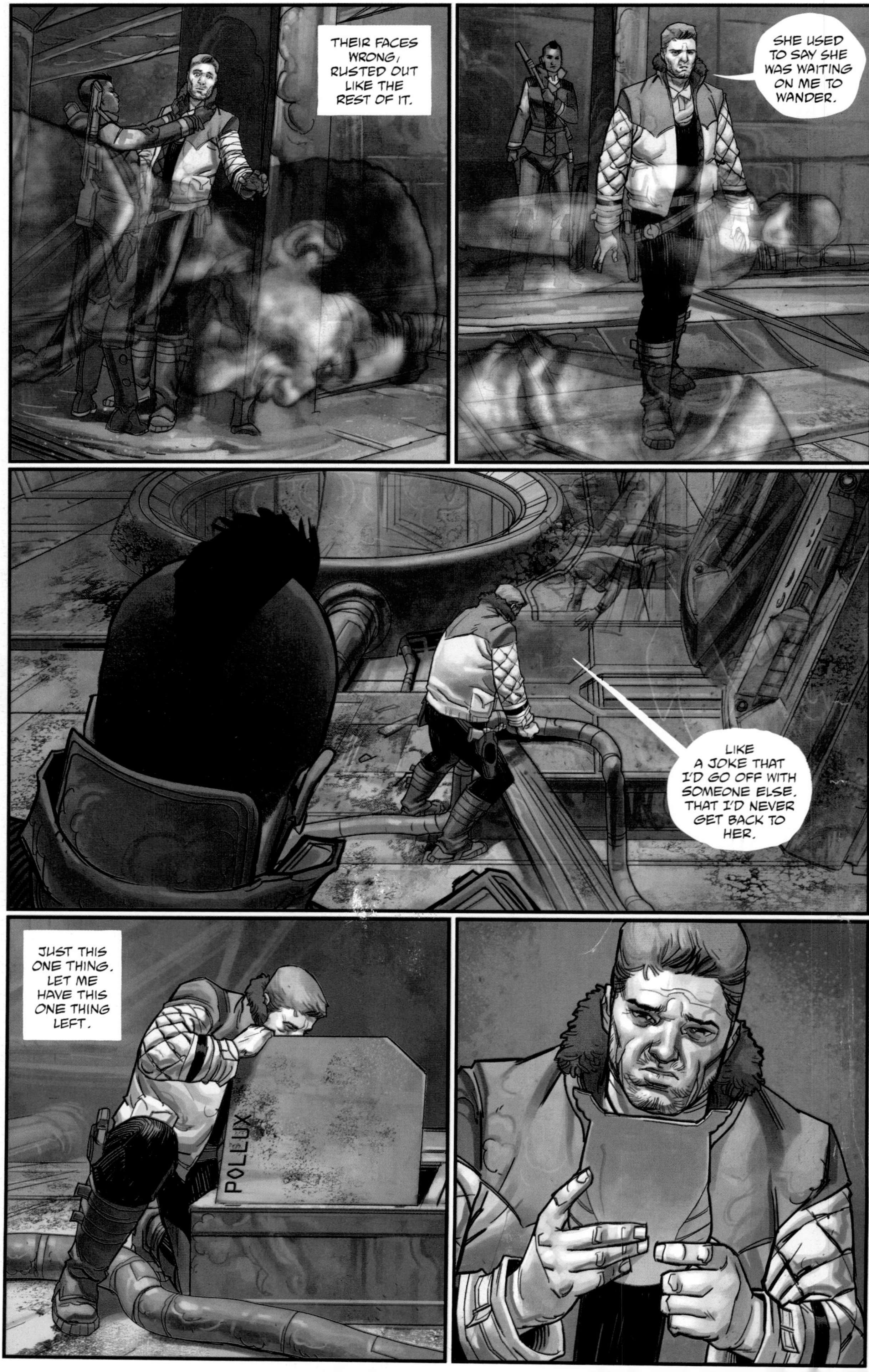
THEIR FACES WRONG, RUSTED OUT LIKE THE REST OF IT.
SHE USED TO SAY SHE WAS WAITING ON ME TO WANDER.
LIKE A JOKE THAT I'D GO OFF WITH SOMEONE ELSE. THAT I'D NEVER GET BACK TO HER.
JUST THIS ONE THING. LET ME HAVE THIS ONE THING LEFT.
POLLUX

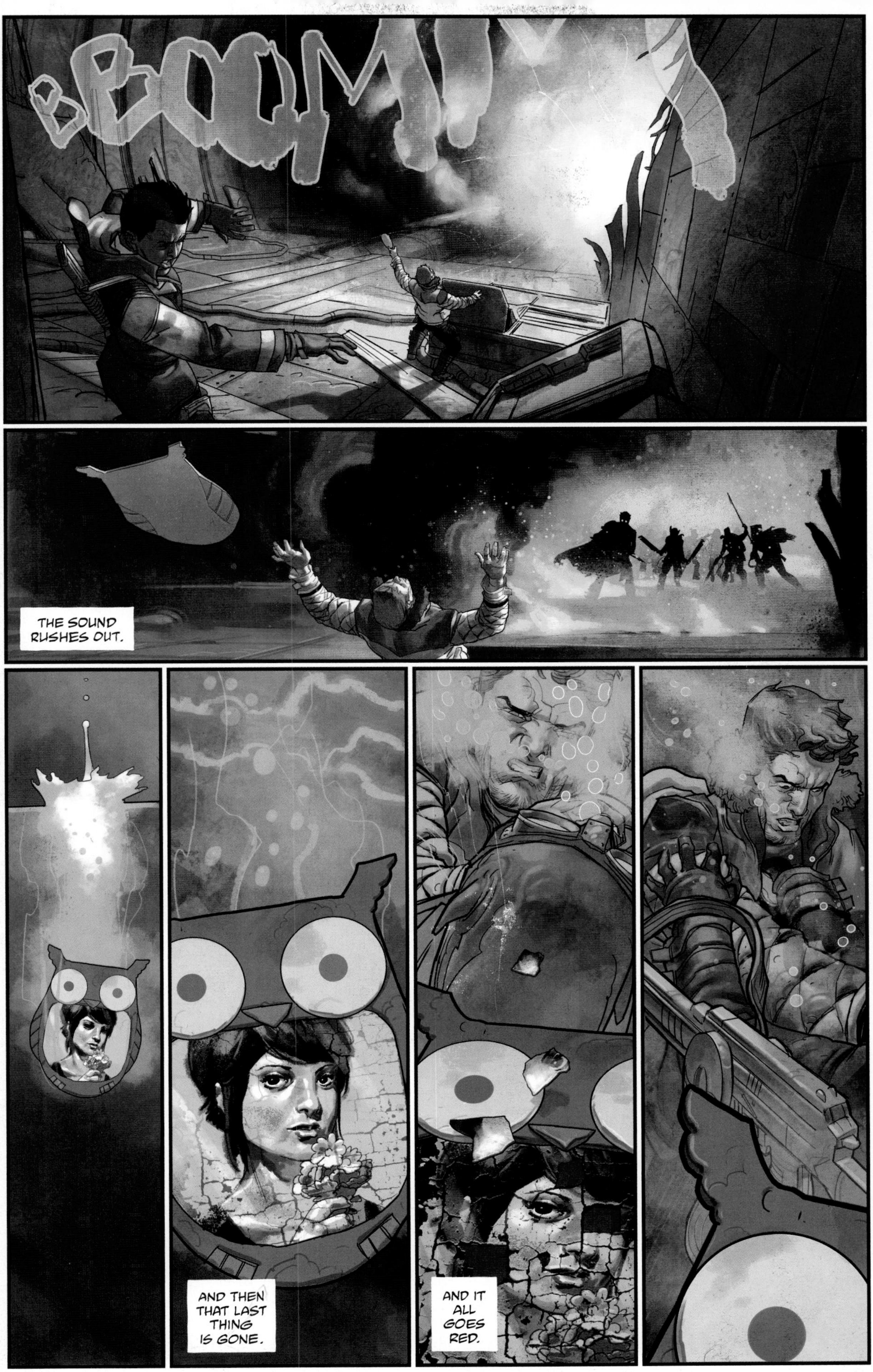
BOOM!
THE SOUND RUSHES OUT.
AND THEN THAT LAST THING IS GONE.
AND IT ALL GOES RED.

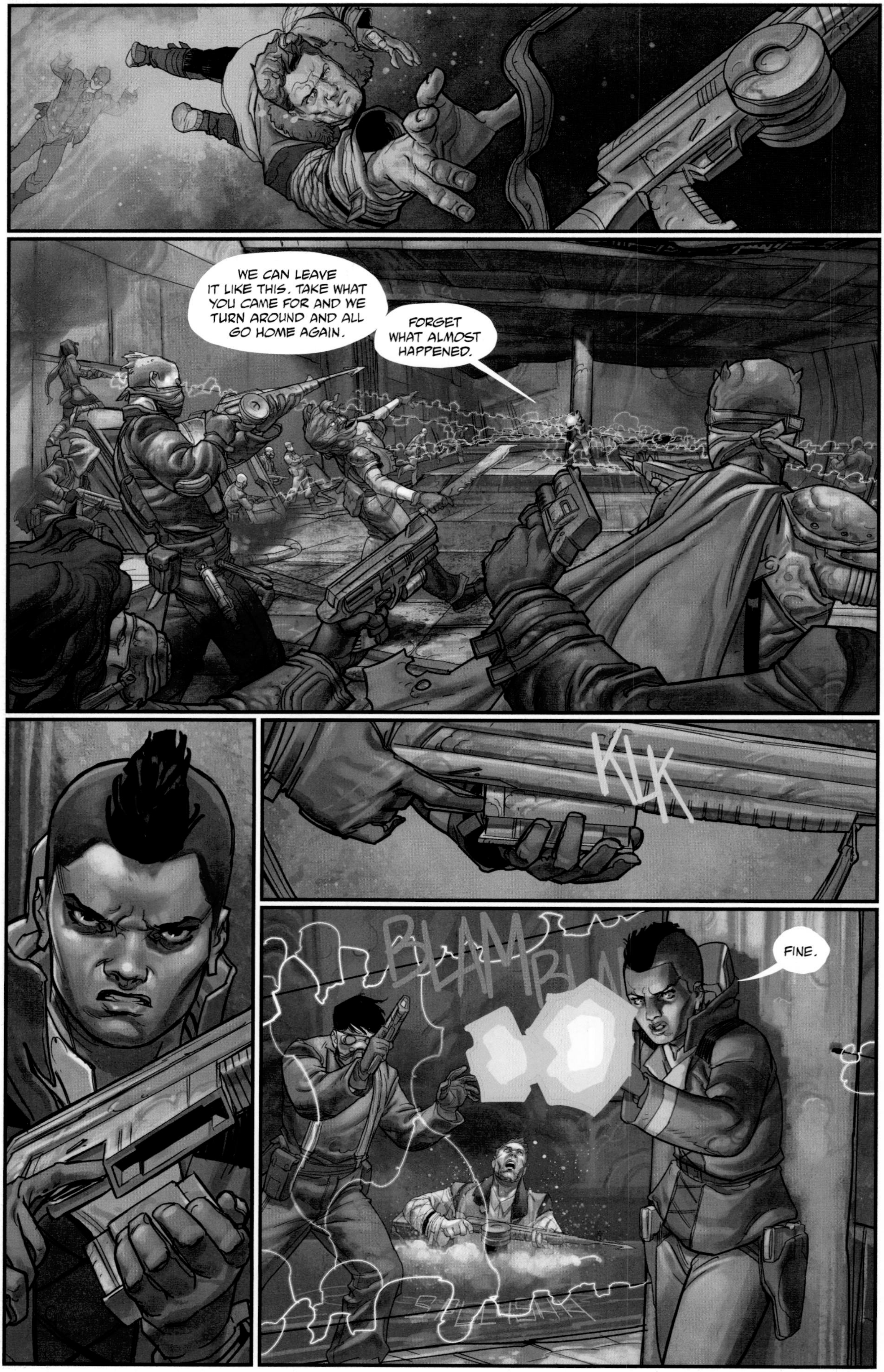

WE CAN LEAVE IT LIKE THIS. TAKE WHAT YOU CAME FOR AND WE TURN AROUND AND ALL GO HOME AGAIN.
FORGET WHAT ALMOST HAPPENED.
KLK
BLAM
FINE.

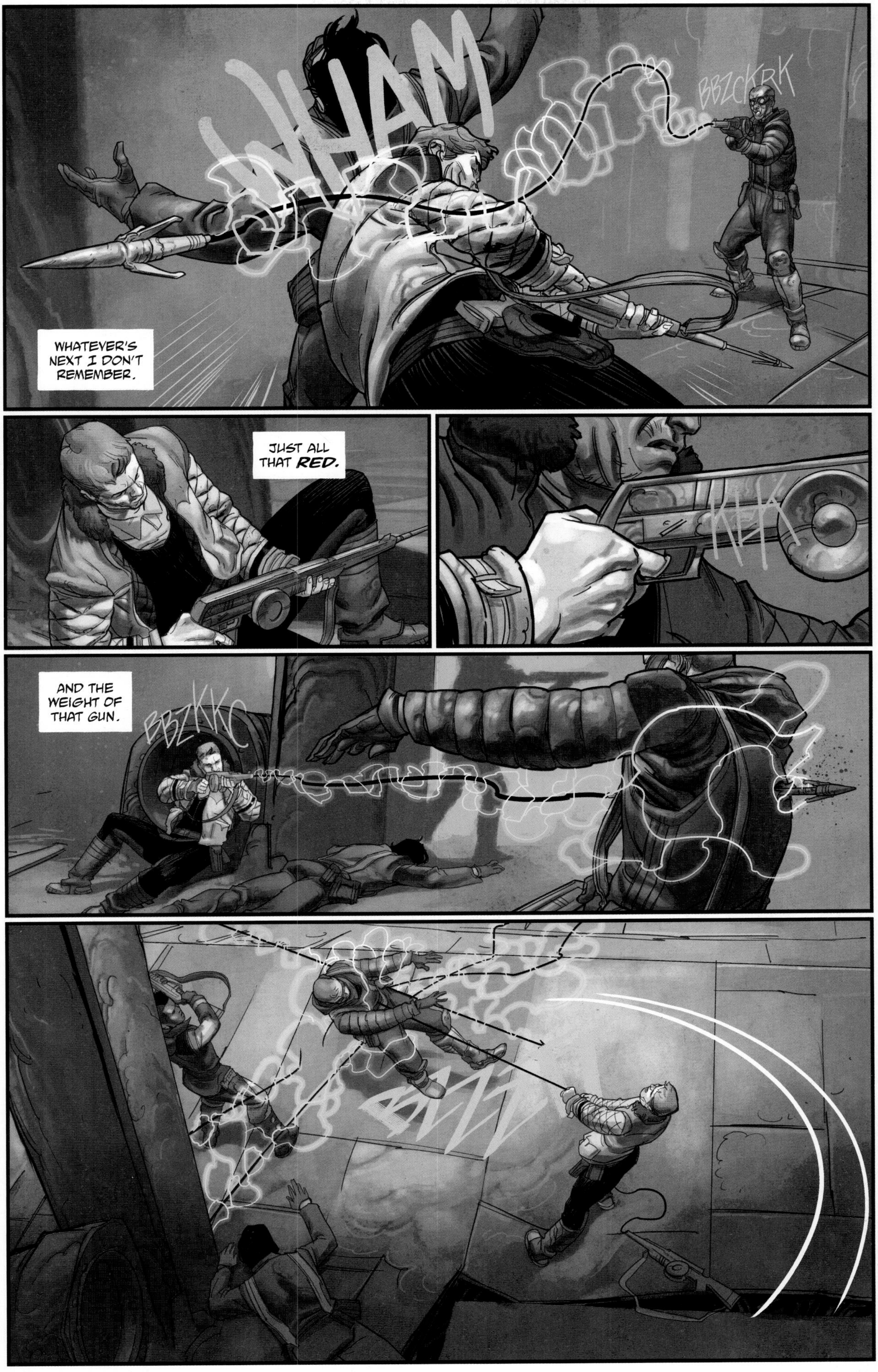
WHAM
BBZCKRK
WHATEVER'S NEXT I DON'T REMEMBER.
JUST ALL THAT **RED.**
KLIK
AND THE WEIGHT OF THAT GUN.
BBZKKC
BZZZ

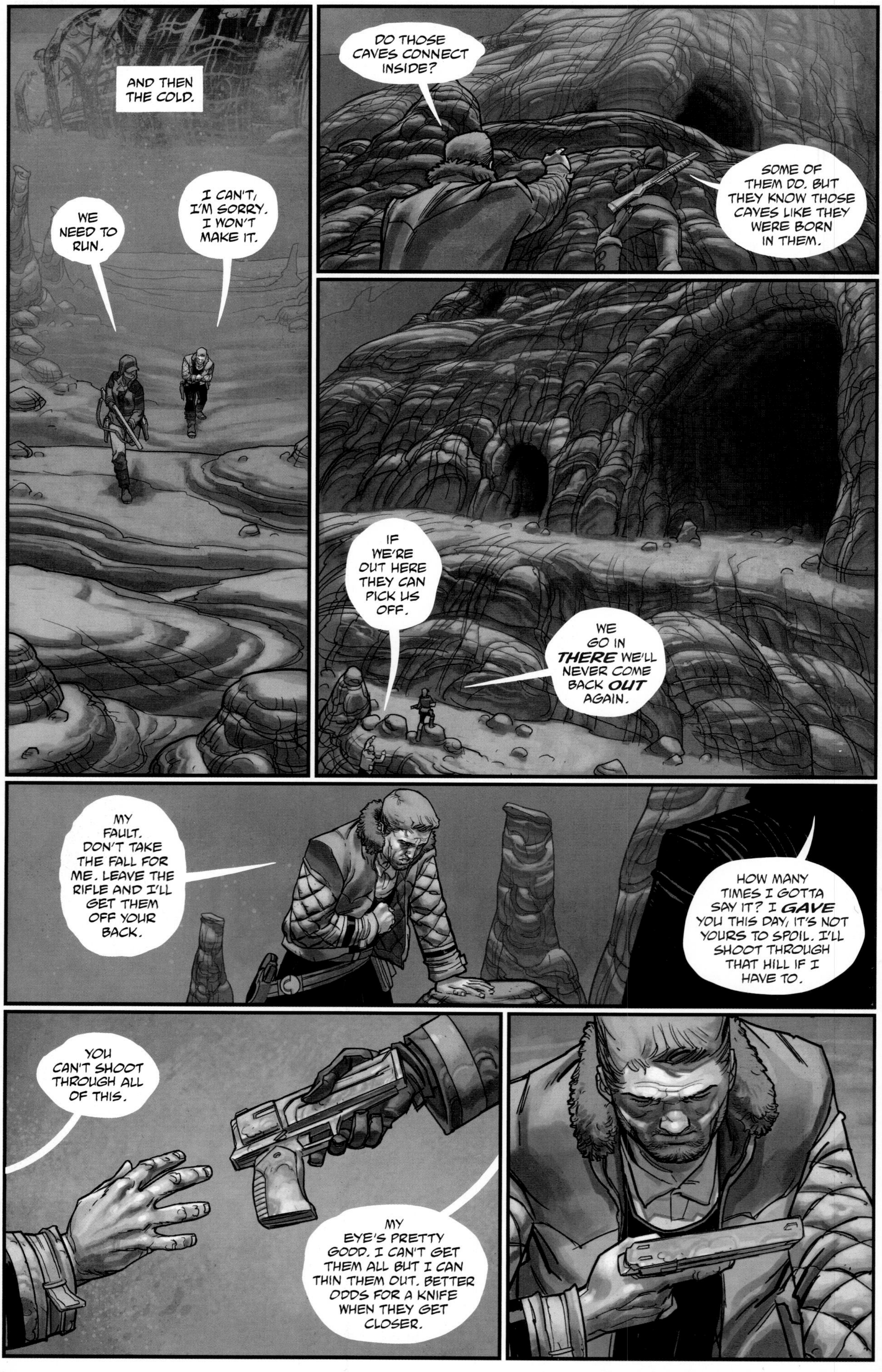
AND THEN THE COLD.
WE NEED TO RUN.
I CAN'T, I'M SORRY. I WON'T MAKE IT.
DO THOSE CAVES CONNECT INSIDE?
SOME OF THEM DO. BUT THEY KNOW THOSE CAVES LIKE THEY WERE BORN IN THEM.
IF WE'RE OUT HERE THEY CAN PICK US OFF.
WE GO IN THERE WE'LL NEVER COME BACK OUT AGAIN.
MY FAULT. DON'T TAKE THE FALL FOR ME. LEAVE THE RIFLE AND I'LL GET THEM OFF YOUR BACK.
HOW MANY TIMES I GOTTA SAY IT? I GAVE YOU THIS DAY, IT'S NOT YOURS TO SPOIL. I'LL SHOOT THROUGH THAT HILL IF I HAVE TO.
YOU CAN'T SHOOT THROUGH ALL OF THIS.
MY EYE'S PRETTY GOOD. I CAN'T GET THEM ALL BUT I CAN THIN THEM OUT. BETTER ODDS FOR A KNIFE WHEN THEY GET CLOSER.

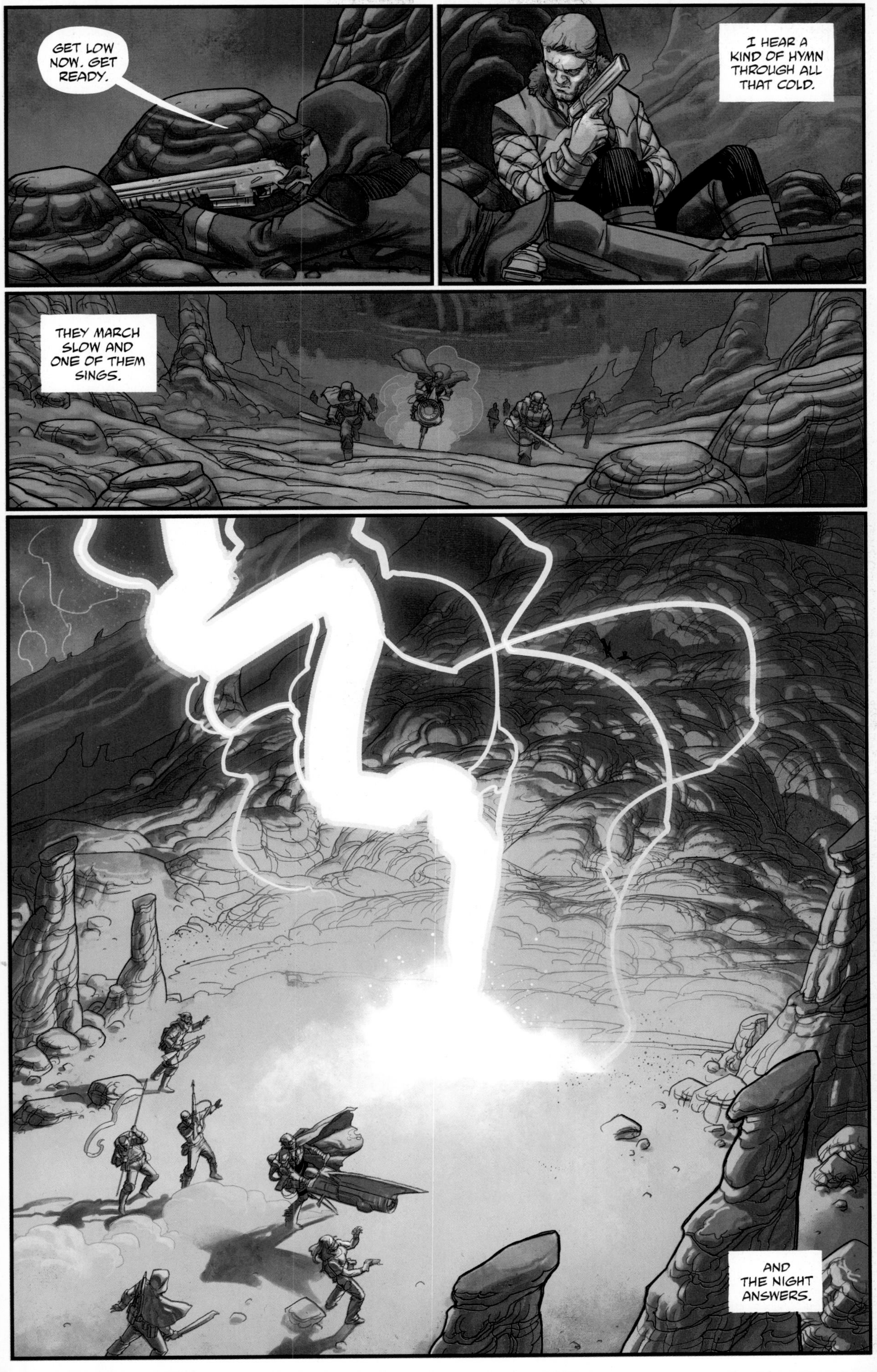
GET LOW NOW. GET READY.
I HEAR A KIND OF HYMN THROUGH ALL THAT COLD.
THEY MARCH SLOW AND ONE OF THEM SINGS.
AND THE NIGHT ANSWERS.

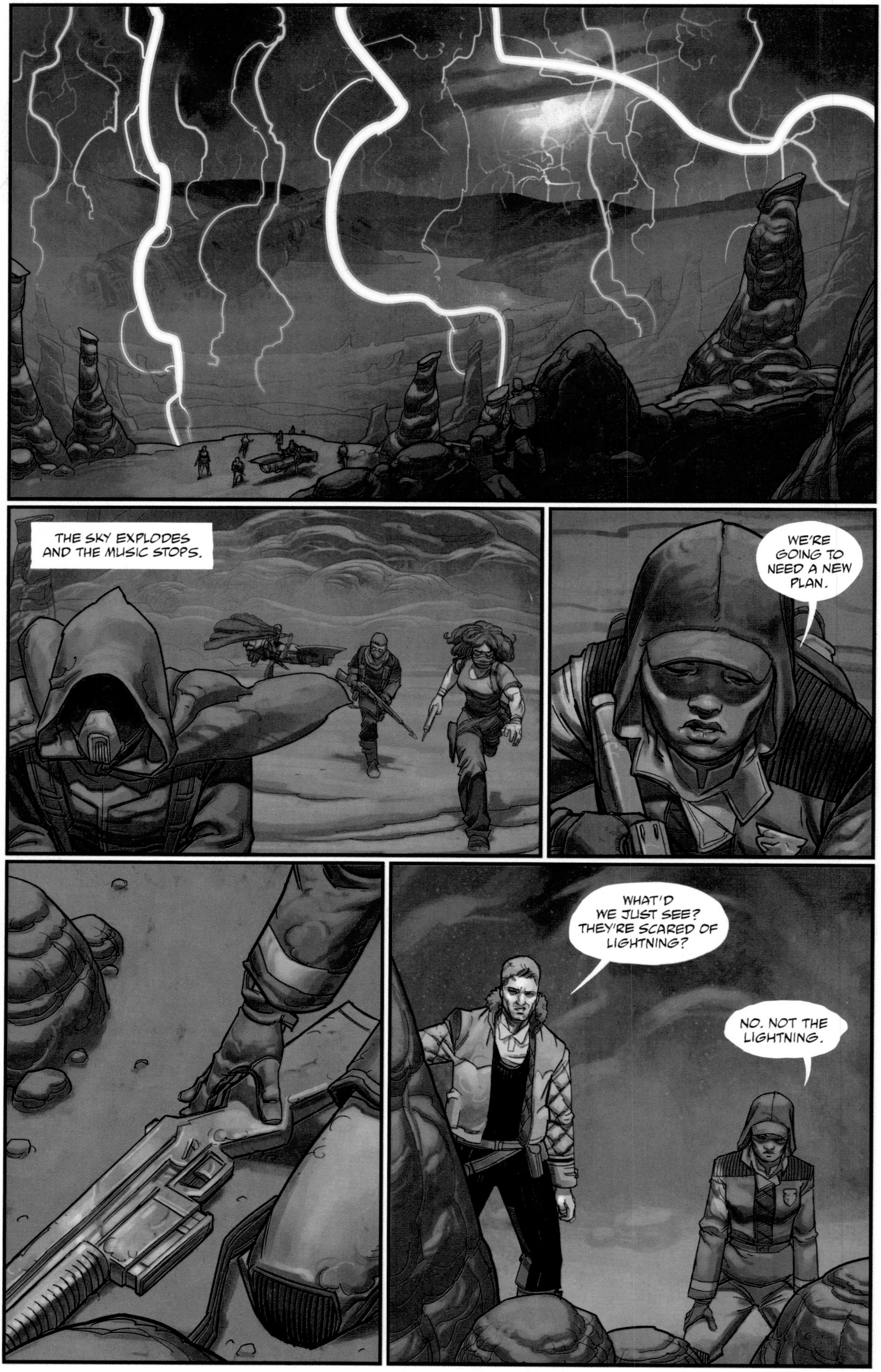
THE SKY EXPLODES AND THE MUSIC STOPS.
WE'RE GOING TO NEED A NEW PLAN.
WHAT'D WE JUST SEE? THEY'RE SCARED OF LIGHTNING?
NO. NOT THE LIGHTNING.

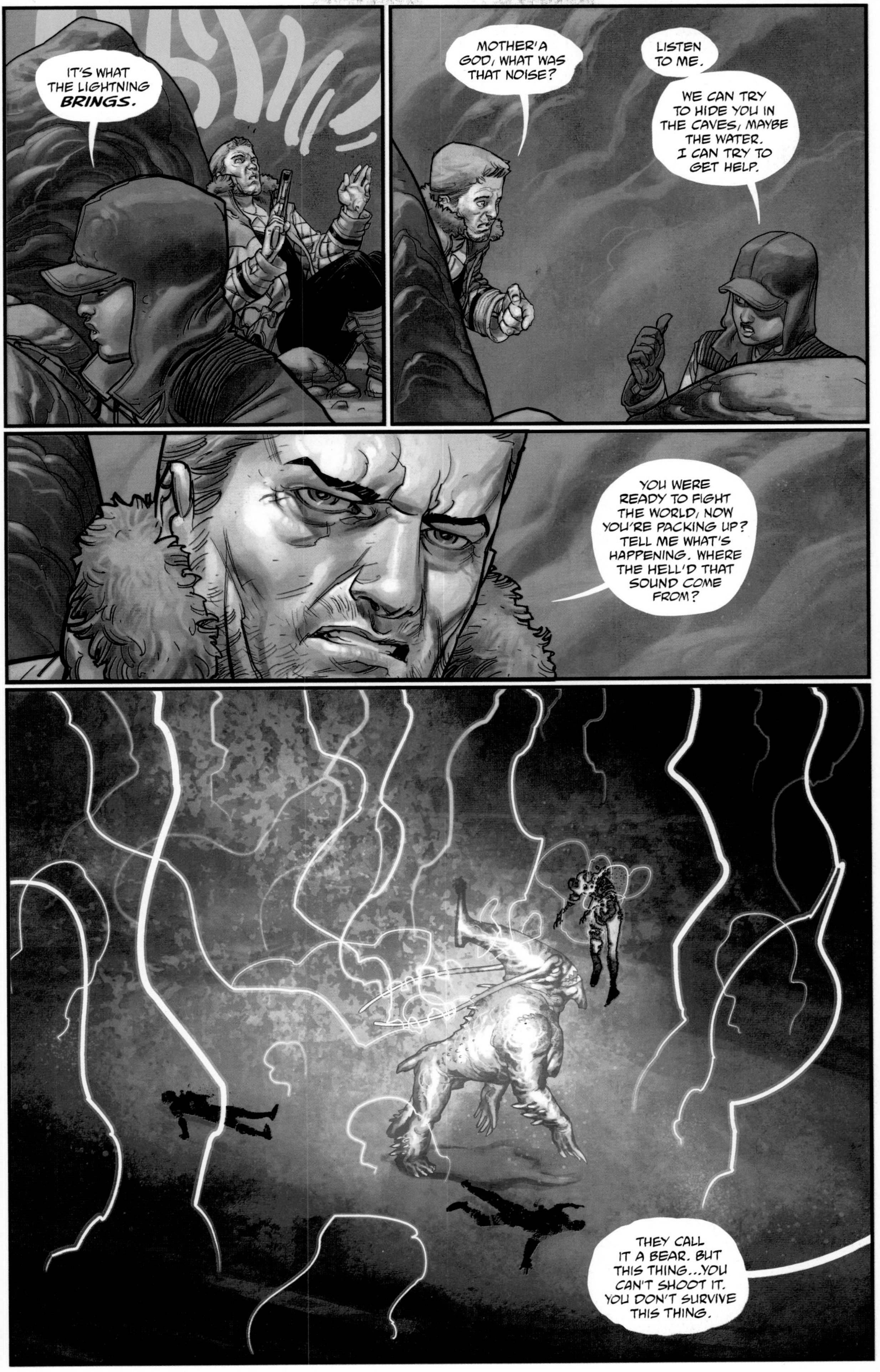
IT'S WHAT THE LIGHTNING **BRINGS.**
MOTHER'A GOD, WHAT WAS THAT NOISE?
LISTEN TO ME.
WE CAN TRY TO HIDE YOU IN THE CAVES, MAYBE THE WATER. I CAN TRY TO GET HELP.
YOU WERE READY TO FIGHT THE WORLD, NOW YOU'RE PACKING UP? TELL ME WHAT'S HAPPENING. WHERE THE HELL'D THAT SOUND COME FROM?
THEY CALL IT A BEAR. BUT THIS THING... YOU CAN'T SHOOT IT. YOU DON'T SURVIVE THIS THING.

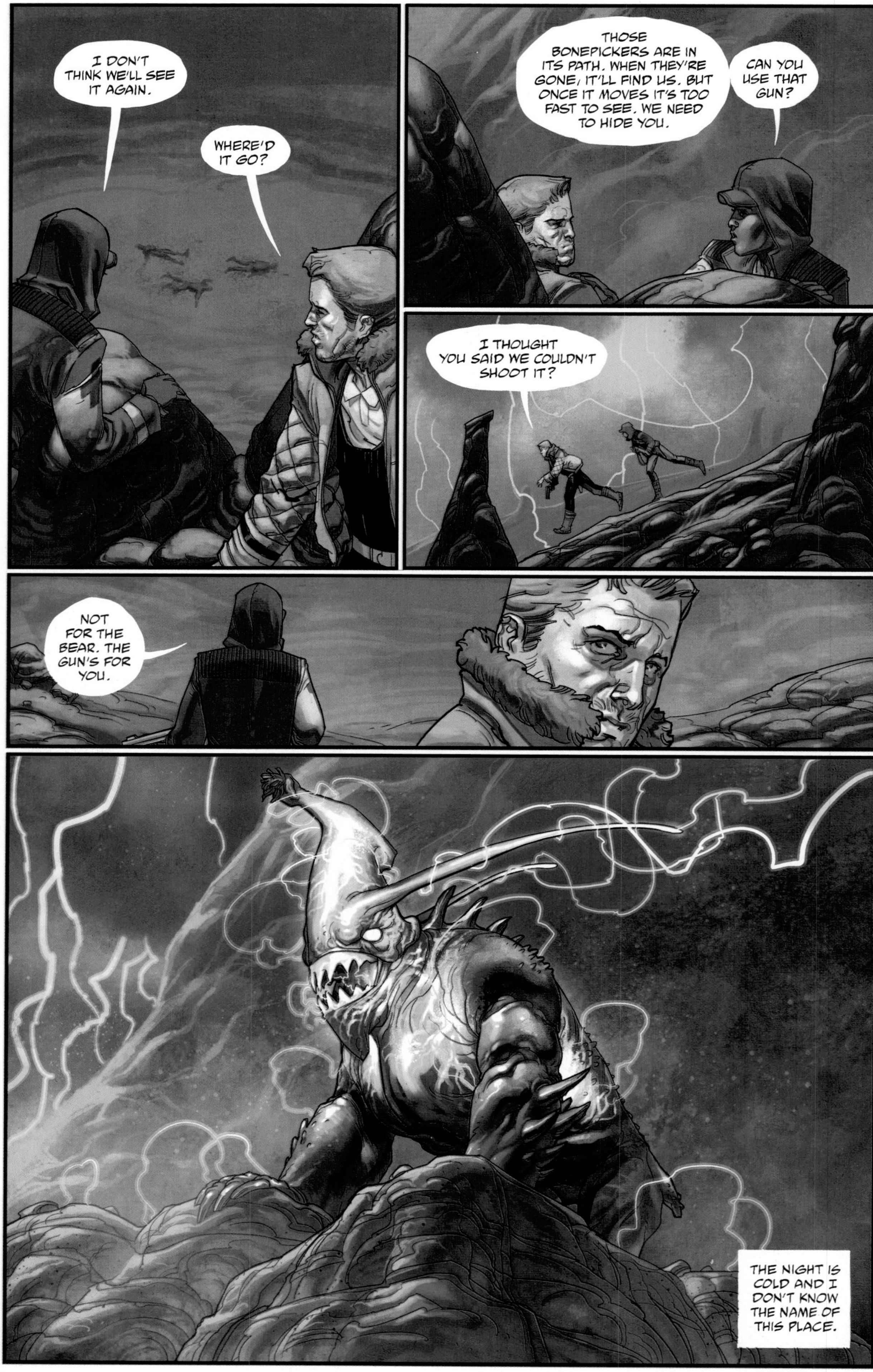
I DON'T THINK WE'LL SEE IT AGAIN.
WHERE'D IT GO?
THOSE BONEPICKERS ARE IN ITS PATH. WHEN THEY'RE GONE, IT'LL FIND US. BUT ONCE IT MOVES IT'S TOO FAST TO SEE. WE NEED TO HIDE YOU.
CAN YOU USE THAT GUN?
I THOUGHT YOU SAID WE COULDN'T SHOOT IT?
NOT FOR THE BEAR. THE GUN'S FOR YOU.
THE NIGHT IS COLD AND I DON'T KNOW THE NAME OF THIS PLACE.

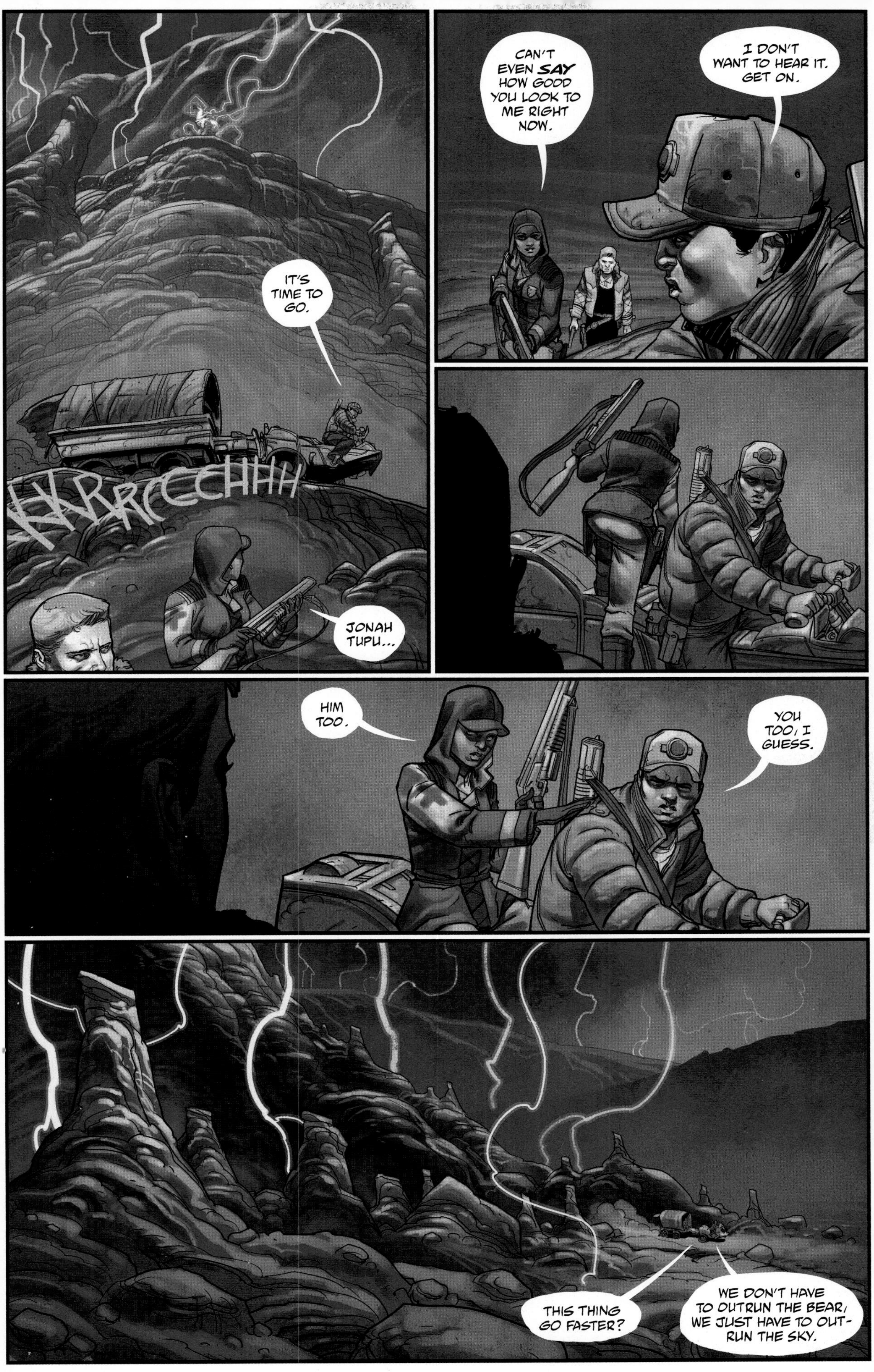
IT'S TIME TO GO.
KKRRCCHHH
JONAH TUPU...
CAN'T EVEN SAY HOW GOOD YOU LOOK TO ME RIGHT NOW.
I DON'T WANT TO HEAR IT. GET ON.
HIM TOO.
YOU TOO, I GUESS.
THIS THING GO FASTER?
WE DON'T HAVE TO OUTRUN THE BEAR, WE JUST HAVE TO OUT-RUN THE SKY.

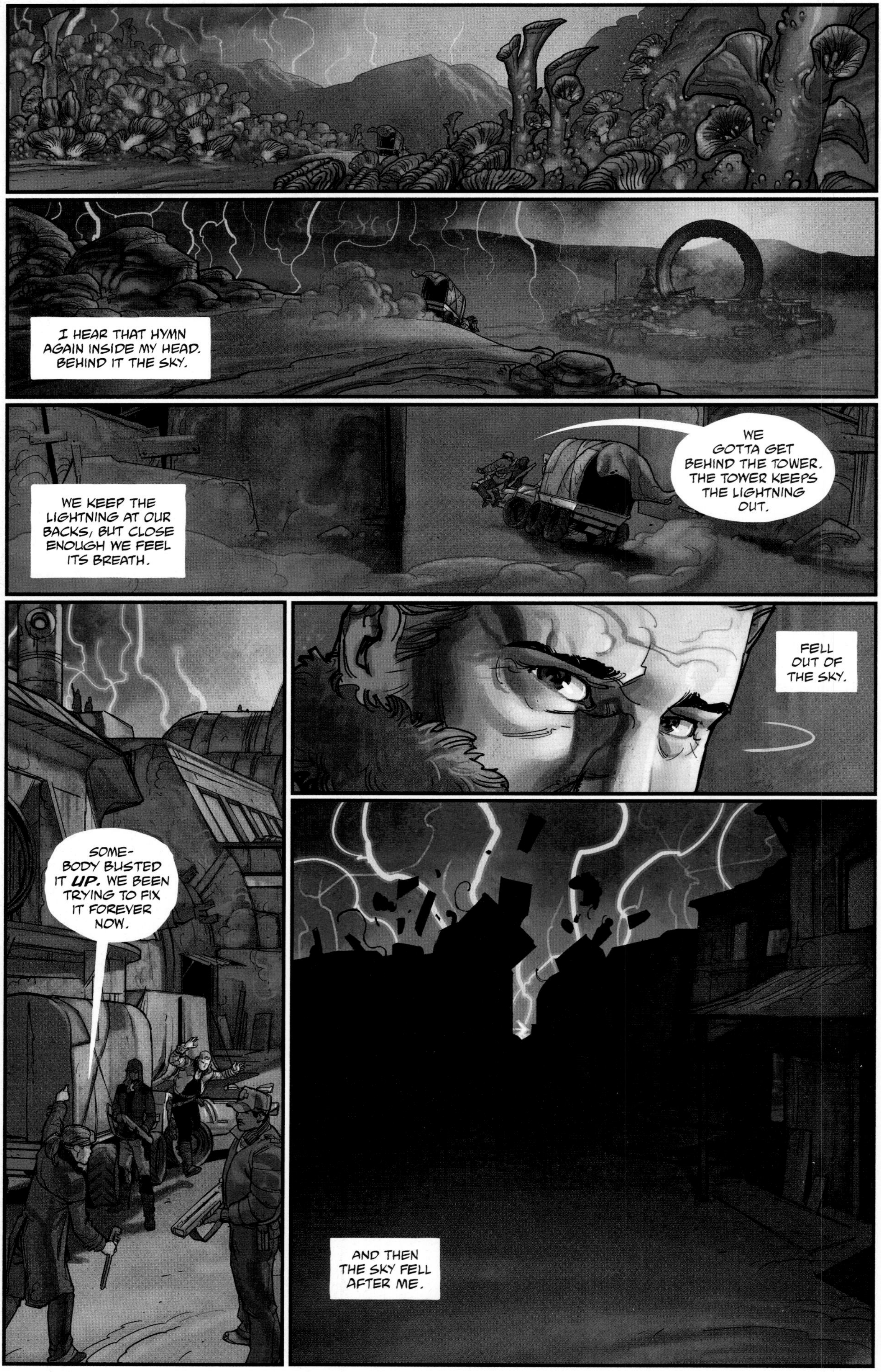
I HEAR THAT HYMN AGAIN INSIDE MY HEAD. BEHIND IT THE SKY.
WE KEEP THE LIGHTNING AT OUR BACKS, BUT CLOSE ENOUGH WE FEEL ITS BREATH.
WE GOTTA GET BEHIND THE TOWER. THE TOWER KEEPS THE LIGHTNING OUT.
SOME-BODY BUSTED IT UP. WE BEEN TRYING TO FIX IT FOREVER NOW.
FELL OUT OF THE SKY.
AND THEN THE SKY FELL AFTER ME.

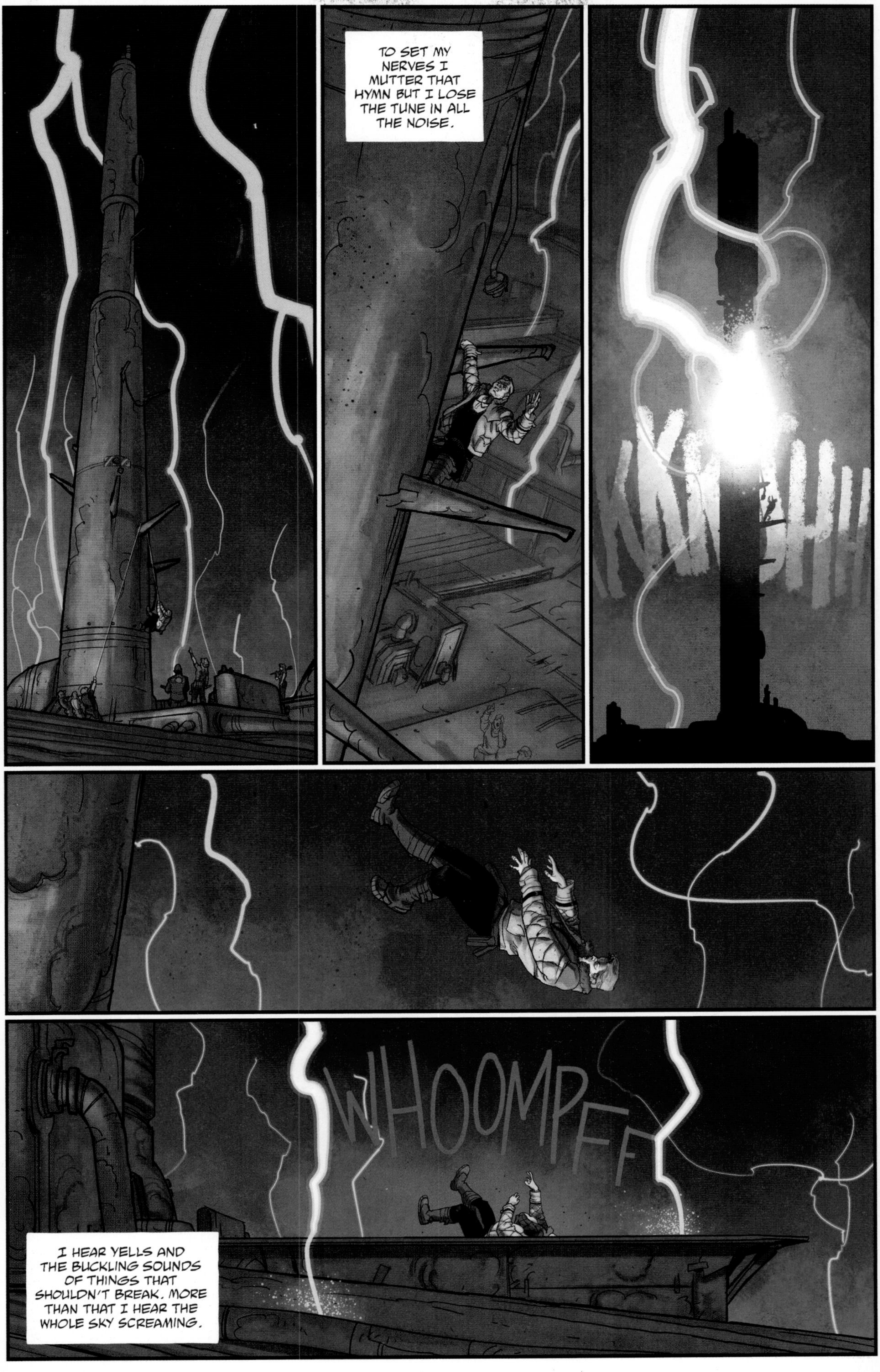
TO SET MY NERVES I MUTTER THAT HYMN BUT I LOSE THE TUNE IN ALL THE NOISE.
WHOOMPFF
I HEAR YELLS AND THE BUCKLING SOUNDS OF THINGS THAT SHOULDN'T BREAK. MORE THAN THAT I HEAR THE WHOLE SKY SCREAMING.

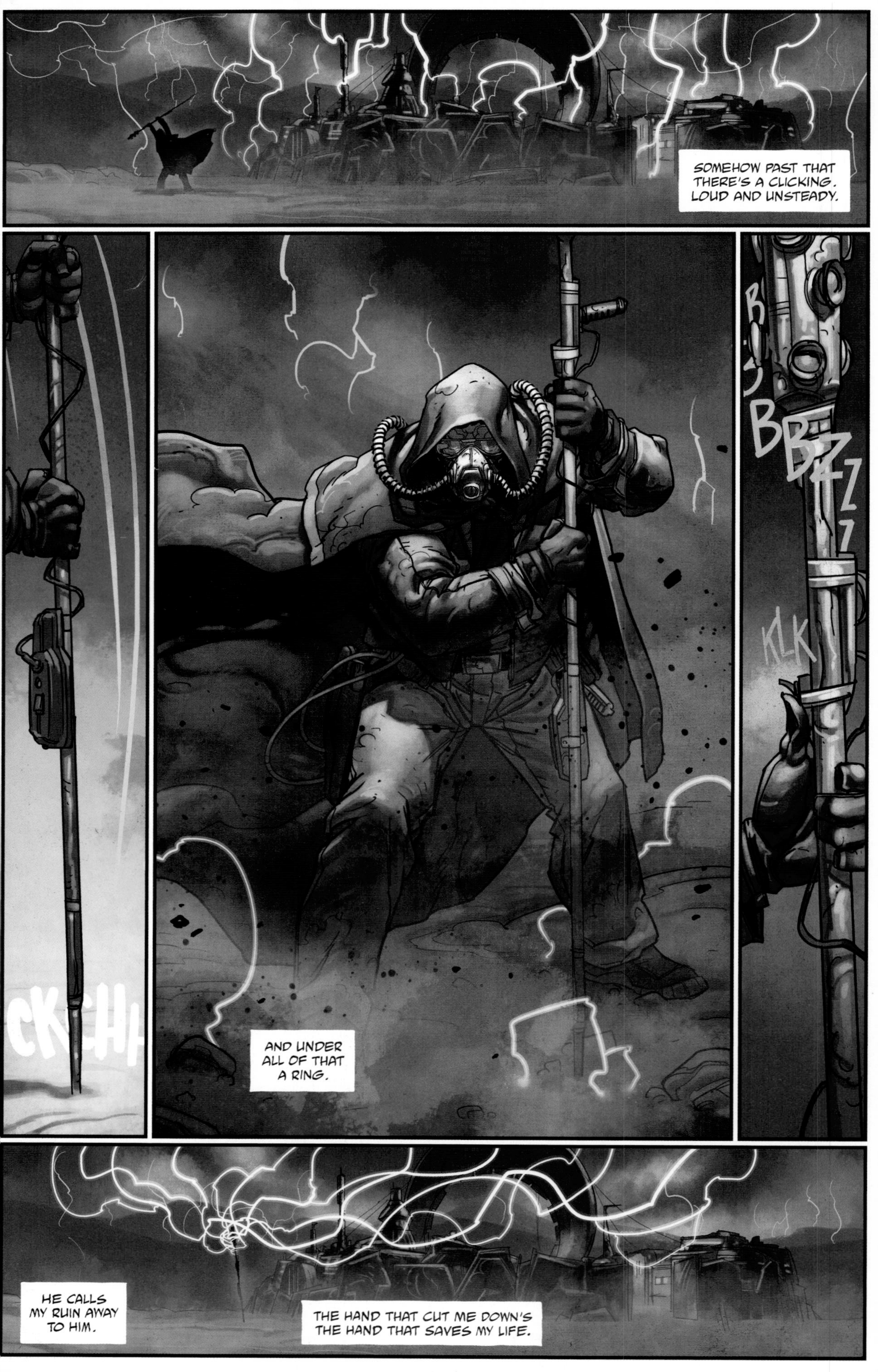
SOMEHOW PAST THAT THERE'S A CLICKING. LOUD AND UNSTEADY.
CKCHH
AND UNDER ALL OF THAT A RING.
BBZZZ
KLK
HE CALLS MY RUIN AWAY TO HIM.
THE HAND THAT CUT ME DOWN'S THE HAND THAT SAVES MY LIFE.

NEAR THE TOP I FEEL MY GUTS BLEED AND MY EYES GET HOT.

BUT THERE'S NO ONE ELSE HERE THAT DESERVES THIS.

XKCAHK

BZZZZZZTT

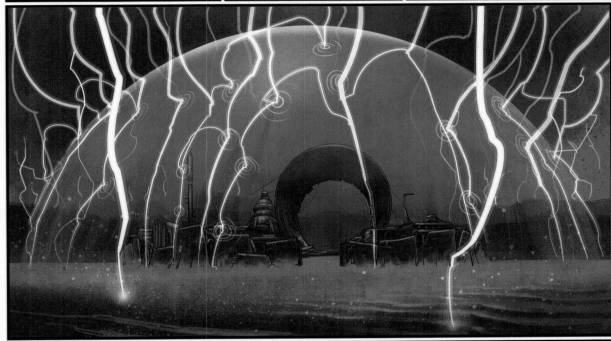

IF HE HEARS THEM CHEER, HE DOESN'T ANSWER.

SO...

...TELL ME ABOUT YOUR GIRL.

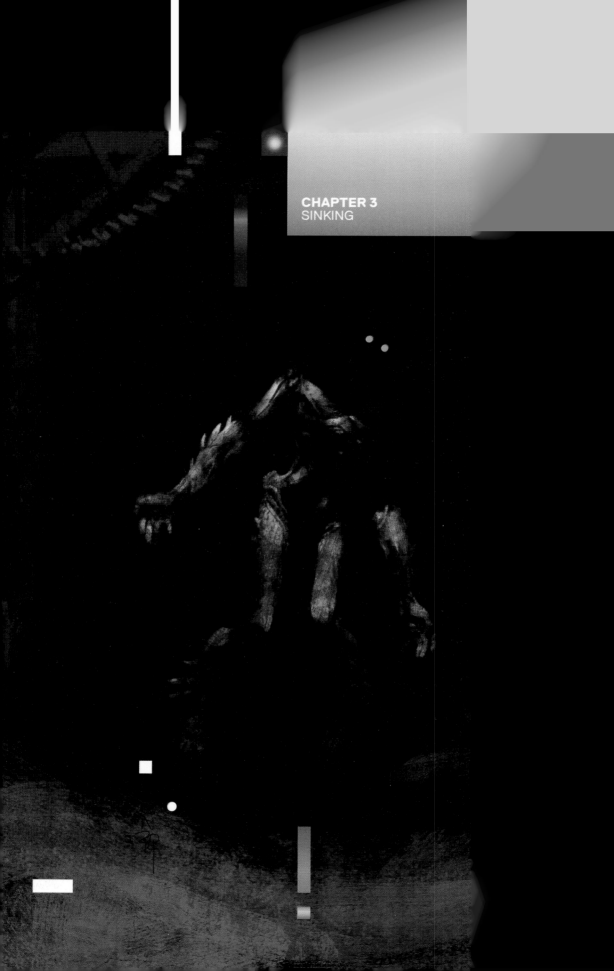

CHAPTER 3
SINKING

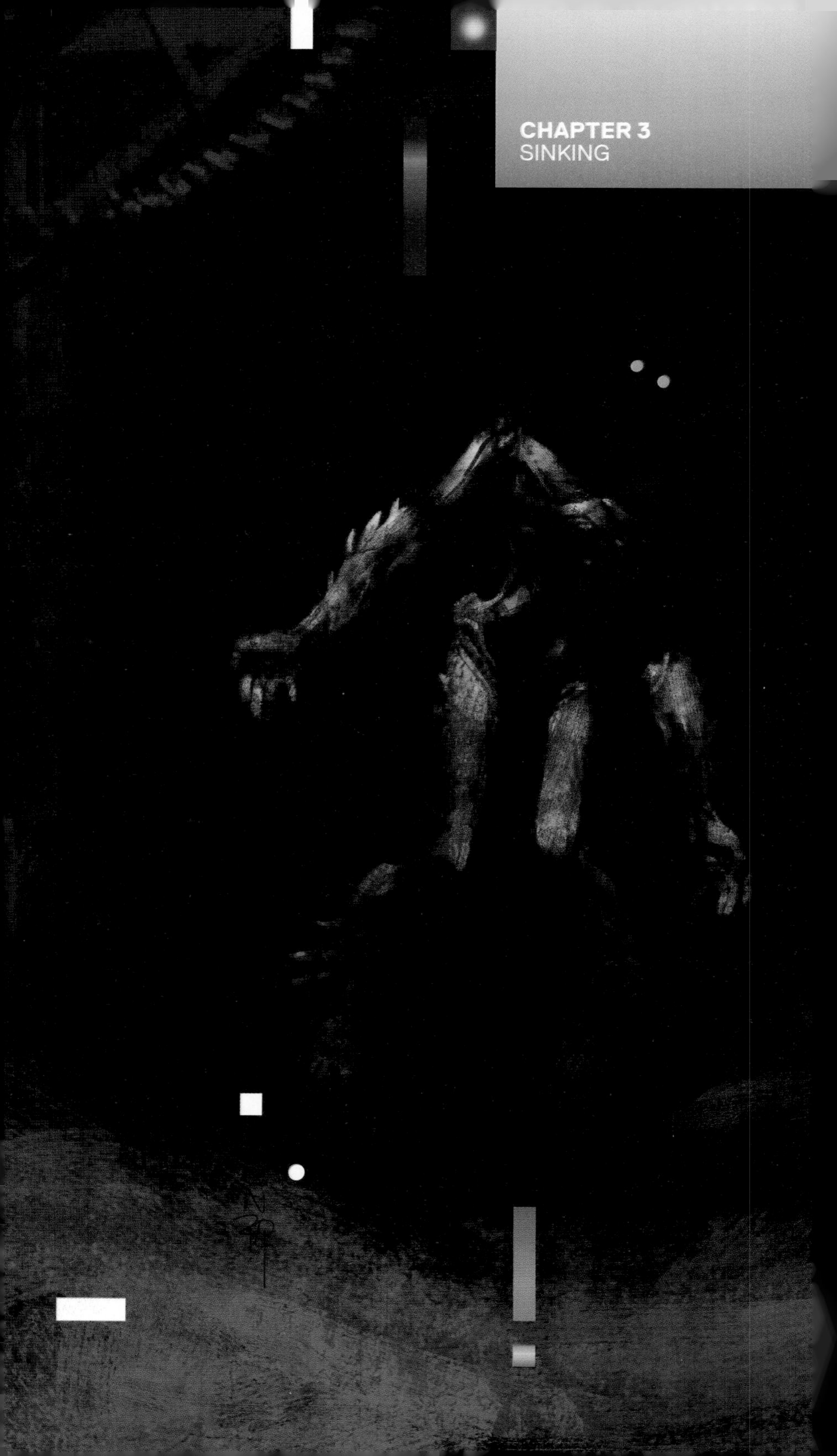

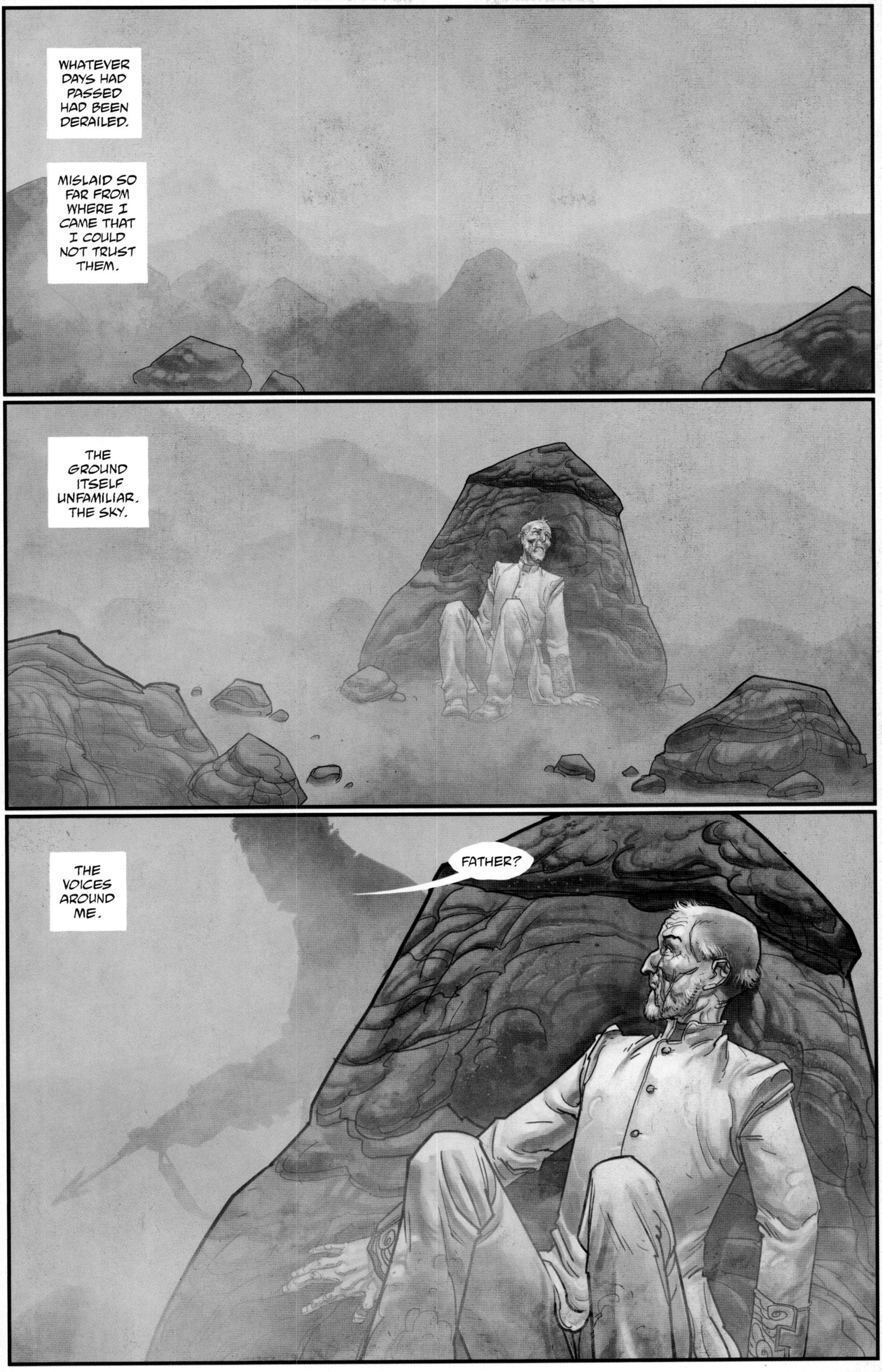
WHATEVER DAYS HAD PASSED HAD BEEN DERAILED.
MISLAID SO FAR FROM WHERE I CAME THAT I COULD NOT TRUST THEM.
THE GROUND ITSELF UNFAMILIAR. THE SKY.
THE VOICES AROUND ME.
FATHER?

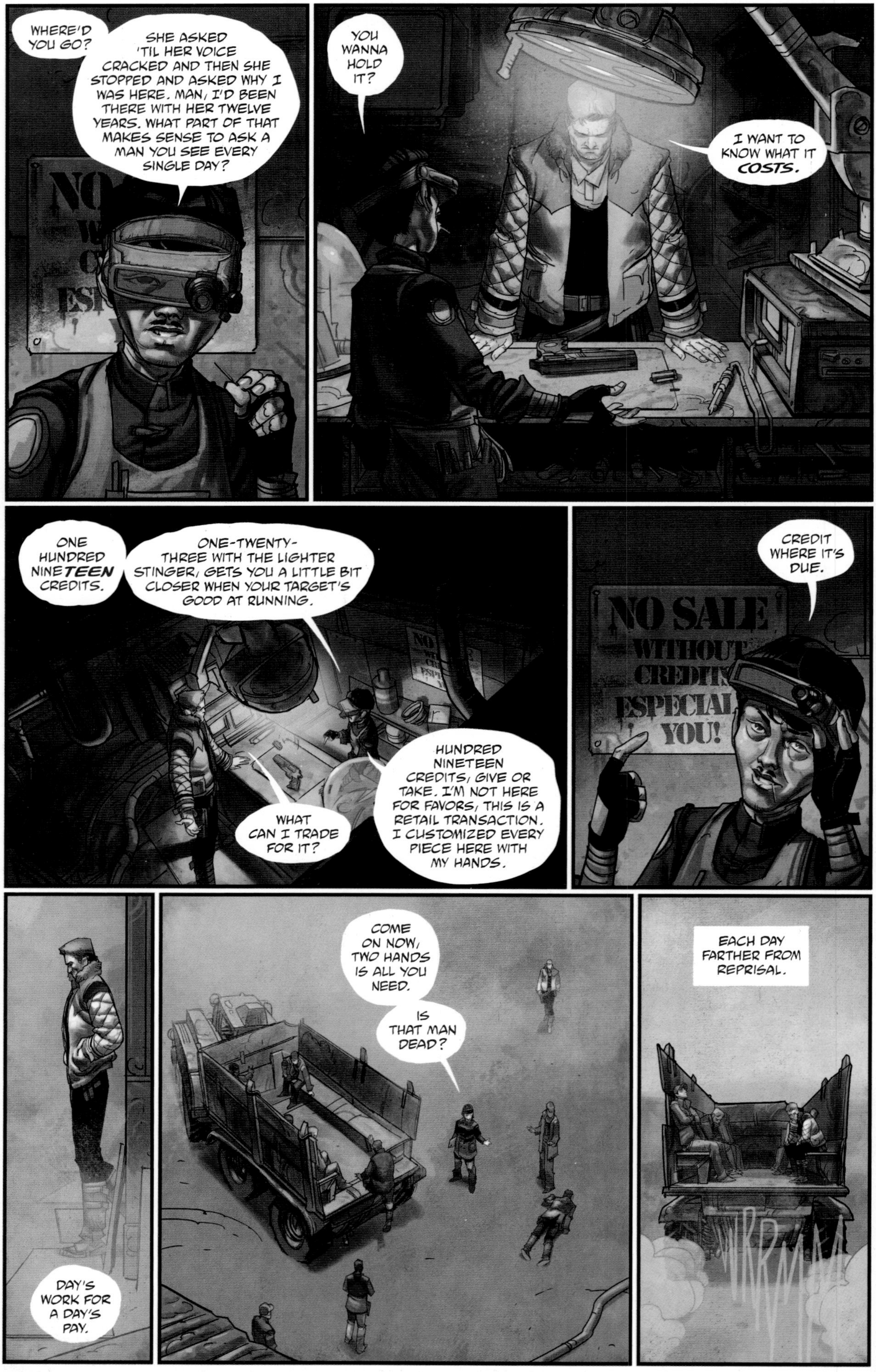
WHERE'D YOU GO?
SHE ASKED 'TIL HER VOICE CRACKED AND THEN SHE STOPPED AND ASKED WHY I WAS HERE. MAN, I'D BEEN THERE WITH HER TWELVE YEARS. WHAT PART OF THAT MAKES SENSE TO ASK A MAN YOU SEE EVERY SINGLE DAY?
YOU WANNA HOLD IT?
I WANT TO KNOW WHAT IT *COSTS.*
ONE HUNDRED NINE*TEEN* CREDITS.
ONE-TWENTY-THREE WITH THE LIGHTER STINGER, GETS YOU A LITTLE BIT CLOSER WHEN YOUR TARGET'S GOOD AT RUNNING.
WHAT CAN I TRADE FOR IT?
HUNDRED NINETEEN CREDITS, GIVE OR TAKE. I'M NOT HERE FOR FAVORS, THIS IS A RETAIL TRANSACTION. I CUSTOMIZED EVERY PIECE HERE WITH MY HANDS.
CREDIT WHERE IT'S DUE.
NO SALE WITHOUT CREDITS ESPECIAL YOU!
DAY'S WORK FOR A DAY'S PAY.
COME ON NOW, TWO HANDS IS ALL YOU NEED.
IS THAT MAN DEAD?
EACH DAY FARTHER FROM REPRISAL.
WRRMM

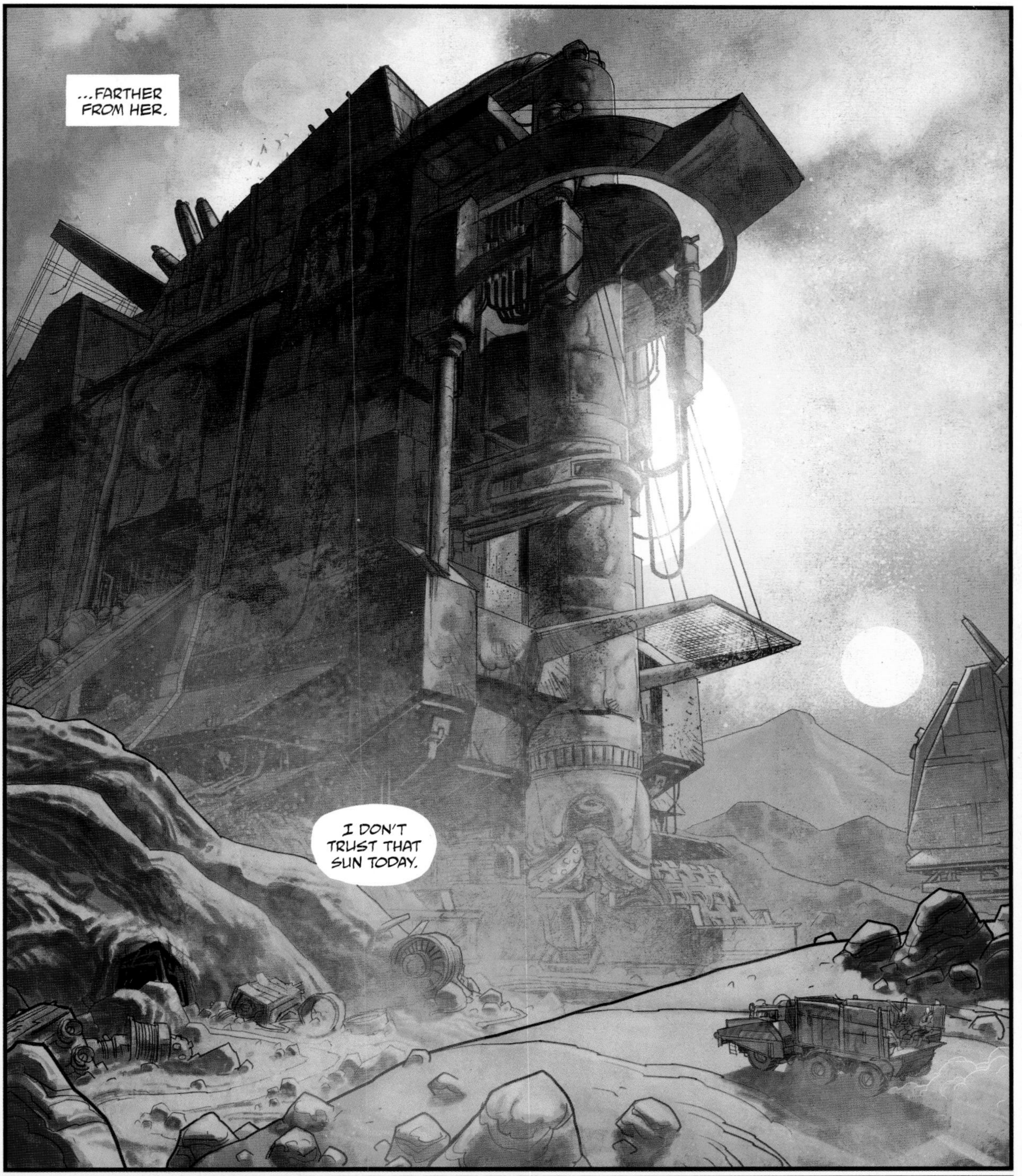
...FARTHER FROM HER.
I DON'T TRUST THAT SUN TODAY.

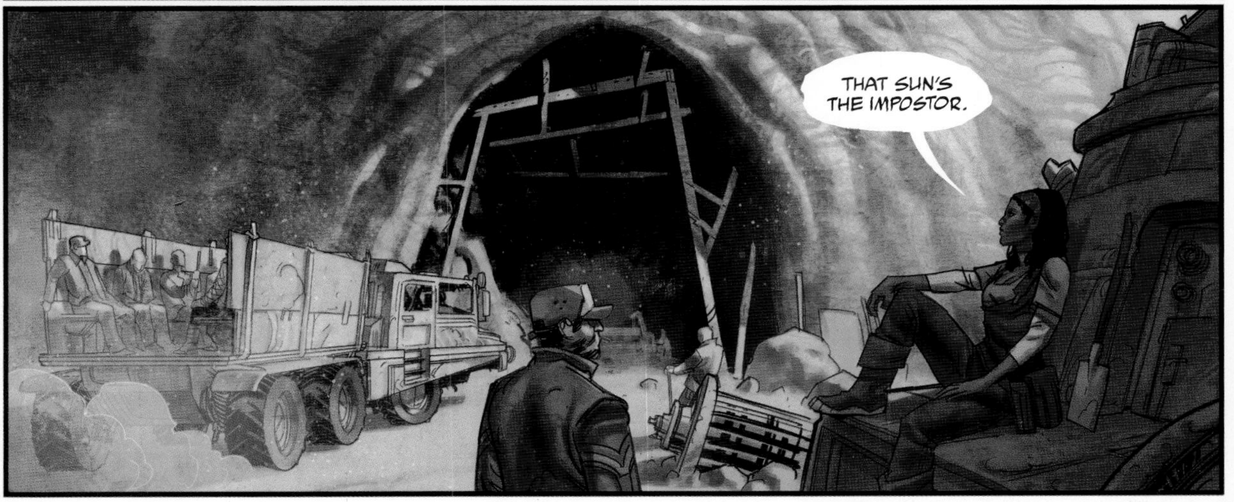
THAT SUN'S THE IMPOSTOR.

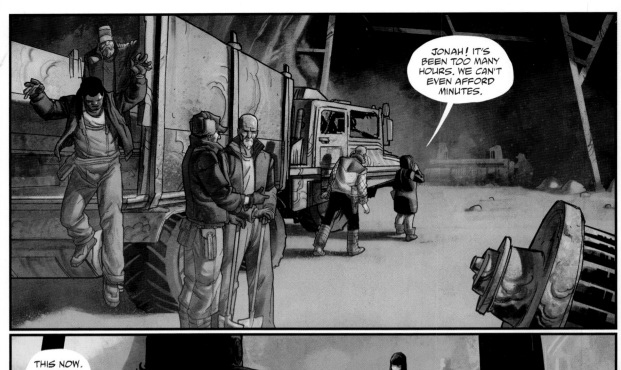

JONAH! IT'S BEEN TOO MANY HOURS. WE CAN'T EVEN AFFORD MINUTES.

THIS NOW. SHOULD BE RIGHT.

GOTTA TEST IT OUT. ANY ONE'A YOU WANNA CHANCE YOUR HEALTH FOR AN EXTRA HOUR'S PAY?

I'LL DO IT.

NO SIR, YOU WILL **NOT.** YOU'RE ABOUT THE BEST I GOT, I WOULDN'T RISK YOUR HANDS FOR A MONTH WITH THAT BOY IN TOWN THAT DON'T SPEAK ENGLISH.

THIS ONE'S NOT ADDED UP, YET. YOU WANNA RAISE YOUR STOCK, NEW GUY? OR SHUT IT DOWN?

NO WAY TO TEST IT THAT DON'T RISK A FUNERAL?

NOT AT OUR DAY'S BUDGET.

AT LEAST THE DARK'S FAMILIAR.

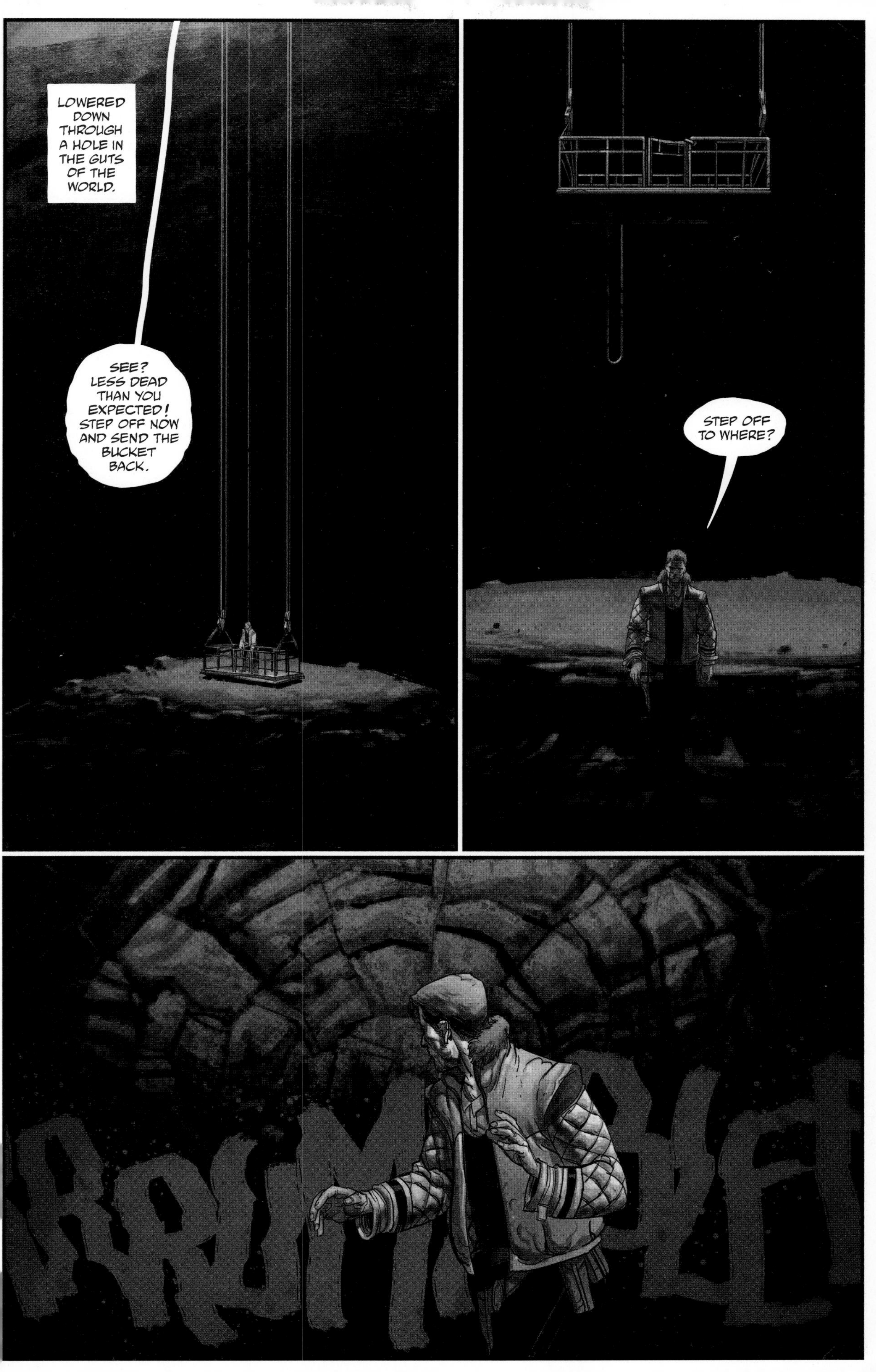
LOWERED DOWN THROUGH A HOLE IN THE GUTS OF THE WORLD.
SEE? LESS DEAD THAN YOU EXPECTED! STEP OFF NOW AND SEND THE BUCKET BACK.
STEP OFF TO WHERE?

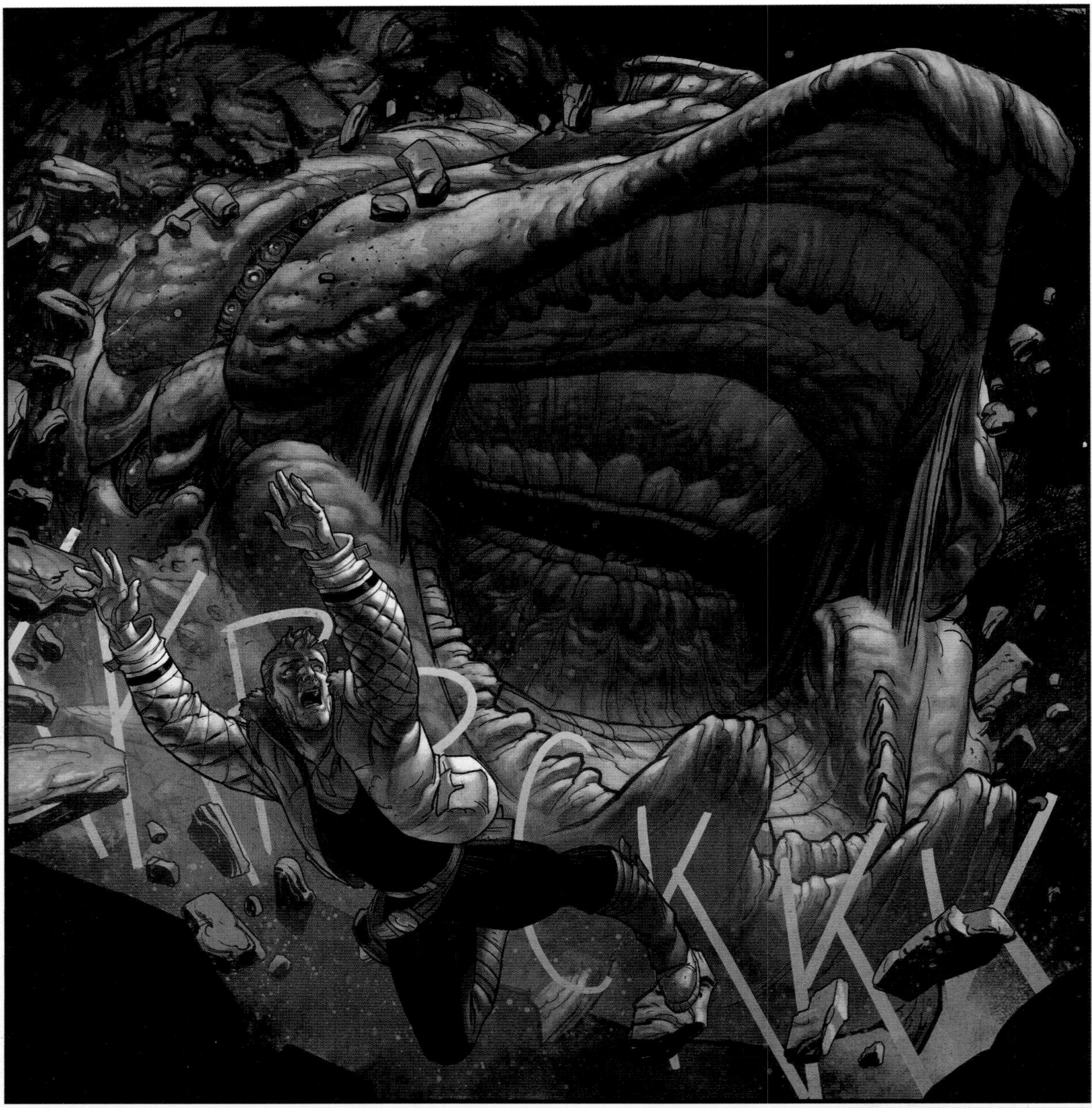

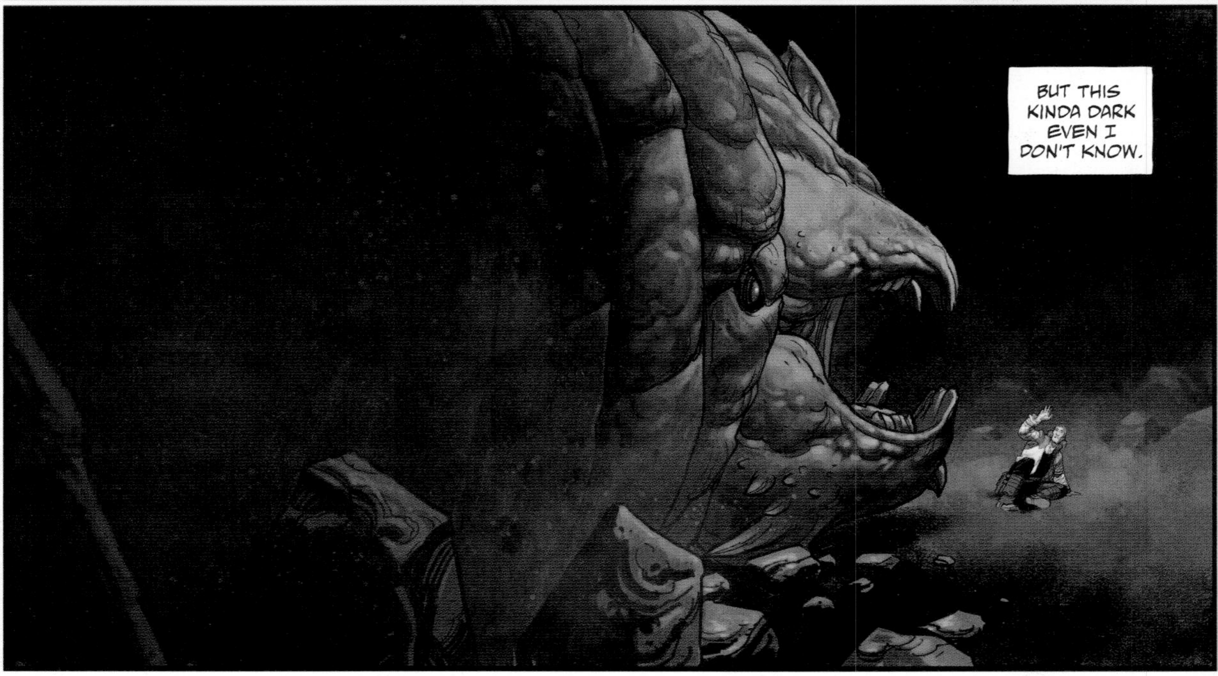
BUT THIS KINDA DARK EVEN I DON'T KNOW.

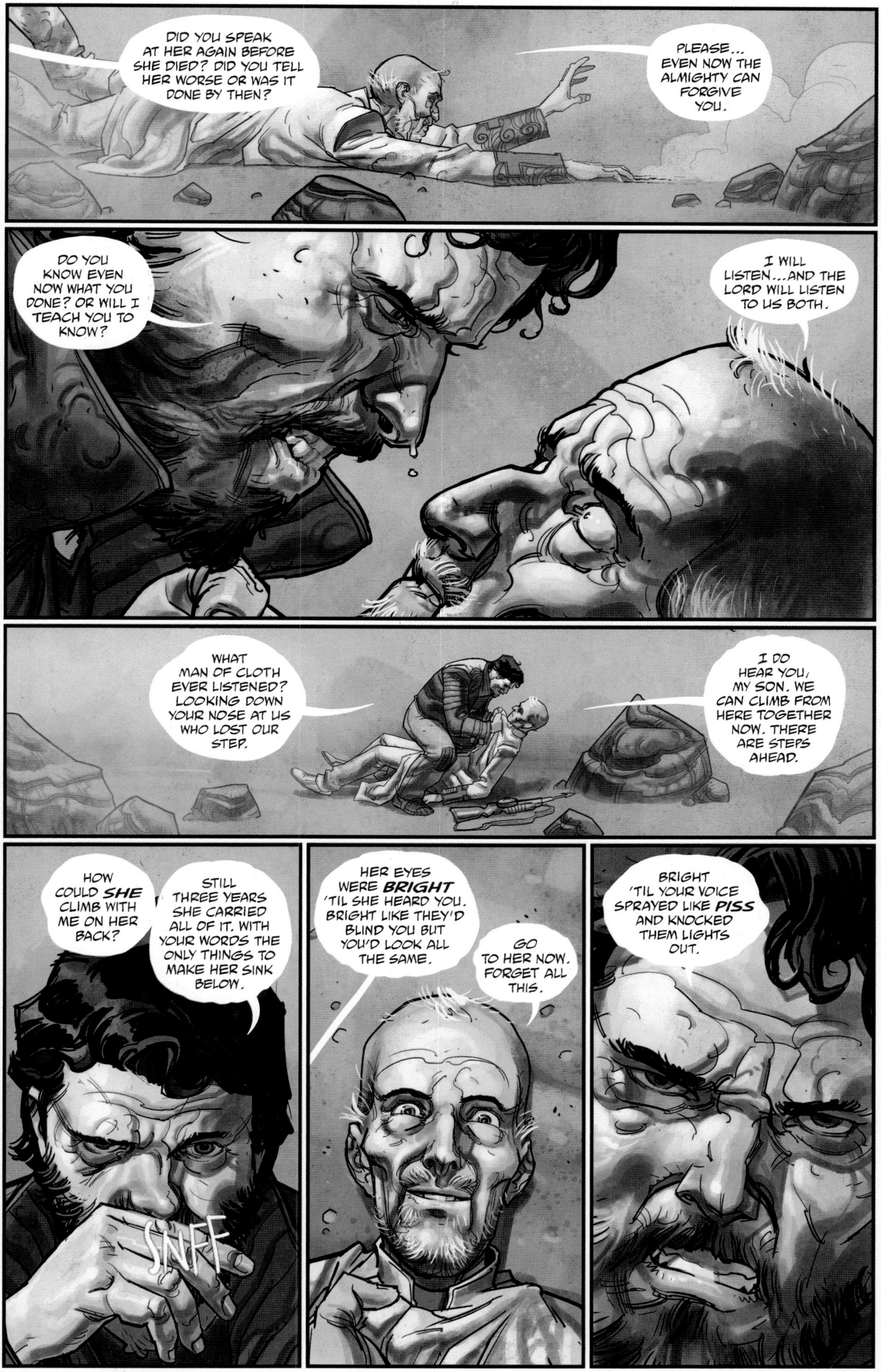
DID YOU SPEAK AT HER AGAIN BEFORE SHE DIED? DID YOU TELL HER WORSE OR WAS IT DONE BY THEN?
PLEASE... EVEN NOW THE ALMIGHTY CAN FORGIVE YOU.
DO YOU KNOW EVEN NOW WHAT YOU DONE? OR WILL I TEACH YOU TO KNOW?
I WILL LISTEN... AND THE LORD WILL LISTEN TO US BOTH.
WHAT MAN OF CLOTH EVER LISTENED? LOOKING DOWN YOUR NOSE AT US WHO LOST OUR STEP.
I DO HEAR YOU, MY SON. WE CAN CLIMB FROM HERE TOGETHER NOW. THERE ARE STEPS AHEAD.
HOW COULD SHE CLIMB WITH ME ON HER BACK?
STILL THREE YEARS SHE CARRIED ALL OF IT. WITH YOUR WORDS THE ONLY THINGS TO MAKE HER SINK BELOW.
SNFF
HER EYES WERE BRIGHT 'TIL SHE HEARD YOU. BRIGHT LIKE THEY'D BLIND YOU BUT YOU'D LOOK ALL THE SAME.
GO TO HER NOW. FORGET ALL THIS.
BRIGHT 'TIL YOUR VOICE SPRAYED LIKE PISS AND KNOCKED THEM LIGHTS OUT.

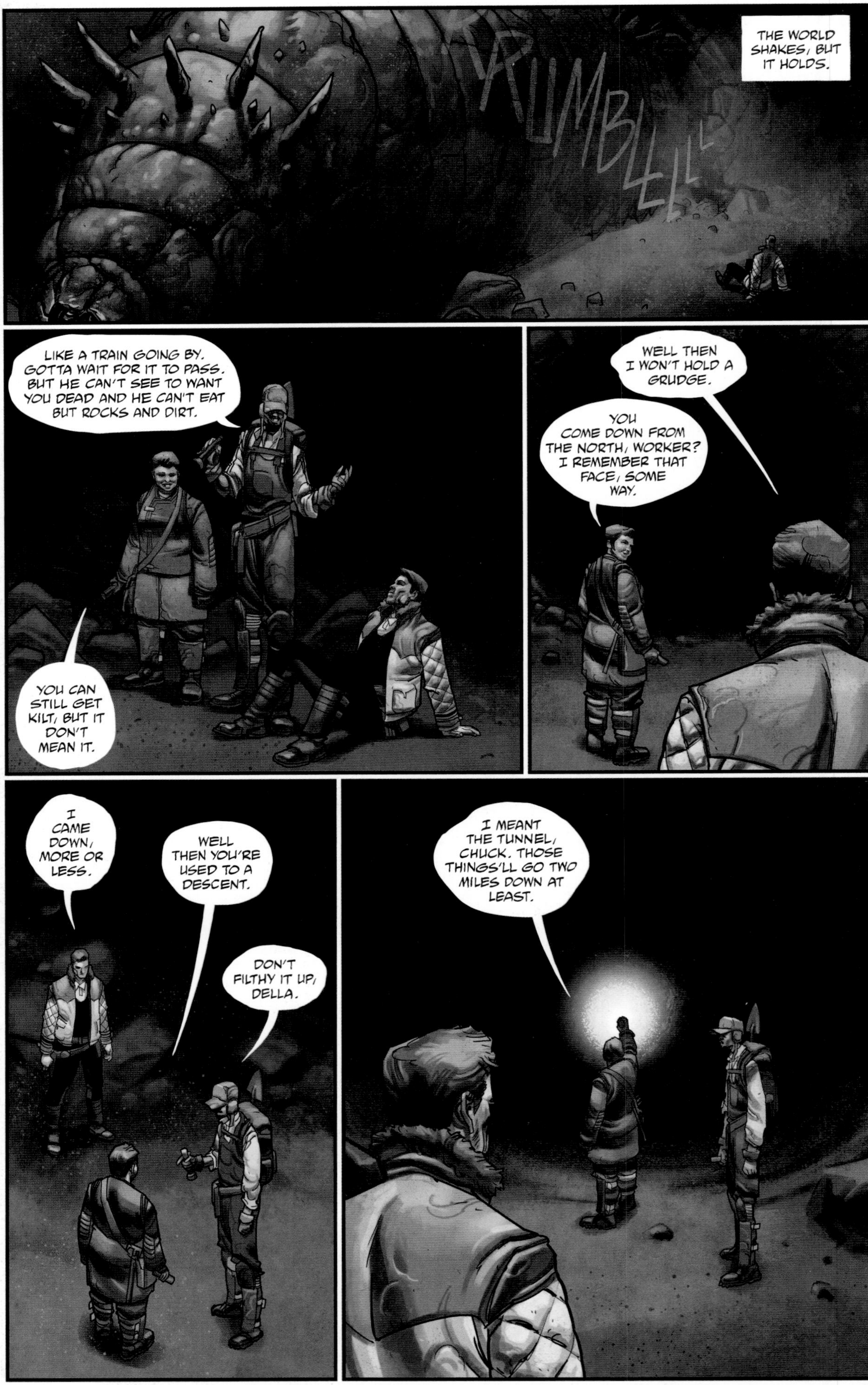
THE WORLD SHAKES, BUT IT HOLDS.
RUMBLELLL
LIKE A TRAIN GOING BY. GOTTA WAIT FOR IT TO PASS. BUT HE CAN'T SEE TO WANT YOU DEAD AND HE CAN'T EAT BUT ROCKS AND DIRT.
YOU CAN STILL GET KILT, BUT IT DON'T MEAN IT.
WELL THEN I WON'T HOLD A GRUDGE.
YOU COME DOWN FROM THE NORTH, WORKER? I REMEMBER THAT FACE, SOME WAY.
I CAME DOWN, MORE OR LESS.
WELL THEN YOU'RE USED TO A DESCENT.
DON'T FILTHY IT UP, DELLA.
I MEANT THE TUNNEL, CHUCK. THOSE THINGS'LL GO TWO MILES DOWN AT LEAST.

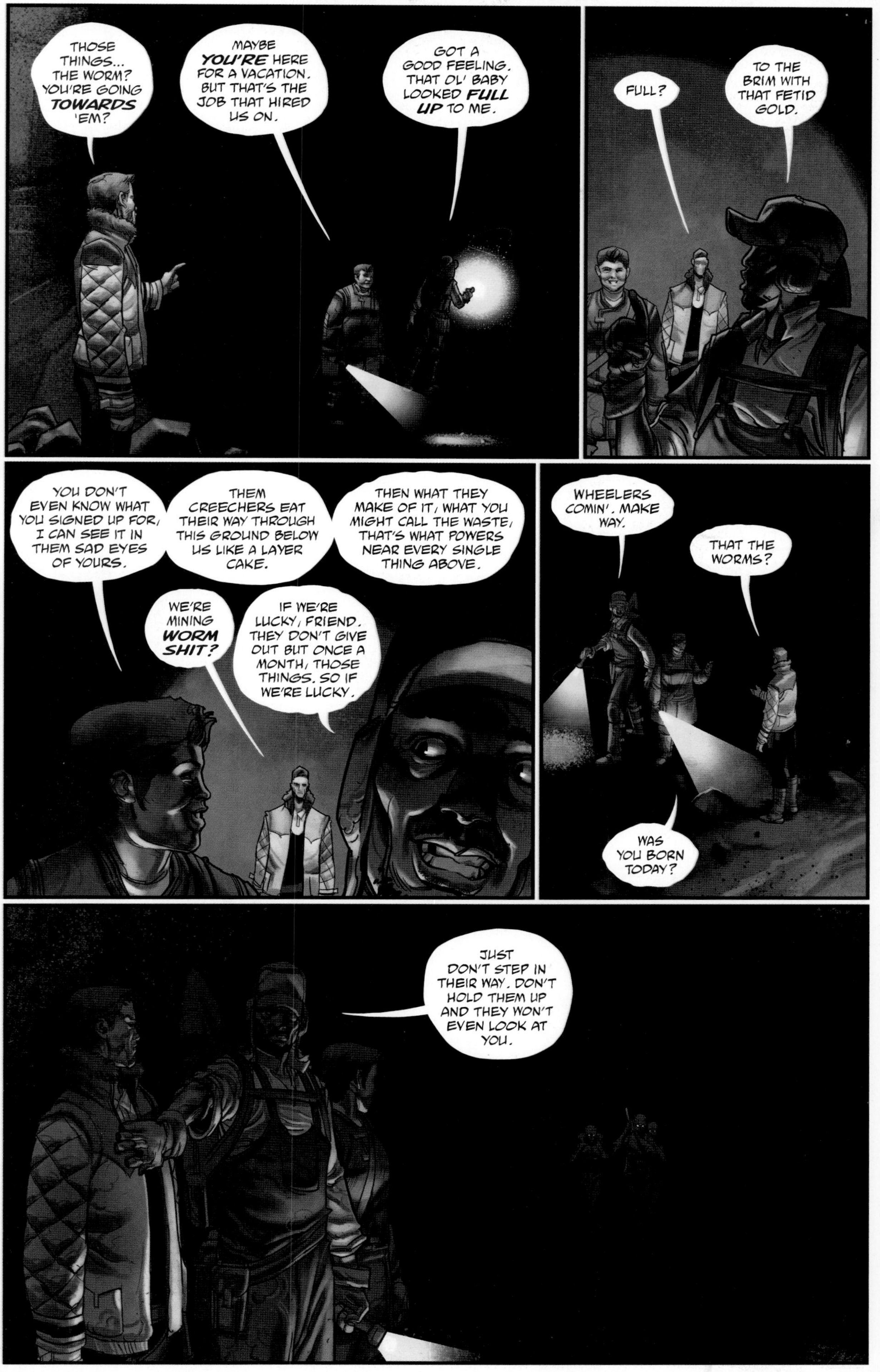
THOSE THINGS... THE WORM? YOU'RE GOING TOWARDS 'EM?
MAYBE YOU'RE HERE FOR A VACATION. BUT THAT'S THE JOB THAT HIRED US ON.
GOT A GOOD FEELING. THAT OL' BABY LOOKED FULL UP TO ME.
FULL?
TO THE BRIM WITH THAT FETID GOLD.
YOU DON'T EVEN KNOW WHAT YOU SIGNED UP FOR, I CAN SEE IT IN THEM SAD EYES OF YOURS.
THEM CREECHERS EAT THEIR WAY THROUGH THIS GROUND BELOW US LIKE A LAYER CAKE.
THEN WHAT THEY MAKE OF IT, WHAT YOU MIGHT CALL THE WASTE, THAT'S WHAT POWERS NEAR EVERY SINGLE THING ABOVE.
WE'RE MINING WORM SHIT?
IF WE'RE LUCKY, FRIEND. THEY DON'T GIVE OUT BUT ONCE A MONTH, THOSE THINGS. SO IF WE'RE LUCKY.
WHEELERS COMIN'. MAKE WAY.
THAT THE WORMS?
WAS YOU BORN TODAY?
JUST DON'T STEP IN THEIR WAY. DON'T HOLD THEM UP AND THEY WON'T EVEN LOOK AT YOU.

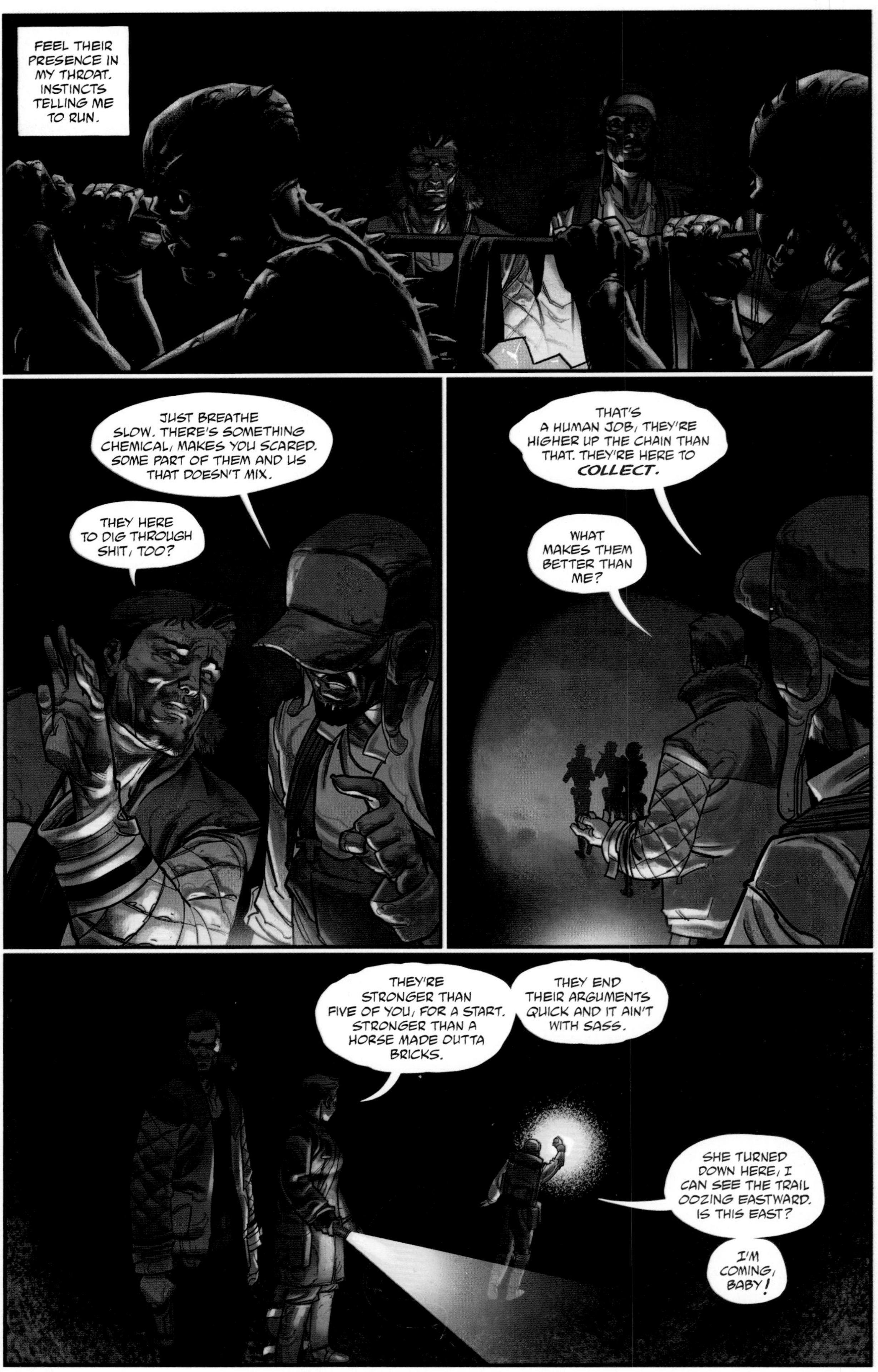
FEEL THEIR PRESENCE IN MY THROAT. INSTINCTS TELLING ME TO RUN.
JUST BREATHE SLOW. THERE'S SOMETHING CHEMICAL, MAKES YOU SCARED. SOME PART OF THEM AND US THAT DOESN'T MIX.
THEY HERE TO DIG THROUGH SHIT, TOO?
THAT'S A HUMAN JOB, THEY'RE HIGHER UP THE CHAIN THAN THAT. THEY'RE HERE TO COLLECT.
WHAT MAKES THEM BETTER THAN ME?
THEY'RE STRONGER THAN FIVE OF YOU, FOR A START. STRONGER THAN A HORSE MADE OUTTA BRICKS.
THEY END THEIR ARGUMENTS QUICK AND IT AIN'T WITH SASS.
SHE TURNED DOWN HERE, I CAN SEE THE TRAIL OOZING EASTWARD. IS THIS EAST?
I'M COMING, BABY!

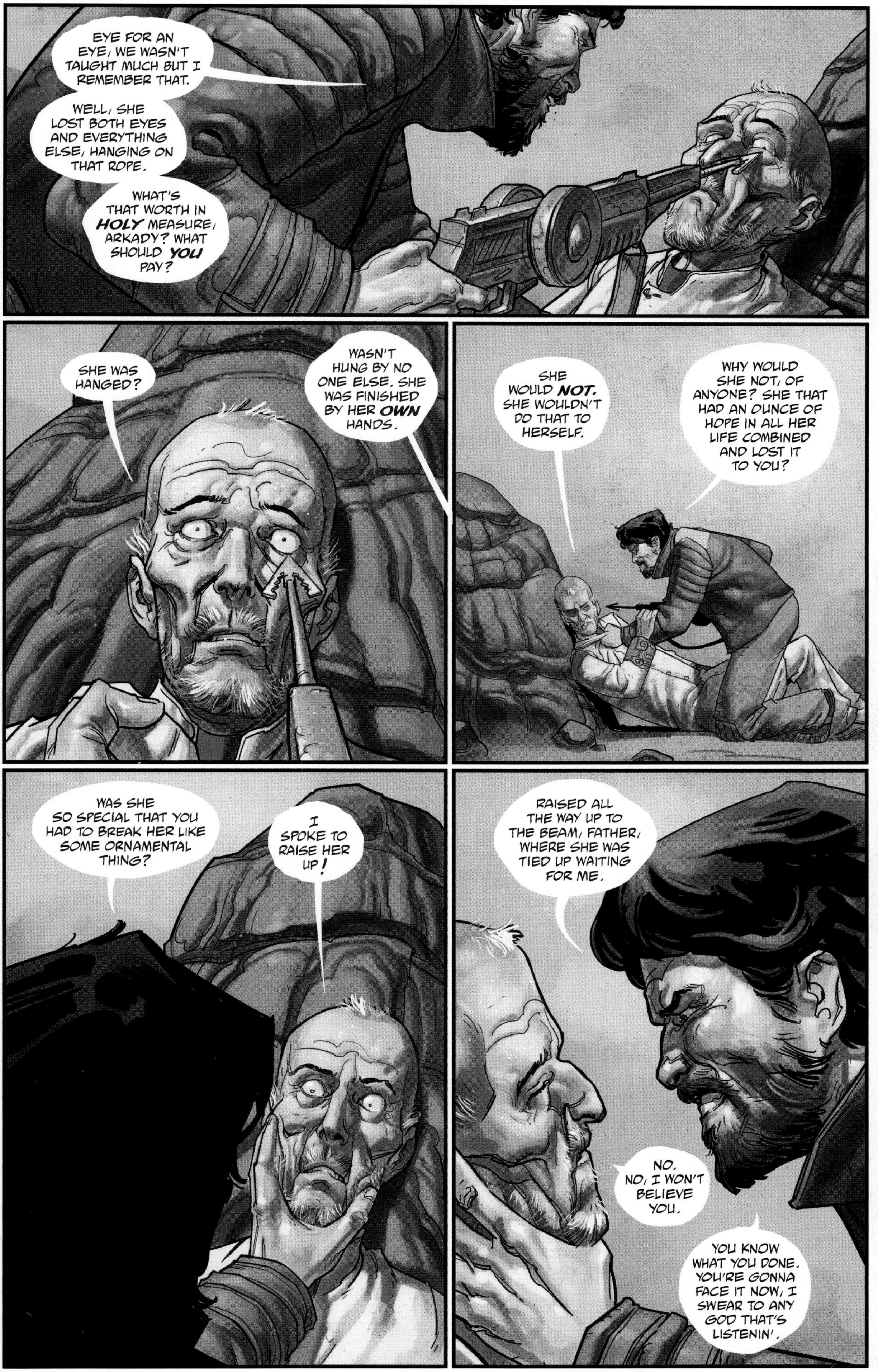
EYE FOR AN EYE, WE WASN'T TAUGHT MUCH BUT I REMEMBER THAT.
WELL, SHE LOST BOTH EYES AND EVERYTHING ELSE, HANGING ON THAT ROPE.
WHAT'S THAT WORTH IN HOLY MEASURE, ARKADY? WHAT SHOULD YOU PAY?
SHE WAS HANGED?
WASN'T HUNG BY NO ONE ELSE. SHE WAS FINISHED BY HER OWN HANDS.
SHE WOULD NOT. SHE WOULDN'T DO THAT TO HERSELF.
WHY WOULD SHE NOT, OF ANYONE? SHE THAT HAD AN OUNCE OF HOPE IN ALL HER LIFE COMBINED AND LOST IT TO YOU?
WAS SHE SO SPECIAL THAT YOU HAD TO BREAK HER LIKE SOME ORNAMENTAL THING?
I SPOKE TO RAISE HER UP!
RAISED ALL THE WAY UP TO THE BEAM, FATHER, WHERE SHE WAS TIED UP WAITING FOR ME.
NO. NO, I WON'T BELIEVE YOU.
YOU KNOW WHAT YOU DONE. YOU'RE GONNA FACE IT NOW, I SWEAR TO ANY GOD THAT'S LISTENIN'.

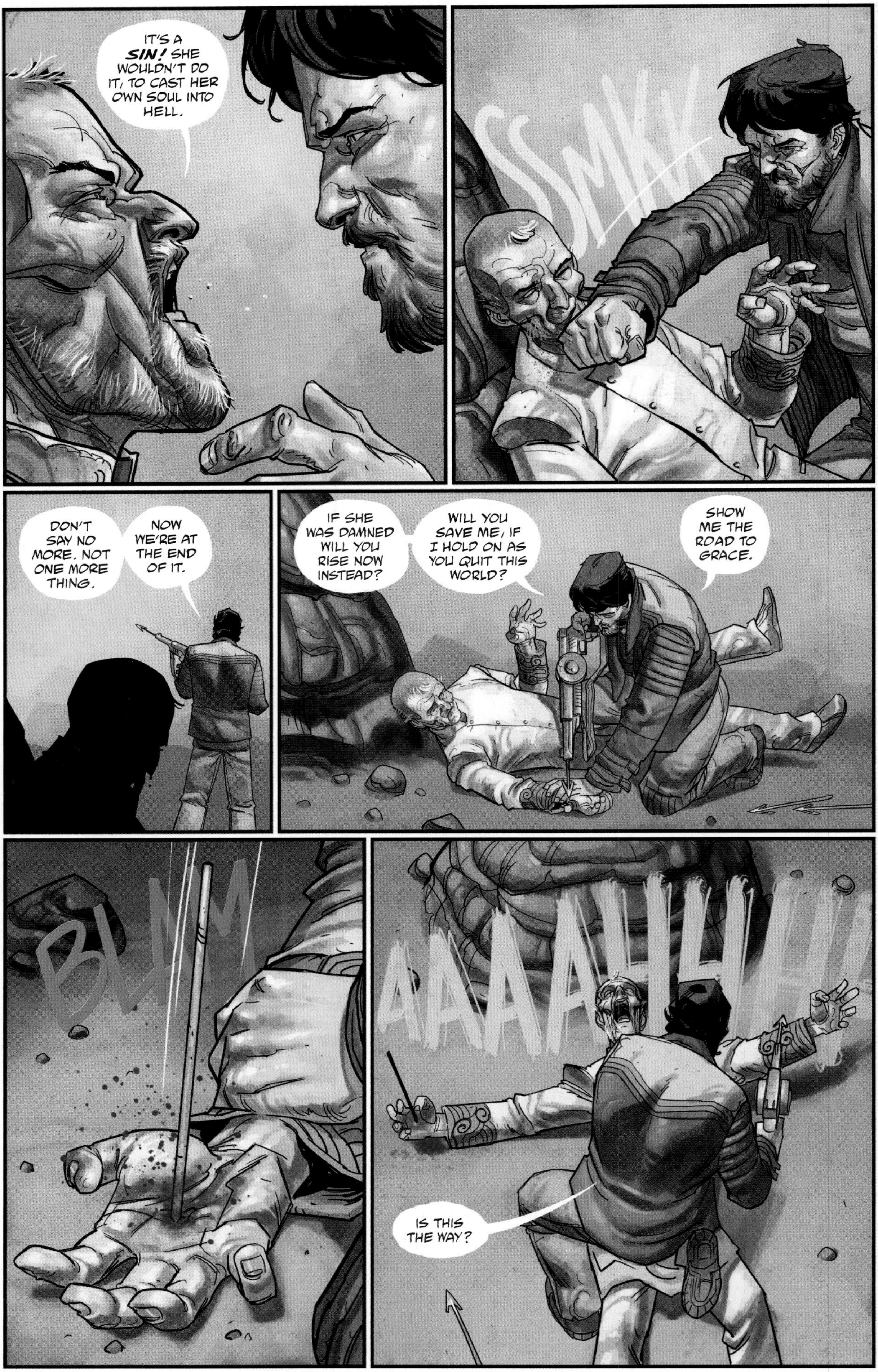
IT'S A SIN! SHE WOULDN'T DO IT, TO CAST HER OWN SOUL INTO HELL.
SSMKK
DON'T SAY NO MORE. NOT ONE MORE THING.
NOW WE'RE AT THE END OF IT.
IF SHE WAS DAMNED WILL YOU RISE NOW INSTEAD?
WILL YOU SAVE ME, IF I HOLD ON AS YOU QUIT THIS WORLD?
SHOW ME THE ROAD TO GRACE.
BLM
AAAAHH!
IS THIS THE WAY?

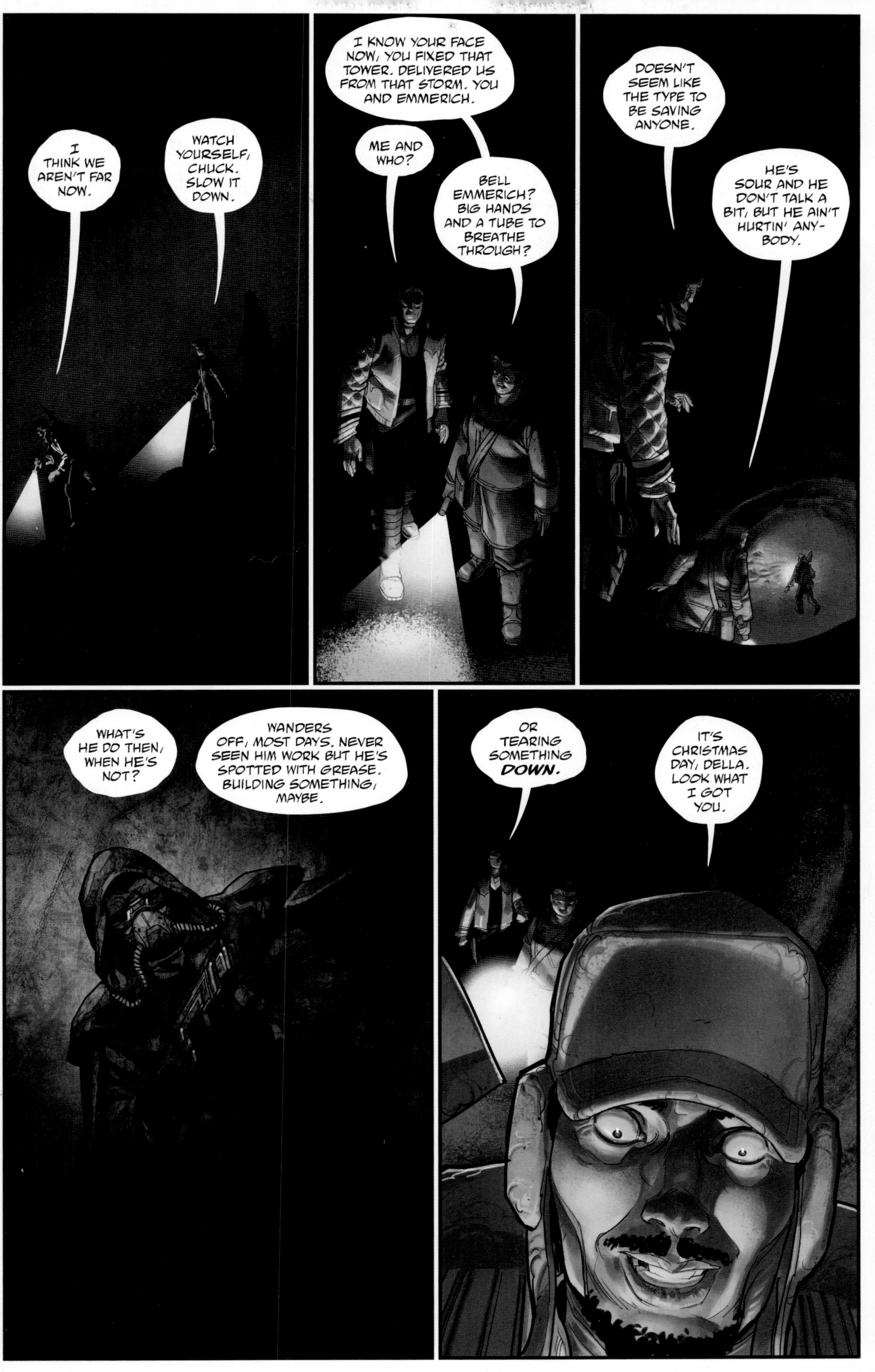
I THINK WE AREN'T FAR NOW.
WATCH YOURSELF, CHUCK. SLOW IT DOWN.
I KNOW YOUR FACE NOW, YOU FIXED THAT TOWER. DELIVERED US FROM THAT STORM. YOU AND EMMERICH.
ME AND WHO?
BELL EMMERICH? BIG HANDS AND A TUBE TO BREATHE THROUGH?
DOESN'T SEEM LIKE THE TYPE TO BE SAVING ANYONE.
HE'S SOUR AND HE DON'T TALK A BIT, BUT HE AIN'T HURTIN' ANY-BODY.
WHAT'S HE DO THEN, WHEN HE'S NOT?
WANDERS OFF, MOST DAYS. NEVER SEEN HIM WORK BUT HE'S SPOTTED WITH GREASE. BUILDING SOMETHING, MAYBE.
OR TEARING SOMETHING **DOWN.**
IT'S CHRISTMAS DAY, DELLA. LOOK WHAT I GOT YOU.

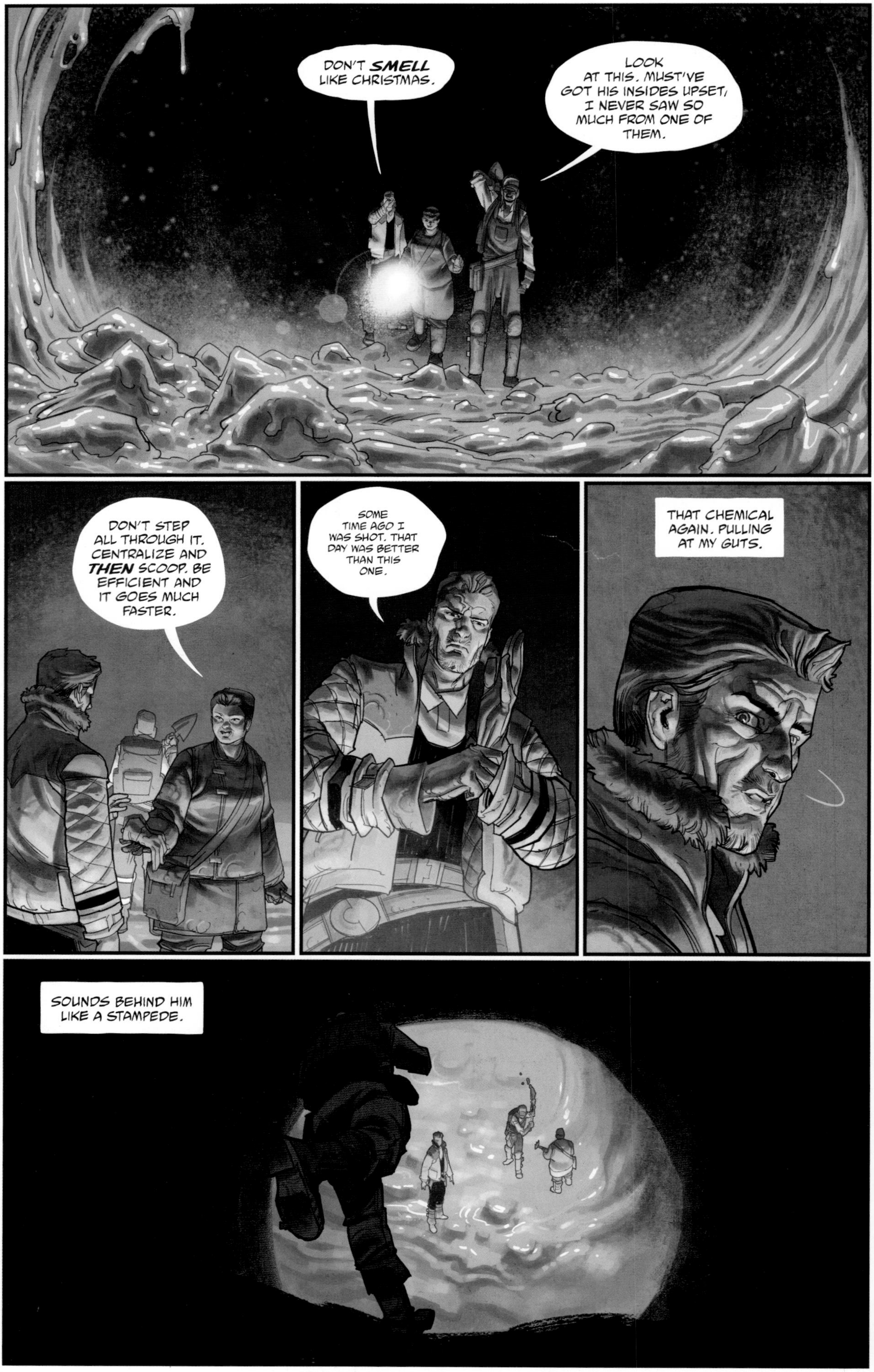
DON'T SMELL LIKE CHRISTMAS.
LOOK AT THIS. MUST'VE GOT HIS INSIDES UPSET, I NEVER SAW SO MUCH FROM ONE OF THEM.
DON'T STEP ALL THROUGH IT. CENTRALIZE AND THEN SCOOP. BE EFFICIENT AND IT GOES MUCH FASTER.
SOME TIME AGO I WAS SHOT. THAT DAY WAS BETTER THAN THIS ONE.
THAT CHEMICAL AGAIN. PULLING AT MY GUTS.
SOUNDS BEHIND HIM LIKE A STAMPEDE.

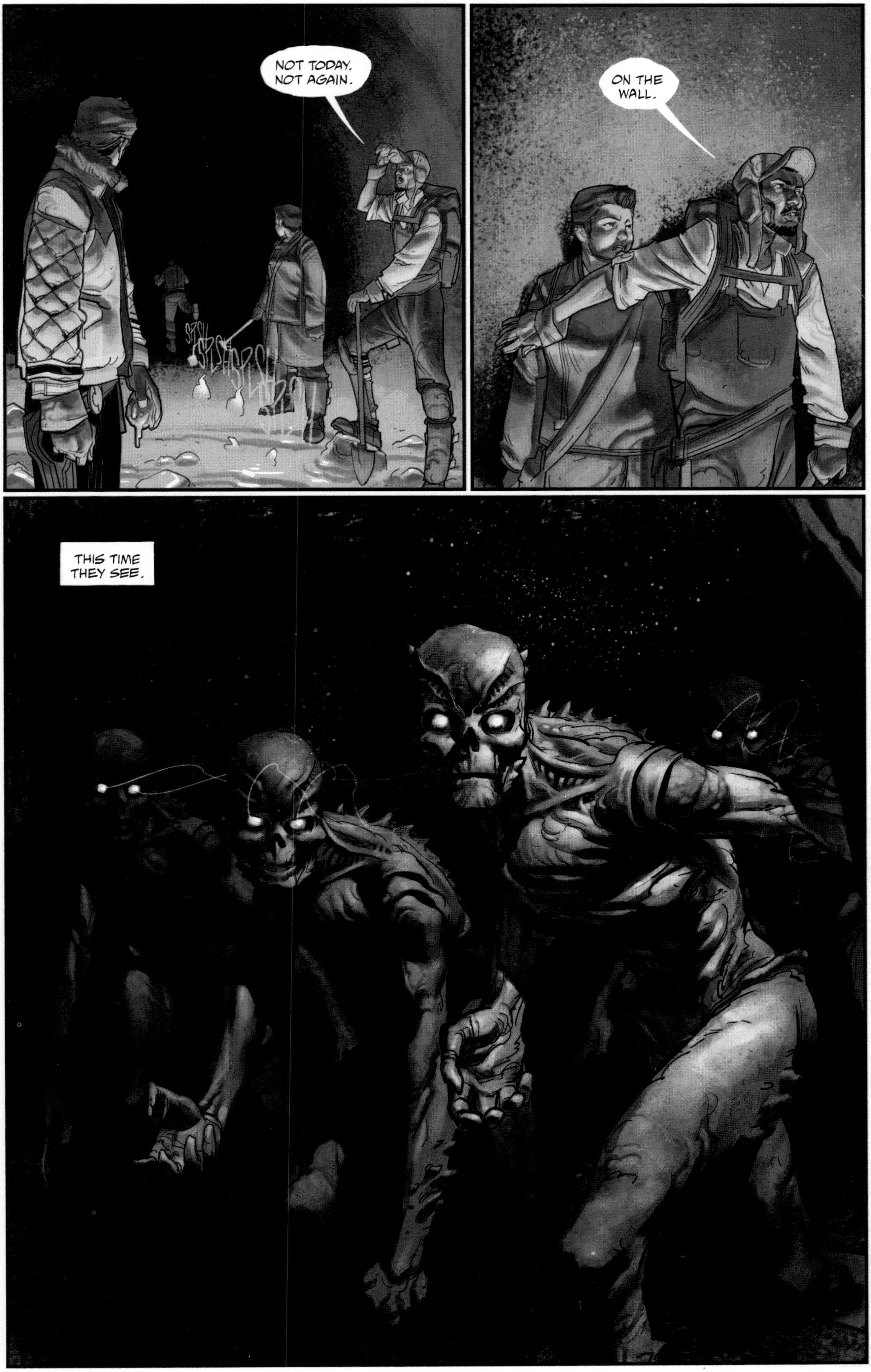
NOT TODAY.
NOT AGAIN.
ON THE
WALL.
THIS TIME
THEY SEE.

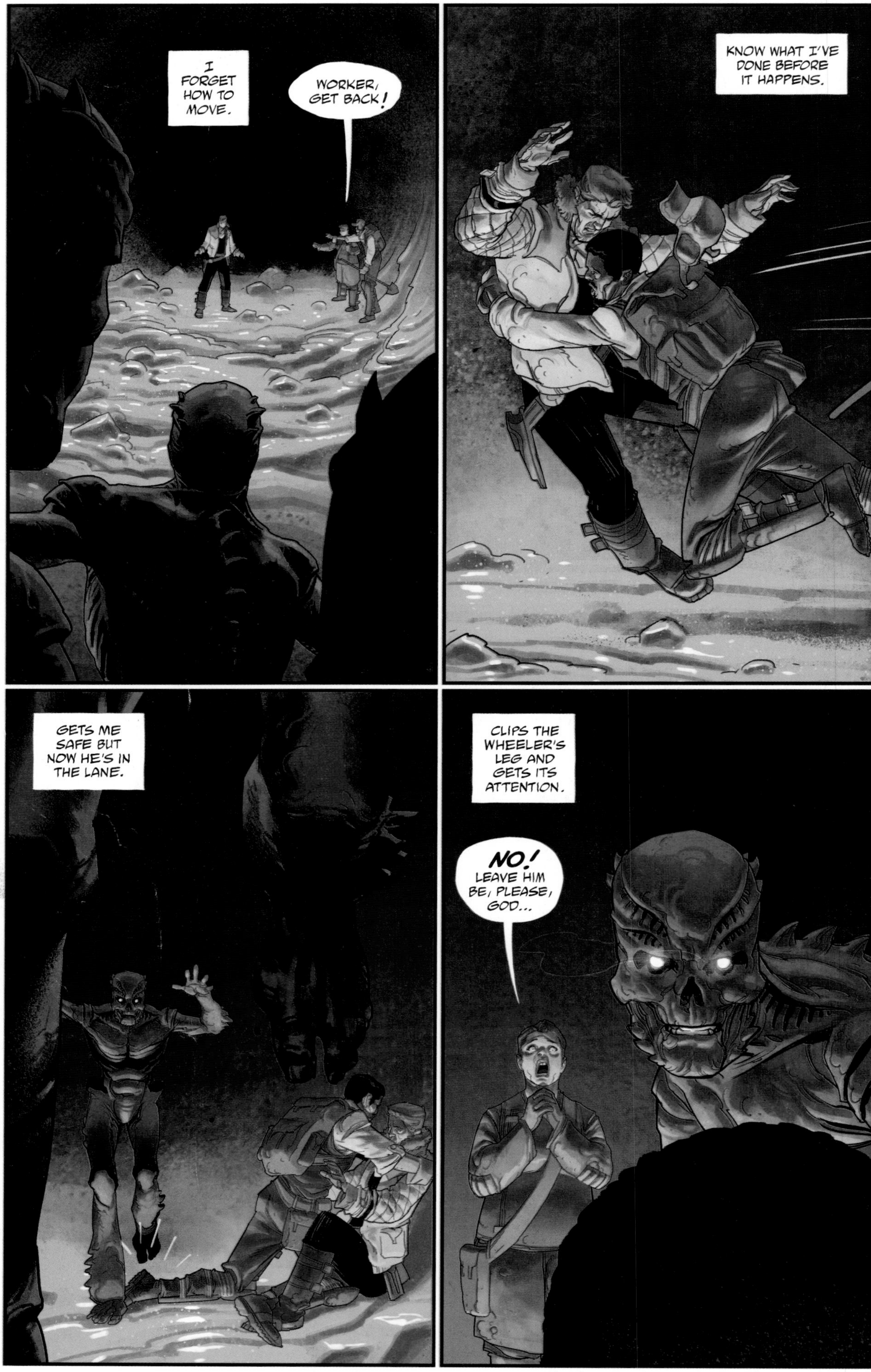
I FORGET HOW TO MOVE.
WORKER, GET BACK!
KNOW WHAT I'VE DONE BEFORE IT HAPPENS.
GETS ME SAFE BUT NOW HE'S IN THE LANE.
CLIPS THE WHEELER'S LEG AND GETS ITS ATTENTION.
NO! LEAVE HIM BE, PLEASE, GOD...

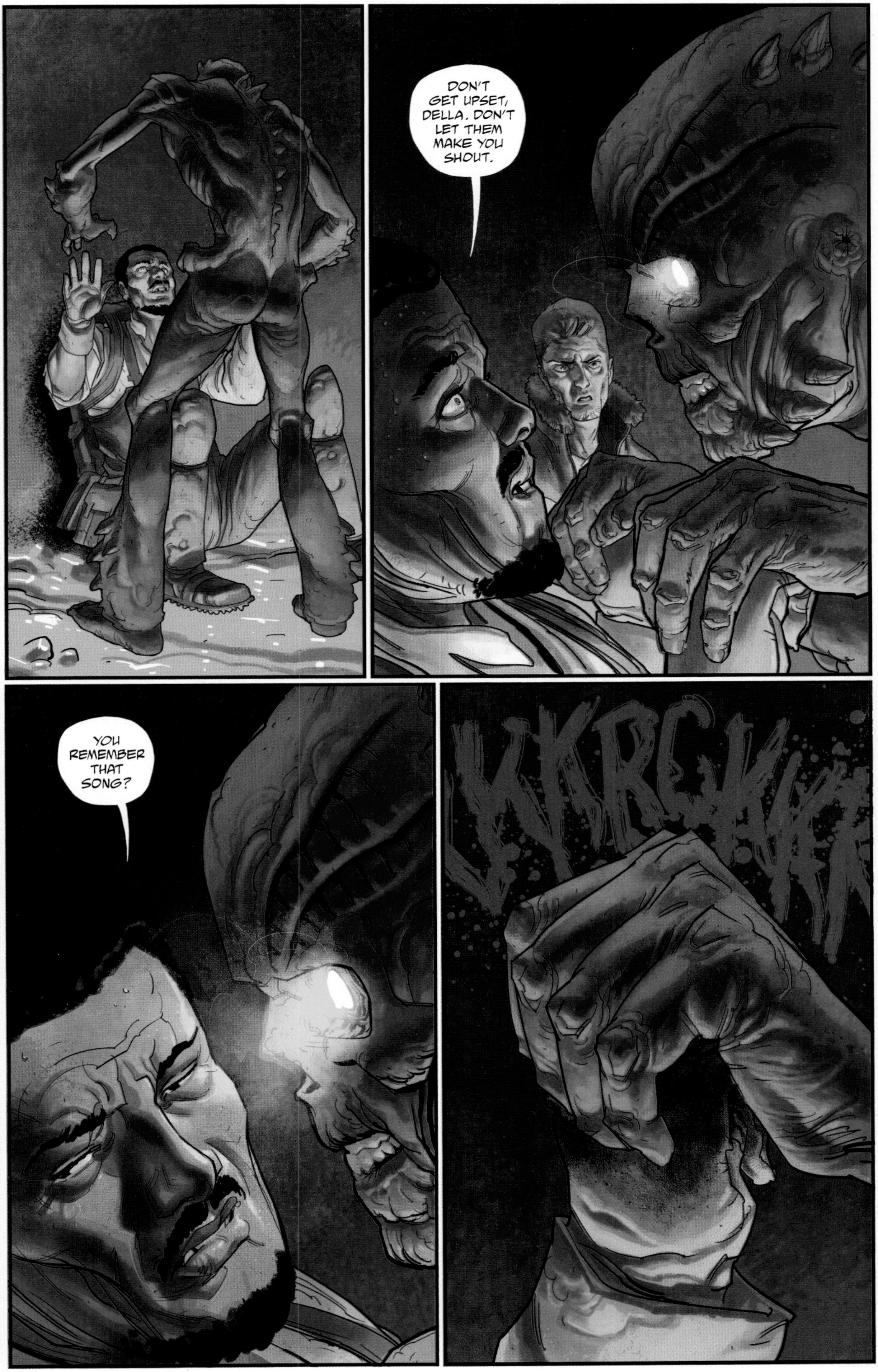
DON'T GET UPSET, DELLA. DON'T LET THEM MAKE YOU SHOUT.
YOU REMEMBER THAT SONG?
KKRCKKK

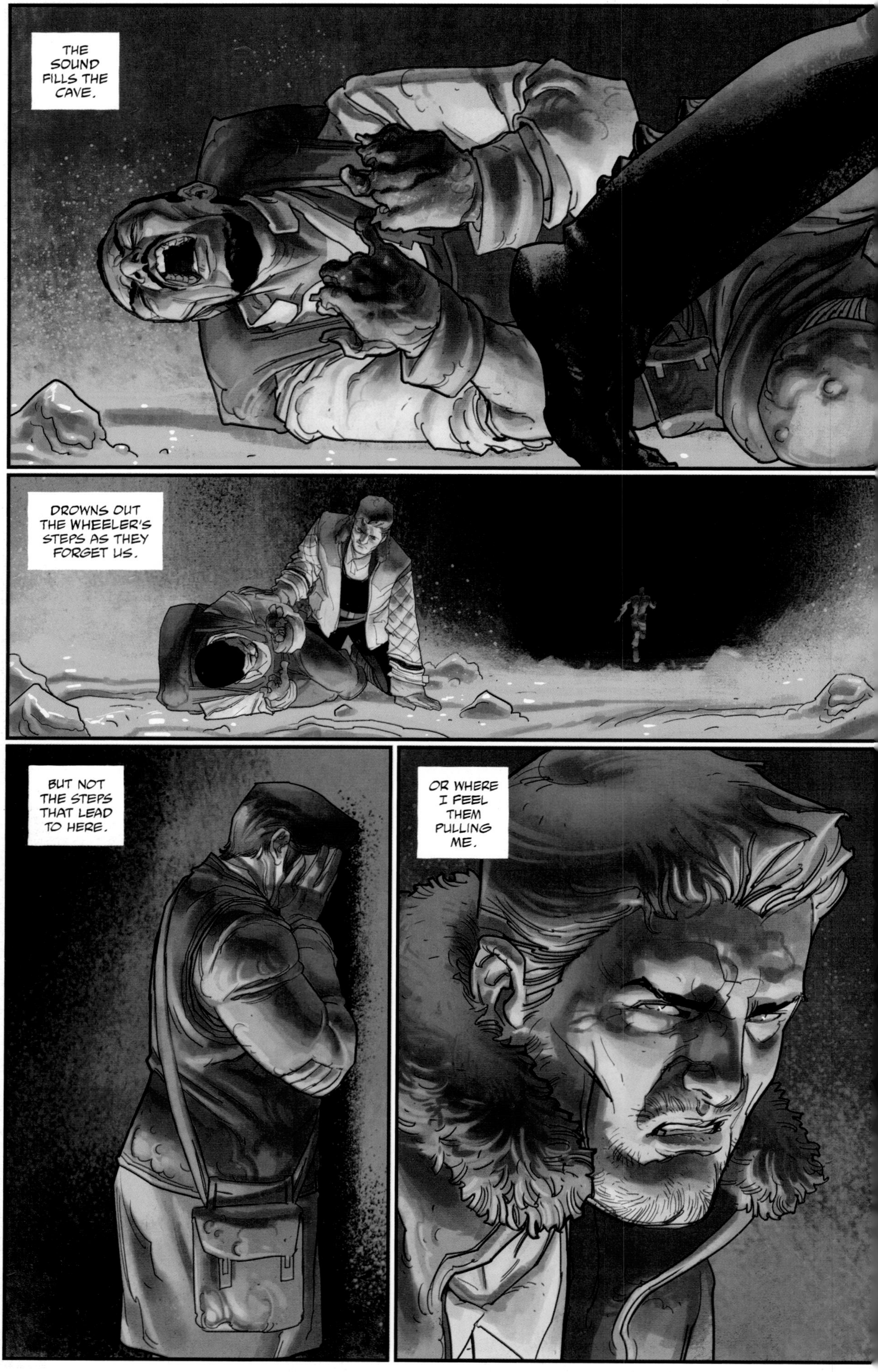
THE SOUND FILLS THE CAVE.
DROWNS OUT THE WHEELER'S STEPS AS THEY FORGET US.
BUT NOT THE STEPS THAT LEAD TO HERE.
OR WHERE I FEEL THEM PULLING ME.

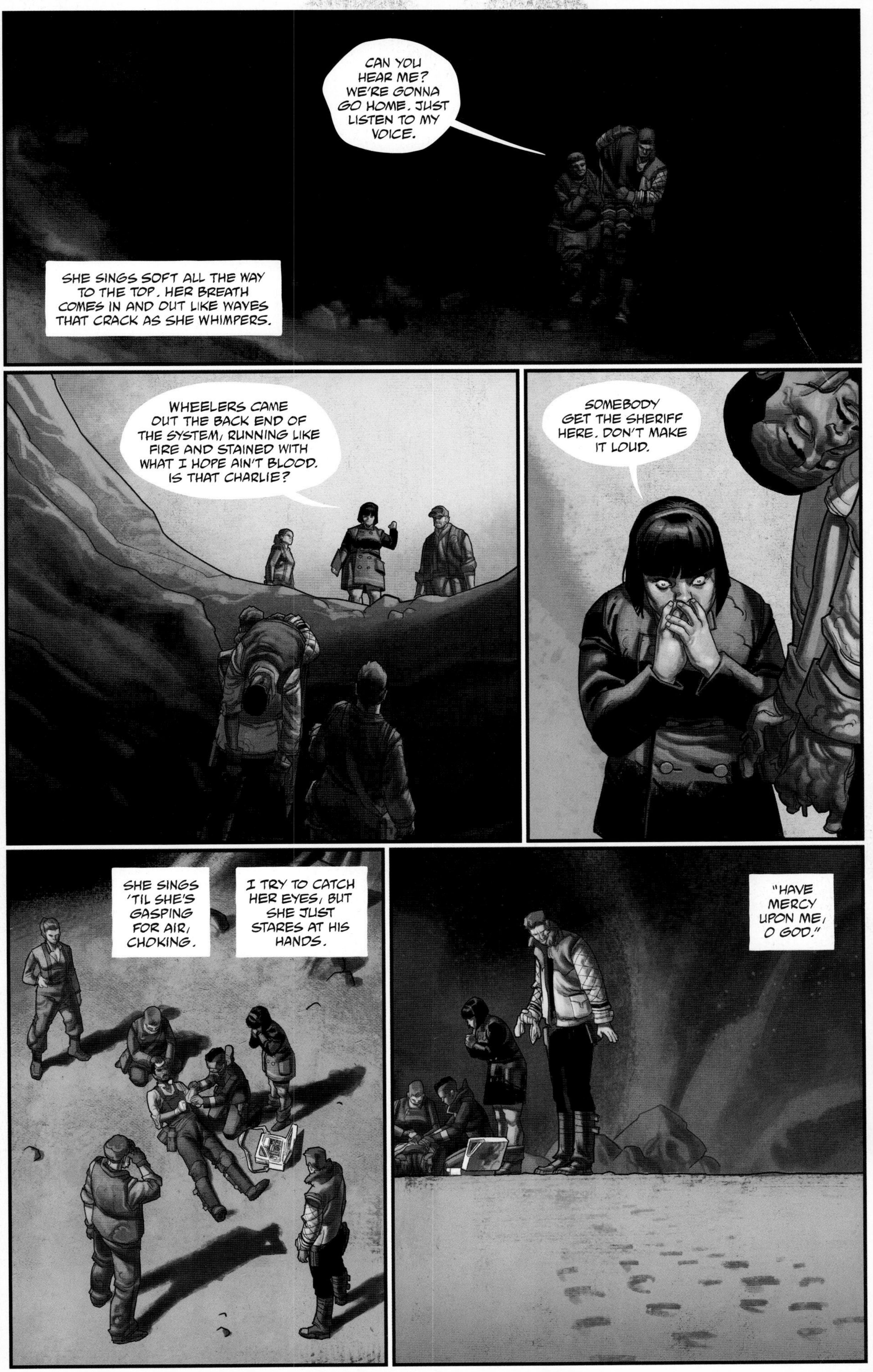
CAN YOU HEAR ME? WE'RE GONNA GO HOME. JUST LISTEN TO MY VOICE.
SHE SINGS SOFT ALL THE WAY TO THE TOP. HER BREATH COMES IN AND OUT LIKE WAVES THAT CRACK AS SHE WHIMPERS.
WHEELERS CAME OUT THE BACK END OF THE SYSTEM, RUNNING LIKE FIRE AND STAINED WITH WHAT I HOPE AIN'T BLOOD. IS THAT CHARLIE?
SOMEBODY GET THE SHERIFF HERE. DON'T MAKE IT LOUD.
SHE SINGS 'TIL SHE'S GASPING FOR AIR, CHOKING.
I TRY TO CATCH HER EYES, BUT SHE JUST STARES AT HIS HANDS.
"HAVE MERCY UPON ME, O GOD."

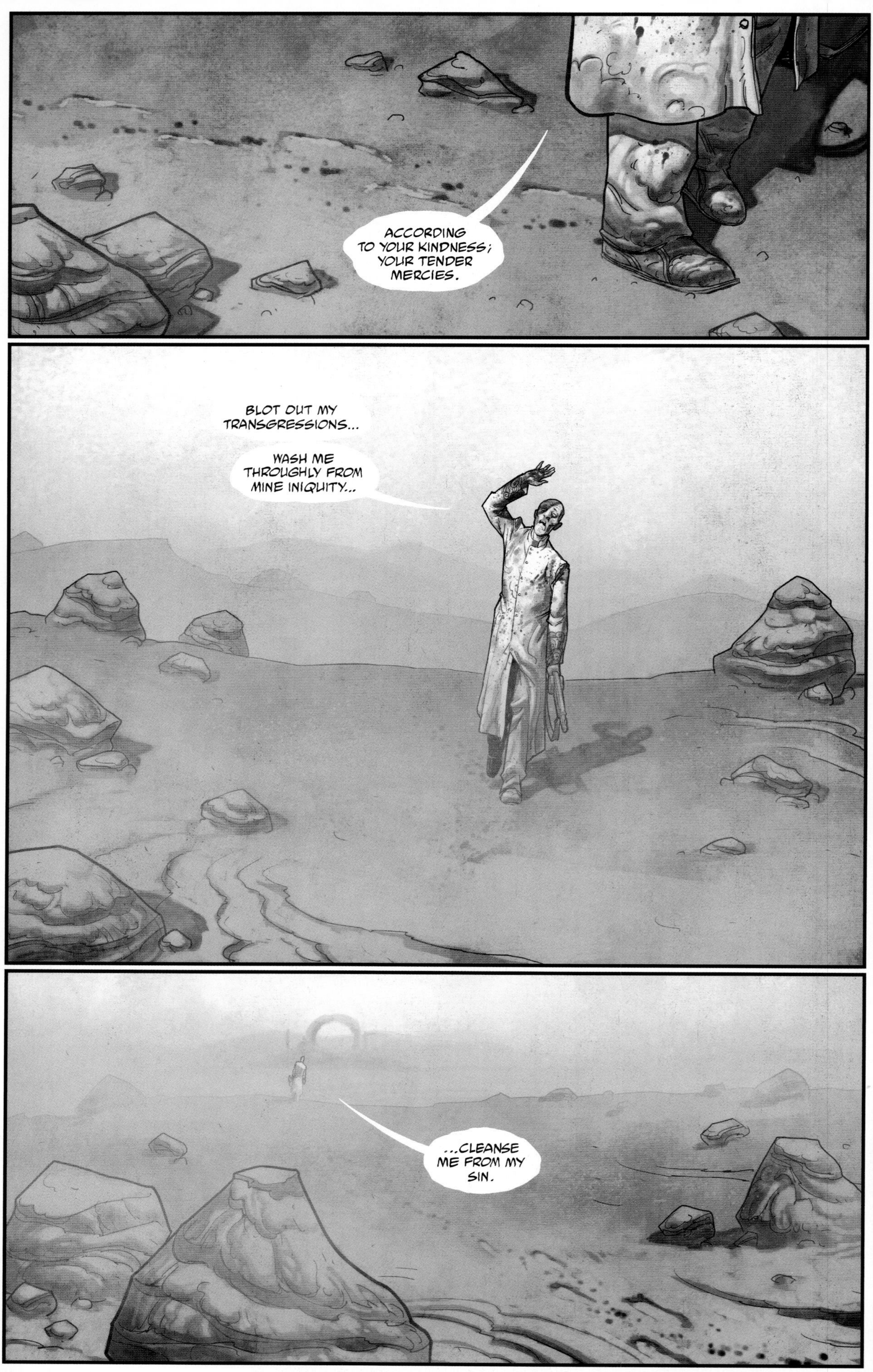
ACCORDING TO YOUR KINDNESS; YOUR TENDER MERCIES.
BLOT OUT MY TRANSGRESSIONS...
WASH ME THROUGHLY FROM MINE INIQUITY...
...CLEANSE ME FROM MY SIN.

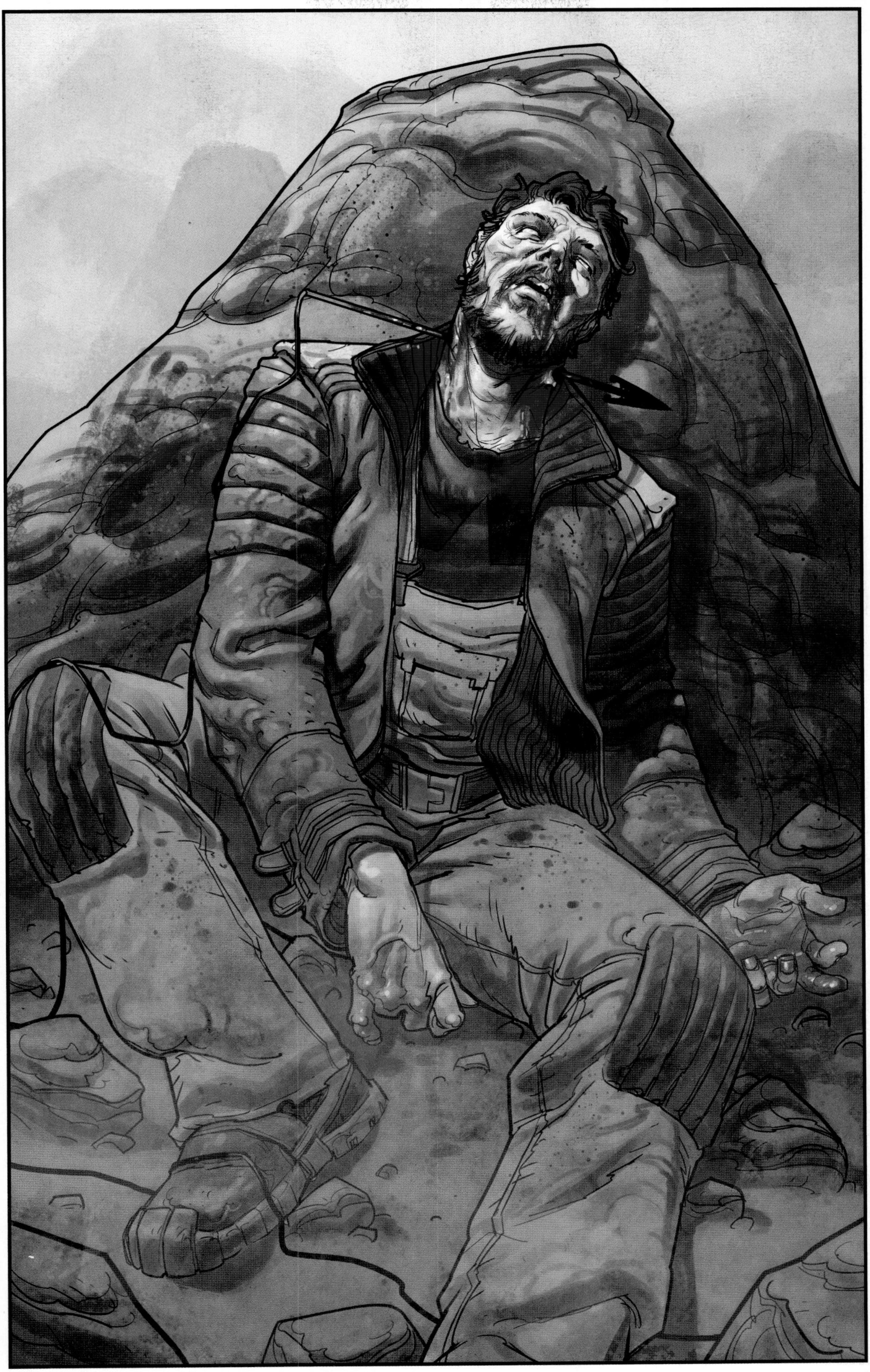

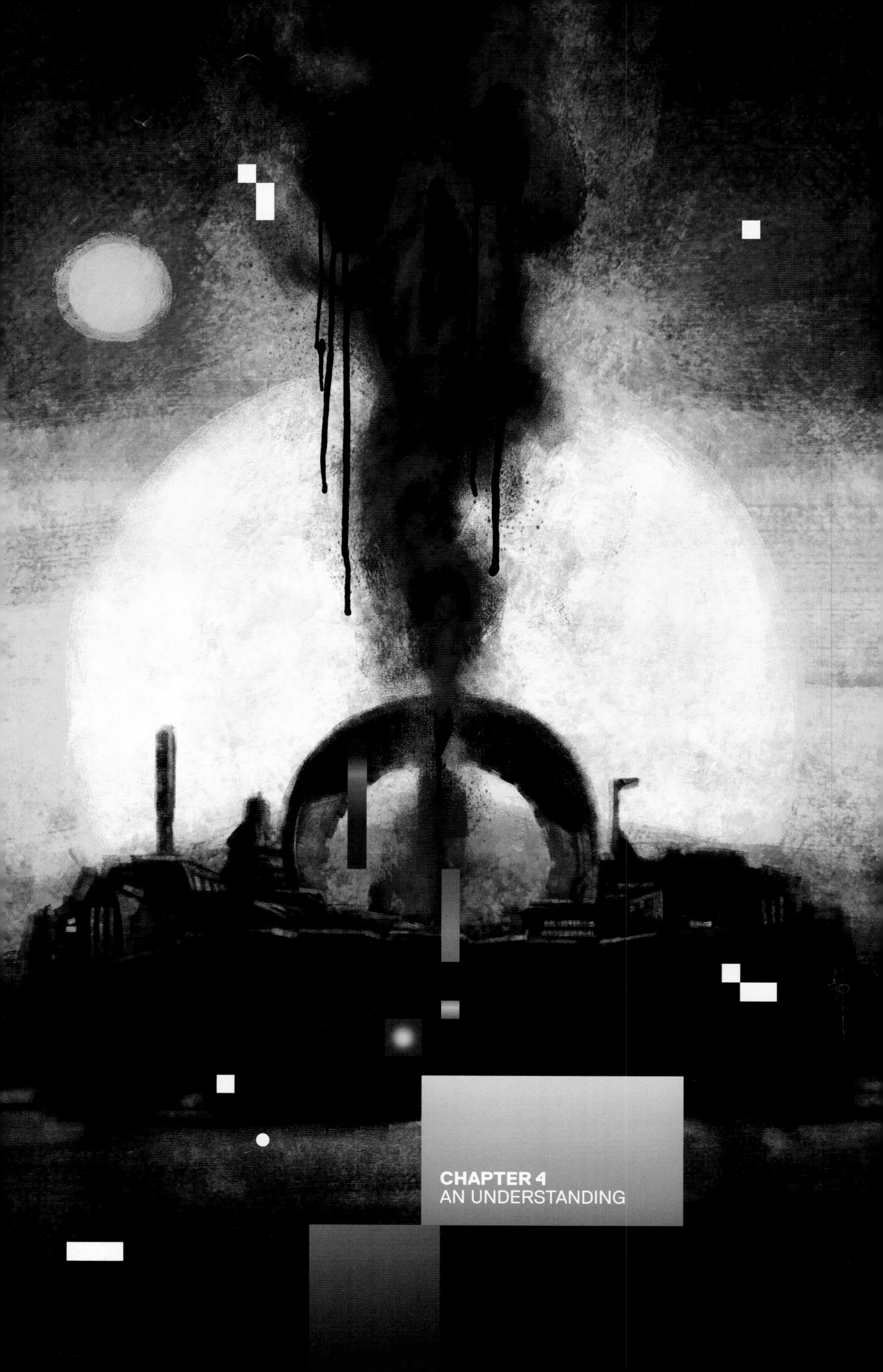

CHAPTER 4
AN UNDERSTANDING

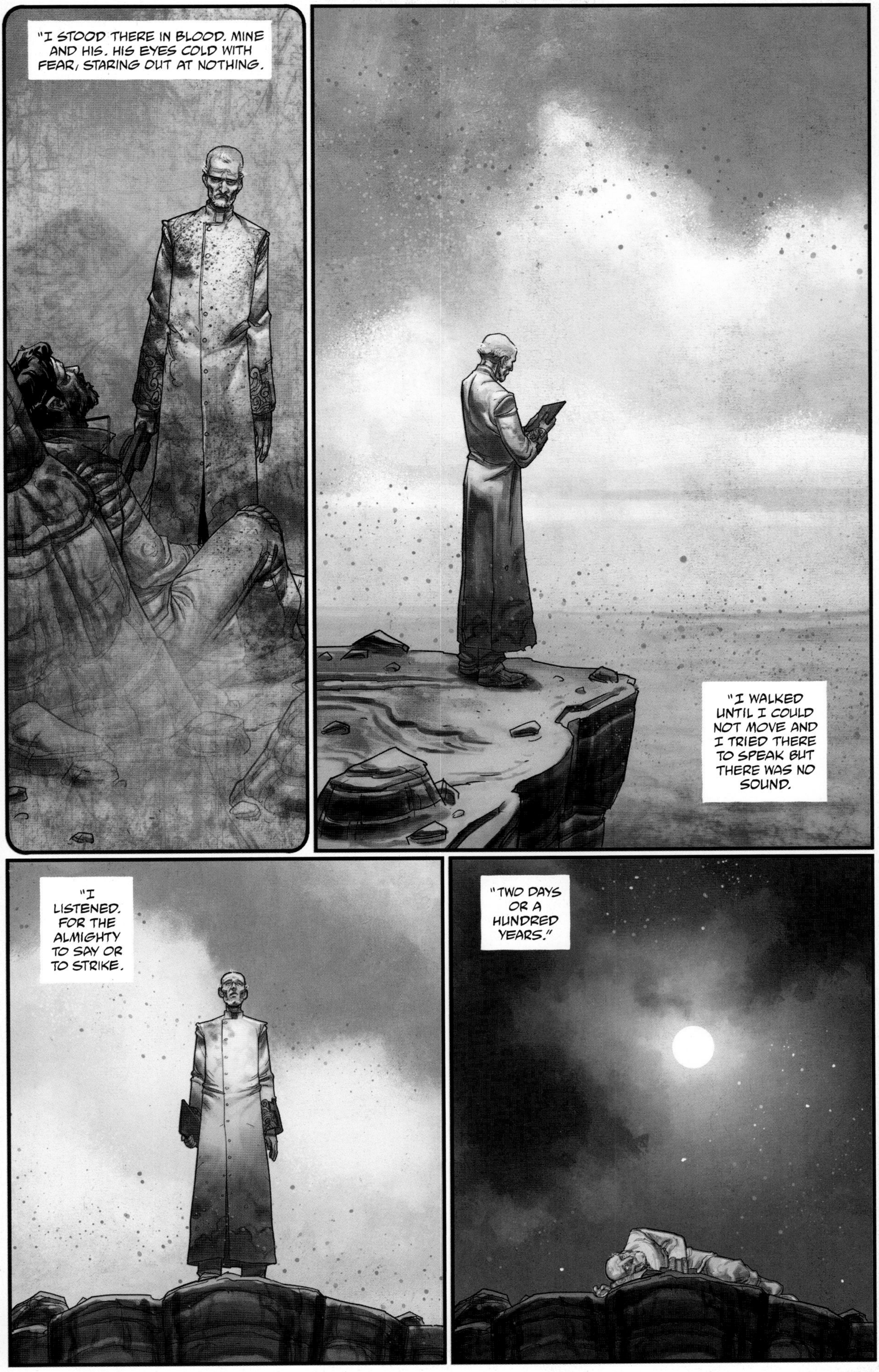
"I STOOD THERE IN BLOOD. MINE AND HIS. HIS EYES COLD WITH FEAR, STARING OUT AT NOTHING.
"I WALKED UNTIL I COULD NOT MOVE AND I TRIED THERE TO SPEAK BUT THERE WAS NO SOUND.
"I LISTENED. FOR THE ALMIGHTY TO SAY OR TO STRIKE.
"TWO DAYS OR A HUNDRED YEARS."

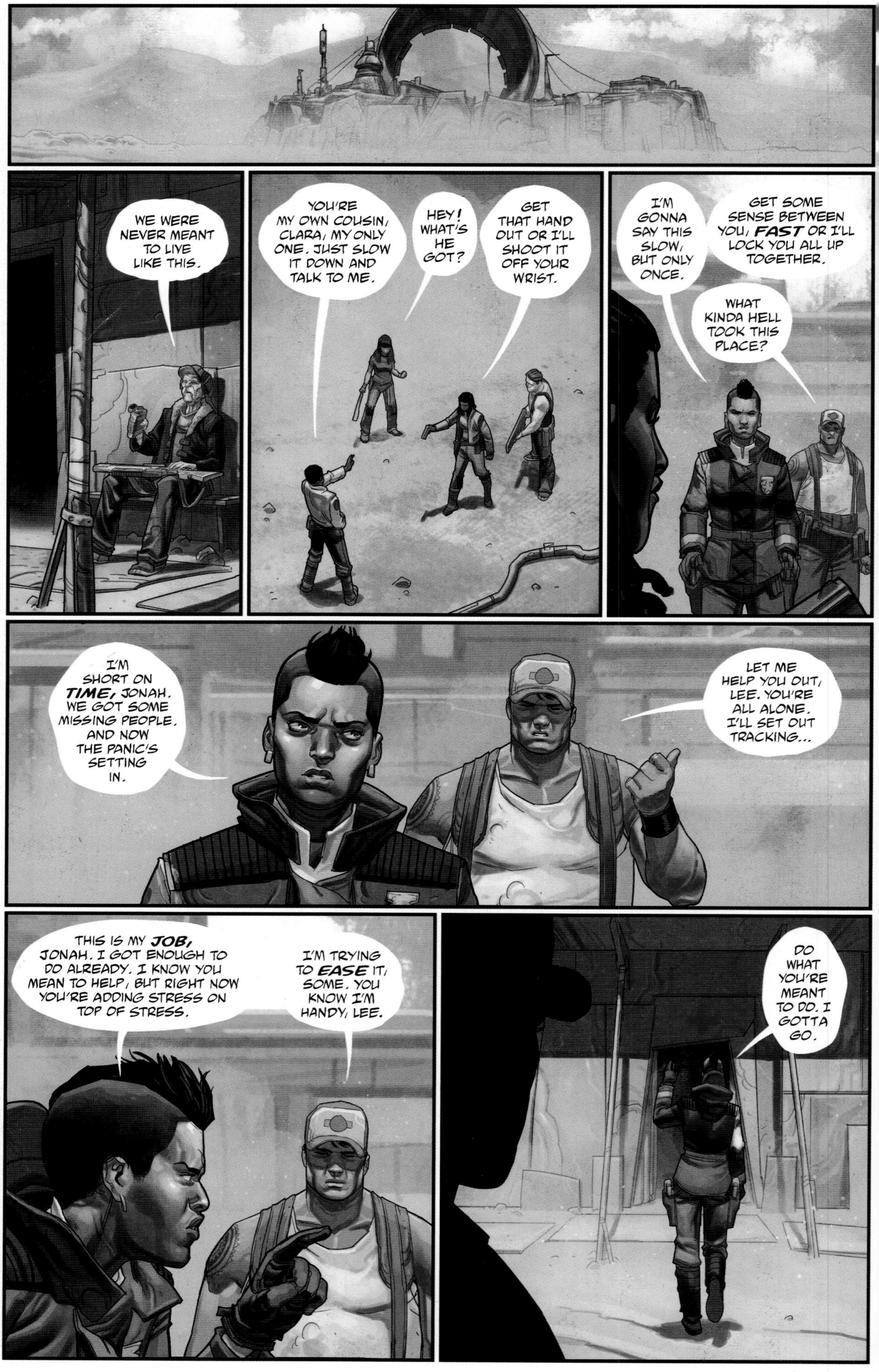
WE WERE NEVER MEANT TO LIVE LIKE THIS.
YOU'RE MY OWN COUSIN, CLARA, MY ONLY ONE. JUST SLOW IT DOWN AND TALK TO ME.
HEY! WHAT'S HE GOT?
GET THAT HAND OUT OR I'LL SHOOT IT OFF YOUR WRIST.
I'M GONNA SAY THIS SLOW, BUT ONLY ONCE.
GET SOME SENSE BETWEEN YOU, FAST OR I'LL LOCK YOU ALL UP TOGETHER.
WHAT KINDA HELL TOOK THIS PLACE?
I'M SHORT ON TIME, JONAH. WE GOT SOME MISSING PEOPLE. AND NOW THE PANIC'S SETTING IN.
LET ME HELP YOU OUT, LEE. YOU'RE ALL ALONE. I'LL SET OUT TRACKING...
THIS IS MY JOB, JONAH. I GOT ENOUGH TO DO ALREADY. I KNOW YOU MEAN TO HELP, BUT RIGHT NOW YOU'RE ADDING STRESS ON TOP OF STRESS.
I'M TRYING TO EASE IT, SOME. YOU KNOW I'M HANDY, LEE.
DO WHAT YOU'RE MEANT TO DO. I GOTTA GO.

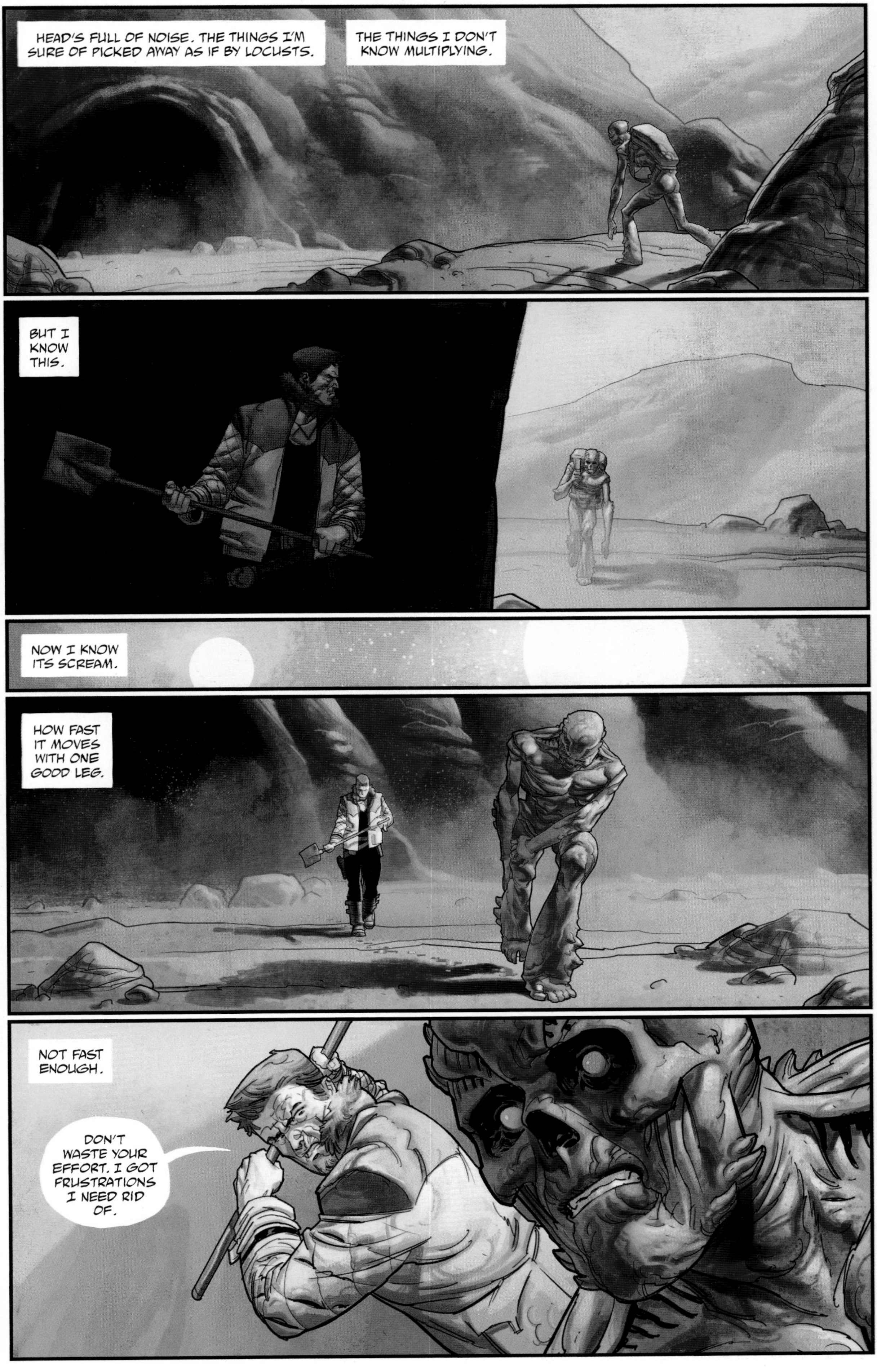
HEAD'S FULL OF NOISE. THE THINGS I'M SURE OF PICKED AWAY AS IF BY LOCUSTS.
THE THINGS I DON'T KNOW MULTIPLYING.
BUT I KNOW THIS.
NOW I KNOW ITS SCREAM.
HOW FAST IT MOVES WITH ONE GOOD LEG.
NOT FAST ENOUGH.
DON'T WASTE YOUR EFFORT. I GOT FRUSTRATIONS I NEED RID OF.

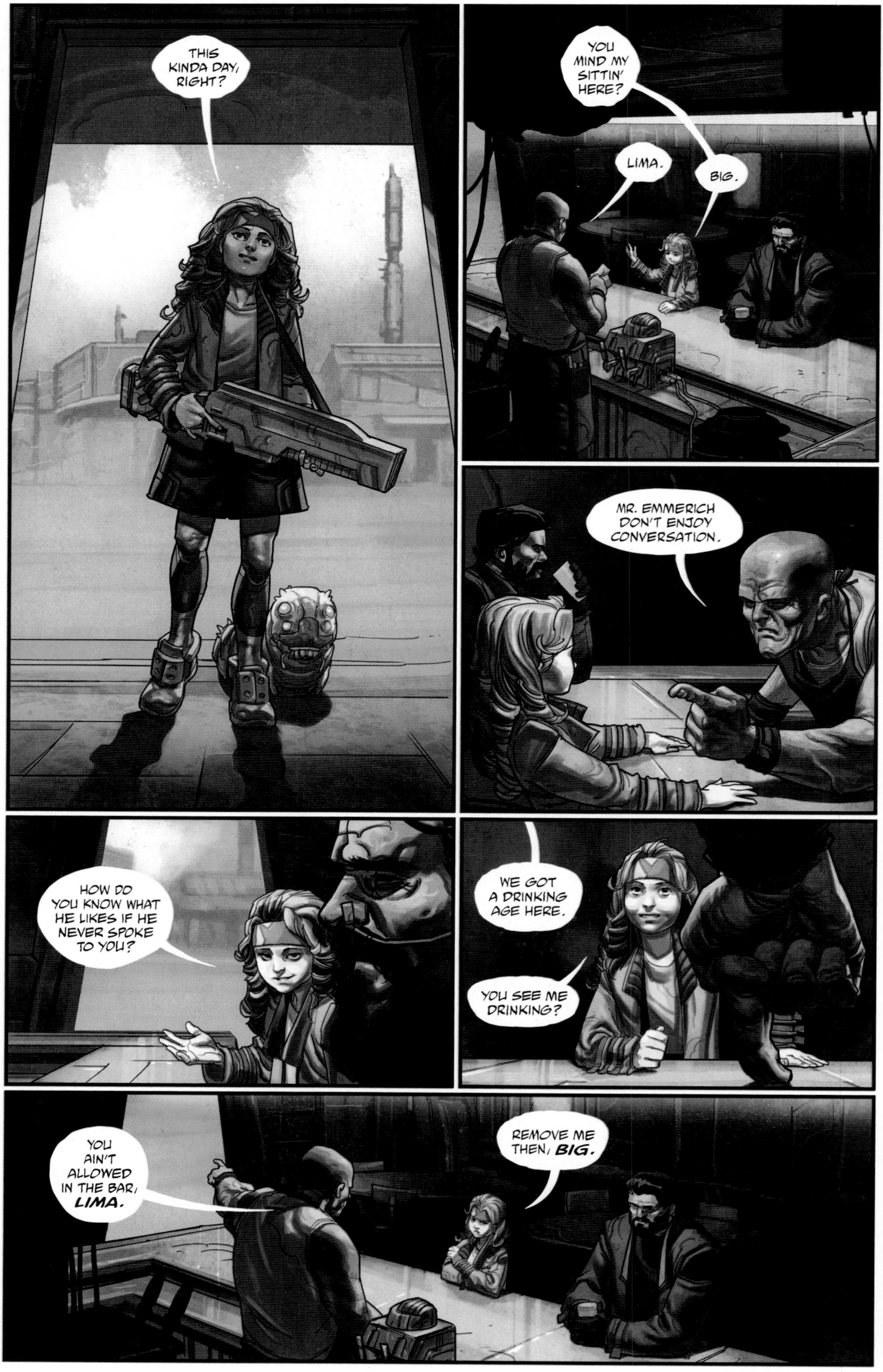
THIS KINDA DAY, RIGHT?
YOU MIND MY SITTIN' HERE?
LIMA.
BIG.
MR. EMMERICH DON'T ENJOY CONVERSATION.
HOW DO YOU KNOW WHAT HE LIKES IF HE NEVER SPOKE TO YOU?
WE GOT A DRINKING AGE HERE.
YOU SEE ME DRINKING?
YOU AIN'T ALLOWED IN THE BAR, **LIMA.**
REMOVE ME THEN, **BIG.**

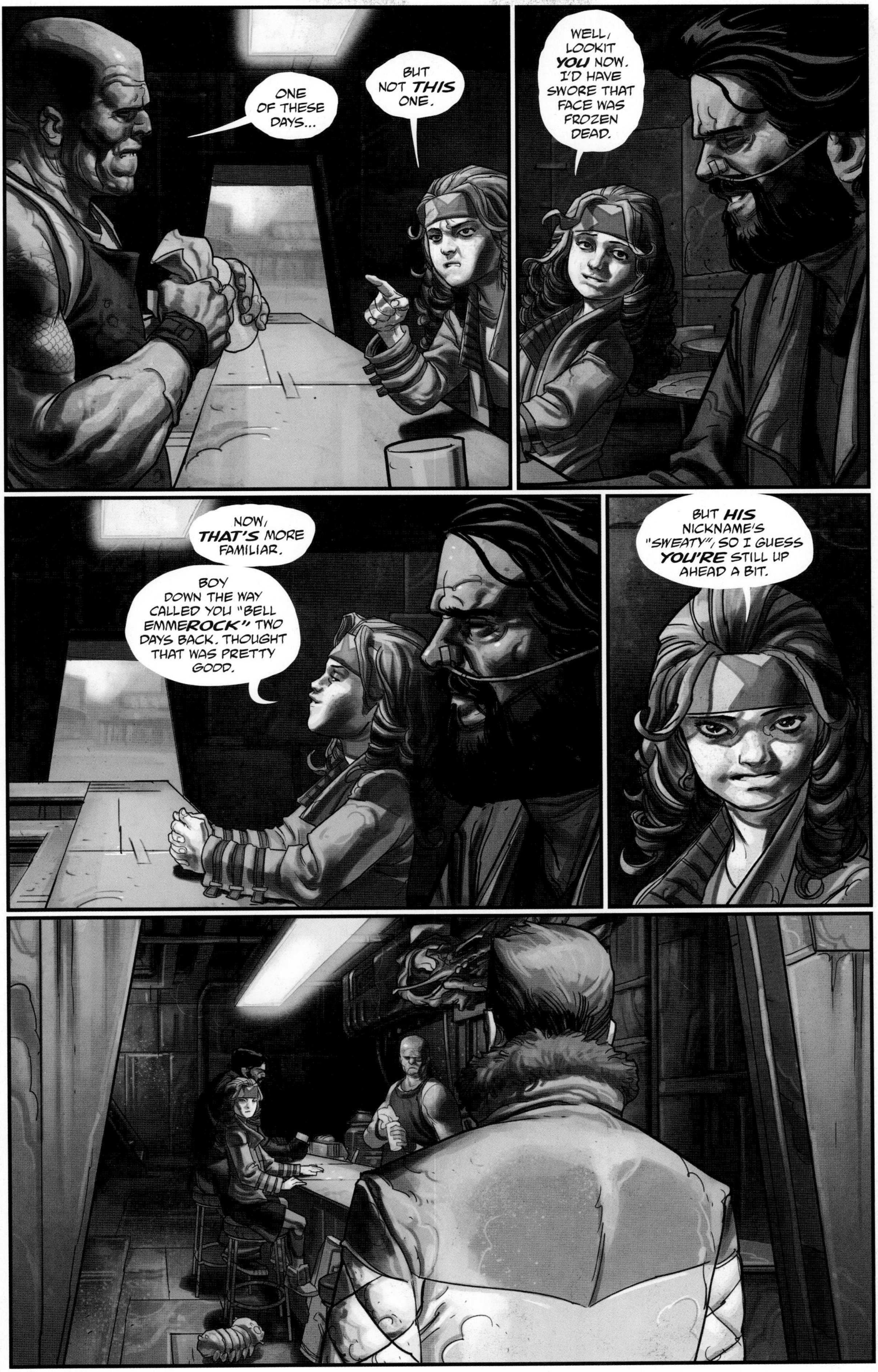
ONE OF THESE DAYS...
BUT NOT THIS ONE.
WELL, LOOKIT YOU NOW. I'D HAVE SWORE THAT FACE WAS FROZEN DEAD.
NOW, THAT'S MORE FAMILIAR.
BOY DOWN THE WAY CALLED YOU "BELL EMMEROCK" TWO DAYS BACK. THOUGHT THAT WAS PRETTY GOOD.
BUT HIS NICKNAME'S "SWEATY", SO I GUESS YOU'RE STILL UP AHEAD A BIT.

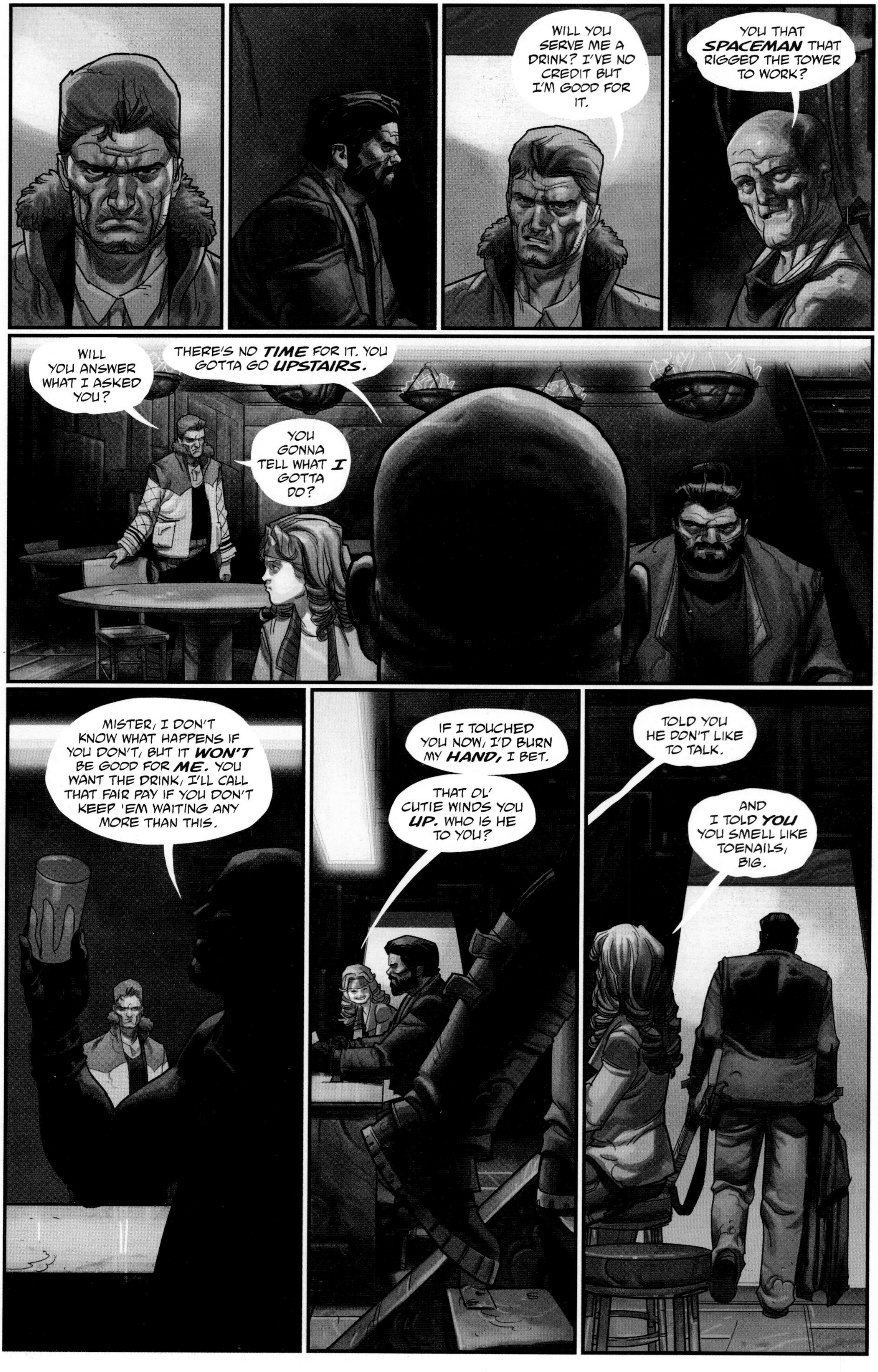
WILL YOU SERVE ME A DRINK? I'VE NO CREDIT BUT I'M GOOD FOR IT.
YOU THAT SPACEMAN THAT RIGGED THE TOWER TO WORK?
WILL YOU ANSWER WHAT I ASKED YOU?
THERE'S NO TIME FOR IT. YOU GOTTA GO UPSTAIRS.
YOU GONNA TELL WHAT I GOTTA DO?
MISTER, I DON'T KNOW WHAT HAPPENS IF YOU DON'T, BUT IT WON'T BE GOOD FOR ME. YOU WANT THE DRINK, I'LL CALL THAT FAIR PAY IF YOU DON'T KEEP 'EM WAITING ANY MORE THAN THIS.
IF I TOUCHED YOU NOW, I'D BURN MY HAND, I BET.
THAT OL' CUTIE WINDS YOU UP. WHO IS HE TO YOU?
TOLD YOU HE DON'T LIKE TO TALK.
AND I TOLD YOU YOU SMELL LIKE TOENAILS, BIG.

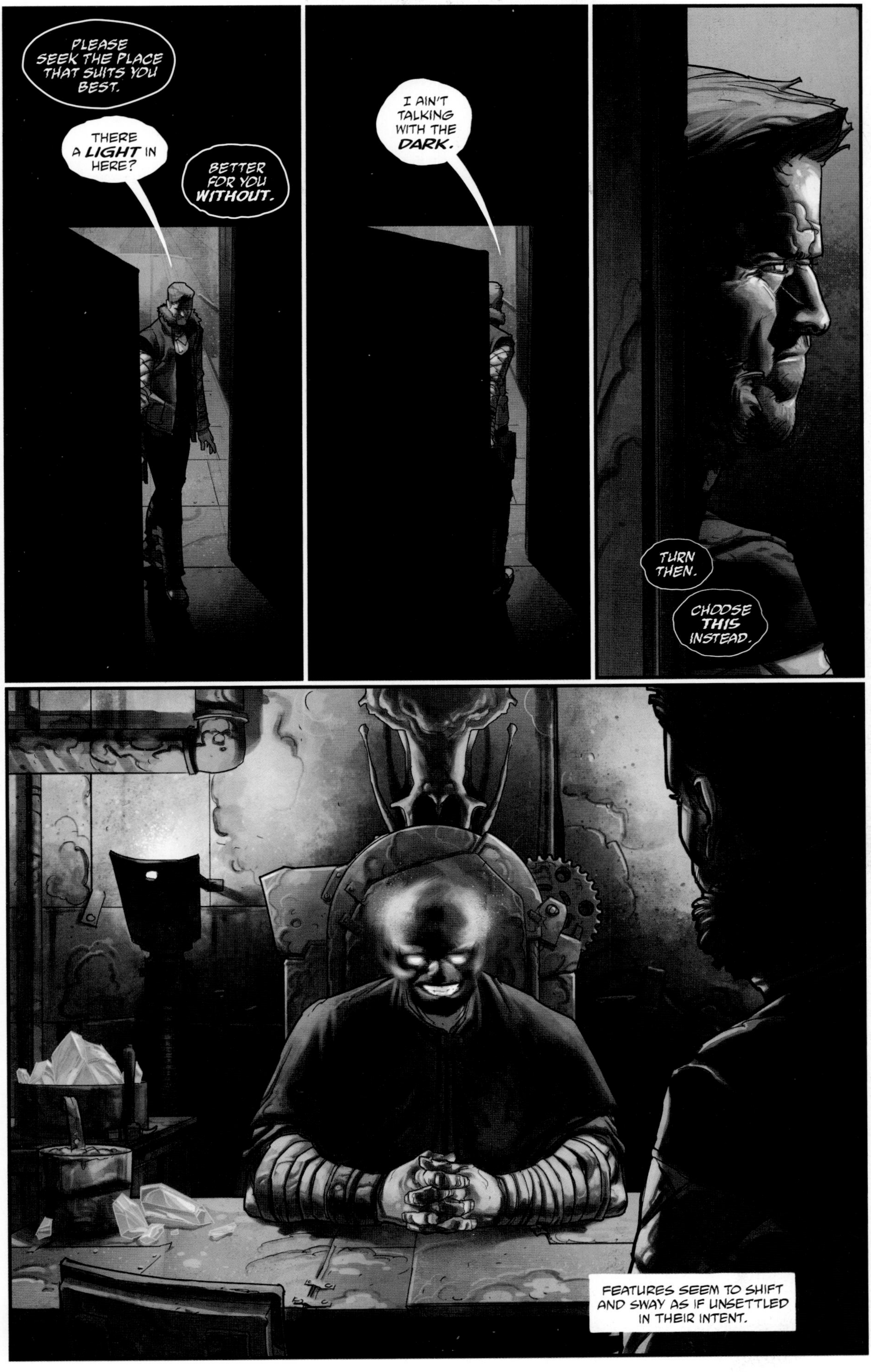
PLEASE SEEK THE PLACE THAT SUITS YOU BEST.
THERE A LIGHT IN HERE?
BETTER FOR YOU WITHOUT.
I AIN'T TALKING WITH THE DARK.
TURN THEN.
CHOOSE THIS INSTEAD.
FEATURES SEEM TO SHIFT AND SWAY AS IF UNSETTLED IN THEIR INTENT.

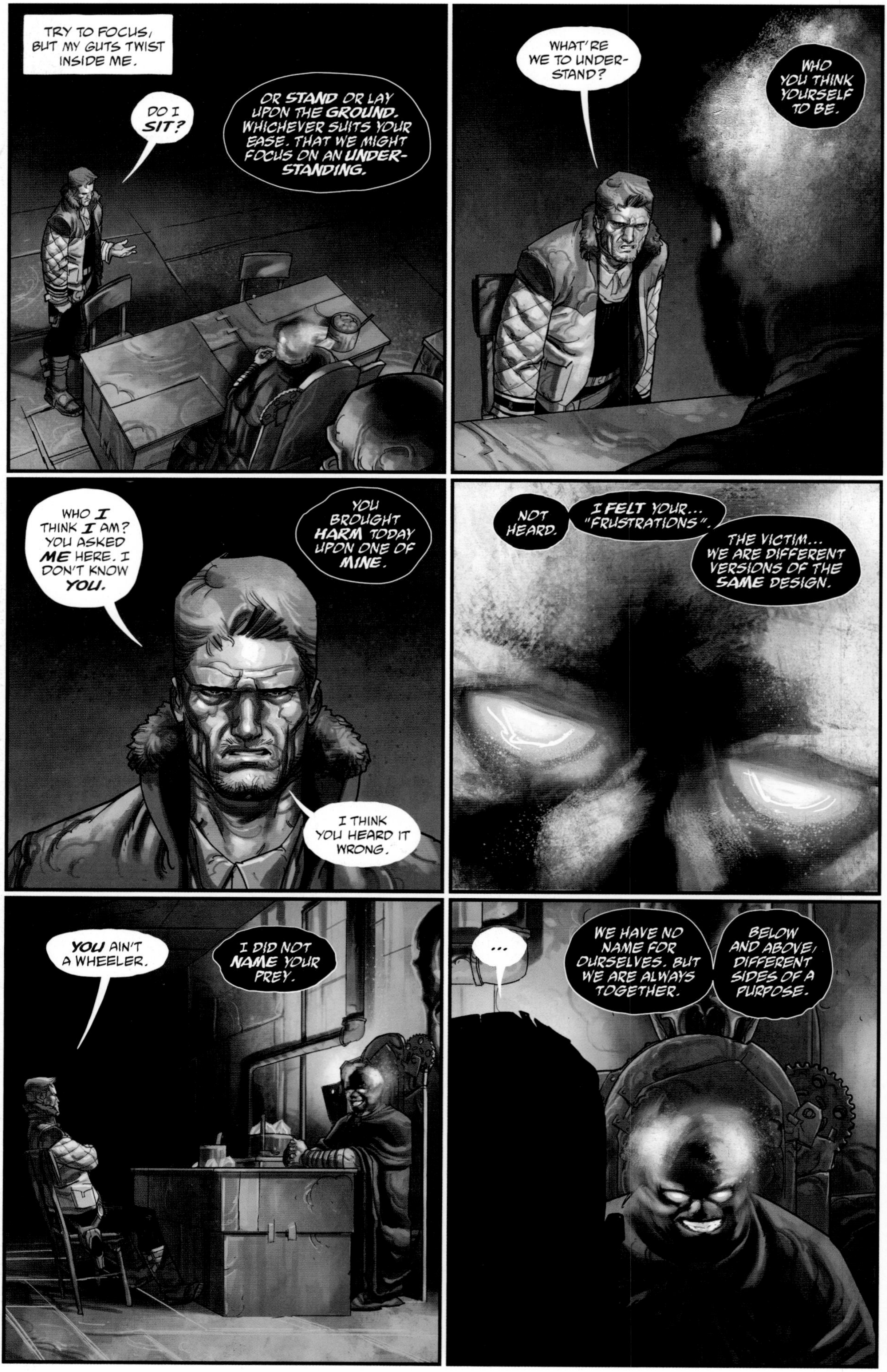
TRY TO FOCUS, BUT MY GUTS TWIST INSIDE ME.
DO I SIT?
OR STAND OR LAY UPON THE GROUND. WHICHEVER SUITS YOUR EASE. THAT WE MIGHT FOCUS ON AN UNDER-STANDING.
WHAT'RE WE TO UNDER-STAND?
WHO YOU THINK YOURSELF TO BE.
WHO I THINK I AM? YOU ASKED ME HERE. I DON'T KNOW YOU.
YOU BROUGHT HARM TODAY UPON ONE OF MINE.
I THINK YOU HEARD IT WRONG.
NOT HEARD.
I FELT YOUR... "FRUSTRATIONS".
THE VICTIM... WE ARE DIFFERENT VERSIONS OF THE SAME DESIGN.
YOU AIN'T A WHEELER.
I DID NOT NAME YOUR PREY.
...
WE HAVE NO NAME FOR OURSELVES. BUT WE ARE ALWAYS TOGETHER.
BELOW AND ABOVE, DIFFERENT SIDES OF A PURPOSE.

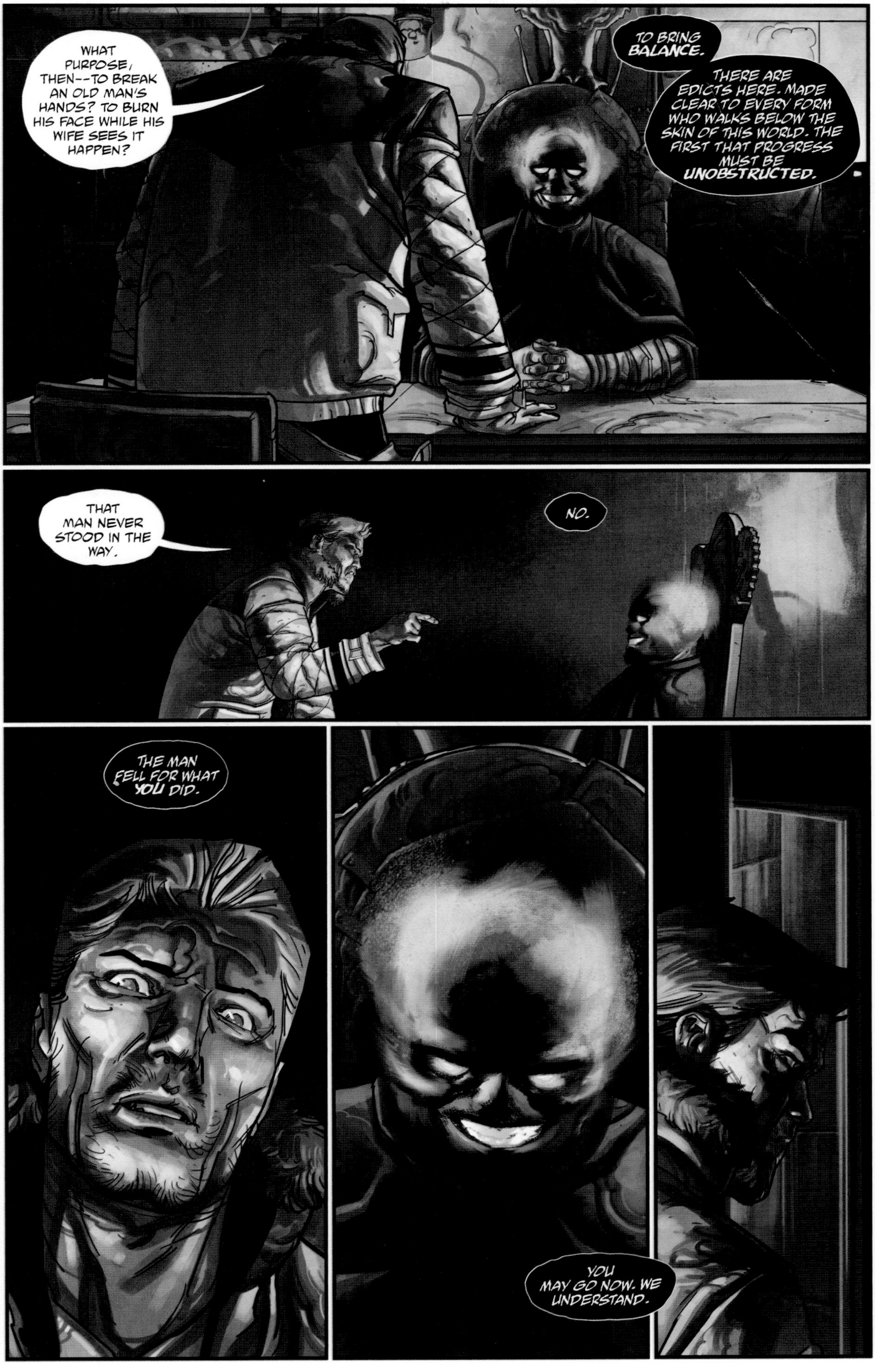
WHAT PURPOSE, THEN--TO BREAK AN OLD MAN'S HANDS? TO BURN HIS FACE WHILE HIS WIFE SEES IT HAPPEN?
TO BRING BALANCE.
THERE ARE EDICTS HERE. MADE CLEAR TO EVERY FORM WHO WALKS BELOW THE SKIN OF THIS WORLD. THE FIRST THAT PROGRESS MUST BE UNOBSTRUCTED.
THAT MAN NEVER STOOD IN THE WAY.
NO.
THE MAN FELL FOR WHAT YOU DID.
YOU MAY GO NOW. WE UNDERSTAND.

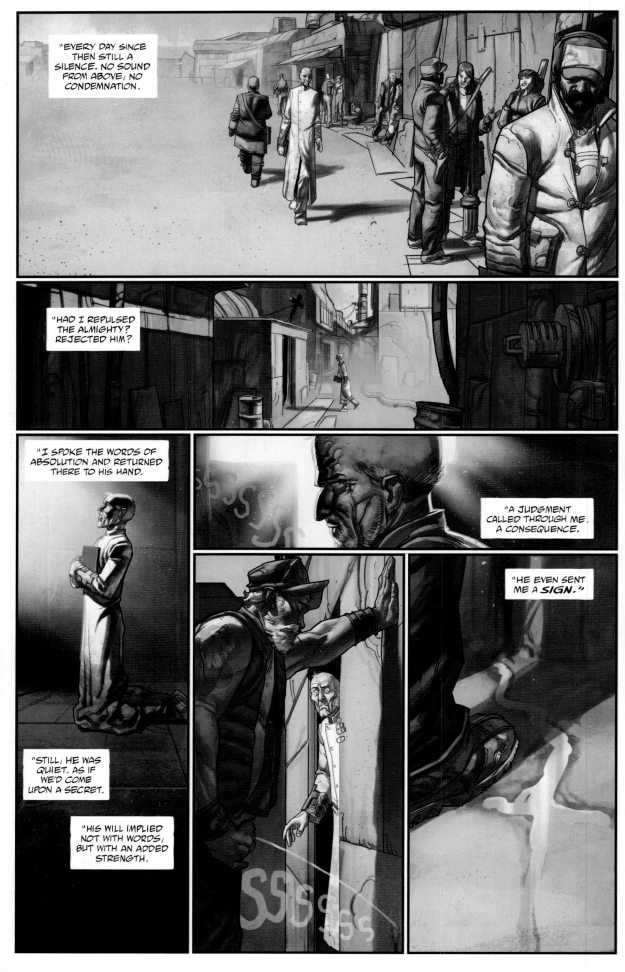

"EVERY DAY SINCE THEN STILL A SILENCE. NO SOUND FROM ABOVE, NO CONDEMNATION.

"HAD I REPULSED THE ALMIGHTY? REJECTED HIM?

"I SPOKE THE WORDS OF ABSOLUTION AND RETURNED THERE TO HIS HAND.

"A JUDGMENT CALLED THROUGH ME. A CONSEQUENCE.

"HE EVEN SENT ME A *SIGN*."

"STILL, HE WAS QUIET. AS IF WE'D COME UPON A SECRET.

"HIS WILL IMPLIED NOT WITH WORDS, BUT WITH AN ADDED STRENGTH.

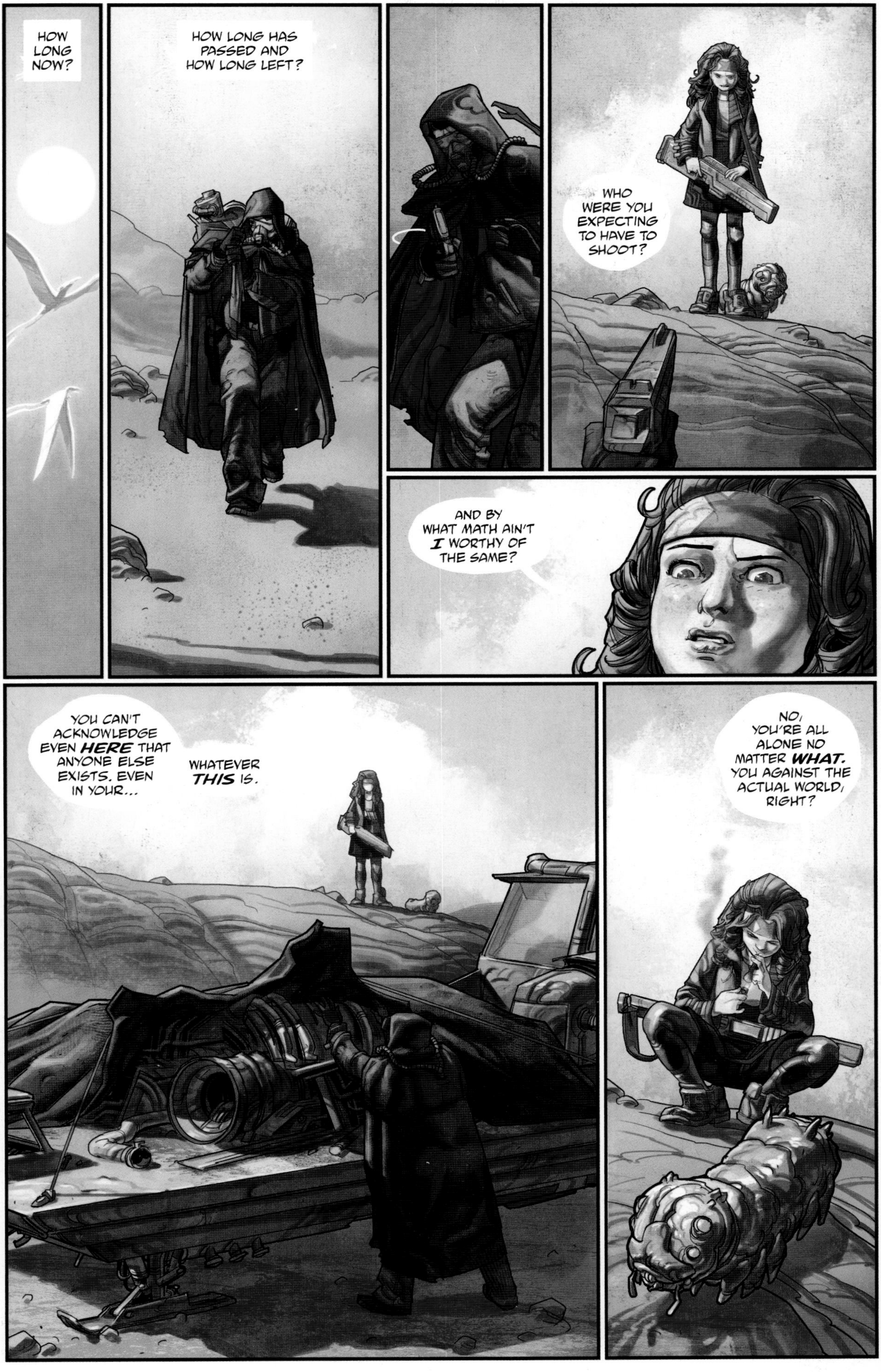
HOW LONG NOW?
HOW LONG HAS PASSED AND HOW LONG LEFT?
WHO WERE YOU EXPECTING TO HAVE TO SHOOT?
AND BY WHAT MATH AIN'T I WORTHY OF THE SAME?
YOU CAN'T ACKNOWLEDGE EVEN HERE THAT ANYONE ELSE EXISTS. EVEN IN YOUR...
WHATEVER THIS IS.
NO, YOU'RE ALL ALONE NO MATTER WHAT. YOU AGAINST THE ACTUAL WORLD, RIGHT?

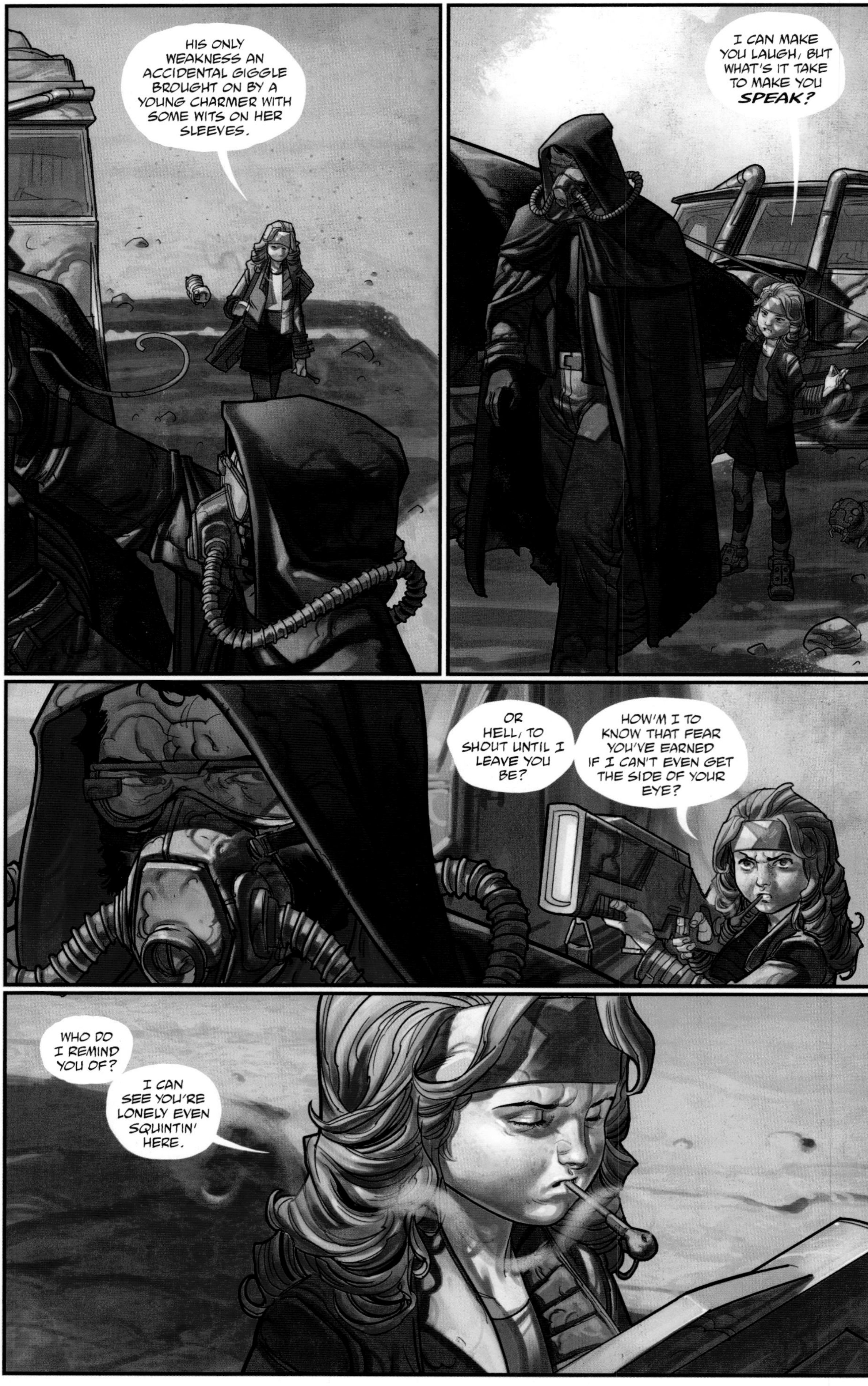
HIS ONLY WEAKNESS AN ACCIDENTAL GIGGLE BROUGHT ON BY A YOUNG CHARMER WITH SOME WITS ON HER SLEEVES.
I CAN MAKE YOU LAUGH, BUT WHAT'S IT TAKE TO MAKE YOU **SPEAK?**
OR HELL, TO SHOUT UNTIL I LEAVE YOU BE?
HOW'M I TO KNOW THAT FEAR YOU'VE EARNED IF I CAN'T EVEN GET THE SIDE OF YOUR EYE?
WHO DO I REMIND YOU OF?
I CAN SEE YOU'RE LONELY EVEN SQUINTIN' HERE.

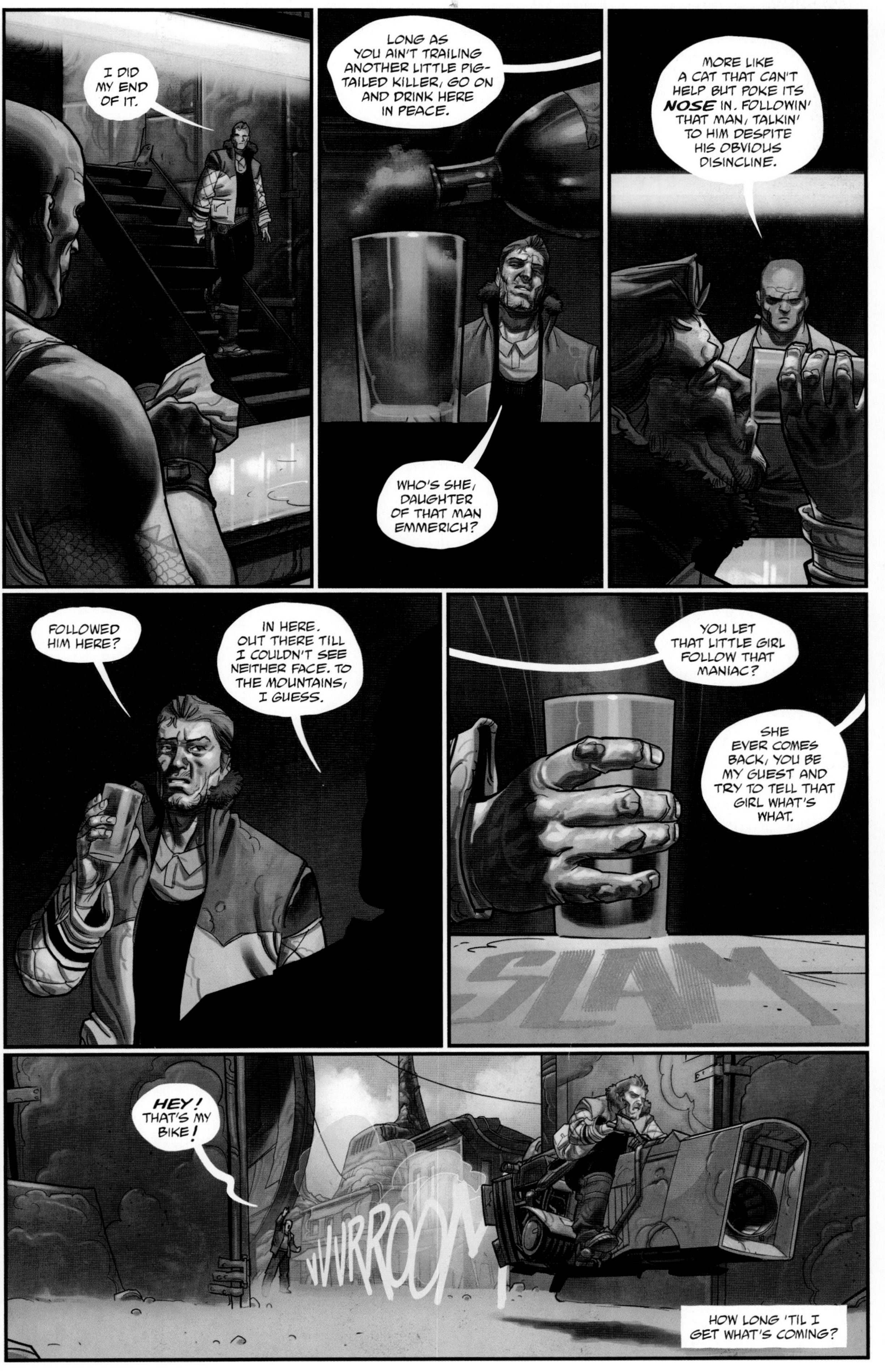
I DID MY END OF IT.
LONG AS YOU AIN'T TRAILING ANOTHER LITTLE PIG-TAILED KILLER, GO ON AND DRINK HERE IN PEACE.
WHO'S SHE, DAUGHTER OF THAT MAN EMMERICH?
MORE LIKE A CAT THAT CAN'T HELP BUT POKE ITS NOSE IN. FOLLOWIN' THAT MAN, TALKIN' TO HIM DESPITE HIS OBVIOUS DISINCLINE.
FOLLOWED HIM HERE?
IN HERE. OUT THERE TILL I COULDN'T SEE NEITHER FACE. TO THE MOUNTAINS, I GUESS.
YOU LET THAT LITTLE GIRL FOLLOW THAT MANIAC?
SHE EVER COMES BACK, YOU BE MY GUEST AND TRY TO TELL THAT GIRL WHAT'S WHAT.
SLAM
HEY! THAT'S MY BIKE!
VVVRROOM
HOW LONG 'TIL I GET WHAT'S COMING?

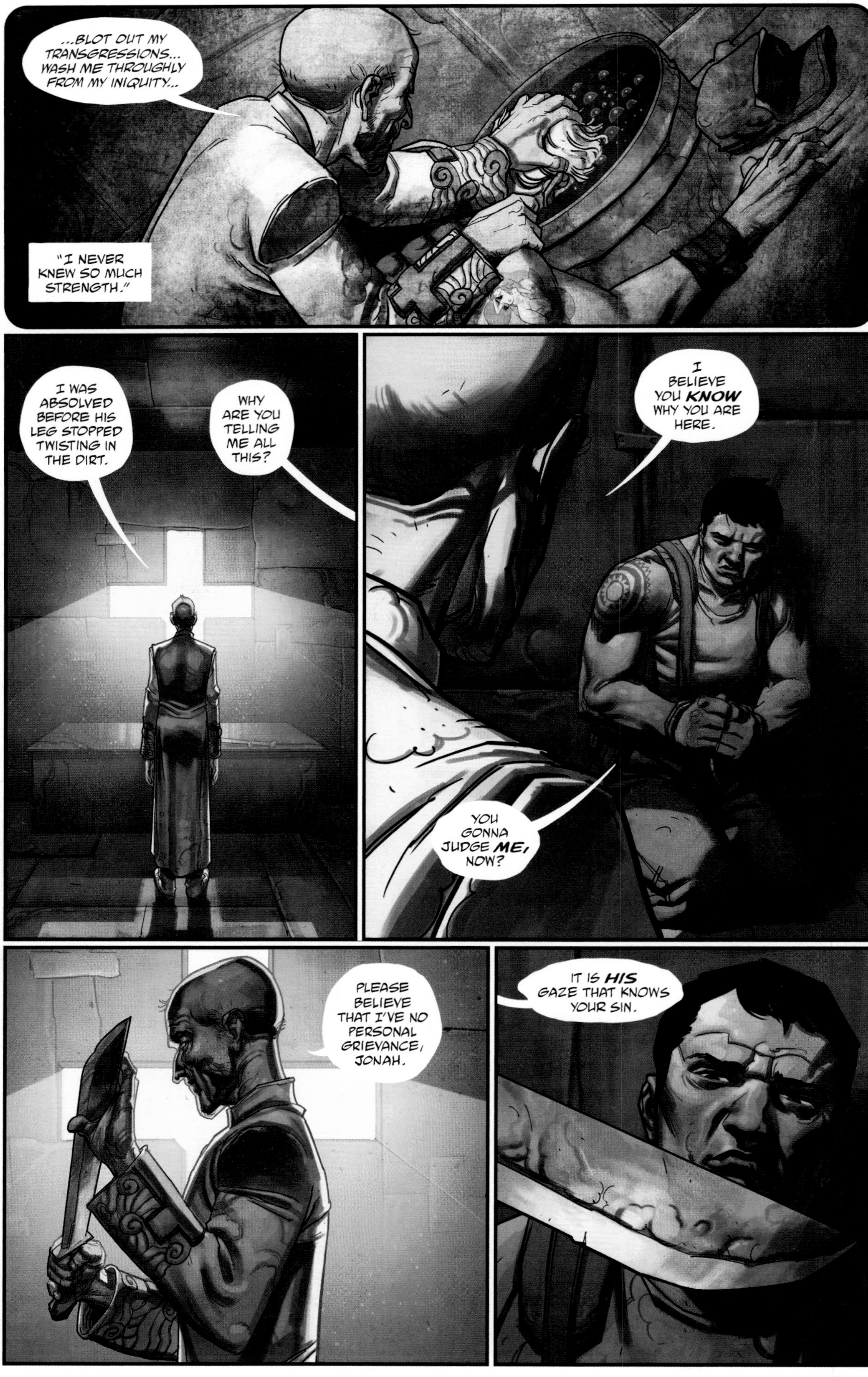
...BLOT OUT MY TRANSGRESSIONS... WASH ME THROUGHLY FROM MY INIQUITY...
"I NEVER KNEW SO MUCH STRENGTH."
I WAS ABSOLVED BEFORE HIS LEG STOPPED TWISTING IN THE DIRT.
WHY ARE YOU TELLING ME ALL THIS?
I BELIEVE YOU KNOW WHY YOU ARE HERE.
YOU GONNA JUDGE ME, NOW?
PLEASE BELIEVE THAT I'VE NO PERSONAL GRIEVANCE, JONAH.
IT IS HIS GAZE THAT KNOWS YOUR SIN.

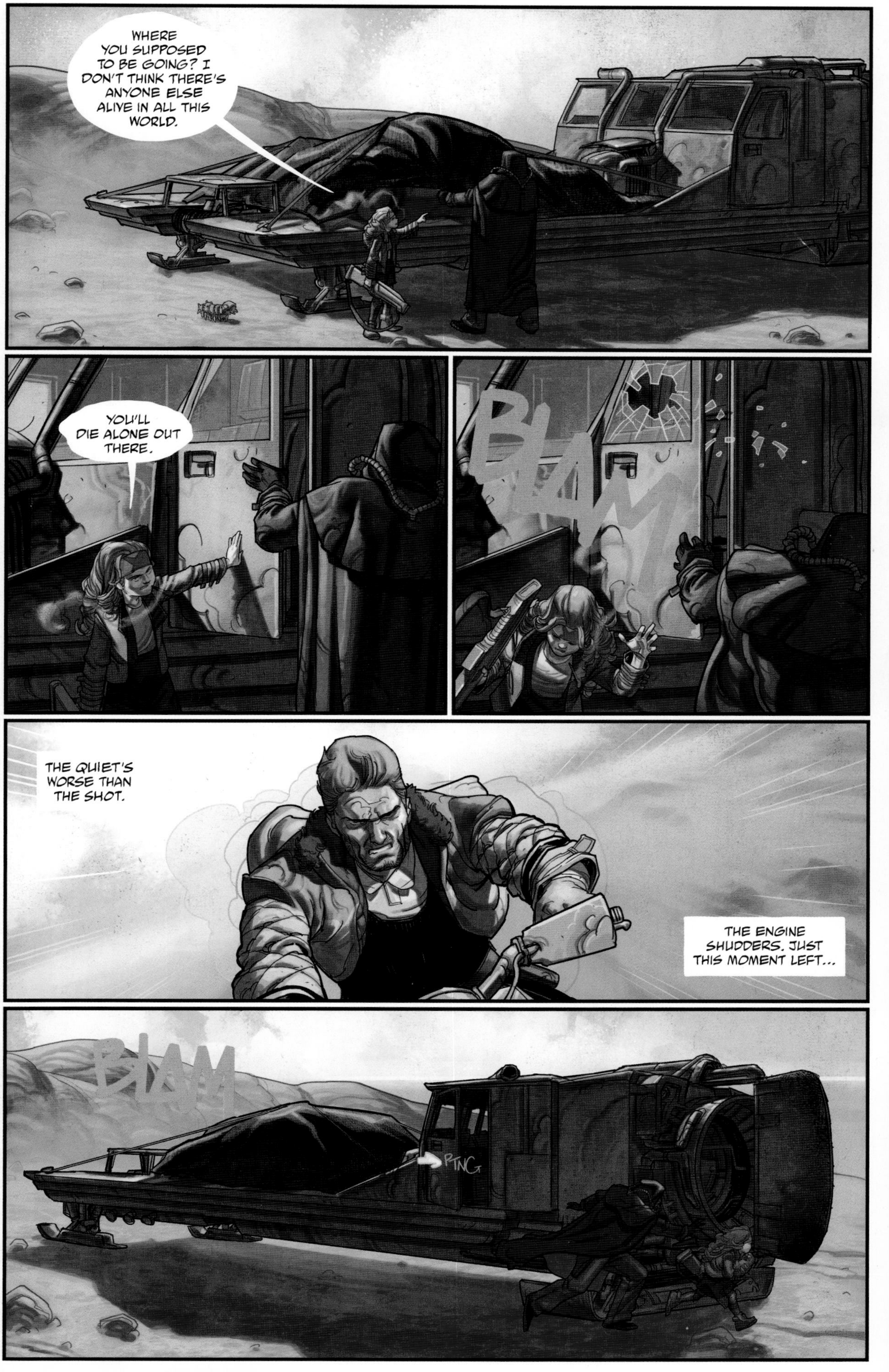
WHERE YOU SUPPOSED TO BE GOING? I DON'T THINK THERE'S ANYONE ELSE ALIVE IN ALL THIS WORLD.
YOU'LL DIE ALONE OUT THERE.
BLAM
THE QUIET'S WORSE THAN THE SHOT.
THE ENGINE SHUDDERS. JUST THIS MOMENT LEFT...
BLAM
PTNG

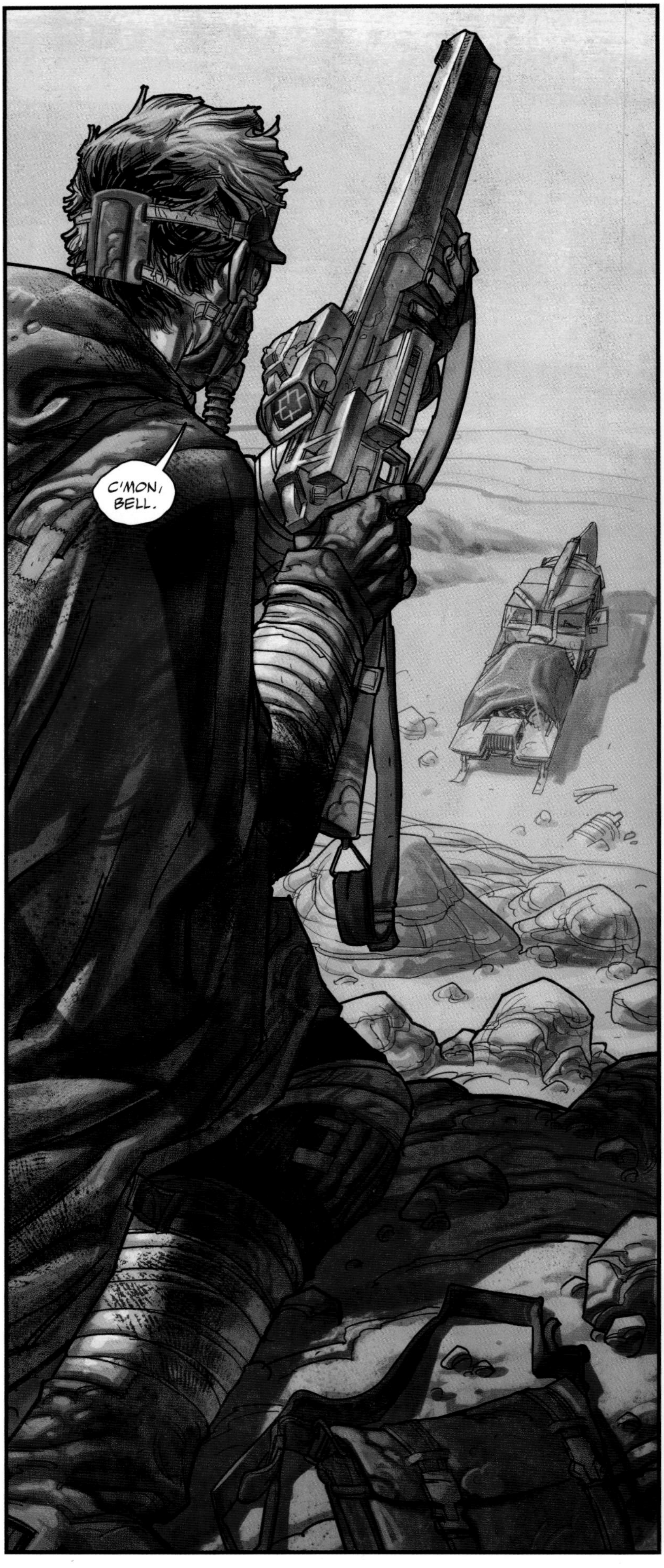
C'MON, BELL.
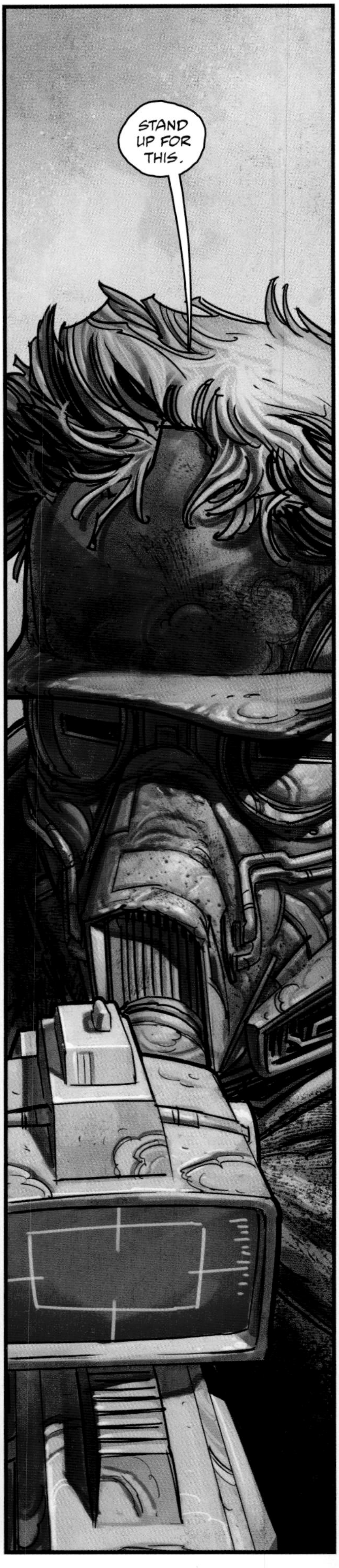
STAND UP FOR THIS.

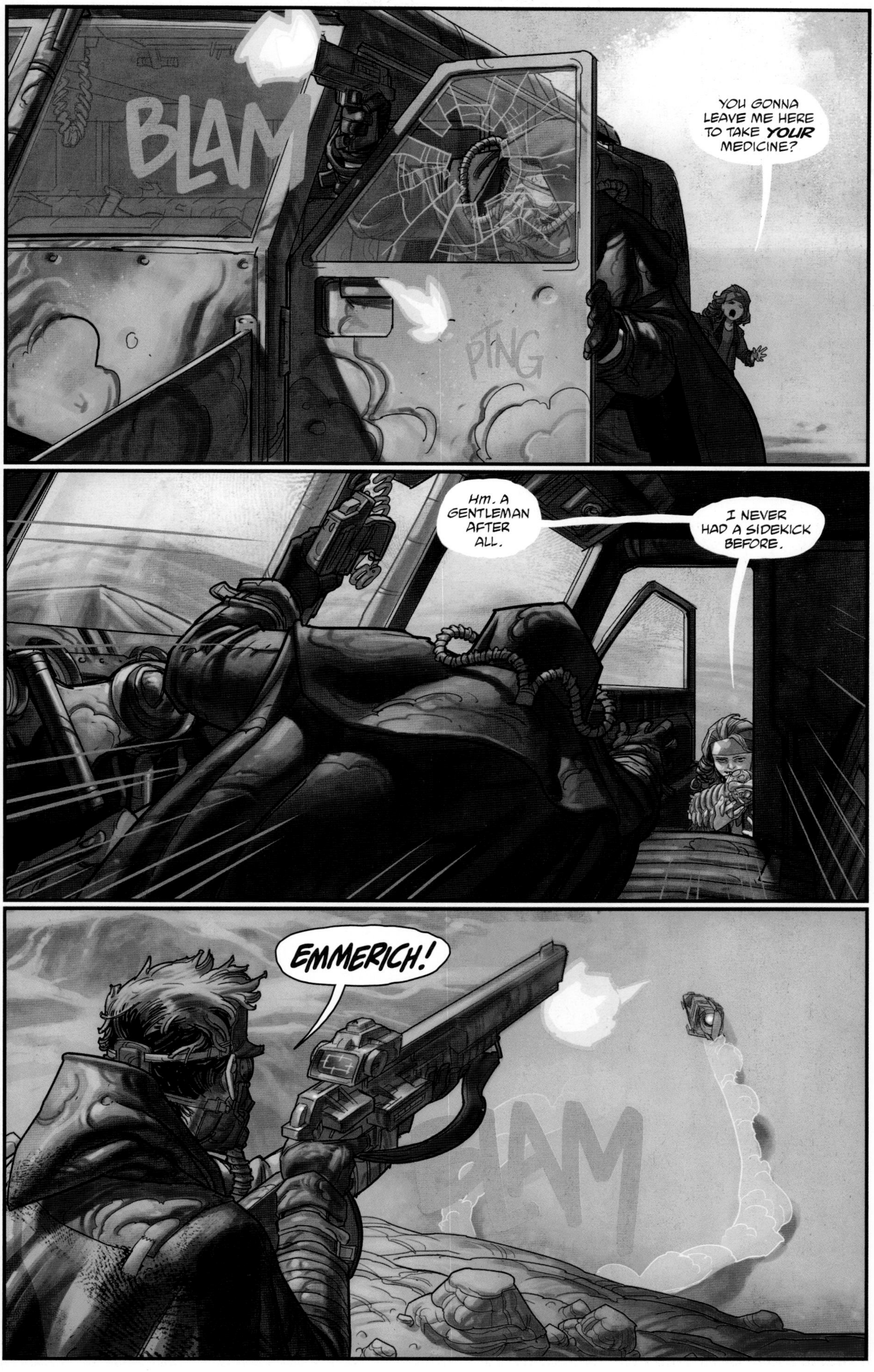
BLAM
YOU GONNA LEAVE ME HERE TO TAKE *YOUR* MEDICINE?
PTING
Hm. A GENTLEMAN AFTER ALL.
I NEVER HAD A SIDEKICK BEFORE.
EMMERICH!
BLAM

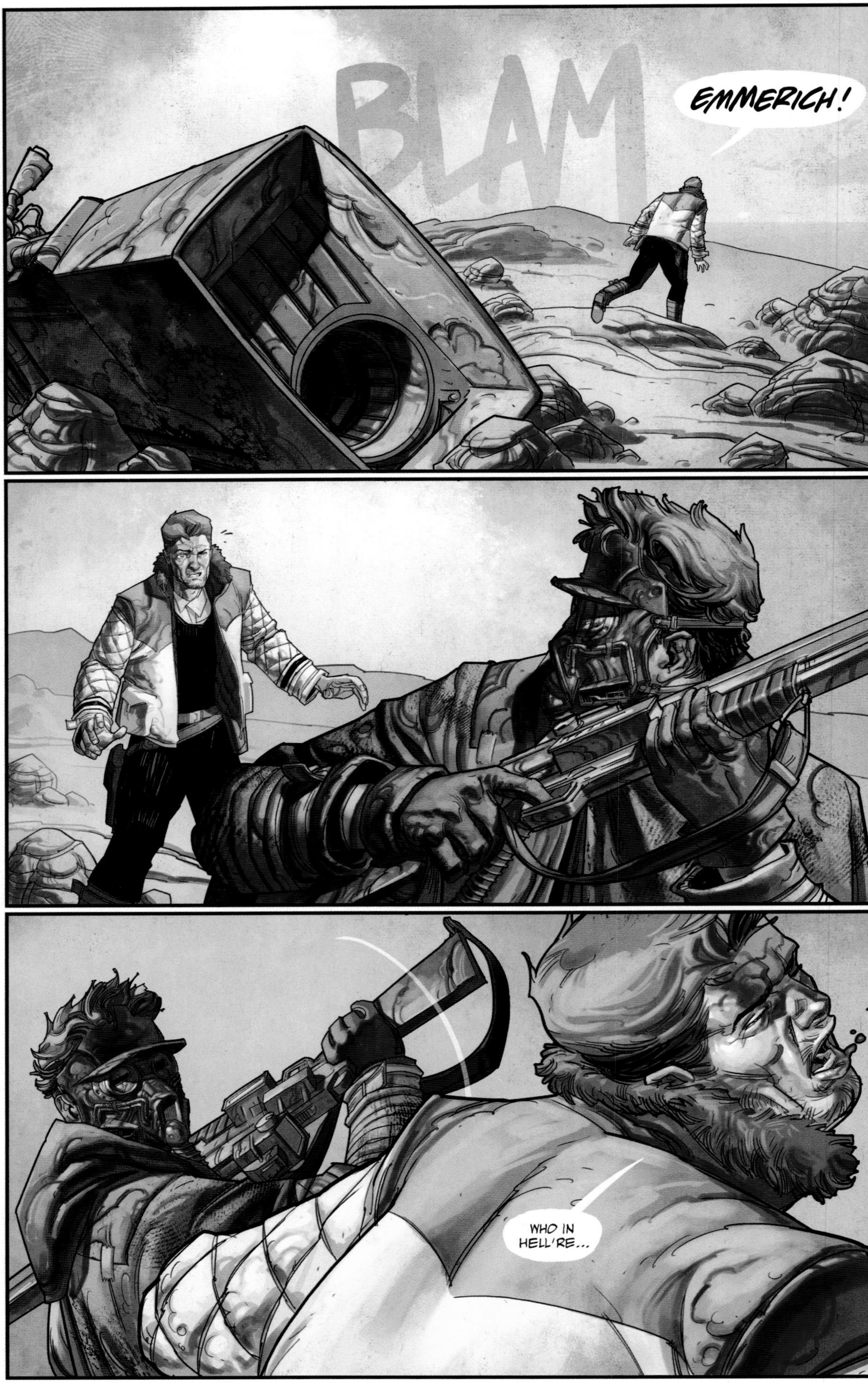
BLAM
EMMERICH!
WHO IN HELL'RE...

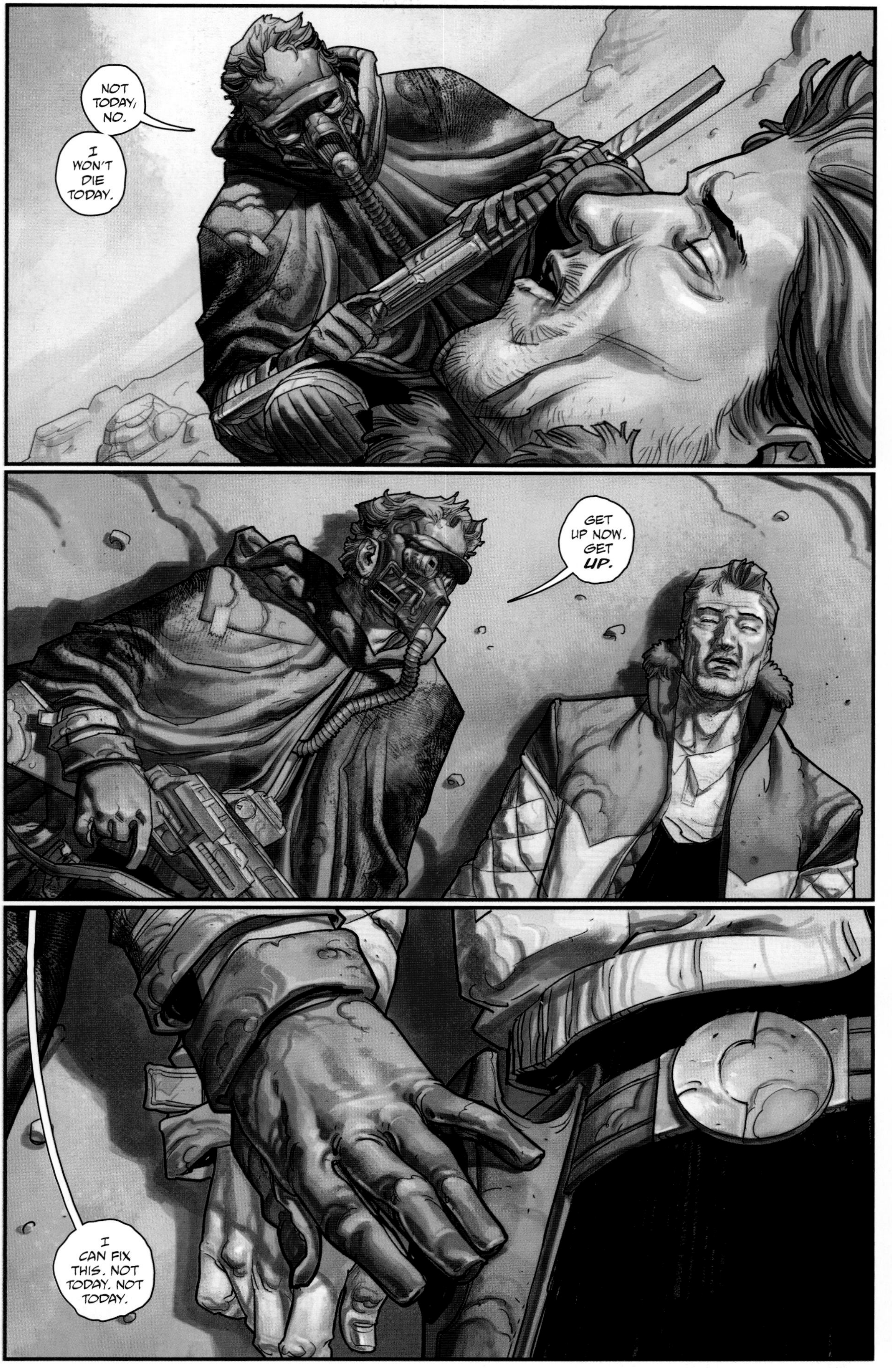
NOT TODAY, NO.
I WON'T DIE TODAY.
GET UP NOW. GET UP.
I CAN FIX THIS. NOT TODAY. NOT TODAY.

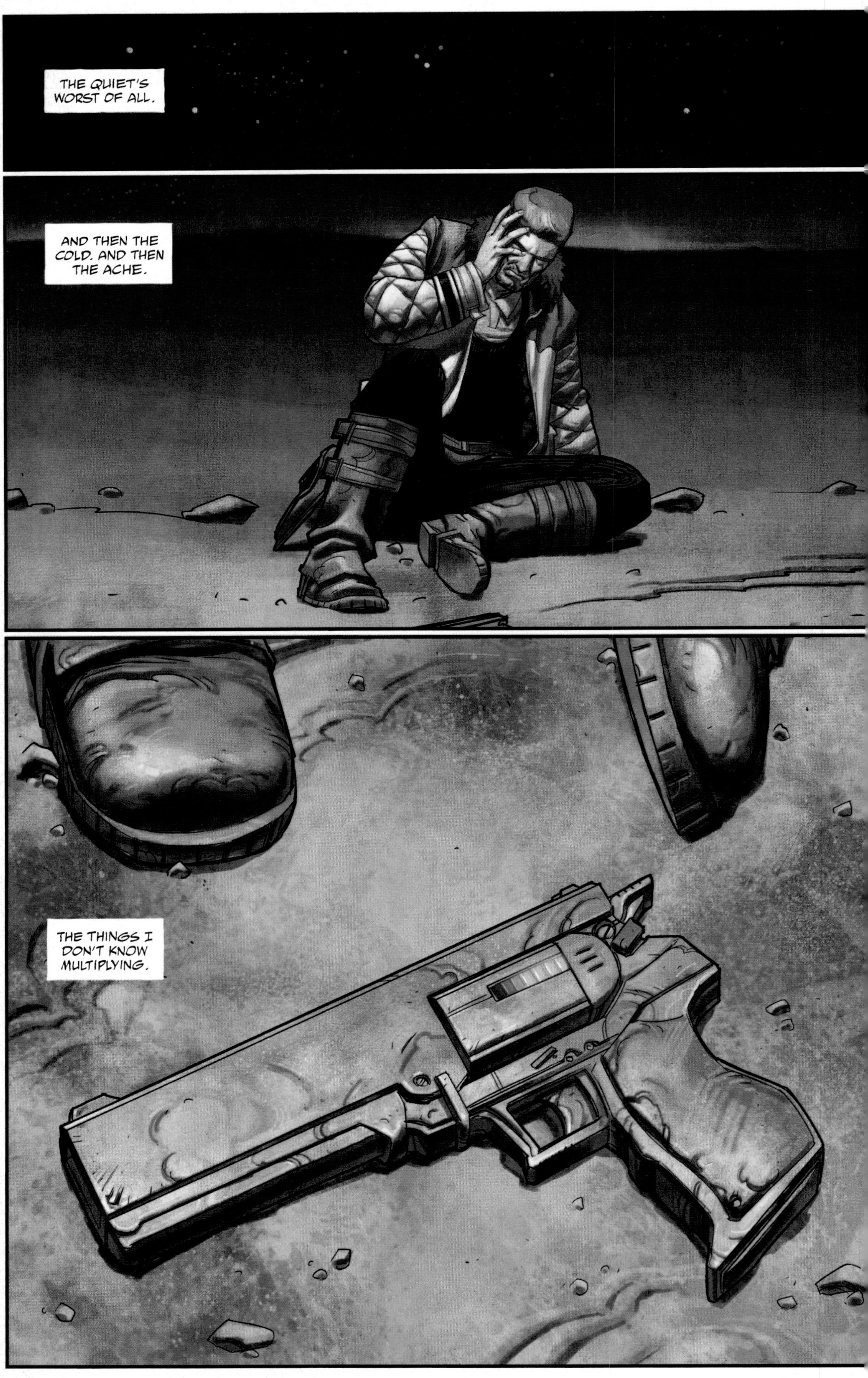
THE QUIET'S WORST OF ALL.
AND THEN THE COLD. AND THEN THE ACHE.
THE THINGS I DON'T KNOW MULTIPLYING.

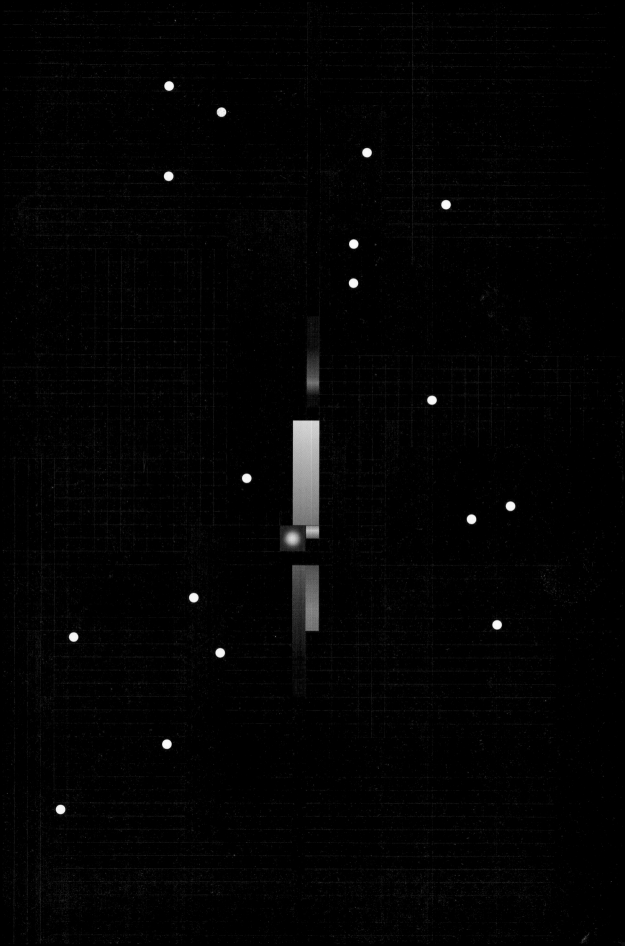

CHAPTER 5
GO

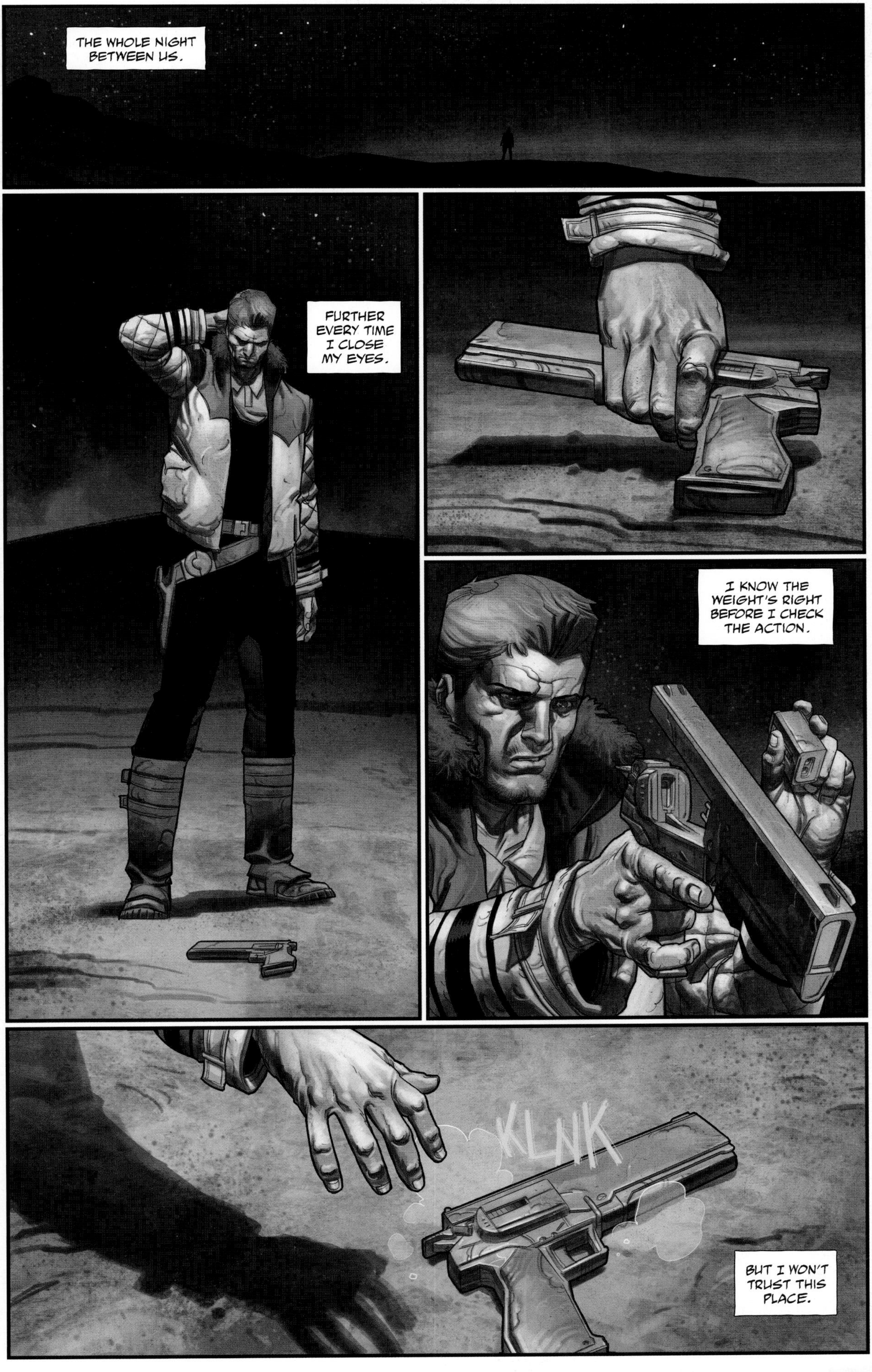
THE WHOLE NIGHT BETWEEN US.
FURTHER EVERY TIME I CLOSE MY EYES.
I KNOW THE WEIGHT'S RIGHT BEFORE I CHECK THE ACTION.
KLNK
BUT I WON'T TRUST THIS PLACE.

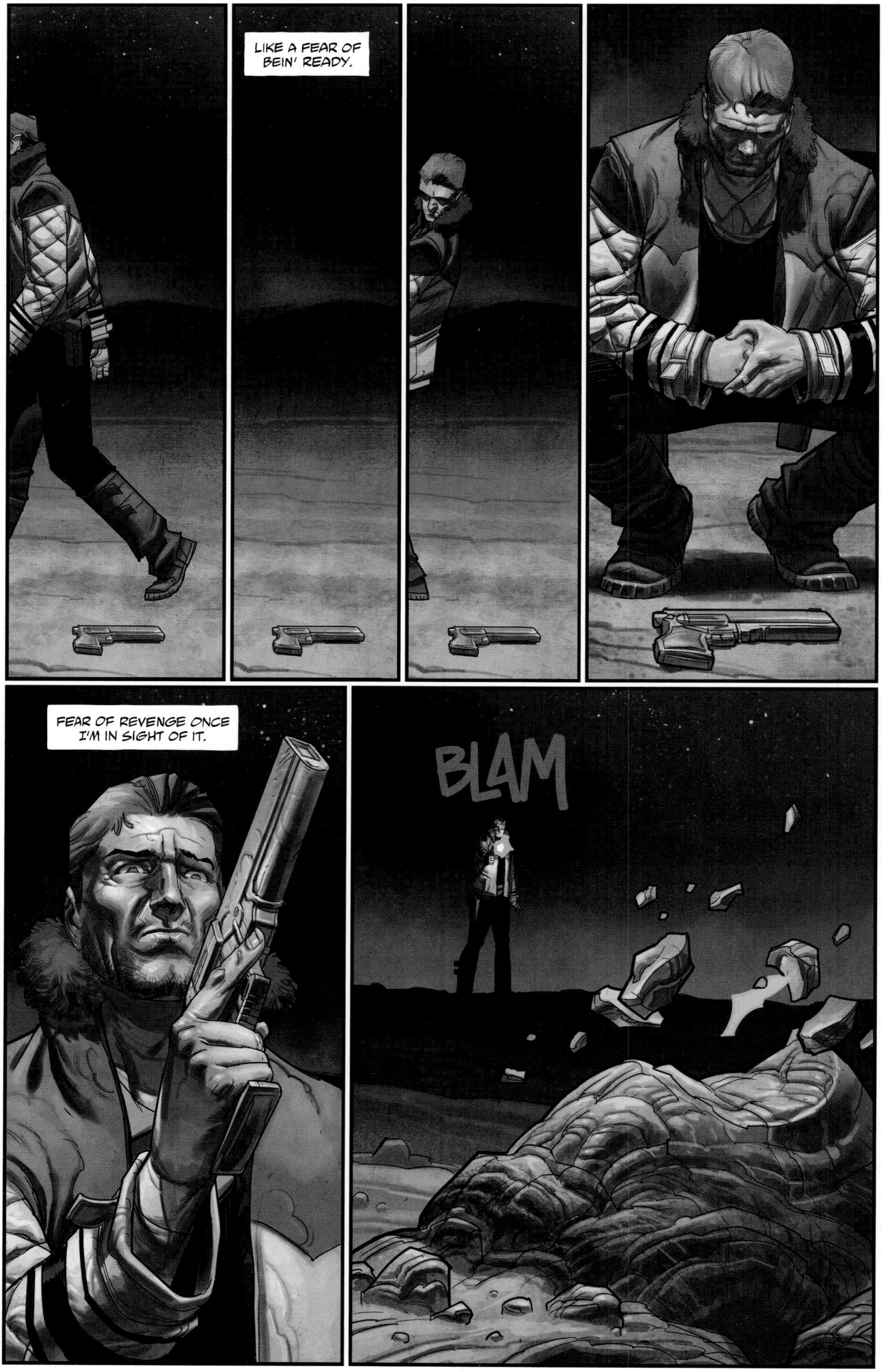
LIKE A FEAR OF BEIN' READY.
FEAR OF REVENGE ONCE I'M IN SIGHT OF IT.
BLAM

A FEAR OF WHAT'S AFTER.

CAREFUL NOW, CHUCK... LEMME GET THE RIGHT GRIP.

SOME KINDA BERRY, WHERE'D YOU GET THIS? IS IT FROZEN?

I DIDN'T FREEZE IT. JUST HOW THEY TASTE, THE CRAZY THINGS.

THAT FOOL PRIEST HAS FINALLY SAID THE LAST WRONG THING.

I'M FINE HERE, DELLA. YOU GET THE SHERIFF.

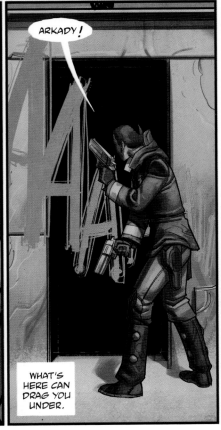

ARKADY!

WHAT'S HERE CAN DRAG YOU UNDER.

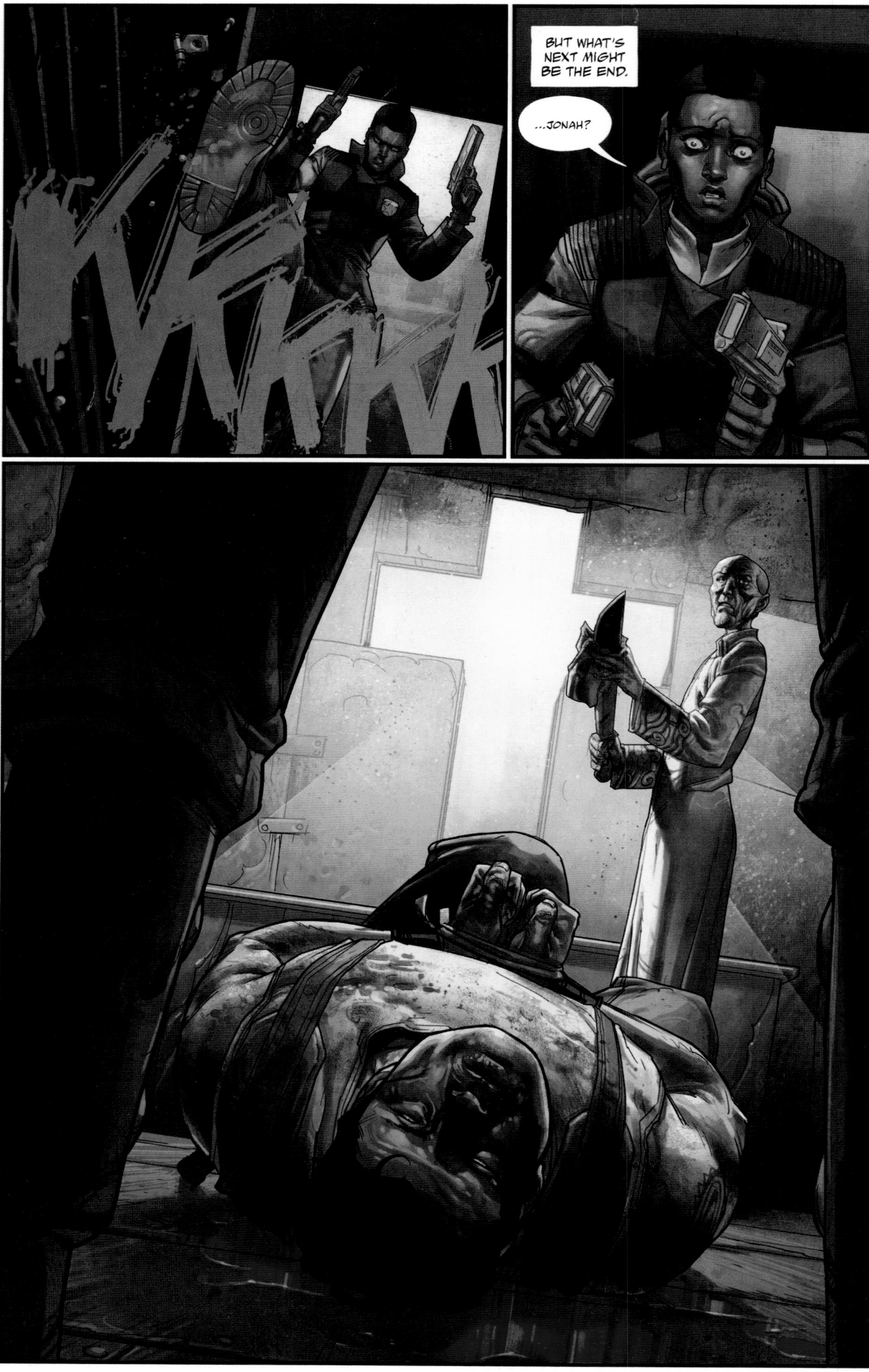
BUT WHAT'S NEXT MIGHT BE THE END.
...JONAH?

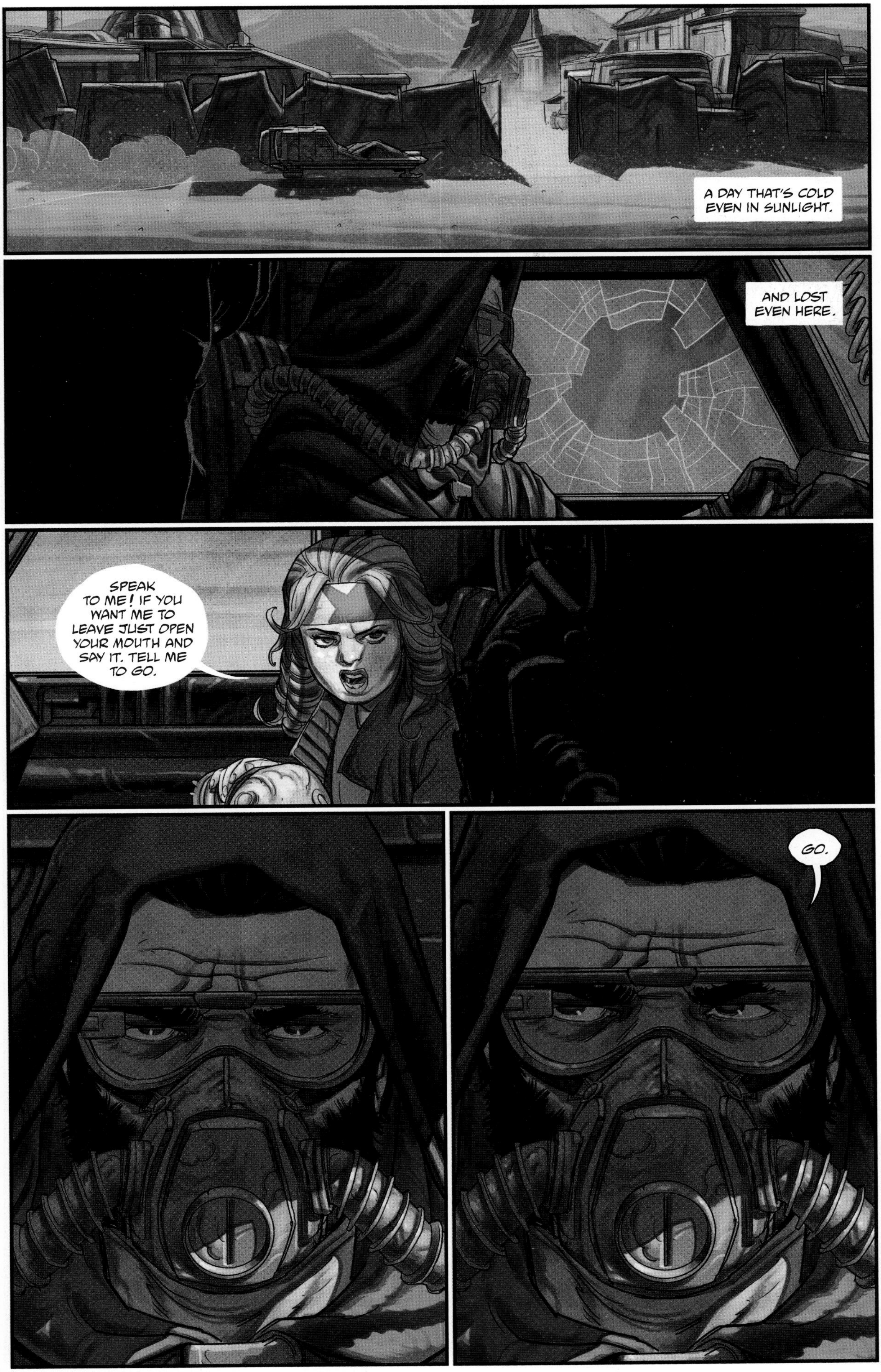

A DAY THAT'S COLD EVEN IN SUNLIGHT.
AND LOST EVEN HERE.
SPEAK TO ME! IF YOU WANT ME TO LEAVE JUST OPEN YOUR MOUTH AND SAY IT. TELL ME TO GO.
GO.

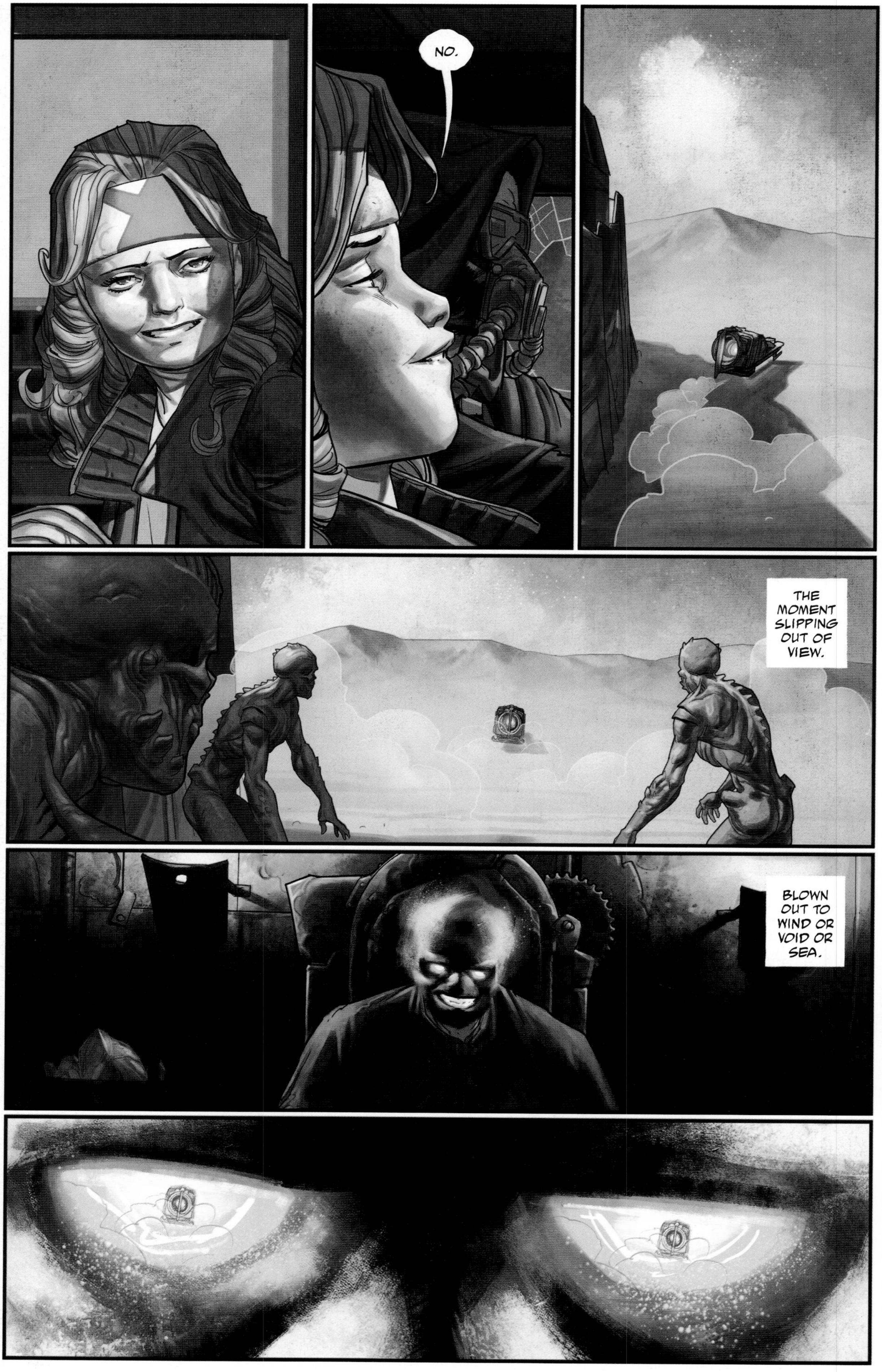
NO.
THE MOMENT SLIPPING OUT OF VIEW.
BLOWN OUT TO WIND OR VOID OR SEA.

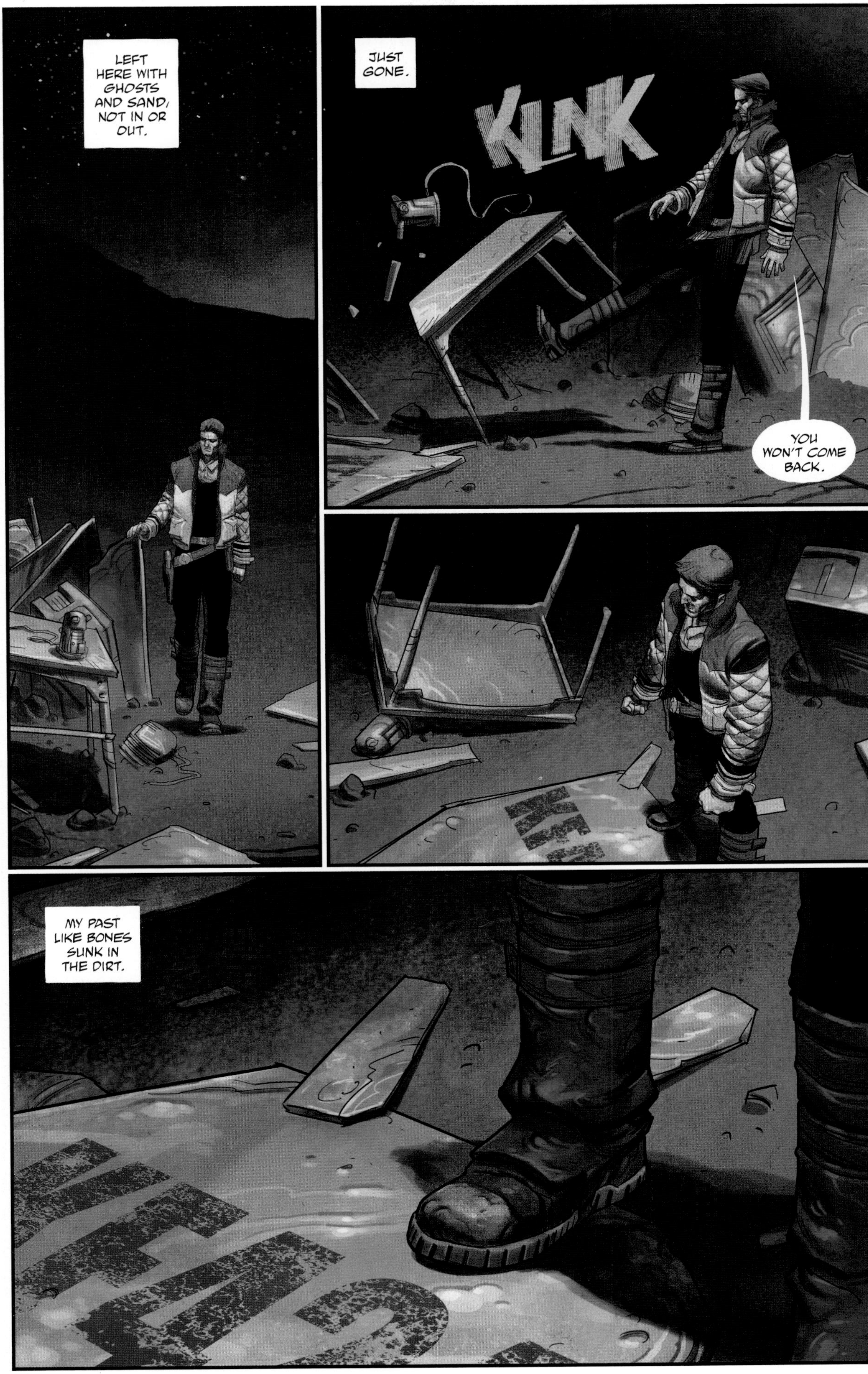

LEFT HERE WITH GHOSTS AND SAND, NOT IN OR OUT.
JUST GONE.
KLINK
YOU WON'T COME BACK.
MY PAST LIKE BONES SUNK IN THE DIRT.

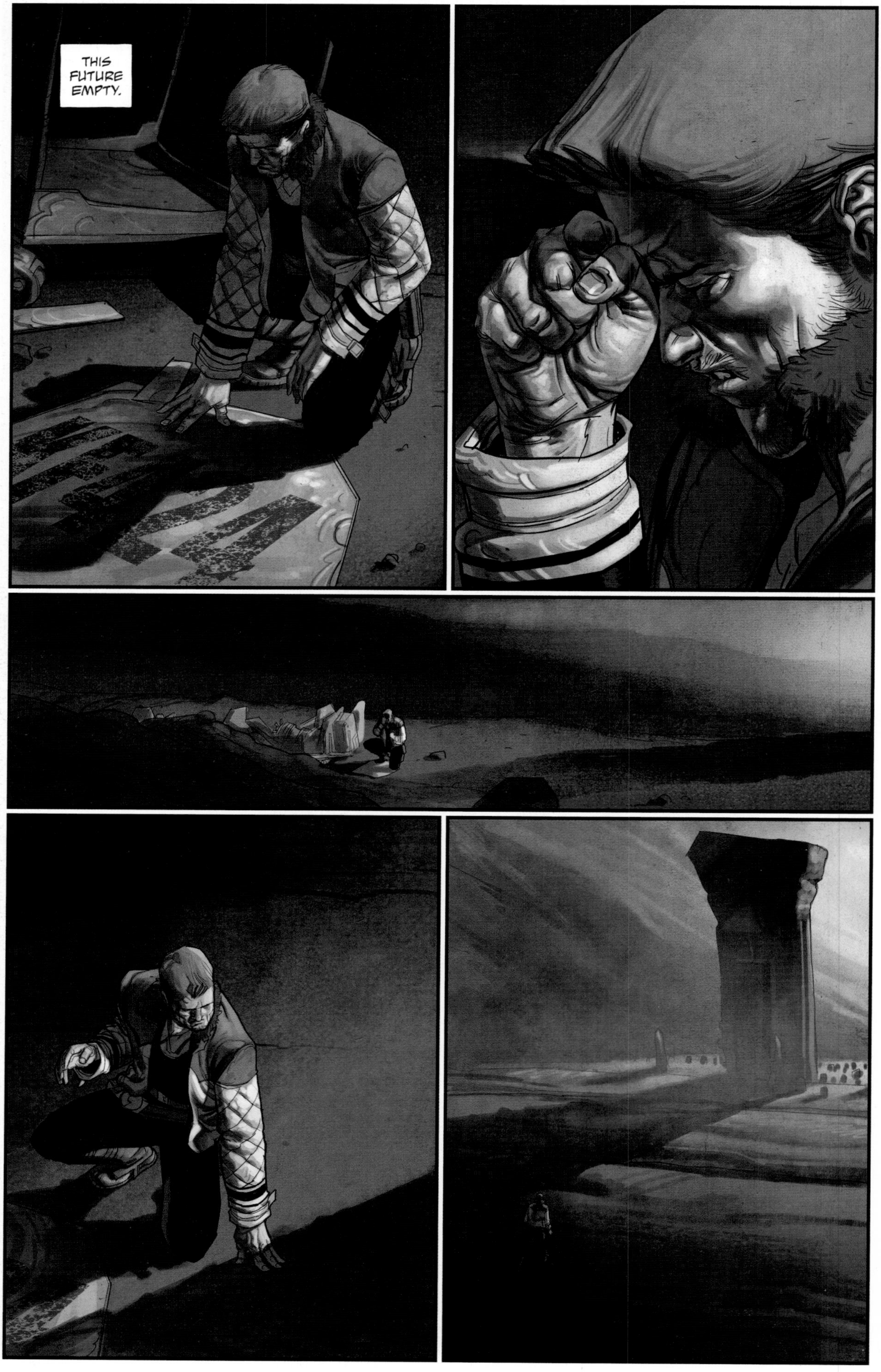
THIS FUTURE EMPTY.

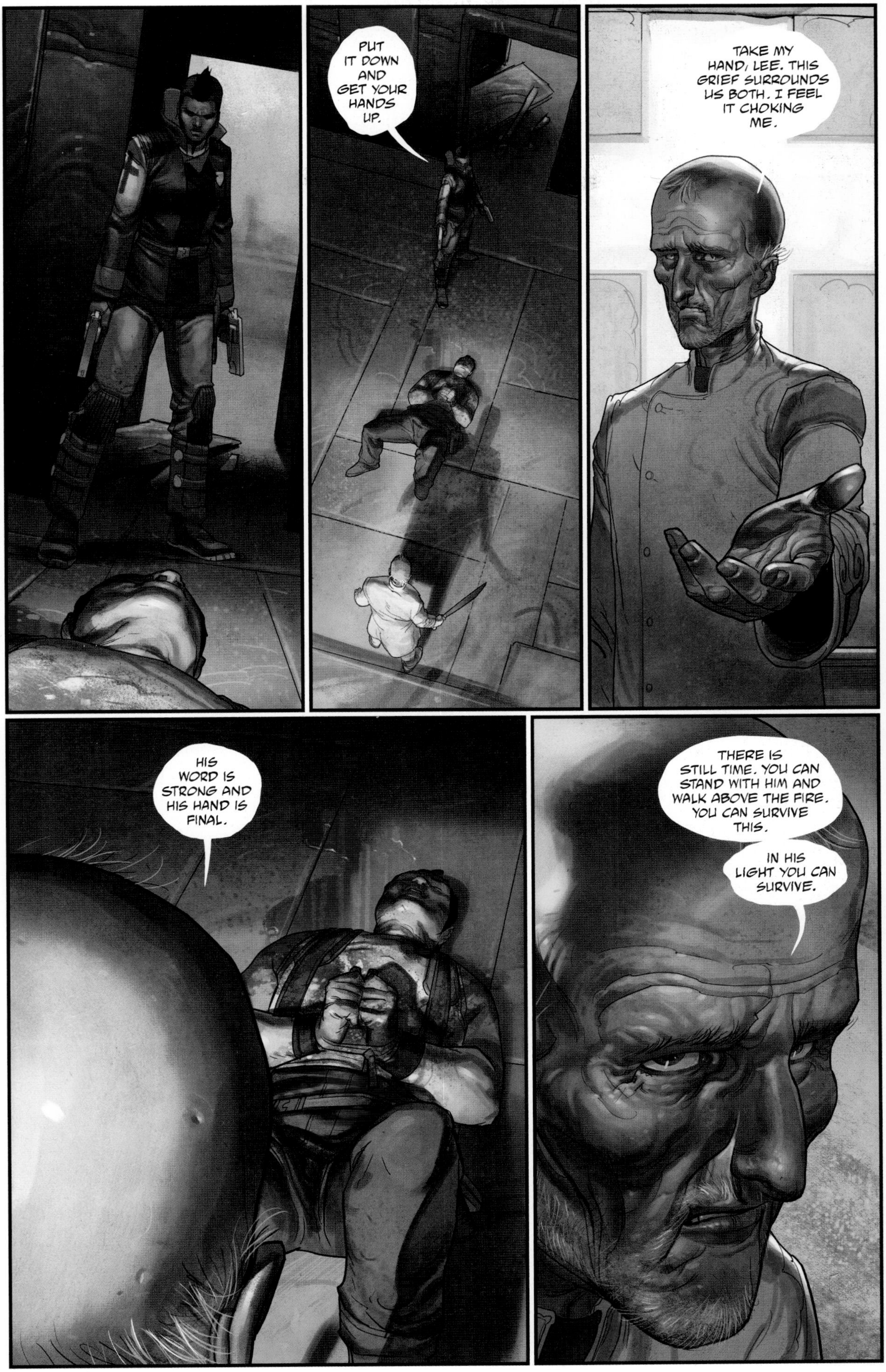
PUT IT DOWN AND GET YOUR HANDS UP.
TAKE MY HAND, LEE. THIS GRIEF SURROUNDS US BOTH. I FEEL IT CHOKING ME.
HIS WORD IS STRONG AND HIS HAND IS FINAL.
THERE IS STILL TIME. YOU CAN STAND WITH HIM AND WALK ABOVE THE FIRE. YOU CAN SURVIVE THIS.
IN HIS LIGHT YOU CAN SURVIVE.

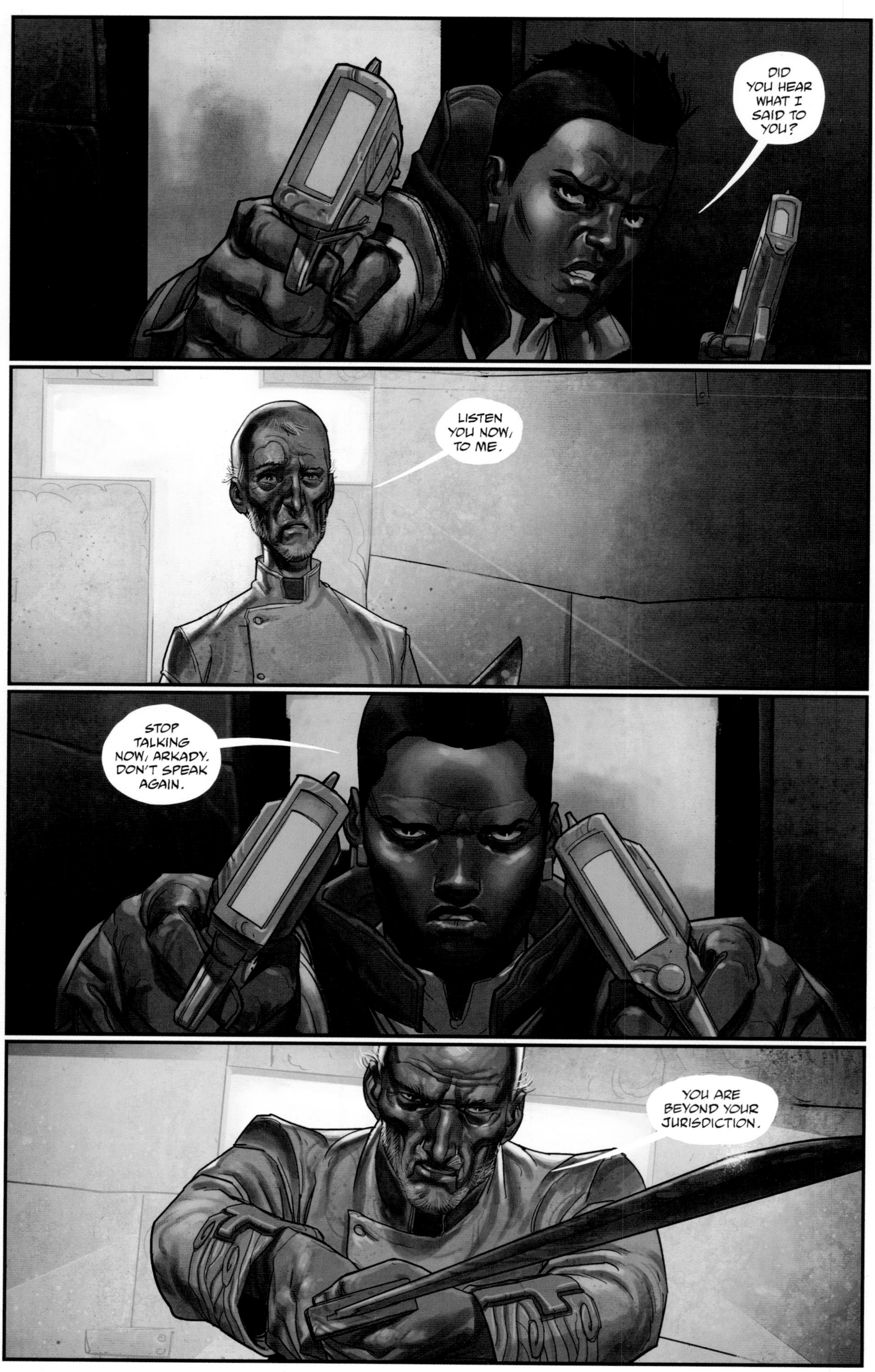
DID YOU HEAR WHAT I SAID TO YOU?
LISTEN YOU NOW, TO ME.
STOP TALKING NOW, ARKADY. DON'T SPEAK AGAIN.
YOU ARE BEYOND YOUR JURISDICTION.

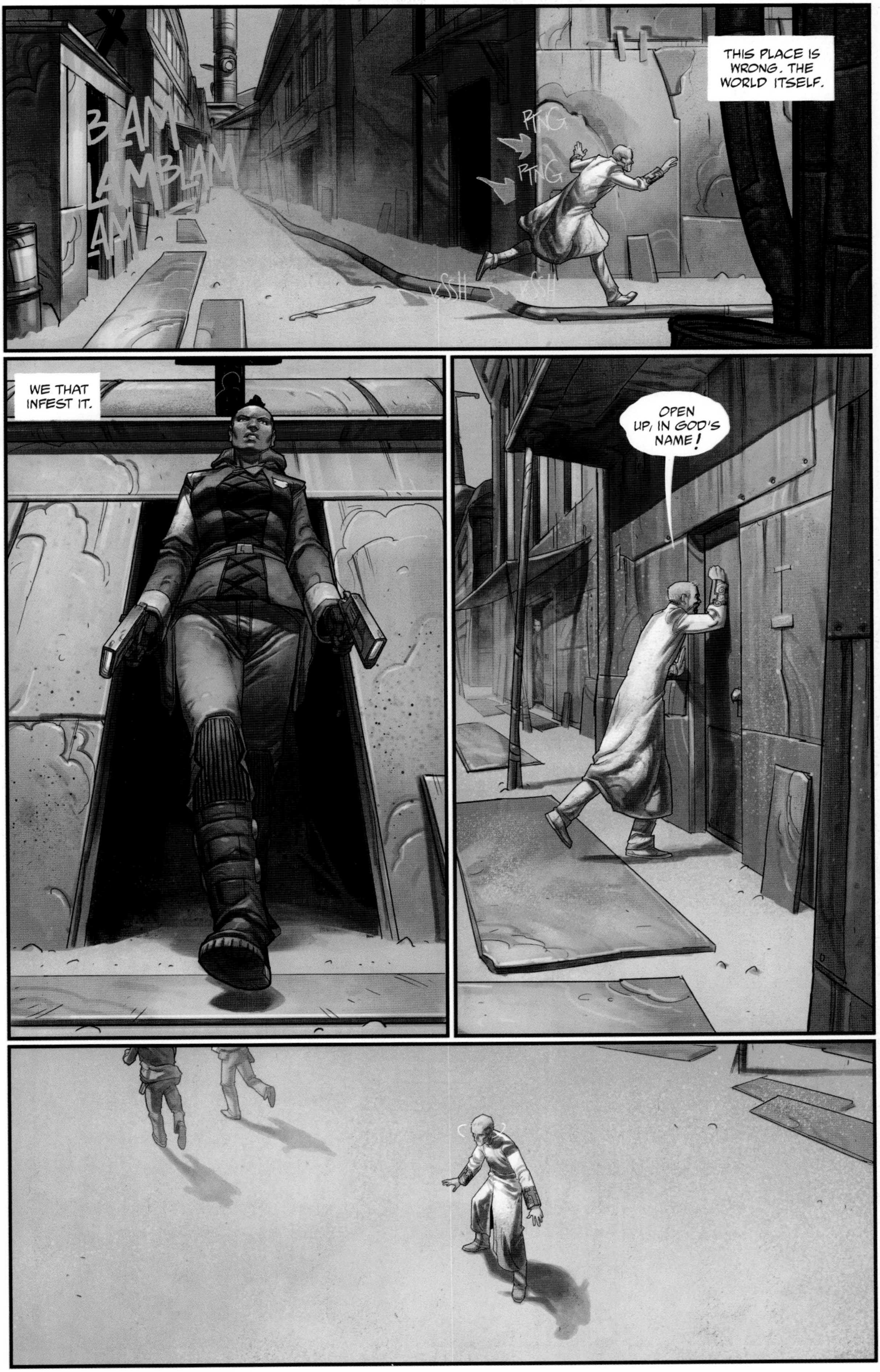
THIS PLACE IS WRONG. THE WORLD ITSELF.
BLAM BLAMBLAM BLAM
PTNG
PTNG
KSSH
KSSH
WE THAT INFEST IT.
OPEN UP, IN GOD'S NAME!

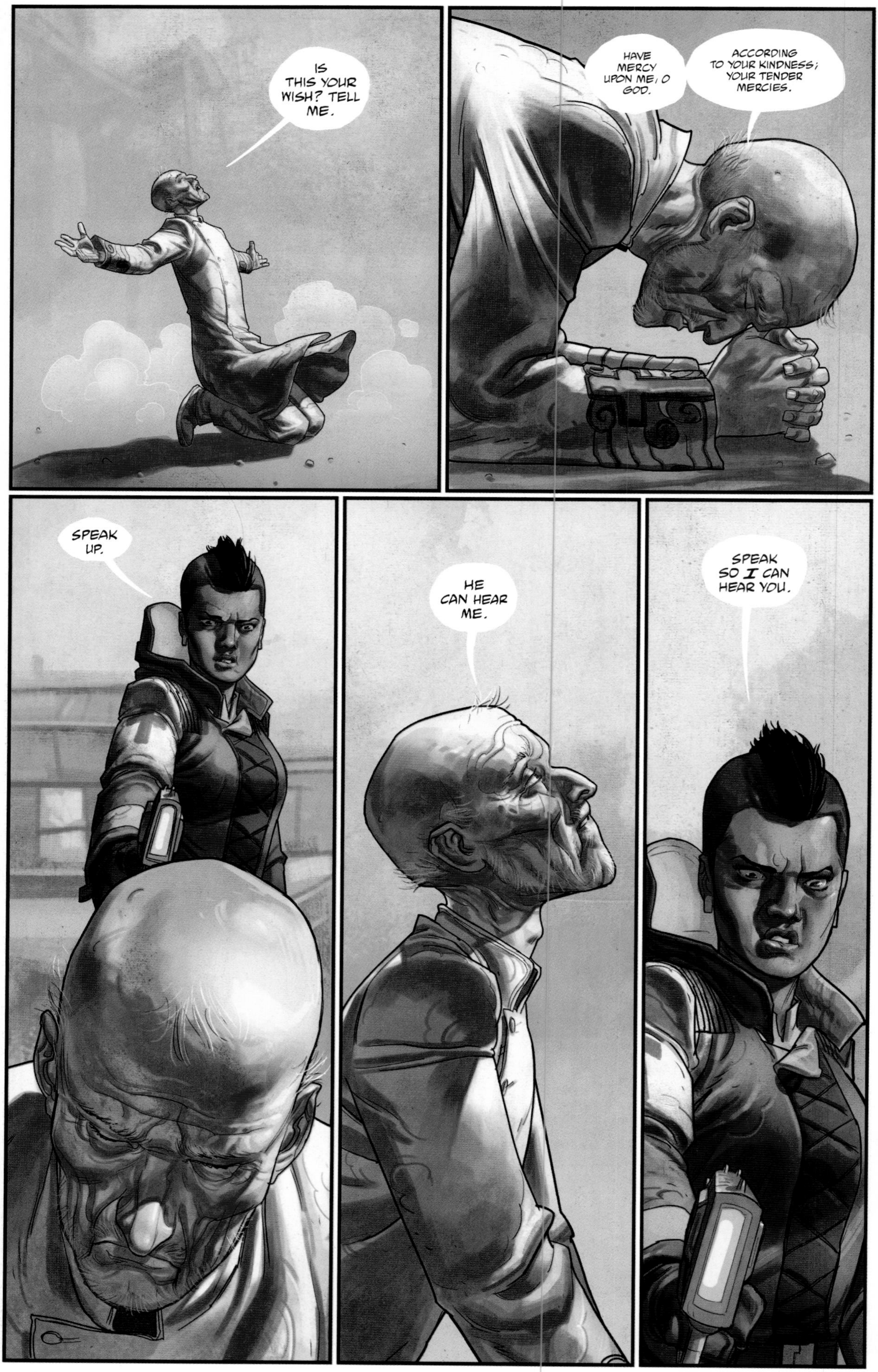
IS THIS YOUR WISH? TELL ME.
HAVE MERCY UPON ME, O GOD.
ACCORDING TO YOUR KINDNESS; YOUR TENDER MERCIES.
SPEAK UP.
HE CAN HEAR ME.
SPEAK SO I CAN HEAR YOU.

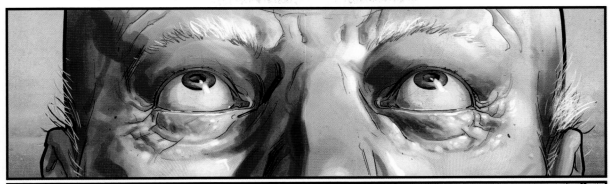

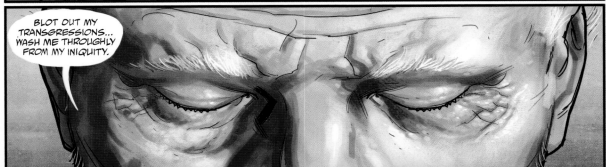

BLOT OUT MY TRANSGRESSIONS... WASH ME THROUGHLY FROM MY INIQUITY.

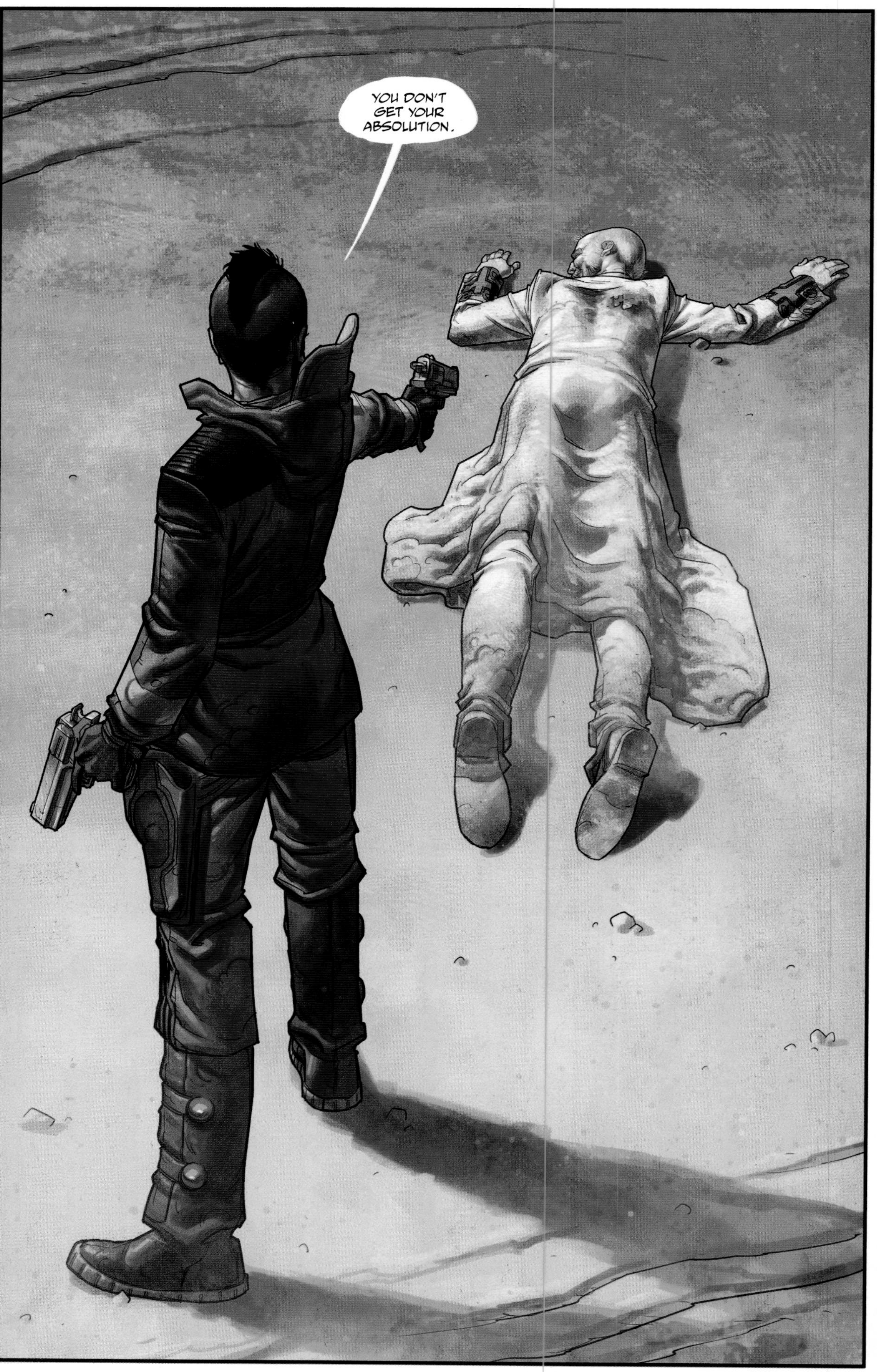
YOU DON'T GET YOUR ABSOLUTION.

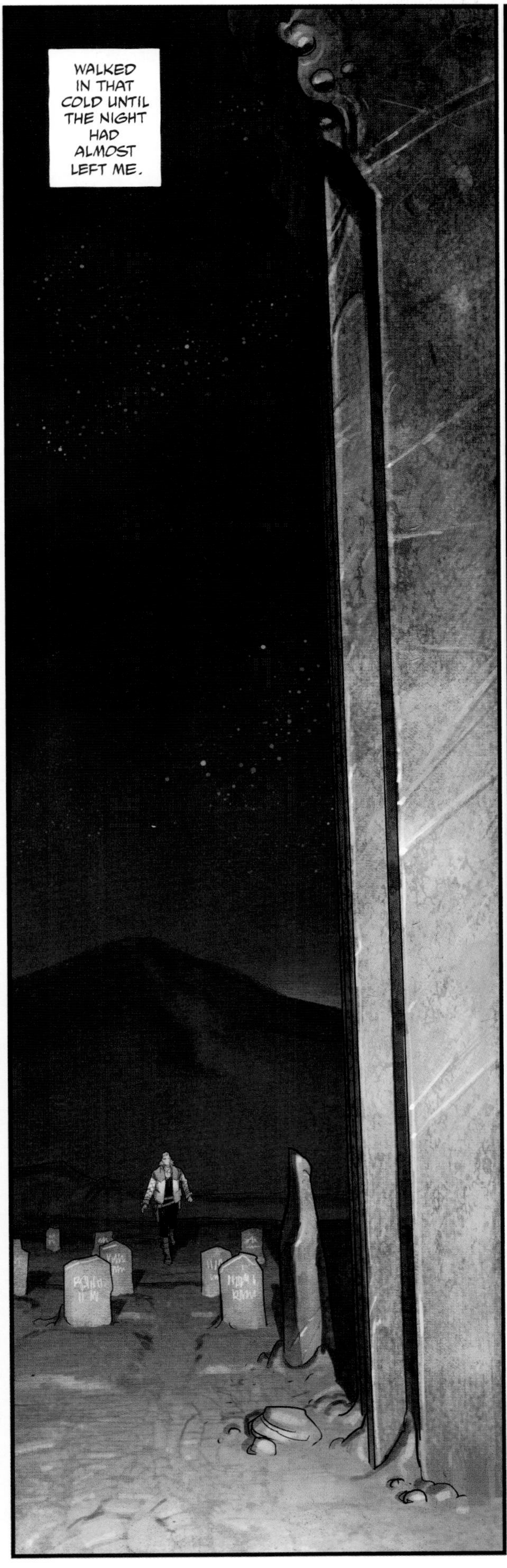
WALKED IN THAT COLD UNTIL THE NIGHT HAD ALMOST LEFT ME.
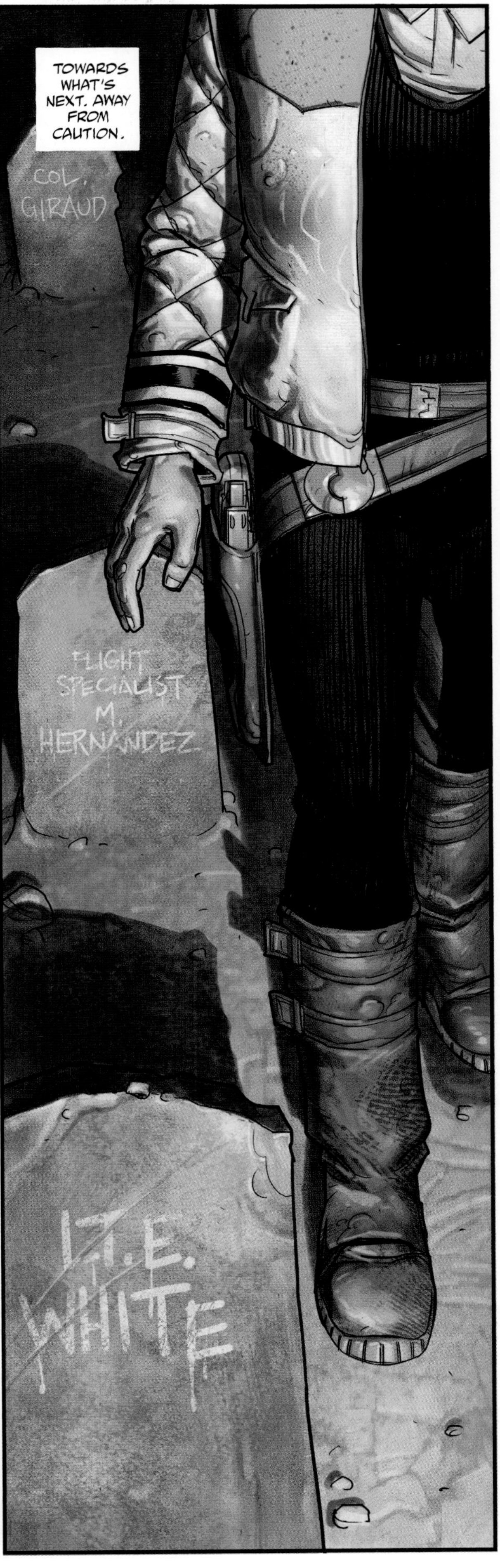
TOWARDS WHAT'S NEXT. AWAY FROM CAUTION.
COL. GIRAUD
FLIGHT SPECIALIST M. HERNANDEZ
LT. E. WHITE

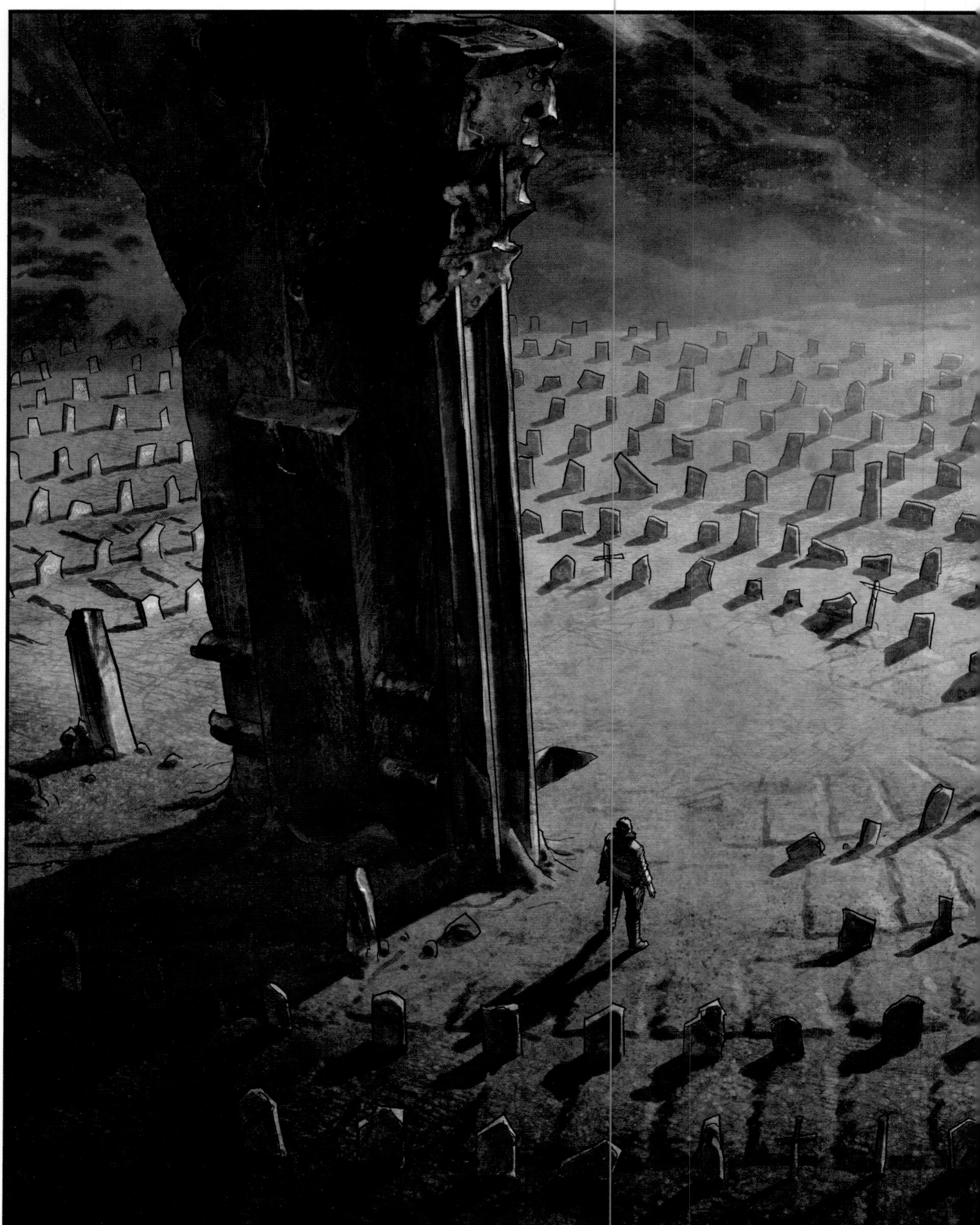

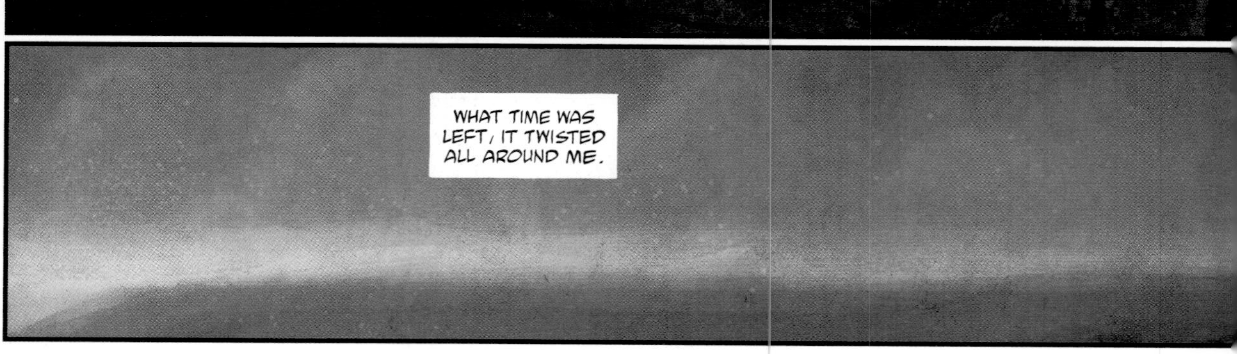
WHAT TIME WAS LEFT, IT TWISTED ALL AROUND ME.

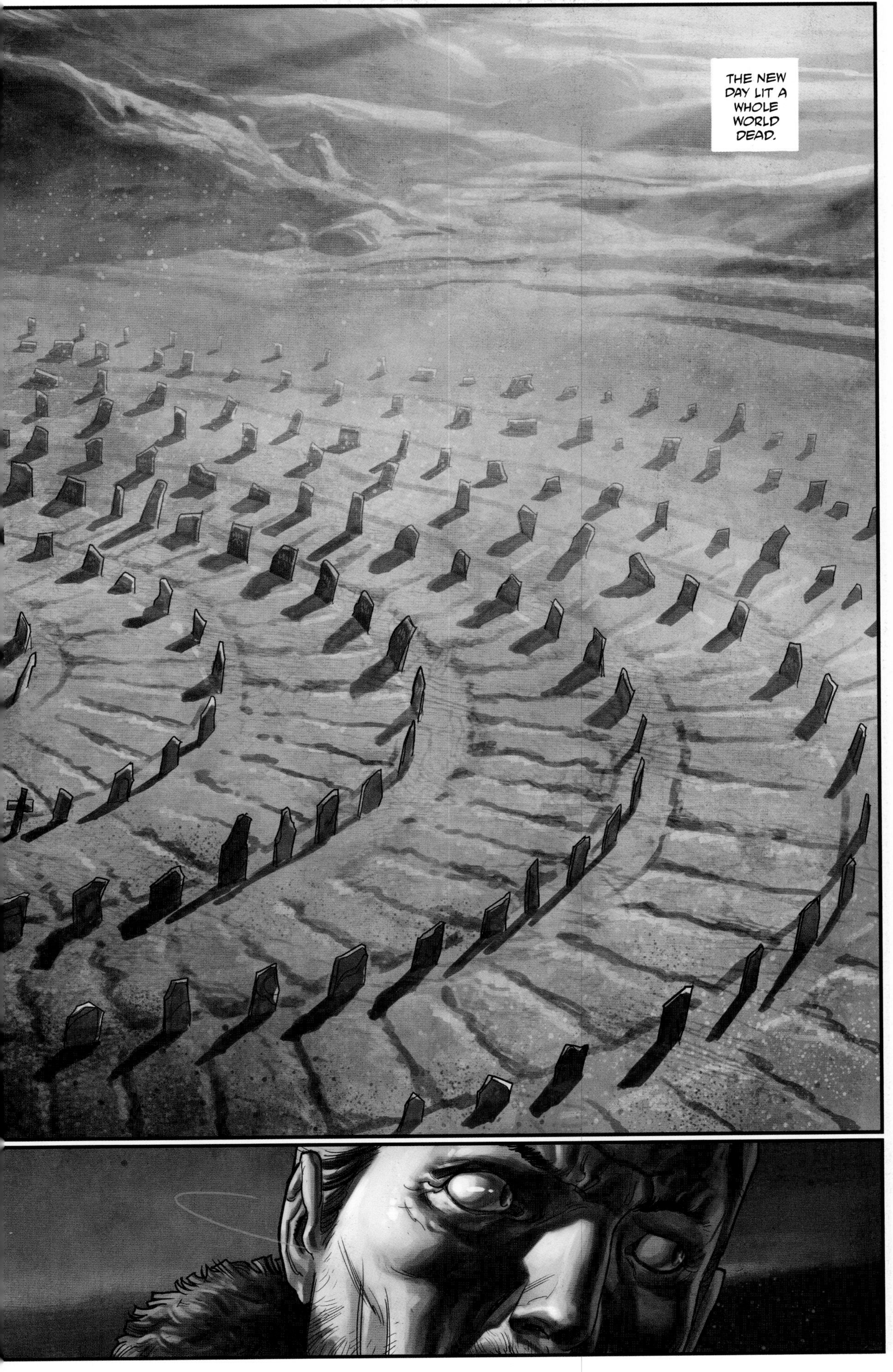
THE NEW DAY LIT A WHOLE WORLD DEAD.

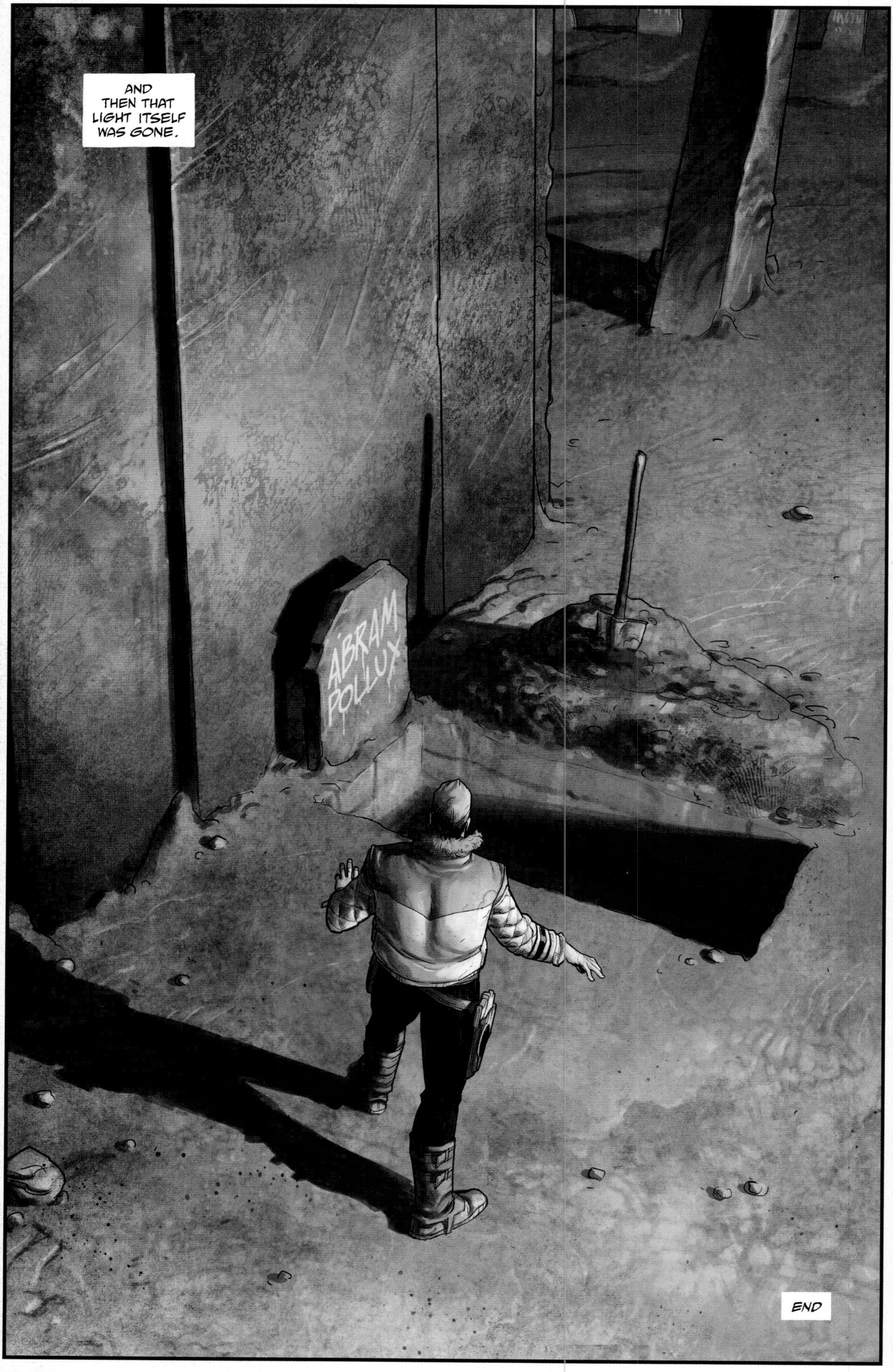
AND THEN THAT LIGHT ITSELF WAS GONE.
ABRAM POLLUX
END

COVER
GALLERY

Esad Ribic, Cliff Chiang, Jason Latour,
Becky Cloonan, Marko Djurdjević,
Rafael Albuquerque, and Skottie Young

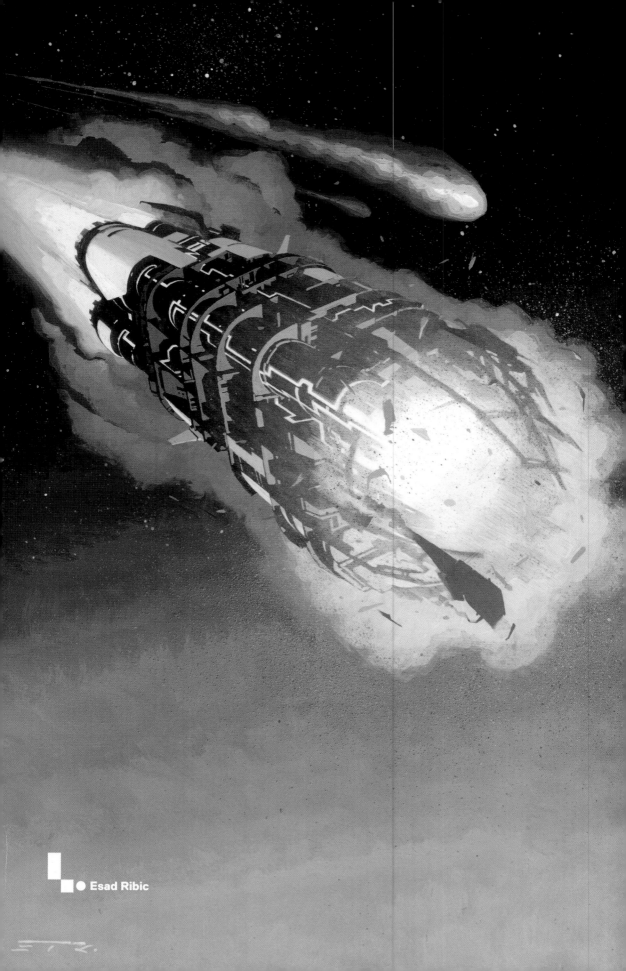

Esad Ribic

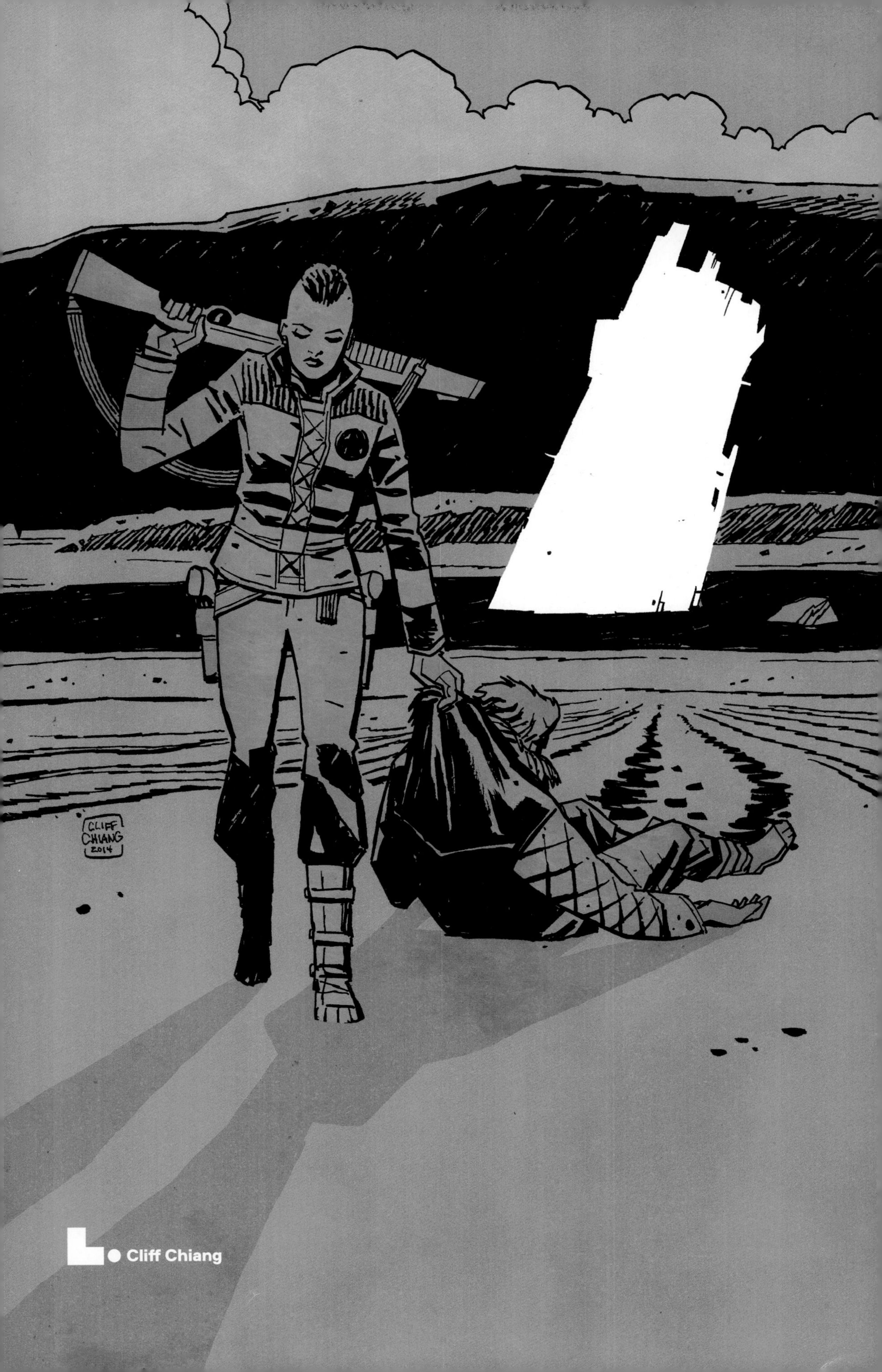
CLIFF CHIANG 2014

Cliff Chiang

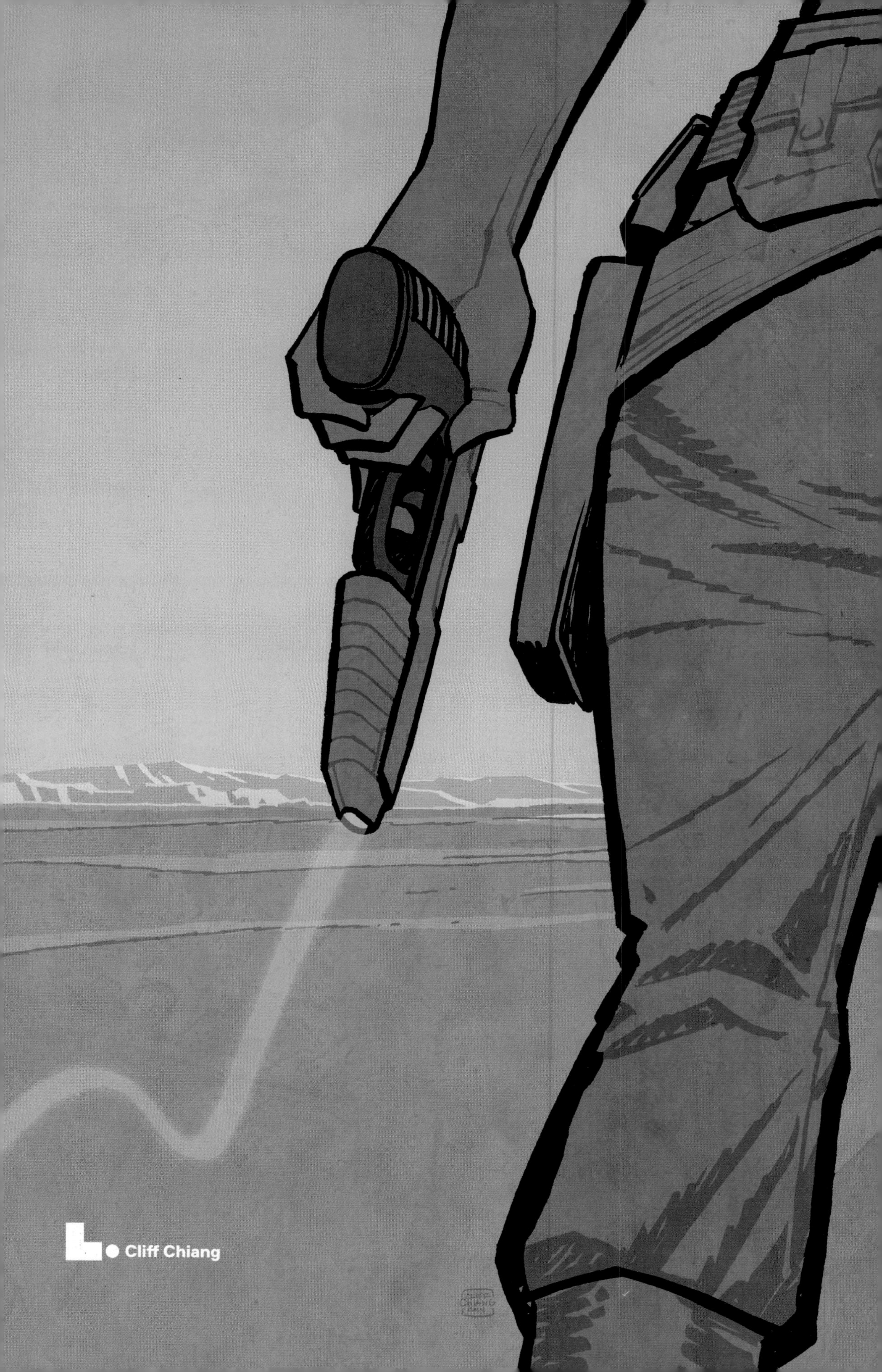
Cliff Chiang

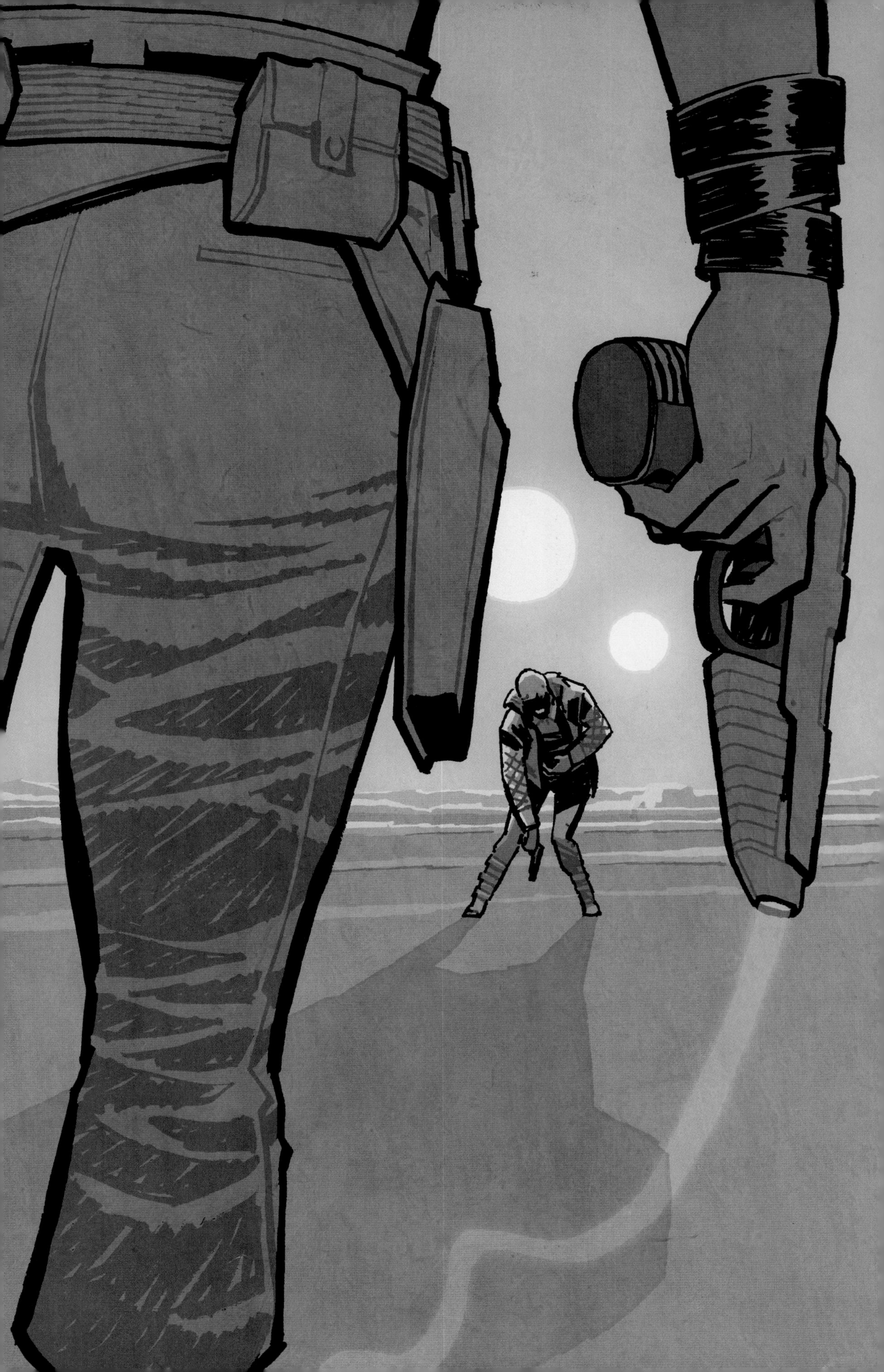

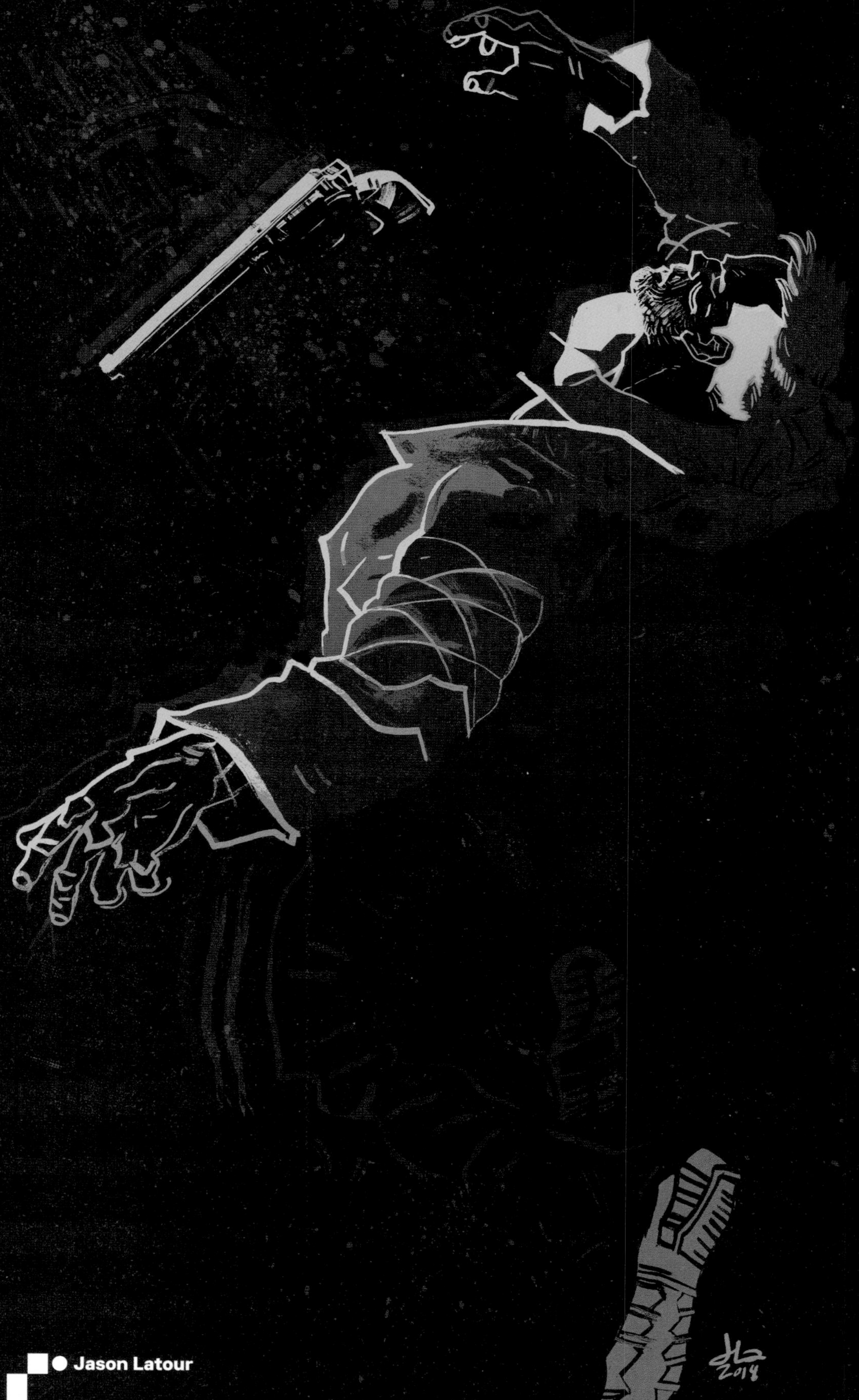

Jason Latour

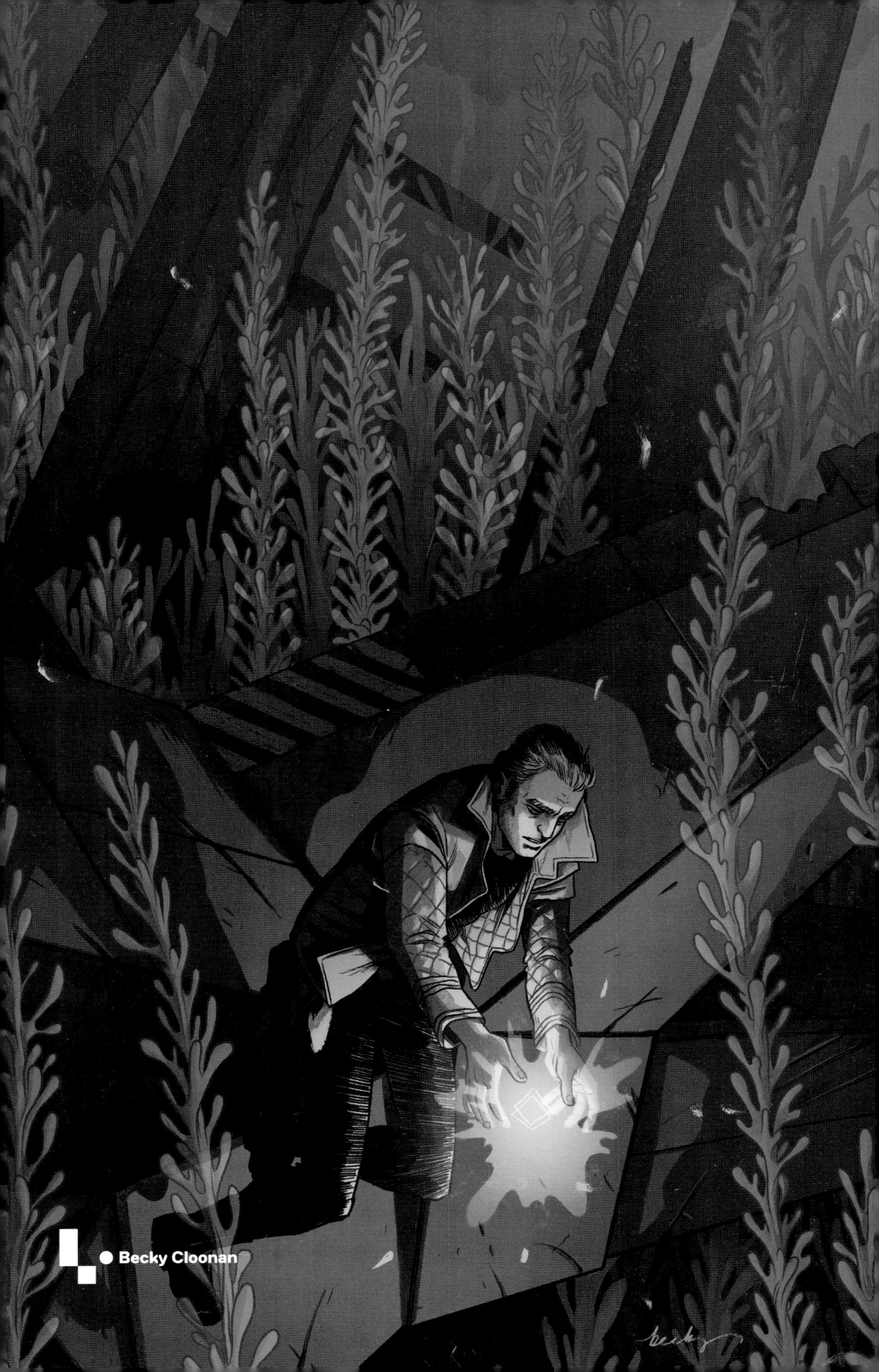
Becky Cloonan
becky

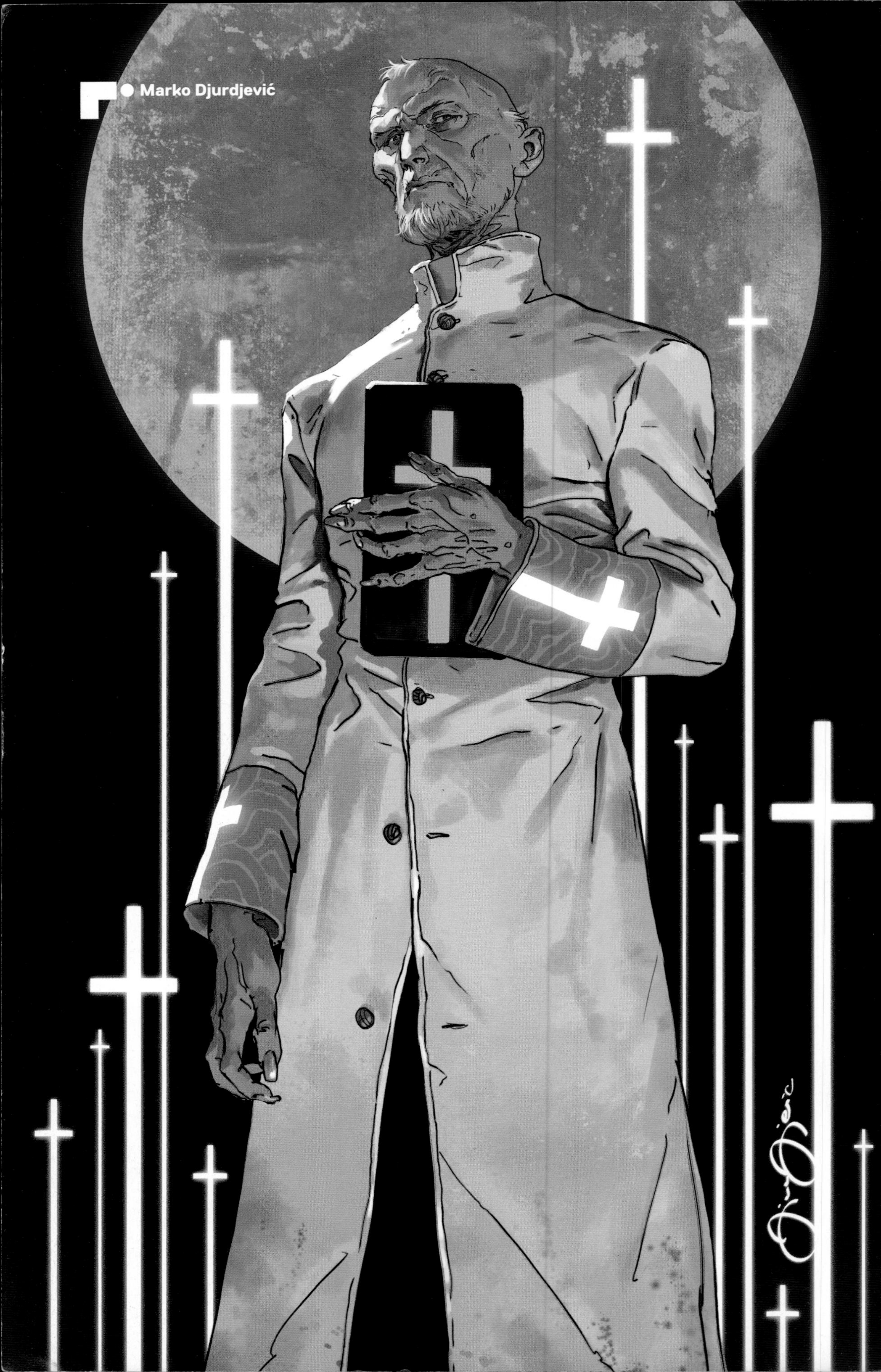
Marko Djurdjević

Rafael Albuquerque

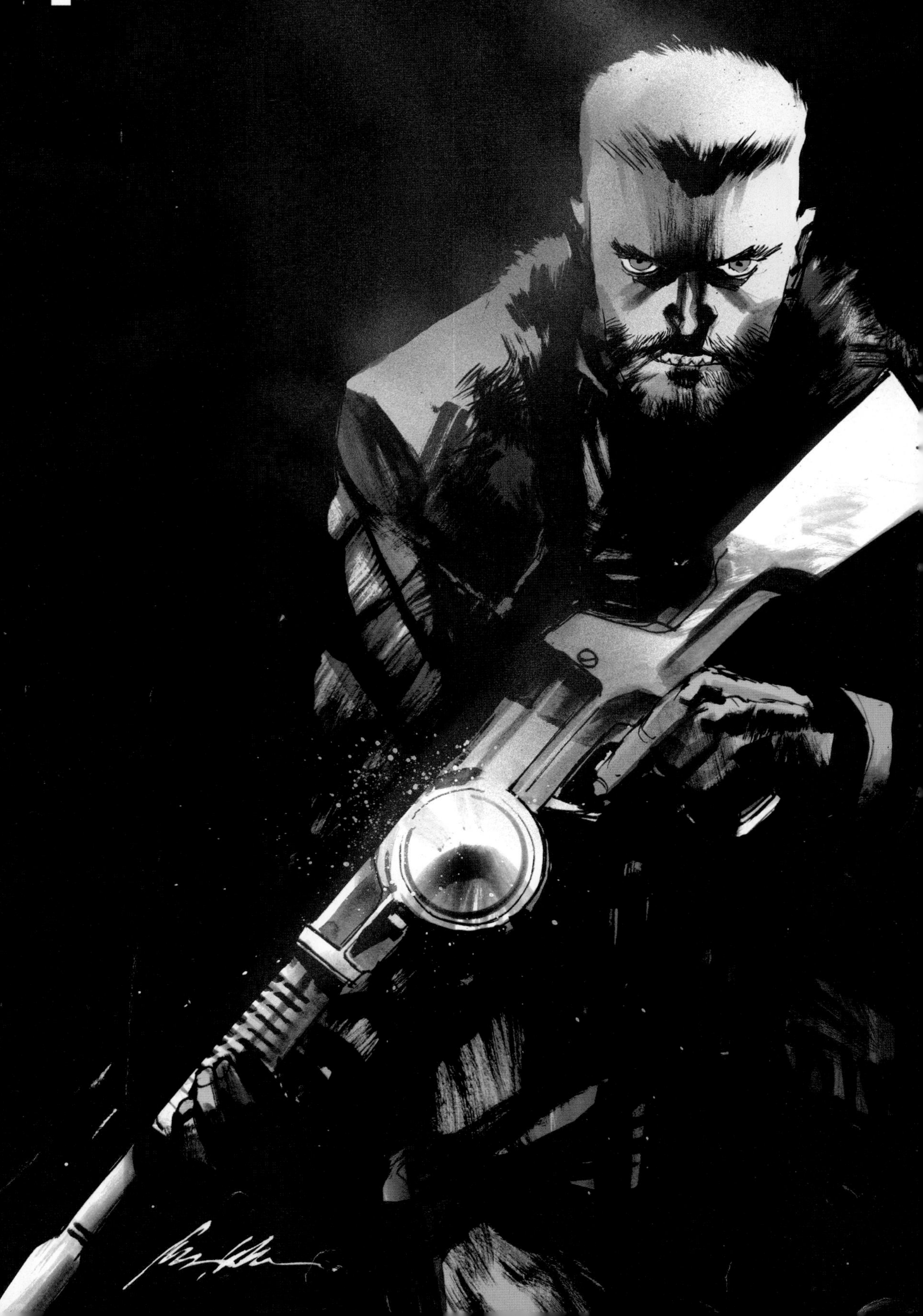

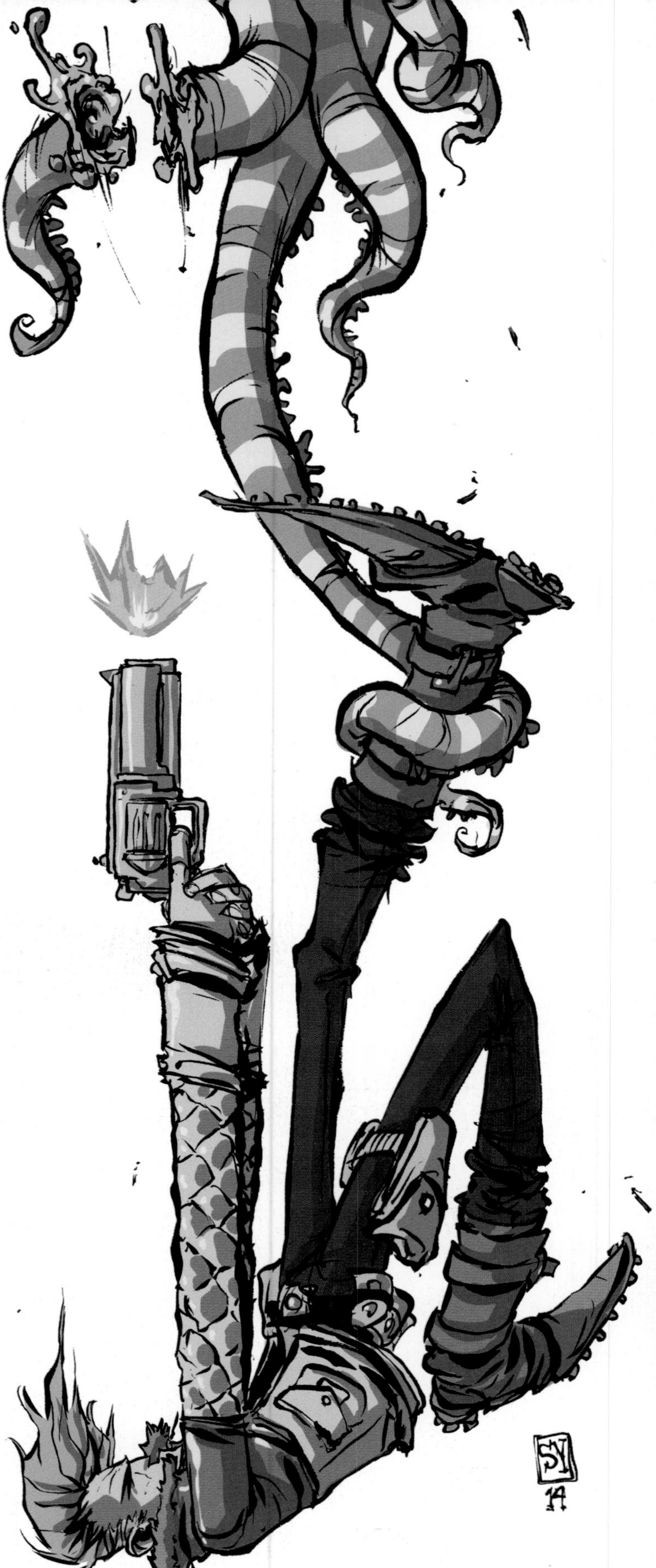

Skottie Young

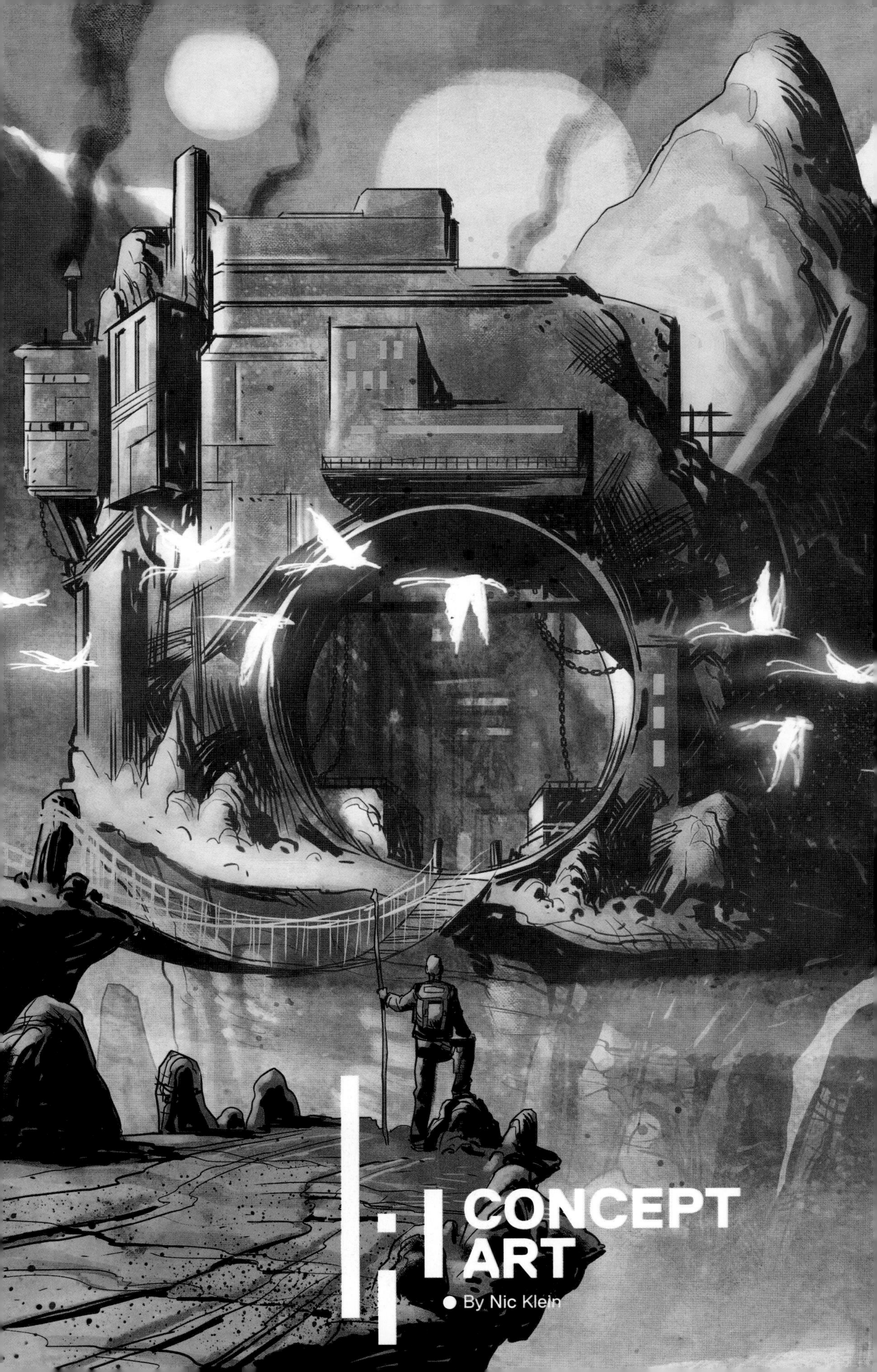
CONCEPT
ART
By Nic Klein

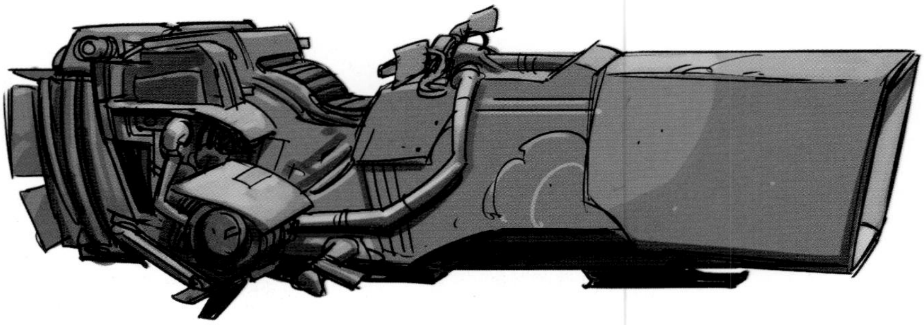

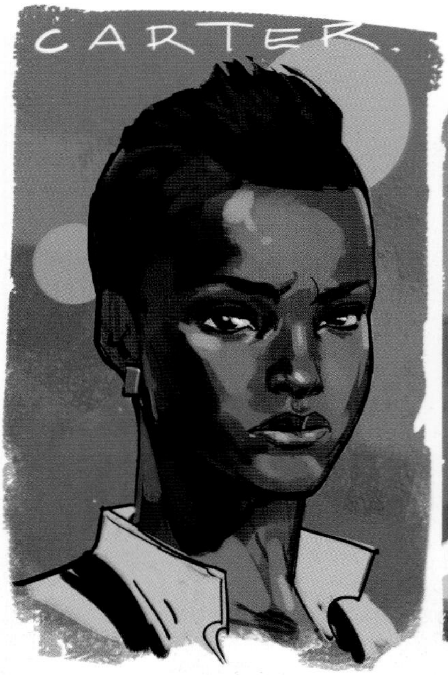
CARTER.

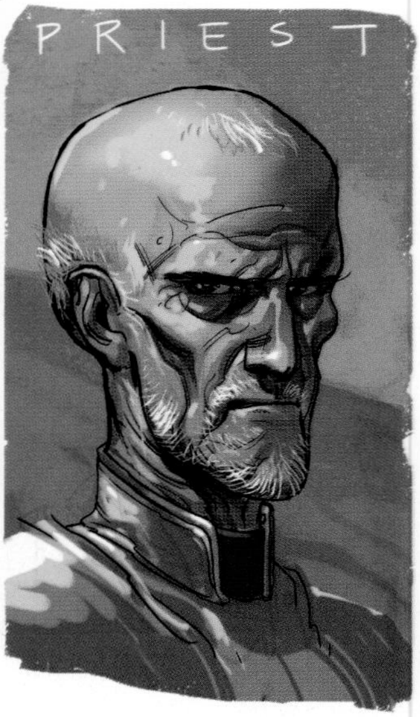
PRIEST

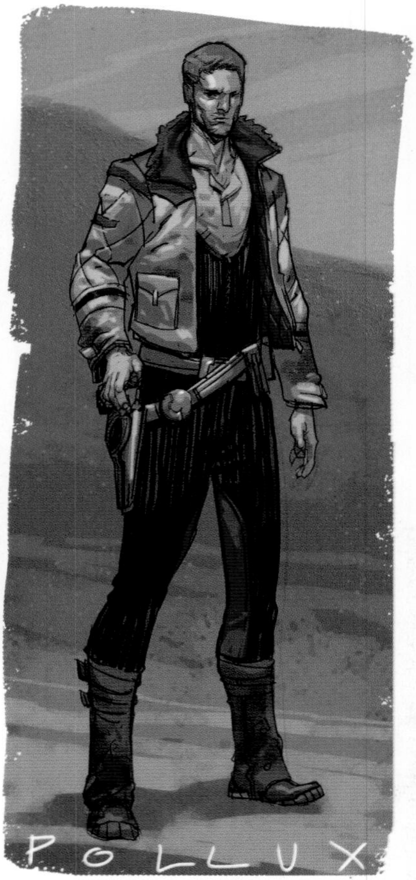
POLLUX

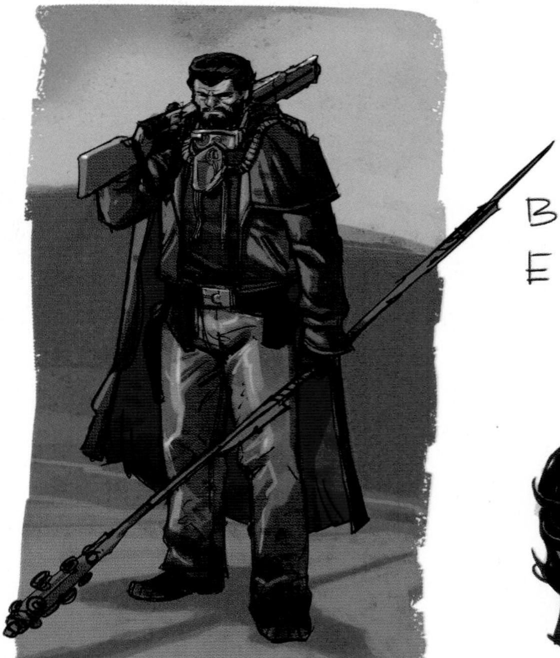

BELL
EMMERICH

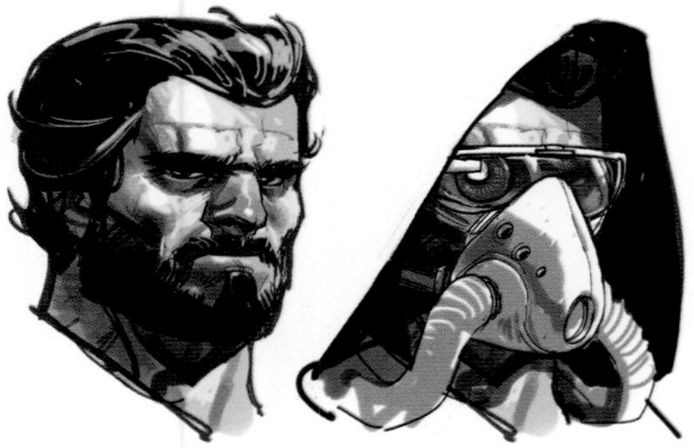

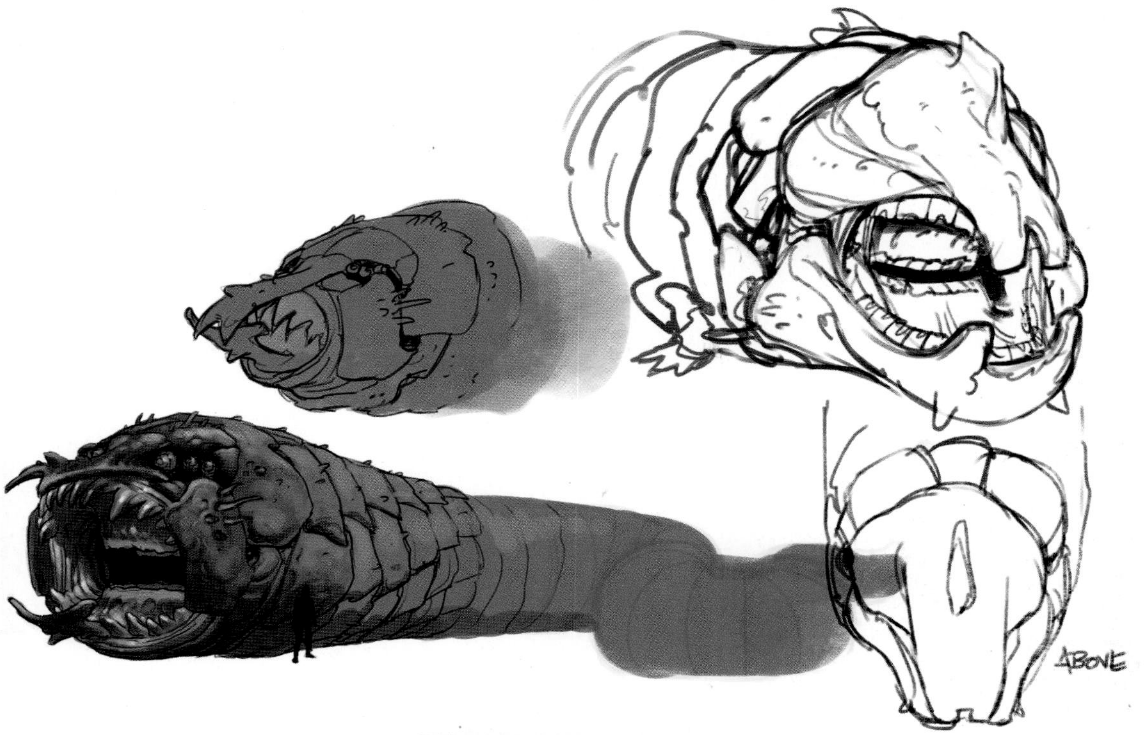
ABOVE

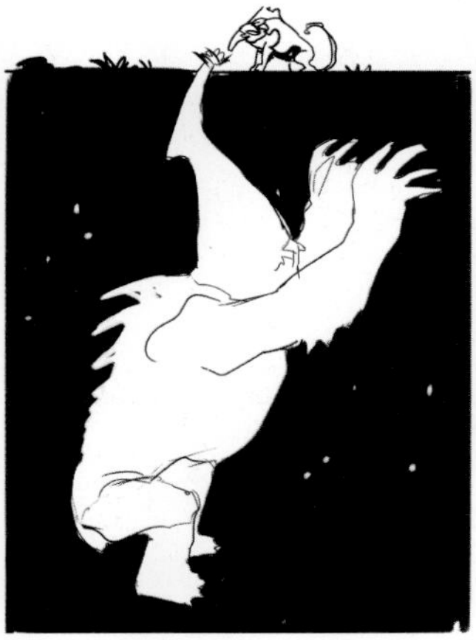

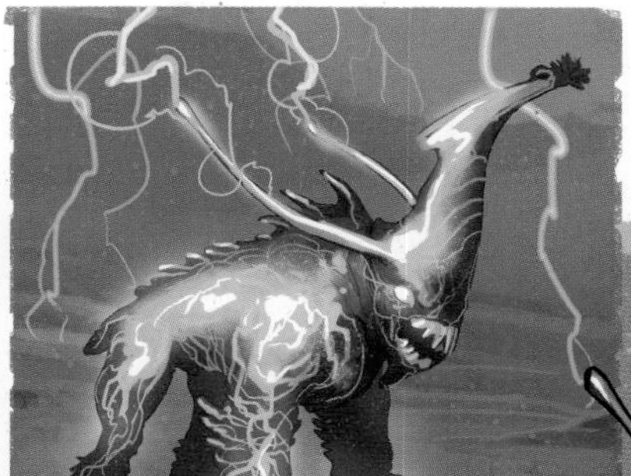

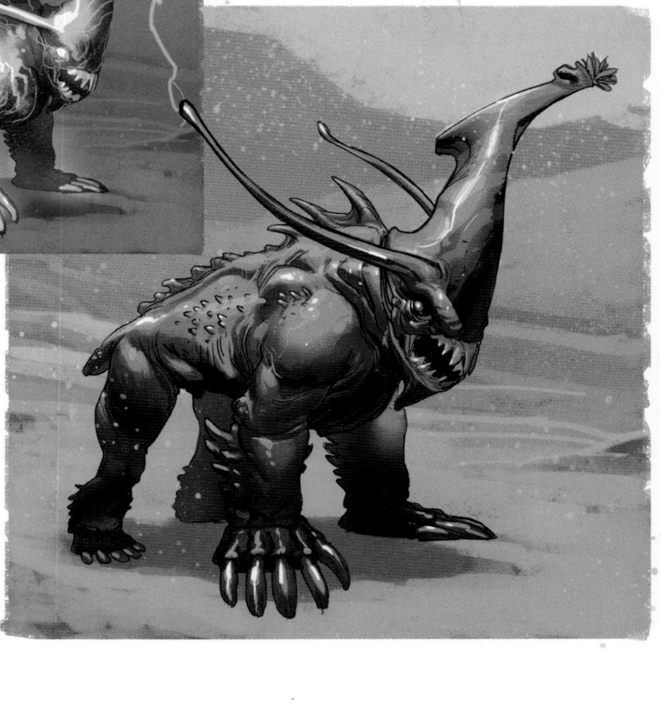

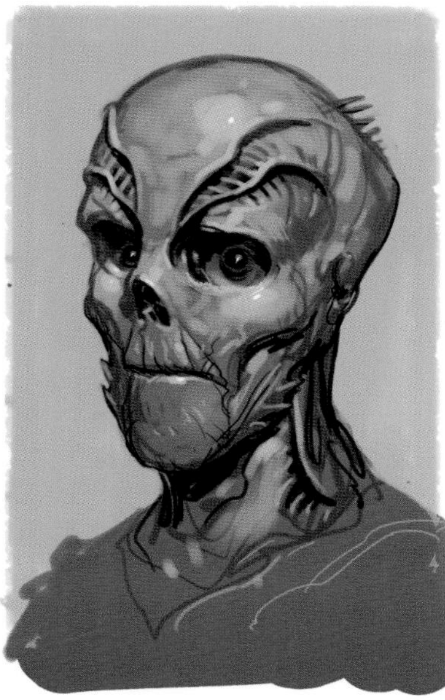

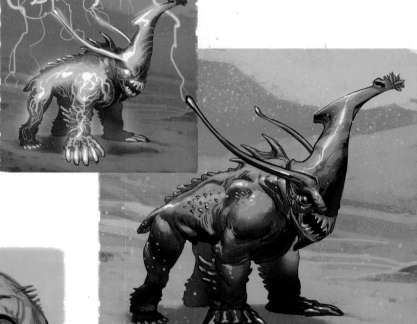

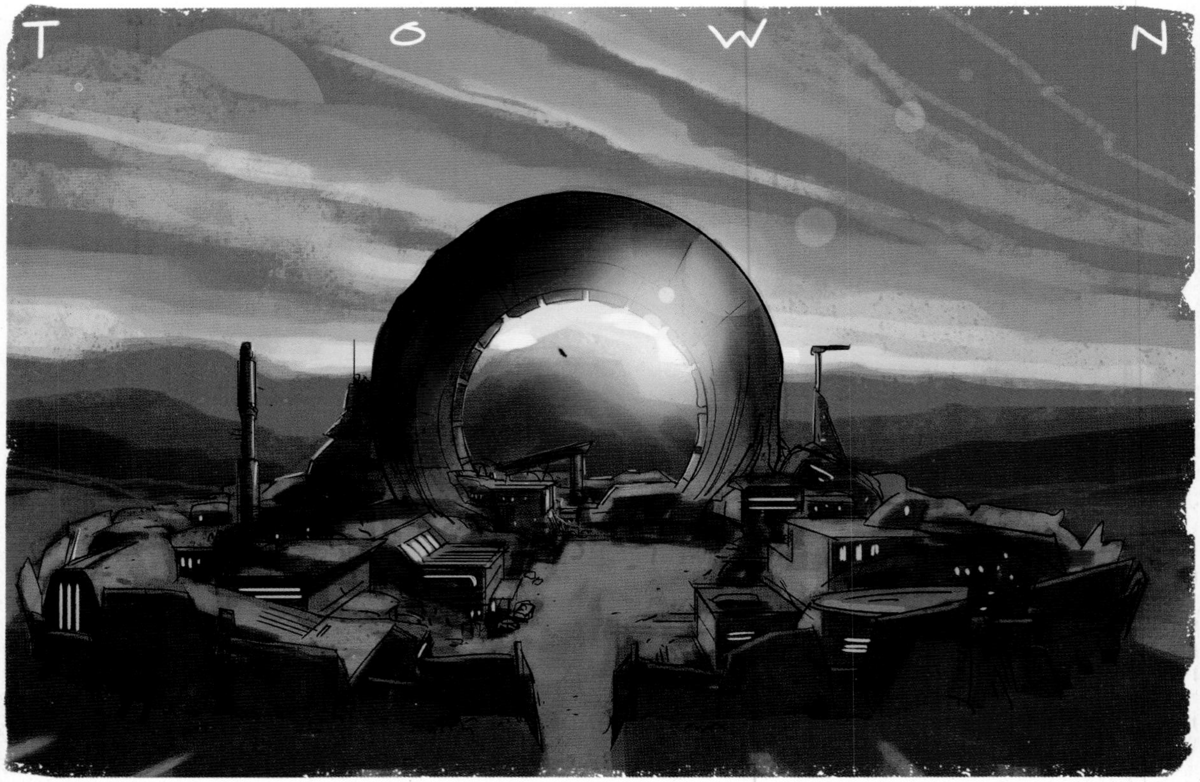
T O W N

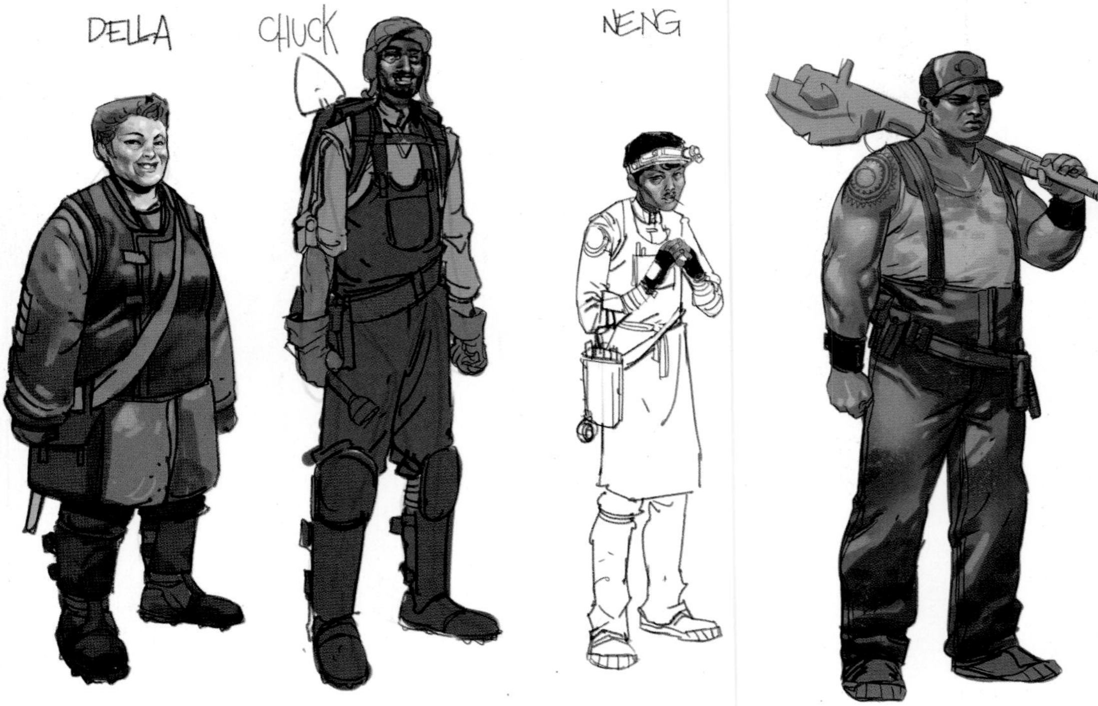
DELLA
CHUCK
NENG